Home Country

ERNIE PYLE

**WILLIAM SLOANE
ASSOCIATES, INC.**
Publishers   *New York*

Contents

Foreword

This is Ernie Pyle's fifth book; that is, the fifth to appear between boards. By another reckoning it is his first, for it was written before the others. During the years 1935 to 1940, Ernie and That Girl who rode with him (his wife, Jerry) were crisscrossing North America in search of material for a daily newspaper column. In that period he turned out about a million and a half words. Not all of these are here, but an effort has been made to include his best-remembered writings of those years. Scholars who may seek to trace the origins of the style or stance or philosophy—or whatever it may have been—that eventually made Ernie Pyle almost universally read and revered in America may find good hunting here. It is not at these, however, but rather at those who simply like good reading, that this collection is aimed.

Ernie's newspaper career had alternated, since its beginning in 1923, between desk work and what is known in the business as "leg" work. In 1932 he was called in from a four-year stint as aviation columnist of the Washington *Daily News* and made managing editor of the paper. It was a confining job, and after three years of it he managed to talk his employers into letting him use his legs once more, this time experimentally as a roving reporter with no destination and no assignment other than "a piece a day." The pieces ran at first only in the Washington *News,* later in some of the other Scripps-Howard newspapers, presently in all of them, and finally in papers outside that chain.

People who encountered Ernie's column only during the war years may discover in these pages why it had already become, in peacetime, a daily favorite of millions.

HOME COUNTRY

Home in Indiana

Chapter I

I DON'T KNOW WHETHER YOU KNOW THAT LONG, SAD wind that blows so steadily across the thousands of miles of Midwest flatlands in the summertime. If you don't, it will be hard for you to understand the feeling I have about it. Even if you do know it, you may not understand.

To me the summer wind in the Midwest is one of the most melancholy things in all life. It comes from so far and blows so gently and yet so relentlessly; it rustles the leaves and the branches of the maple trees in a sort of symphony of sadness, and it doesn't pass on and leave them still. It just keeps coming, like the infinite flow of Old Man River. You could—and you do—wear out your lifetime on the dusty plains with that wind of futility blowing in your face. And when you are worn out and gone, the wind—still saying nothing, still so gentle and sad and timeless—is still blowing across the prairies, and will blow in the faces of the little men who follow you, forever.

One time in 1935, when I was driving across Iowa, I became conscious of the wind and instantly I was back in character as an Indiana farm boy again. Like dreams came the memories the wind brought. I lay again on the ground under the shade trees at noontime, with my half hour for rest before going back to the fields, and the wind and the sun and the hot country silence made me sleepy, and yet I couldn't sleep for the wind in the trees. The wind was like the afternoon ahead that would never end, and the days and the summers and even the lifetimes that would flow on forever, tiredly, patiently.

Maybe it's a bad job, my trying to make you see something that only I can ever feel. It is just one of those small impressions that form in a child's mind, and grow and stay with him through a lifetime, even shaping a part of his character and manner of thinking, and he can never explain it.

There's another impression that has come up with me out of childhood: I have a horror of snakes that verges on the irrational. I'm not afraid of being killed by a snake. It isn't that kind of fear. It's a horrible, unnatural mania for getting away, and it is induced equally by a six-inch garden snake and a six-foot rattler.

Ask my mother. She'll tell you the snake story, probably. In all the years, she never failed to tell it over again when I came home on a visit.

I was a little fellow, maybe four or five. My father was plowing at the far end of our farm, a half mile from the house. I was walking along behind the plow, barefooted, in the fresh soft furrow. He had just started the field, and was plowing near a weedy fence row. Red wild roses were growing there. I asked my father for his pocketknife so I could cut some of the roses to take back to the house. He gave it to me and went on plowing. I sat down in the grass and started cutting off the roses.

Then it happened in a flash. A blue racer came looping through the grass at me. I already had my horror of snakes at that tender age—it must have been born in me. I screamed, threw away the knife, and ran as fast as I could. Then I remembered it was my father's knife. I crept back over the plowed ground till I found it. He had heard me scream and had stopped. I gave him the knife and started back to the house.

I approached the house from the west side, where there was an old garden all grown up in high weeds. I stopped on the far side and shouted for my mother. When she came out to see what I wanted, I asked her to come and get me. She said I should come on through by myself. I couldn't have done that if it had killed me not to. She ordered me to come through, and I began to cry. She told me that if I didn't stop crying and didn't come through, she would whip me. I couldn't stop, and I couldn't come through. So she came and got me. And she whipped me—one of the two times, I believe, that she ever whipped me.

· 4 ·

That evening when my father came in from the fields, she told him about the crazy boy who wouldn't walk through the weeds and had to be whipped. And then my father told her about the roses and the knife and the snake. It was the roses, I think, that hurt her so. My mother cried for a long time that night after she went to bed.

It has been more than thirty years since that happened, but to this day when I go home my mother sooner or later will say, "Do you remember the time I whipped you because you wouldn't walk through the weeds?" And then she will tell me the story, just as I have told it here, and along toward the end she always manages to get the hem of her apron up around her eyes, just in case she should need it, which she always does.

My mother would rather drive a team of horses in the field than cook a dinner. But in her lifetime she has done very little of the first and too much of the latter. She has had only three real interests—my father, myself, and her farm work. Nothing else makes much difference to her. And yet, when I left home in my late teens, to be gone forever except for brief visits, she was content for me to go, because she knew I was not happy on the farm.

My mother is living proof that happiness is within yourself; for a whole lifetime she has done nothing but work too hard, and yet I'm sure she has been happy. She loves the farm there outside Dana, Indiana. She wouldn't think of moving to town, as the other "retired" farmers do. She would rather stay home now and milk the cows than to go to the state fair. She is the best chicken raiser and cake baker in the neighborhood. She loves to raise chickens and hates to bake cakes.

After she and my father had been married thirty years, they took a trip east and saw Niagara Falls. She didn't want to go and was glad to get back home, but did admit she enjoyed the trip. The highlight of the journey, which included Washington and New York, was a night in a tourist cabin near Wheeling, West Virginia. It was fixed so nice inside, she said, just like home. She talks about it yet.

My mother probably knows as little about world affairs as any woman in our neighborhood. Yet she is the broadest-minded and most liberal of the lot. I don't remember her ever telling me I couldn't do something. She always told me what she thought was right, and what was wrong, and then it was up to me. When I was about sixteen I forgot and left my corncob pipe lying on the window sill one day when I went to school. When I got home that night, she handed me the pipe and said, "I see you're smoking now." I said, "Yes." And that was all there was to that. She thinks it's awful for women to smoke, but I imagine if she had a daughter who smoked she'd think it was all right.

She is a devout Methodist and a prohibitionist. Yet she and my father voted for Al Smith in 1928, because they thought he was a better man than Hoover. Some of their neighbors wouldn't speak to them for months because they voted for a Catholic and a wet, but they didn't care. They are always doing things they think are right.

My mother has quite a temper. I remember once when the liniment man came, and said we hadn't paid him for a bottle of liniment. My mother said we had. The man said we hadn't. So my mother went and got the money, opened the screen door, and threw it in his face. He never came back.

She always tells people just what she thinks. A good many of our neighbors have deservedly felt the whip of her tongue, and they pout over it a while, but whenever they're in trouble they always thaw out and come asking for help. And of course get it. My mother is the one the neighbors always call on when somebody gets sick, or dies, or needs help of any kind. She has practically raised a couple of kids besides myself. She has always been the confidante of the young people around there.

I started driving a team of horses in the fields when I was nine. I remember that first day perfectly. My mother had gone to a club meeting, but she came home in the middle of the afternoon and brought me a lunch of bread and butter and sugar out to the field. And also, I suppose, she wanted to make sure I hadn't been dragged to death under the harrow.

She played the violin when she was younger, but she gave it up after I took one term of lessons. I gave it up too. You should have heard me.

My mother doesn't realize it, but her life has been the life of a real prairie pioneer. You could use her in a book, or paint her picture, as one of the sturdy stock of the ages who have always done the carrying-on when the going was tough.

She isn't so well any more, but she seems to work harder than ever. We try to get her to rest, but she says, "Oh, the work has to be done." We say, "Yes, but you don't have to do it. Supposing you were gone; the work would still be here, but you wouldn't have to do it." But she doesn't understand what we mean.

Perhaps you have heard of my father. He is the man who put oil on his brakes when they got to squeaking, then drove to Dana and ran over the curb and through a plate-glass window and right into a dry-goods store.

My father is also the man who ran with Roosevelt in 1932. He ran for township trustee, was the only Democrat in the county who lost, and was probably the happiest man who listened to election returns that night. He couldn't think of anything worse than being township trustee. The reason he lost was that all the people figured that if he was trustee he wouldn't have time to put roofs on their houses and paint their barns and paper their dining rooms and fix their chimneys, and do a thousand and one other things for them. I guess when my father is gone that whole neighborhood will just sort of fall down.

He used to work as a hired hand way over on the other side of the Wabash River. When he was courting my mother, every Sunday he would drive a horse six miles to the river, row a boat across, and then ride a bicycle ten miles to my mother's house. At midnight he started to reverse the process. Mother figured he either loved her or else was foolish and needed somebody to look after him, so she married him.

My father has never lived anywhere except on a farm, and yet I don't think he ever did like the farm very well. He has been happiest, I think, since he started renting out the farm. Ever since then he has been carpentering and handy-manning all about the neighborhood. He is a wizard with tools, where other people are clumsy. He is a carpenter at heart.

Once when he was a young man, my father did start out to see

· 7 ·

the world. He went to Iowa to cut broom corn, but broke a leg and had to come home. He never went anywhere again till he was fifty-five, when he went to California to see his brother. He sat up all the way in a day coach. Later he went to New York, so he has seen both oceans.

When he was in Washington he kept butting his head against those big glass cases that hold exhibits in the Smithsonian Institute. The glass was polished so clean he couldn't see it. We all thought it was awfully funny. He got a splitting headache from it.

We got our first automobile in 1914. We kept it up in the north end of the wagon shed, right behind the wagon. At the south end of the wagon shed there was a big gravel pit. One day we came home from town, my mother and I got out at the house, and father went to put the car away. We saw him make the circle in the barn lot, and then drive into the north end of the shed. The next instant, the south end of the shed simply burst open, a wagon came leaping out, and with one great bound was over the cliff and down in the gravel pit. My father said he never did know exactly what happened.

He is a very quiet man. He has never said a great deal to me all his life, and yet I feel that we have been very good friends. He never gave me much advice, or told me to do this or that, or not to. He bought me a Ford roadster when I was about sixteen, and when I wrecked it a couple of weeks later he never said a word. But he didn't spare me either; I worked like a horse from the time I was nine. ●

He never shows much emotion, and he has never seen a big-league ball game. Yet my mother came home one afternoon during a World Series, and caught him sitting in front of the radio, all by himself, clapping and yelling for all he was worth.

My father is now getting a little deaf. Mother says he can always hear what he isn't supposed to hear. If my father doesn't like people, he never says anything about it. It he does like people, he never says much about that either. He is very even-tempered. If he has an enemy in this whole country, I have yet to hear about it.

He doesn't swear or drink or smoke. He is honest, in letter and in spirit. He is a good man without being at all annoying about it. He used to smoke cigars, but he quit the Fourth of July that

Johnson fought Jeffries in Reno—I think it was 1908. The event didn't have anything to do with it. His holiday cigar simply made him sicker than usual that day, so he quit.

My Aunt Mary was born thirty years too soon. Jim Williams should draw one of his "Out Our Way" cartoons about her. If she was forty, instead of seventy, I am sure she would be in Congress now. She always did want to be in politics and national affairs, and she does plenty of first-rate original thinking too. Yet she never went beyond the eighth grade in school.

Aunt Mary was past forty when she married. I remember when Uncle George first started going with her. She lived at our house then, and he would come to take her riding before breakfast. He drove a fractious sorrel mare hitched to a two-wheeled racing sulky with just a little seat on it. He would stop out in the road and yell till we were all awake, then Aunt Mary would go out and get in with him. She was ashamed to ride up and down the road in a racing sulky on a tiny little seat with a man before breakfast, but she liked Uncle George, so she went.

And then I remember the night they were married. There were a lot of people at our house that night. I was a little shaver, but I had sense enough to know that as soon as the knot was tied the kissing would start. So I hid behind the couch. Sure enough, as soon as the ceremony was over, Aunt Mary, crying as though she had just buried Uncle George instead of marrying him, wanted to kiss everybody in the place, especially me. And I couldn't be found. The search got so frantic I finally came out to get kissed and have it over with.

Uncle George lived on a farm, but he wasn't a farmer—he was a dreamer. He would fuss all day around his garden and his flowers, and play his beautiful big black square piano, and order freight-car loads of lime and fertilizer he couldn't pay for, and talk by the hour about his prize sweet corn, and spend whole half days studying the flower and seed catalogues he had sent away for. My Uncle George was a great man and he worked like a Trojan, but he never got anything done and Aunt Mary had to make the living. She did a nice job of it, too. She raised hundreds of chickens, and she raised her own hogs and cows, and through twenty years she kept the treasury from going flat. She worked from four in the morning till nine at night, and found time to go to a couple of weekly clubs and run the country church besides. She even bought an automobile as early as 1915 and learned to drive it, and drive it well too, when she was fifty years old. Uncle George never would drive the damn thing, so she had to haul him around too.

Then Uncle George died. Aunt Mary was sixty years old. She had been born on a farm, raised on a farm, had never been off the farm. But she was alert, she had more energy than a buzz saw, and she was tall and straight despite a lifetime of killing work. And she was generous and kind. And so, at sixty, she went to Indianapolis all alone, to make her way in the world. And she did make it. She worked at all kinds of jobs. She worked as supervisor in a girls' reform school. She worked in a restaurant. She took care of a sick woman. She worked as a housekeeper. And today at seventy she is still working. Not only making her own way, as we say of boys just out of college, but helping keep a lot of other people, just as she always has.

In the city, Aunt Mary had time and opportunity to keep up with what was going on in the world even better than she did before. She knew all about the New Deal, and was in favor of it. Most farm people and churchmen are fundamentalists, but my Aunt Mary would have to take only a couple of jumps to be a full-fledged socialist. She has pretty advanced social ideas, and if she was forty instead of seventy I'll bet she'd make the capitalists holler. She still has all her old energy. When she writes letters her mind runs so far ahead of her pen that she leaves out half the words.

But her main interest still lay in the little community where she lived for sixty years. Every letter to her had to tell how Minnie's chickens were doing, and who wasn't at church last Sunday, and when Edith is going to have her baby, and what Grace's new dress looks like. About twice a year she went back for a few days, and those few days were real happiness for her. And people would say to her what a shame she had to go back so soon and she would say, philosophically, but spirited-like too, "Yes, I'd sure love to stay, but I've got my own way to make, you know."

And here she is, at seventy, still hammering away at life and getting the best of it. She makes a lot of us younger ones look cheap.

Bob came past in his dad's car and picked me up. We drove down the road half a mile to the creek in Mr. Webster's pasture where I used to fish. Mr. Webster had been dead more than twenty years, but everybody still called it "Mr. Webster's pasture."

I had fished in that creek hundreds of times, but this was the first time I'd ever gone down there in an auto. I always used to walk, in my bare feet. It had been twenty years, I guess, since I had fished there. The creek never was very big, and it hadn't grown any in twenty years. You could jump across it almost any place. It was muddy too, and grass had grown up all along the banks.

We stopped the car at a little cement bridge and got out. Bob said there were fish there. The hole must have been five feet across, and all of a foot deep. Bob had dug the worms and had them in a tomato can, just as we used to carry them. When I fished down there last, Bob's parents hadn't even heard of him. And now he was bigger than I was. He was about to finish high school and was going to Chicago to be an artist. I wondered if he'd be coming back to fish twenty years afterward. Maybe he'd come back and paint a picture of Mr. Webster's pasture.

"Do you still know how to bait a hook?" Bob asked. I said, "Sure," and shoved the worm down over the hook. Bob watched me, as though I was a woman and couldn't bear it. I felt sorry for the worm, but I didn't say anything. I didn't remember having any feeling about hurting a worm when I was little. When I was through I spit on the bait and threw the line in.

The fish were biting pretty good for Bob and me—better than I remembered their biting in the old days. We caught about thirty in an hour. Only eight were big enough to save, and they weren't really big enough, but we had to take something home. I caught the two biggest sunfish, and Bob caught a cat, but it wasn't so big as my sunfish. After a while they stopped biting, and we pulled in our lines and got in the car and drove home. The old creek down in Mr. Webster's pasture didn't even know the great fisherman had been away for twenty years, I suppose. And for that matter, I don't suppose it knew he ever came back.

My mother wrote me that they had a new car. Well, not exactly a new car—you might call it a sort of secondhand car, she said. But it was pretty.

A new car wouldn't have done them any harm; the old one was eight years old. You could hardly start it in the winter, and my father was always taking out the back seat so he could carry his tools there. It looked pretty bad on the outside too. A new car had been discussed for more than six months. My father and mother were to trade in their old car, and Aunt Mary, who was finally coming over from Indianapolis to live with them, was to pay the cash balance.

There had been some difference of opinion over what the new car should be. There being only three of them to decide, it boiled down to the simple proposition that it would be one of three makes. There was no question that each of the three had its fine points. But still they couldn't decide. My advice was asked, by letter. I replied cautiously that they were, in my opinion, on the right track, and they certainly couldn't go wrong on any one of the three.

Finally the weight of approval seemed to crystallize in Aunt Mary's choice. But they reckoned without the shoe dealer from Clinton. I don't know how he heard about them, but one day he pulled up in the driveway in his last-year's car. He had driven it only five thousand miles, and it was a plum-green color, and very shiny, and the minute my folks saw it everything was off. "Let's go to Indianapolis and show it to your sister," the shoe dealer said.

So my folks got on their good clothes, and they climbed in and drove the eighty miles to Indianapolis. They got there just at lunchtime. Aunt Mary was so glad to see them that at first she didn't notice the car. They all stayed for lunch. My mother had taken over three frying chickens, a cake, and a quart of cream, so they wouldn't be imposing on the people Aunt Mary worked for. After lunch, they all went for a ride in the car.

Aunt Mary was a little hard to sell. But my family and the shoe dealer pointed out to her such indispensable added attractions as the cigar lighter (nobody in the family smoked), the two wind-shield wipers, the radio (I was ready to bet that within a week my father would get to listening and run the car into the ditch), the two taillights (nobody who is anybody has a car with just one taillight nowadays, you know), and the curved nickel shields for the rear tires. Mother pointed out especially the beautiful plum-green color of it. She didn't tell me in the letter whether the car had an engine or not.

Anyway, the gadgets won, and the upshot was that when they left for home the shoe dealer had sold his automobile. I felt sure they would get a lot of pleasure out of this car. They'd had only three in twenty-two years. And I suggested to my father that he pick up an old fourth-hand car with a box on the back (and with two taillights, of course) to haul his tools around in, so he wouldn't spoil the seats on the new job.

Washington
Interlude

Chapter
II
SIX THOUSAND MILES BEHIND US, AND THE WHITE
glow in the night of the Capitol dome ahead. Six thousand miles
of Canada and the United States, without getting lost by as much
as a block. And here, within eight miles of the White House, we
went through a place called Merryfield, Virginia, which we had
never heard of before, and had to stop and ask the way.

It was in the soft warm spring of 1923 that I first saw Washington. I was a cub reporter, and the editor had compassionately
invited me to stay at his hotel until I found a place to live. We
were walking to work that first morning, walking with the world
ahead of me, walking through McPherson Square, so green and
pretty, with people sitting leisurely on the benches even as early
as seven o'clock, and the editor said to me, "You'll probably like
Washington. But let me warn you: don't stay here too long. It's
a nice easygoing city and people get in a rut, and if you stay till
you get to liking it too well, you'll never leave. You'll just settle
down to a pleasant routine and never amount to anything."

When I came back in 1935, I had been heeding that editor's
advice for a dozen years, always getting out of Washington. But
somehow or other I kept coming back. Maybe it was the city that
pulled me back, or maybe it was some stubborn part of me that
didn't want to amount to anything. Anyhow, here I was again.

In appearance the Washington of 1935 was very different from
the Washington of that morning a dozen years earlier, but the
character of the place seemed to have changed hardly at all, and
there was still the same easy enchantment in the streets and the

· 14 ·

trees. Washington is really a big city that has achieved small-townishness in character. It has the personal liberty of that most cosmopolitan of all cities, New York, without its cruelty and lonesomeness.

I have often wondered how Washington achieved the appearance and the niceties of a small town, while retaining the best features of the big city. Anyone who sends in the correct answer, plus ten dollars in gold, can have my expired season pass to the American League ball games. My own guess is: Washington, on the edge of the real South, naturally has some of the South's delightful slothfulness. A good big percentage of the population came there from somewhere else—many of them from small towns. Physically, Washington is broad and smooth, its parks are big and numerous, its streets are wide and its buildings low, and the result is spaciousness. Many of its people live in apartment houses, hence the city doesn't spread all over the eastern seaboard. A good part of its population is in comfortable circumstances, so that the pinched look and the anxious stare and the goad of hurry, hurry, hurry seldom settles on the citizens of Washington. The whole thing, summed up, makes for easy living.

When a fellow has been shooting around the country and then goes back to Washington and walks down the street, all the people he knows stop and shake hands and say, "How was the trip?" So you say, "Oh, fine," and you chat for a minute or two.

Up in the new Supreme Court building a handsome young man stopped and said, "You don't know who I am, do you?" I didn't, so he told me he used to be a Western Union messenger and ran messages for me.

Down at the District jail, I saw a friend of many years who was waiting to be tried for murder. He was glad to see me, and I to see him, and to see that he looked better than he had in years.

Crossing the street, I heard somebody yell at me. It was a man standing on the corner counting cars. I asked him what for. He said he was doing it on relief, because the traffic bureau wanted the figures. He used to be a taxi driver, and I knew him well. A lot of taxi drivers are my friends.

In a restaurant I walked over to Gene Vidal, who was head of the Federal Bureau of Air Commerce, and I said, "Well, you think you're such a hot dresser, just take a look at me." I had on that combination that always makes people say, "Who do you like in the third at Belmont today?" Mr. Vidal just gave my green sweater a jerk, and then let on as if he thought the outfit was funny. But I could tell he was really burned up.

A fellow stopped me on the street and said, "I'm the man whose poem you wouldn't publish last winter." I started to square off and make what little defense I could, but he said he just wanted to say hello, and he didn't suppose he ever would get it published anywhere.

So, you see, when I sit at home in the evening reading in the original Greek and thinking about my friends and what a diversified lot they are, I feel very proud of them, and proud of myself too, for knowing them. Of course I just dismiss all those who stop and say, "Have you been away?" or "Where are you working now?" or who want to talk about what *they've* been doing.

The new Supreme Court building will never be complete till they put a couple of Saint Bernard dogs out front to carry rum to the travelers stricken with snow blindness trying to reach the entrance.

I paid a visit to this nine-million-dollar Parthenon. It sits back, majestically, half a block from the street. This half block is one vast expanse of glittering, sheet-white marble pavement. The bright sun spatters down on this white marble and comes right back up again into your face. It is like a sunny day on a field of snow. You know how some people have to sneeze when they look at the sun. Well, this white marble reflection started to get me, and I gave off a couple of tentative snorts, and then I went at it in earnest. Sneeze, wheeze, sneeze. There were other people around and I was embarrassed until I heard them starting to sneeze too. By that time my eyes had begun to water, everything had turned red, and I was half blind. I couldn't see the other sneezers, but I could hear them to right, to left, and all around, like delegates to the International Hay Fever Convention. With handkerchiefs over our eyes, and tears on our cheeks, we finally reached the shade of the main doorway, and safety.

The building was closed, all except the main corridor. But when I told them I was a poor boy, without any papa or mama, who had walked all the way from Mississippi just to see this wonderful new building, they got out a special guide and took me all over the place.

The only big word I can think of to describe it is "magnificent," but when you utter that word in those marble halls it rattles around like a dry bean—it is such an inadequate word. In my common opinion, the building is too grand, too magnificent. It is like having a twenty-room house just for me and my dog. Practically everything is marble—outside, inside, the walls, the floors. More marble was used in this than in any other building ever built in this world—more than seventeen hundred freight-car loads.

Inside, the building is such a maze of stairs and doors and wide white corridors that you can easily lose your way. You can't help feeling there is too much apple for the seed. In size the Supreme Court chamber itself bears about the same ratio to the entire building as does the watch pocket to a pair of pants. It holds two hundred eighty-three spectators, ten per cent more than the old chamber in the Capitol. The nine justices' suites occupy only a small portion of the building's whole space. There are countless offices for clerks and minor officials of the court, and even a handsome office just for the attorney general when he journeys up that way. There is a high-ceilinged library, half as long as the building, for the use of lawyers. Then there is a smaller library for the justices. There are a huge private dining room, a luncheon room, and a pantry and kitchen that could supply a hotel. And a cafeteria for the public. And immense conference rooms, all dark-oaked and red-velveted and crystal-chandeliered. And even the basement corridors are of marble.

I would like to know what Mr. Justice Brandeis thought of this pomp of Rome that has come to Washington. But I suppose I shall never know.

Some people get medals, some get money, and some wind up a long life of virtue and endeavor by getting hissed at in public. That's me.

It happened one noon in a Washington restaurant where I was to meet a girl for lunch. While I stood just inside the doorway, looking around for her, I gradually became aware of a clucking noise off to my right. It turned out to be the girl in the cloakroom, saying over and over, monotonously, yet eagerly, "Check your hat, check your hat, check your hat, sir?"

I turned and shook my head, then went outside to wait. But it was chilly, and after a minute or so, I decided to go back in, get a table, and wait there for my luncheon guest. The hostess was at the door, and while I was telling her what I had in mind, the clucking noise at my right was vigorously resumed, and continued—clickety-clack. I didn't turn around that time, for I knew what it was. Furthermore, I wasn't checking my hat that day, for the plain and simple reason that I didn't want to. Hasn't a man got a right in this country not to check his hat if he doesn't want to? I thought he had, but now I'm sure I don't know, and I'll appreciate any advice upon just what is expected of a man with a hat.

Anyhow, the hostess said she'd get me a table. As I walked behind her, I could hear the clucking noise following me for a few steps. Then all of a sudden it stopped, there was one-fourth of a second's silence, and then:

"Sssssssssssss! ! ! !"

I stopped dead. I did a military about-face. I fixed a G-man glare at the cloakroom window, and held it. The girl was guilty all right, but I'll give her credit—she was quick. There crossed her face just one fleeting, surprised look of being caught, and then she raised her brows, inclined her head, and said, "Check your hat, sir?" I turned and went to my table, blubbering to the hostess something about being hissed at, but she apparently thought I was just a New Dealer talking to himself, and paid no attention.

The thing got to preying on my mind in the next few days. Sometimes I would walk along, and throw out my chest its full half inch, thinking what a guy I was—the only one in the capital of the United States, perhaps, who had ever had the distinction of being hissed at by a hat-check girl. But at other times I would go deep into melancholia and shame. I blushed when the radiator hissed in the mornings. I was disgraced, I had a stigma. People knew about it, and pointed. I was a lank, outcast black cat in an alley full of gray ones. And even in the presence of people who didn't know, I was beaten and afraid. I knew, whether they did or not. What it would do to me in the end I could only guess. It was all so confused in my mind. I thought and thought about it, and only one thing stood out clearly: that I wished I had gone back, right at the time, and given that girl a good big push in the face.

Perhaps every person in this world has in his list of acquaintances a man or woman who is the inventor type. I don't mean the professional inventor, who actually makes models and gets patents and reaps big fortunes, or the poor but honest inventor who is always being cheated out of his ideas by big corporations. I mean the casual inventor, who otherwise appears quite sound, who pops up every day or so with a grand idea and never does anything about it except tell his friends.

An acquaintance of mine had a new scheme for pipe smokers. He would have a large vat of burning tobacco in the basement, like a furnace. Then he would have small conveyer pipes running from the furnace up through the walls, carrying the smoke to all parts of the house. In each room he would have several plug-in stations, like electric-light wall plugs, only higher. Each smoker would be equipped with a pipestem stuck on the end of a six- or eight-foot hose. There would be one for each member of the family, and several for guests. When anybody wanted to smoke, he would just plug into the nearest wall socket, sit down, and start puffing.

A fellow I know in Cleveland would have a trough running clear around the edge of the dining-room table to catch the crumbs. He thought it up one night when the cracker he was eating broke in two, dropped onto his napkin, slid off, and shattered on the rug. He saw then that napkins were no good, and that there'd have to be something better. In the bottom of the trough, he would have an endless conveyer, always moving, so that the crumbs would instantly be carried out of sight. His wife thought his idea didn't go far enough. She would solve the problem by having no boards on the floor, so you could just drop crumbs, cigarette ashes, and apple cores clear through into the basement, where the janitor would take care of them. Or if you had no janitor, you could clear them out in the spring. ●

A young woman I knew had an idea that sounded crazy on the surface, but which, upon being analyzed, was exceedingly practical. Since both she and I were disinclined to do anything about it, the idea will probably be taken up by some big manufacturing company, and a fortune made. But we were the kind that money isn't everything to. Her idea was founded on the experience that round skillets are the bunk. You can never get what you're cooking into them and, furthermore, the heat from the gas burner is always in the center or on one side, and you have to keep shoving the skillet around so everything will cook. A big sirloin steak, as she pointed out, is not round, but long and narrow. Just try to wrap one into a round skillet some time. So she would make her skillet rectangular. And to go with it, she would make the burners on stoves rectangular also, instead of the present circular cluster. Thus they would fit the skillet. I think she had something there, and my advice to her was to see a lawyer right away.

It must be tough to discover a new chain of mountains, and not even be able to see them. That's what happened to a certain group of explorers. They couldn't see the mountains because they were under water.

The discoverers were Commander L. V. Kielhorn, of the United States Coast Guard, and his crew aboard the cutter *Chelan*. Mine was the first public announcement of the find. At first I was inclined to be proud that I had the honor of telling the world about this great discovery. But after analyzing the thing, I'm not sure that it makes any difference whether the world knows, or even whether the mountains were ever discovered. It seems to me I'd rather find a five-dollar bill on the sidewalk than a chain of mountains under water.

This new mountain ridge is about two hundred thirty miles long. It starts on the north side of the Aleutian Islands, in the northern Pacific, runs north into the Bering Sea for a hundred twenty miles, then swings west for a hundred ten miles. There it suddenly ends—simply drops off for eleven thousand feet right down to the bottom of the ocean. During most of its 230-mile length, the top of the mountain ridge is about nine hundred feet under water. In places peaks rise to within two hundred forty feet of the top.

The men on the Coast Guard boat reported their discovery to Washington by radio. Washington took it calmly enough. And as far as I know, right there is where the matter still stands.

In one of my annual checkups to see if the Bureau of Engraving and Printing was getting away with any of the money it makes, I ran into an appalling thing. In six weeks the bureau had printed and delivered, for the Christmas rush, two hundred eighteen million revenue stamps to be put on bottles of blended whisky!

Each stamp represents one bottle. That makes nearly two bottles of liquor for every man, woman, and child in the United States, just for the holiday period. If your two bottles are gone before New Year's Eve you might speak to some of those children, who shouldn't be drinking blends anyway.

A great deal of legend had already grown up about the Washington Cathedral, though it wasn't even finished. One was about a laborer who had worked on the cathedral for years and become infused with its spirit and wanted to have his wife buried there. When he was refused, the story goes, he had her cremated, and then one day he dropped the ashes in a barrow of fresh cement, and his wife was forever entombed in the cathedral he loved. Nobody but the man himself, if there was one, knew whether the story was true or not. Bishop James E. Freeman said no such request was ever made of him. But it might have happened before he became bishop. Cathedral officials said it could easily be true, and they thought it probably was.

It is a matter of vexation to me that I must spend my life reading stories about Ely Culbertson and Sidney Lenz and other bridge sharks, and yet I can never find a word in the papers about the feats performed in that noblest of all card games, solitaire. What do I care about Ely and Sidney? Nothing. I have never played a game of bridge in my life, and never intend to. If you play bridge, you have to play with somebody. That cancels it for me. In solitaire, you can miss a play or make a mistake, and nobody in the world knows it but you, and you won't tell. You can sit and look at your cards for hours without batting an eye, and nobody will scowl at you, or cough. You don't have to open your mouth or say a word, except maybe to swear softly to yourself now and then when you get only two aces out.

Solitaire is without fame in its own land. Who invented solitaire? We don't know. Why don't we find out, and build a big monument to him? Who is the champion solitaire player of the world? We don't know. Why don't we find out, and run his picture every Sunday in the magazine sections? Is there a solitaire player who has never cheated? Probably not, but why don't we find out and, if there is, build a legend around him, as we did with George and his hatchet?

Solitaire is wonderful on ships, or on trains, or in bleak hotel rooms where time drags, or at home in the evenings when you have company you don't like. It is also the perfect salve for an inhibited gambling spirit. There are, I imagine, any number of people like myself who have an inborn itch for gambling, but who never gamble because they can't bear to lose. Solitaire is just the thing for us. We can imagine we're playing in a gambling house, and we deal in big figures, and at the end of the evening we've lost $387 and we don't have to pay it.

I stayed one week in a hotel where the light was too dim for reading, the heat went off at seven o'clock, and there wasn't even an old-fashioned rocking chair. So I put on a couple of sweaters, pulled up a hard-bottomed chair, put a pillow on it, and played solitaire. Every night for a week. Altogether, I played about seventy games. I won (got all the cards out) only once. Once, just by little dribbles, I came out slightly ahead for the evening. All the other evenings I went steadily downhill. At the end of the week I was some six hundred dollars in the red. I kept track on the back of an envelope, and when I left I threw the envelope in the wastebasket.

There was a friend of mine who wanted only one thing in this life. She wanted somebody to give her five hundred dollars, with the stipulation that she must use it playing solitaire in a gambling house. If she ever got above five hundred dollars, she would be allowed to quit; otherwise, keep playing till she was broke. She'd never be satisfied till she tried it.

I have talked with solitaire players all over the country. Every one of them seems to know somebody who once played solitaire in a gambling house. But I have yet to meet a person who, himself, had played it in a gambling house. I wonder if you really can.

Once I met an old man on a boat who played constantly. He said he had kept count of his progress for years, and that he was way ahead. He said he could win in a gambling house. He could, it is true, except that they wouldn't let him play. They'd throw him right through the front window. He just moved his cards wherever they'd do the most good, whether they fit or not.

They are a strange corporation of loneliness and close kinship, the women of aviation who sit at home and hear that their husbands are dead. Death comes to other women's husbands too. But no people in this world are so closely linked together as the people of aviation, and it is the long and very real shadow of death that links them. When one woman's husband dies violently, the wives of the living shudder a little for themselves, though not much; and the wives of the already dead come quickly with their sympathy and their memories.

I have tried to analyze the attitude toward death among aviators. I have even tried to analyze my own, for it became in time the same as theirs. Vaguely I feel it is something like this: the pilot knows something might happen, but—oh, well, he's escaped so far, and probably he will this time too. The wives have a greater faith—a conviction of their husbands' superiority. I have never known an aviation wife who didn't consider her husband the greatest pilot in the world. It's too bad when other pilots are killed, she thinks, but that won't happen to my man; he can handle any emergency. Those who have picked up the receiver and heard the awful news know better than that. Among them have been women whose husbands actually were the greatest pilots in the world.

One night my phone rang, and a hurried voice said, "What do

you know about Howard?" I started to make a funny answer to the effect that I knew a lot about him, but something in the voice stopped me. I said, "What do you mean?" "The papers say he's been missing for seventeen hours out west. I can't get any information. Can't you help me?"

There wasn't any information. In the next few weeks hundreds of men, on snowshoes and skis, on horses, in airplanes, hunted the western mountains over, but there was no trace. The missing man was Howard Stark, known in many countries as the greatest blind flier of his day.

Missing—that is aviation at its worst. Sudden news of death is like a knockout blow: it hurts and bewilders and then it gradually diminishes. But missing—that is the torture screw, with each hour that passes giving the screw another turn. You can't resign yourself to grief; you must hang alone by the tips of your hope—dangling, imagining, lying to yourself, waiting.

The night after Howard Stark disappeared, another woman called me. "Is there any news?" she asked. "I couldn't sleep last night. All night I was thinking of Mrs. Stark, and living over my trouble again." Her "trouble" had been on the night mail. Three years earlier her husband had crashed and died, half an hour after kissing her goodbye at the airport.

I have been on hand many times when word of a crash came in. There is nothing romantic about aviation then, to hear pilots cussing with tears in their eyes, to see women wild with grief, or dazed and dry-eyed and staring. One girl I knew was hysterical and pounded her head against the wall. Her grief never really left her. She was gone in less than a year. The doctors would say something else, but I know she died because she didn't want to live.

Another night I sat in the operations office with a woman whose husband had just been burned to death. Instead of going home, she sat, because at that point sitting or going home or anything else was equally unimportant to her. She did not cry. To this day I am proud of myself for having the courage and common sense to ask her if she didn't want a drink of whisky. She wasn't a woman who drank, but at that moment a drink of whisky was exactly what she did want. And we got it for her.

· 24 ·

Almost always the women who are left go back to where their lives entered aviation. They take their children and their loneliness back to the home town, and you don't hear from them again until another woman of the clan knocks for admission to their desolate corporation, and they vote her in, and pray for her.

I had a horrifying adventure with a pair of pants. It began out in St. Paul when I bought my new gray suit. I bought it there because it was in St. Paul that the bottom fell out of my old pants, and because I like to show off as a much-traveled young man, and say casually, "Oh, yes, this tie came from Germany, and I got this green sweater in Portland, Maine, and these gloves in Knoxville, and my white socks in El Centro, California, and these shoes in Indianapolis, and this gray suit I picked up in St. Paul."

It was a nice suit, and it had two pairs of pants—one with buttons up the front, the other with a zipper. I had never had a zipper on a pair of pants, and I thought that was hot stuff. The super-supersalesman, clinching the deal, said, "This is one zipper that works, too, and don't you forget it." So I bought the suit, and was measured for alterations. I picked up the altered suit that evening, and left St. Paul early next morning without trying it on. They had altered it, all right, but they altered it down to the point where I couldn't get into it. It cost six dollars to have it altered back up.

But the real story is about that zipper. It never did work very well. It ran like a cog-wheel train off the track. It made a ripping noise, and you had to pull with all your strength to get it up or down, and it kept getting worse. One day when I put on the suit after it had come from the cleaners, it took me five minutes to close the zipper. That should have been sufficient warning, but my mind was on other things, so I went downtown wearing those pants. During the morning I had occasion to work the zipper and it wouldn't budge. I yanked and I pulled and I tugged, but no go. I pulled so hard that the little metal tab cut a gash in my thumb, and I had to go and wrap it up. Finally I had to call for help. An ex-football player on the Washington *News* staff managed to get it open by wrapping a handkerchief around his thumb and bracing himself while I pulled up on the top of the pants.

By that time I was thoroughly alarmed, and I kept within calling distance of aid all day. It happened twice more before evening. I had to get a government clerk and then a fellow in a garage to help me. When I got home I decided to get out of those pants right away. But I couldn't get them off; the zipper wouldn't move.

We had a dinner guest, a great big fellow, and he thought he could zip the zipper all right. He was just a fool; he couldn't even get it started. He cut his thumb on the metal tab and got mad, and I got mad, and I don't know what might have happened if I hadn't thought of the hammer. I got the hammer and had him slip the claw over the tab, and then while I pulled at the pants with all my might, he pushed down on the hammer. It sort of worked. The zipper came open about half an inch at a time. We were going along pretty good, when suddenly the metal tab collapsed under the strain and bent up in a half circle, and the hammer claw wouldn't stay on it. From then on, after every heave with the hammer, I'd have to work the tab up over the edge of the kitchen table, and he'd hammer it down flat again. We got the zipper open in a little less than half an hour.

I didn't put on the other pair of pants, the one with the buttons. I didn't eat any dinner, either. Didn't feel like dinner, somehow. I just went to bed and turned out the lights and lay there with my jaws clenched, glaring at the darkness. After a while I went to sleep.

South of the
Rio Grande

It was a quarter to nine on a Sunday night in Laredo, Texas. The thermometer at the corner of the plaza said 82; the air was soft and a light breeze washed past. Stars twinkled, a brittle blue in the dark sky. All Laredo was bathed in a sweet odor of orange blossoms, which faded and came back as you walked along. The block-square plaza was thick with green trees, and there was a circular lighted bandstand in the middle. The sidewalks were crowded with walkers, all dark-skinned. Loungers, two by two, lay or sat on the grass. You heard no English spoken, for Laredo was eighty per cent Mexican, or Spanish American, as the transplanted Mexicans prefer to be called. Boys and girls, coatless and hatless, were everywhere. They strolled, and talked, and took their time. But it seemed more than mere strolling around the plaza. There was something different.

Gradually it came to you. The boys were all walking in one direction, and the girls in the other—in twos and sometimes threes, row after row, walking along rather rapidly, like an army on a broken-step march. They never paused—just kept going round and round the square. And then you noticed that the outer edge of the sidewalk, clear around the plaza, was lined with still more young men, standing in a solid row like a picket fence. They stood mostly in silence, watching the girls as they passed.

I asked questions, and I found it was a custom as old as Mexico, which the Mexicans brought over into the United States with them. They call it the "promenade." Every town and city in Mexico has its open block-square plaza with a bandstand in the middle, and cement or gravel walks leading inward from the four corners. Every Sunday night, and in some places every Thursday night too, the young people of the town turn out for the promenade around the plaza. All over Mexico that night girls were parading around plazas in one direction and boys in the other, looking at each other.

The purpose of the promenade is to let the young men see what likely-looking girls there are in town, and many a marriage has come out of the first shy glances in the plaza. In the old days the girls were always chaperoned. If a boy liked a girl's looks, he would turn and fall into step with her and walk along talking—properly chaperoned, of course. Now, even though there weren't any chaperons, I noticed only a few boys joining the girls. The promenade had become more an excuse just to come downtown and stand around.

I stood for a long time watching the girls' faces, and never saw one that would launch a rowboat, let alone a battleship. They were nice faces, but not what we in our country consider beautiful. The girls were all in light summer dresses. Some were quite small, still in short skirts. Some ranged up close to the thirties. Most of them were slim, though now and then you would see a fat one. There must have been five hundred girls parading, and as many boys walking or standing along the walk.

Pretty soon a truck pulled up to the curb. It had loud-speakers on top, and it was tuned to a Mexican radio station, very loudly. The strollers strolled on, to the music, and the crowds stood or sat on the grass, and talked and listened. The parading went on for nearly two hours. Gradually the crowd thinned out. At ten o'clock the music stopped. By ten-fifteen the plaza was empty and dark. The boys had seen the girls, and the girls had seen the boys, and they'd both had their walks, and it was all over for another week.

A girl in a blue tailored suit came up to us in the hotel at Juarez, Mexico, and asked, "Are you Americans?" We said yes, and she sat down and started talking. Then her husband came over, and it turned out he was an American rassler. They had been in Mexico about a month, under a Mexican manager, working the small towns out of Tampico, rassling two or three times a week.

They were from Salt Lake City. The rassler's name was Dory Detton. Dory's father was a rassler, and the three sons were all rasslers. Dory went to the University of Utah, and made good grades too, but three years back he had quit school to go into professional rassling. He wished now he'd gone on. His first professional appearance was when he was watching his brother Dean rassle, and the other guy had Dean's head twisted up in the ropes. So Dory, who was just a spectator, forgot himself, jumped into the ring, and knocked this guy cold. Brother Dean thought it was awfully funny.

Dory had had three hundred and twenty matches in three years, and been beaten only a few times, but he sounded like the weekend traffic toll. His skull had been fractured, his right hip smashed, his left shoulder crushed, and his back broken—or at least some vertebrae had been knocked out of place—and it still bothered him. His wife had to work on him all the time. She used to be a beauty operator, so she had strong arms, even though she was just a little thing, and pretty too. After every rassle Dory's back was all out of joint, so she gave him an "adjustment" and got his vertebrae back in place. She carried a kit of doctor's supplies, and what with her adjustments, and massages and bandages and liniments, their room looked like a hospital.

We got interested in Dory, and went to see him rassle. He was a middleweight, but when he got in the ring he looked like one whole end of the Chicago stockyards. The Mexican started right in to slaughter him. I've never seen such a rassle. This Mexican was a wild man; he hit and kicked in the most illegal places, and used his knee, and tried to gouge Dory's eyes out, and twice when Dory had him down he broke loose by biting a hunk out of Dory's leg. The referee tried to stop the Mexican, but the crowd wouldn't let him. They wanted their man to win, and to hell with the details. When Detton had the Mexican down flat and the referee started counting, the crowd would scream "No! No! No!" and the referee would stop and look around, sort of pleading, and finally start his count all over again. Detton won, though, by throwing the Mexican twice. He simply picked him up and put him on his shoulders and jumped up and down with him till he had all the wind knocked out of him, and then laid him on the mat. After the final fall, the crowd screamed at the referee for ten minutes. They could hardly get the next bout under way.

Afterward Dory and his wife came up to our room. He was plenty sore. He said if anybody pulled such dirty stuff on him in the States, he'd knock him out. "But I'm afraid of these crowds," he said. "You've got to fight clean and not too rough, no matter what the other guy's doing. They've cut a couple of American wrestlers all to pieces in the last few months. I figured the only thing to do was get it over with as quick as I could."

I had supposed that all groan-and-grimace boys, like Davy Crockett, were half horse and half alligator, and that you had to talk to them in sign language. But these Dettons were nice people. Both Dory and his wife were young—about twenty-three, I'd judge—and very quiet and serious. Sitting in a hotel room, Dory was even sort of humble. They stayed and talked about half an hour, and then Dory's leg was starting to get sore where the Mexican bit him, and his back was hurting too, so they left.

At four o'clock in the morning I was asleep in the front room of a house in Tamazunchale, a poor little mountain town in the state of San Luis Potosi, deep in tropical Mexico. Outside the window was a banana tree, and beyond it the flowering yard, and the fence, and then the dirt street, full of rocks and mudholes. And on beyond, some thatched houses, and then the river, and then the great mountain, towering close with that looking-down-at-you attitude.

For a while I didn't know whether I was dreaming or awake. I remember lying there a long time, just half listening, letting on to myself that it wasn't real, even after I knew it was. From somewhere, out of the darkness, music was coming. It was so soft, so low, so gentle that for a long time it seemed to be of the same texture as a dream. The utter darkness, and the stillness that comes an hour before dawn, and the terrific quiet that lies just ahead of a thunderstorm, and the few far notes of a muted trumpet flowed and blended into a harmony that was something of nature alone.

I reached for my slippers and couldn't find them, so I got up in my bare feet. I felt my way to the screen door and unhooked it and stepped out onto the porch, down the steps into the yard, and inch by inch, stone by stone, out over the cobbles to the front gate. I could not see the houses, or the street, or the gate I was leaning on, or my hand before me, for it was, as they say down there, as black as the inside of a goat. But I knew the music was not far away; the sound was within a hundred feet of me, up the street.

It was sweet music, sweet and swinging and low, but very sad. It was not jungle music; it wasn't ragged or primitive or poor, like the Indians themselves. It was like our own sentimental waltzes, only sweeter. I could pick out the instruments by the sound. There were four. A flowing, undulating, hushed trombone, and a muted trumpet. Have you ever heard a trumpet played by a Mexican just before dawn—a Mexican who maybe is happy now, but whose heart is a whole legacy of sadness from a saddened people? And a guitar, strummed with tenderness, and by knowing fingers in the dark. And a bass drum. Its sides were loosened, to soften it; it was a faint heartbeat, just holding together the structure of the symphony serenade.

They were serenading a sweetheart, I suppose. Or maybe they were mountain farmers, down for tomorrow's market, full of pulque, just whiling away the hours till dawn. If they spoke between pieces, it was in whispers, for I never heard them. I don't know whether they were boys, or old men. I don't know whether they had on store clothes or dirty Indian "pajamas." I don't know who they were, or what, or why. I never saw them. They never saw me. They had no light. They played as a night bird sings—with their hearts, by instinct, and love.

I had expected Mexico City to be a slow city, but it wasn't. The people on the sidewalks moved no slower than in the States, though the city did absolutely close up at one in the afternoon. Everybody went home for lunch. Nobody ate downtown. At four, people came back and the stores opened again. Working hours were nine to one and four to six-thirty.

Traffic cops' signals were the reverse of ours. If the cop's side was toward you, you stopped. If his face or back was toward you, you went. And how traffic went in Mexico City! A space two feet wide between cars looked like an empty street to a Mexican taxi driver. Taxis swarmed the downtown section like flies. They were just ordinary small sedans, with a colored line drawn clear around on the molding. Some of the lines were blue, some red, some green, and so on. Here's the reason: there were five thousand cabs in Mexico City, which was too many, so the drivers divided themselves into seven sections, each section with its own color. Each color was given one day off a week. Work on your day off and it was a twenty-five-peso fine.

Some people don't suffer from Mexico City's seventy-five-hundred-foot altitude. Others, including me, do. Some have headaches, nosebleeds, and stomach-aches; some can't get their breath; some get tired and sleepy; some want to leap around doing things like a wild man; it makes some people very irritable; some get completely sick. It did all these things to me.

March weather in Mexico City is good—and bad. It is cool at night, though not quite topcoat weather. In the middle of the day the sun beats down fiercely, and you'd better be careful of sunburn. Every afternoon a wind comes up, and with it the dust from the dry bed of nearby Lake Texcoco. By three o'clock the air is thick with sand, and you can hardly breathe. To me this was the most annoying thing about Mexico City; my lips were dry and parched, and my hands were chapped as from a New England frost. The dust season lasts a month or so.

There were two telephone systems, the Ericsson and the Mexican. Both were dial systems. When you answered the telephone you said "Bueno" instead of "Hello." Some people said it *"Bway-no,"* with the accent on the first syllable. Others said it very slowly and philosophically—"Bway-nohhhhh," with the "no" long drawn out.

Hotel bathrooms had sulphur water in the taps. You didn't drink it, but you could brush your teeth in it. A carafe of drinking water was on the table. Men and women sold tickets in the national lottery up and down the sidewalks and in the middle of the streets too. The only matches you could get were little wax ones that made an awful smell. The daily papers printed one page in English, but had only one or two news stories; the rest was filler about such things as a three-legged chicken in Mc-Cook, Nebraska.

Mexico City was beautiful but, it seemed to me, not so beautiful as Washington. It was big too—a million and a quarter—and it was more than six hundred years old. It didn't have subways or elevateds or skyscrapers—its one downtown "skyscraper" was about ten stories, I believe—but it had fine buildings and traffic lights and night clubs. And more statues than Baltimore.

I liked Mexico City mainly because of the people I met. They were intelligent, courteous, and generous about putting themselves out to do things for you. You could taxi anywhere downtown for fourteen cents, our money, and contrary to warnings no driver tried to overcharge me. Its people were park lovers; all classes, old and young, went to the parks at night and on Sundays, and they seemed to have a good time. I liked Mexico City because it was full of old cathedrals and relics of history and lots of frescoes by Diego Rivera painted on walls inside of public buildings; and because there were barefooted Indians right in the heart of town carrying immense loads on their backs; and because when a fellow got a tack in his foot he would sit right down on the curb and fish it out; and because the sidewalks were thronged with Indians selling things (not to tourists, either)—such stuff as peanuts and melons and cigarettes; and because the town was simply lousy with policemen in the snappiest uniforms you ever saw; and because—again contrary to warnings—the beggars didn't bother you, and they were no more frequent than in the States.

And, on the other hand, I disliked Mexico City because the trees were covered with brown dust and everything looked dry and thirsty, and because the altitude made your heart pound, and you had to stop and swell up every now and then to get enough air, until you got used to it. They said even natives had heart trouble from it. I didn't like the trend of architecture that was making Mexico City look like a combination of Hollywood and a futuristic Russian movie. There were at least six new residential "colonies" done in curved corners and nickel strips and setbacks. Even the new downtown buildings were like that. I disliked Mexico City most of all because it wasn't really Mexico, any more than New York is the whole United States.

I disliked Mexico City also because, on the whole, the people didn't like Americans. But then I disliked the Americans for making the Mexicans dislike us. 🌑

Taxco (pronounced Tahsco), a hundred miles south of Mexico City, is very old and primitive, and it's built all over a rough mountainside with ravines and shelves. The maps say the town is five thousand eight hundred fifty feet high, but they don't say which part of town. The upper side must be at least eight hundred feet higher than the lower. I don't believe any two hundred square feet of Taxco are on the same level. Or that any street runs straight more than a third of a block. Or that any row of roofs makes a straight line. When you arrive, you have to take a boy on the running board to show you where to go. Some of the streets are just wide enough for a car and a burro. Most of them look like walking paths rather than streets—and that's exactly what they are. They were built for burros and sandaled men.

Taxco had about five thousand people in 1936, and looked bigger. In the middle of the town was the most dominating piece of architecture I had ever seen—the great cathedral built two hundred years ago by José Borda. He discovered silver there and made more money out of minerals than anyone else in the whole history of Mexico, and then spent it all on this church (and the Borda gardens in Cuernavaca). When he died he didn't have anything, but it must have been worth it. When you look across the ravine at the pinkish old church over there on the mountainside among the white walls and the green trees, its two great towers ascending in massive competition with the mountain peak, you could, I believe, stand there looking as long as at any building in the world.

There were no telephones in Taxco. There were electric lights and a telegraph station, but gas stations had to stay outside of town. Taxco was so perfect that the government had made it what we in the States call a "national monument" and nobody could build anything without the government's approval. The travel literature said Taxco was an "art colony," or a "literary colony." The people who lived there said that was hooey; artists and writers did drift in, but they drifted back out again. Only eight American families were living there permanently, and they were all in business except two.

Not many people had heard of Taxco until the new road came through in 1928. After that it got to be like Niagara Falls, or that foot doctor up in Canada. Some days as many as four hundred Americans would blow into town.

What would become of Taxco in the next few years, I wondered, with tens of thousands of tourists streaming down over the Pan-American Highway to Mexico City and on to Taxco? If tourists got so thick they'd push the burros off into the ravines and you'd hardly be able to see a hog in the street, and if every brown child learned to say "allo" in bad English, then Taxco would be gone. But why, you ask, should I be shooting off the mouth about American sightseers coming to Taxco? Am I a tourist, or am I a tourist? Yes, I know. But at least I wear the same clothes I wear at home, and don't go around in a pink shirt, green jodhpurs, blue spectacles, brown sun helmet, and a pair of field glasses just because I happen to be in Mexico. And I never make any noise.

I had always had a vague impression that just a few buried temples and cities had been found in Mexico. But I found that the country was chock-full of ancient buildings—even cities—all covered by time and weather. For example, I stood on top of the highest pyramid on Monte Alban, just a few miles out of Oaxaca, which is three hundred miles below Mexico City, and saw pyramids all around me—a dozen or more of them, laid out systematically like buildings in a city. And in every direction, as far as I could see, all the hilltops and mountain peaks below me were crowned with one or more irregular mounds. Under every mound was a building of some kind, maybe a thousand years old, maybe five thousand, put there by men who had some kind of scientific civilization approaching ours of today—a civilization that, for some unknown reason, withered and vanished.

I didn't count the mounds within eye's reach, but there were easily a hundred. And this was just one ancient uncovered city. Southern Mexico is strewn with them. Scientists don't have to go out exploring for new mounds. It would take more than the life span of any living scientist to dig into all the known mounds in Mexico. This was what excited me so: to know that maybe in one of these hundreds of mounds was the key to the evolution of all humanity. I could see how a fellow might go crazy and run around tearing at the dirt with his hands, trying to get them all uncovered before he died.

At dinner in a hotel at Guatemala City we sat near a nice-looking elderly couple who were recently arrived tourists. I don't know why they singled us out for their generous offer, but at any rate the gentleman came over, apologized for interrupting, and said they had a delicacy—far more than they could eat—and would like to give us some of it.

The delicacy, it turned out, was boiled iguana. Now, if you ever have seen an iguana, the idea is enough to make your hair stand on end. As far as we could see, it is nothing more or less than a horrible-looking lizard. Many people eat them in Central America, and they are considered very good. The elderly couple had read about them, and being thorough souls who wouldn't pass up an experience, they went to the market, bought one alive, and had the chef cook it.

There wasn't anything we could do, in the circumstances, but accept. We pushed it around the plate, took a few nibbly bites, with our stomach nerves drawn like tight wires, nodded a couple of sickly grins of delight and appreciation, and went upstairs and lay down. It tasted all right, at that—except that I somehow seem to eat with my eyes, instead of my mouth. 🍂

🍂 For two centuries Antigua, twenty-five miles southwest of Guatemala City, was the grandest city between Mexico and Peru. It had seventy thousand people and fifty elaborate churches and monasteries. It glowed with conquest and wealth and a lavish religion. And then in a few minutes, in 1773, an earthquake shook the entire city to the ground. Only three buildings were left wholly standing. In fear of more earthquakes from the towering volcanoes, the capital city was moved to another valley, twenty-five miles away, which was thought to be out of the earthquake belt. And there grew up Guatemala City, the capital of today.

But some of the people would not go. Even now thirteen thousand people were living there among the silent ruins, and they were busy in a quiet way. You sensed this quietness the minute you drove into town. I doubt that people were quiet out of respect for the dead, and yet it might be that the memory of an overwhelming tragedy had touched and tempered the spirits of a people through the years.

The tourist drove clear across town—probably fifty blocks, for the city was large—to the Hotel Manchen at the far edge. Although there were bathtubs and hot water, the hotel admitted to more than a hundred years of existence. Coffee lay drying on the concrete of the patio. Indians without shoes served the meals on outdoor terraces. Flowers were profuse. And over all there was a quiet and a peace which, after the noises of Guatemala City, came over you like a warmth of sun when the clouds pass.

I think the best way, probably the only genuine way, to see Antigua for the first time is to walk—and walk by yourself—wearing dark glasses, for the sun is blindingly bright. First you go up a path back of the hotel, among coffee trees, then through the woods until you come to an opening where you can look down upon the ruined city. You see how the city is laid out; you get the sense of tragedy. Then you walk back down into the town. You go a dozen steps, and you are among the ruins of Antigua. A dozen steps in any direction, almost anywhere in the entire city, and you are among ruins.

To me, "ruins" is a museum word, a tourist-party word, denoting something roped off with a plaque on it, probably with a spiked fence around it, something cold and boring. But the ruins of Antigua were not blocked off; they were not hawked by megaphone or sold at ten cents a handful. They were just there, and you poked around by yourself. They had not retired upon their honors, but were functioning as a part of the daily lives of the people of Antigua. People lived among the cracked walls. You stepped from the lovely tree-shaded plaza into the police station, which looked no different from a police station anywhere in Latin America. But just step to the back door, and you would find a jumble of rock and brick and partly standing walls and cracked domes and hanging sections of roof, just as nature left them in 1773. That was Antigua—behind every modern front, a ruin; within every ruin, a new life.

Most of the ruins were of cathedrals and monasteries, for on them the Spanish lavished their gold and their slave labor, and some of their massive walls stood up when everything around them crumbled. A few of the more lavish church wreckages were kept cleaned and watched over by Indian attendants. Others just stood there, jumbled and old. And some were being used again—for homes, for shops, even parts of them for worship. The convent of San Agustin, on a downtown corner, was now a blacksmith shop. In niches out front still stood the cracked and broken-faced statues of saints. The big public market was within the ruins of the old Jesuit monastery; the Church of the Carmelite Nuns was now the prison for women; a coffee plantation grew among the fallen walls of the Church de la Concepción; the old University of San Carlos was a museum. And so it was all over the city.

It was not the ruins of the great cathedrals that impressed me so much as the prodigious wreckage of small things all around. The far-out streets, paved only with inch-deep dust, were bordered on both sides by partly tumbled stone walls. To right and left they sagged and staggered—vine-covered, some of them. You pushed open the wooden door of the building that was once the Capuchin Monastery. You stepped into a large patio, and all around you were parts of walls and parts of rooms and cracked arches and the silent signs of fury—yet the place was full of people, living there. The sunshine beat in on the lassitude, and a model T Ford truck, without tires, sat in silent ruin along with the sacred bricks of two centuries ago.

They said you could buy a set of old walls for almost nothing. A few people had taken old cracks of stone walls and heaps of broken brick and turned them into mouth-watering private homes, but there weren't many. The one outstanding place—famous even outside of Guatemala—was the home of Dr. Wilson Popenoe, an agronomist and botanist for the United Fruit Company. His work kept him jumping from one country to another, and he was not there at the moment, but friends of ours who were staying in the house as guests asked us to lunch.

When Dr. and Mrs. Popenoe came to Guatemala in 1930 they fell in love with Antigua and bought an old corner ruin—hardly more than a set of walls surrounding some patios. Room by room, patio by patio, they restored it and furnished it as they believed it to have been furnished two hundred years ago. They found vast old beds, intricate wooden statues, rare paintings of the early Spaniards. Mrs. Popenoe died in 1932, but Dr. Popenoe still maintained the house, with a set of barefooted Indian servants always there. I would have liked to own it, but you wouldn't have caught me living in it. The place was just too downright authentic for a twentieth-century fellow like me. I like my antiquity tempered with a little hot water for bathing, a little electricity for reading, a deep chair or two for sitting. By design, the Popenoe house had none of these things. I'm not afraid of earthquakes, but the thought of a cold shower paralyzes me.

They say there is no worse jungle this side of Africa than the Petén in Guatemala. I flew there in a TACA Airlines freighter, which was the only way to get there. Carmelita, the place where we landed, consisted of only an airstrip cut out of the jungle, a thatch-roofed chicle shed, and a handful of brush huts scattered among the trees. There wasn't a floor in the settlement, or a real chair or bed, or a bathtub—not even a tin one.

The Petén jungle comprises one-third of all Guatemala. It is as big as Massachusetts, Delaware, and Connecticut combined, and extends into Yucatán and British Honduras. And it has only seventy-five hundred people. It is full of snakes and monkeys and macaws and fever and mahogany and insects. A horrific density of trees springs up to a solid matted ceiling a hundred feet above the earth. No sunlight gets through. The trails are dark the year round. The ground is an intertwined mat of brush and weeds and lush tropical growth. On the trails, vines and roots as big as your arm twist and writhe like snakes. The relentlessness of nature's growth is almost sinister. You feel it closing in on you all around, and it creates a small terror which some men cannot stand. Even the natives get lost, and each settlement has a horn to blow when someone is missing.

There is only one industry in that part of the world—gathering chicle, which is the base for chewing gum. All the chicle in the world, they told me, comes out of that one jungle area, and everybody who lives there made his living by it. Production was running about two million pounds a year, all taken out by air.

Chicle comes from the wild sapota tree. The sap is called latex, and after it is boiled and hardened it is known as chicle. The men who gather it are *chicleros,* and I'm here to tell you they're nice people—friendly and cheerful and accommodating. Of course, now and then you hear of some Simon Legree foreman who went for a walk in the jungle and didn't come back, but that doesn't happen if you have any decency at all. The chicleros are a mixture of Indian and Spanish and Negro, though sometimes you see one who surely came, light skin and big mustache and all, straight from the Balkans. They live in thatched huts, with walls made of poles stuck in the ground. There are no doors at the openings; no screens. They sleep in hammocks. They have no doctors when they are ill, and their children do not go to school. They dress about as we dress at home in our old work clothes, except that they usually wear leather puttees against snakes (even children wear them) and red bandannas around their heads, gypsy fashion. They speak Spanish, and some who have drifted over from British Honduras speak a little English too.

I arrived just after the chicle season had closed, but most of the chicleros were still around, doing nothing. On my first afternoon half a dozen of them offered to show me how they worked, so they got their ropes and foot spikes and we tracked off into the jungle. This is the way it is done: the chiclero whacks a slanting gash in the tree and spirals it upward around the trunk as high as he can reach. Then he circles his rope around his waist and the tree, adjusting it so that he has about a two-foot slack. Then, with his telephone-lineman's spurs, he starts climbing. Every couple of feet he leans back on his rope, and with first his right and then his left hand, working fast, he whacks with his machete and the chips fly.

When he has finished a tree he has two grooves that run from the bottom to the top, each spiraling the trunk a dozen times or more on its way up. The tree looks like a sixty-foot barber's pole with two sets of stripes crossing each other. These two sets of grooves are so interlaced that a drop of sap, starting at the top, oozes windingly all the way down, until it comes out the final groove at the bottom. Here the chiclero hangs a leather sack. The latex is white. When you slash a tree it immediately starts coming out like perspiration, in little drops that resemble the milk from a milkweed.

A good chiclero can cut forty trees a day. A terribly good man, lucky at finding the best trees, has been known to do a hundred fifty in a long day. He cuts five days a week. On Saturday he collects; he takes a mule with a ten-gallon leather bag hanging on each side, and goes from tree to tree, pouring the small bagfuls of latex into the big bags. And on Sunday he pours the latex into big iron kettles and boils it five hours over an open wood fire. As it cools and hardens, he cuts it into rectangular blocks about the size of an auto battery, each weighing around twenty-two pounds. Before it is hard, he stamps it with a wooden stamp about the size of a postcard, which he has whittled out himself. It has his initials, and identifies the block as his. On Monday certain chicleros are designated to freight the whole camp's chicle blocks to the warehouse at Carmelita—a two days' trip, usually made with a train of ten mules, two hundred pounds to a mule.

The average chiclero gathers about two thousand pounds of chicle in a season, though the best ones can make five thousand or more. At that time their income was running between ten and fifteen dollars a week, out of which they had to repay the contractor for their mules and grub. The life is a hard one. Dampness and cold take their toll in pneumonia and rheumatism, and malaria and dysentery are common. Although these men are born and live and work in the hot tropics, they are so protected from the sun by the dense shade of the jungle that when they go out in the open to work on a new landing field for the planes, they frequently collapse of sunstroke. The chief cause of death among the chicleros is pneumonia, and the second is snakebite. For in that jungle there is the deadly fer-de-lance, or, as it is known locally, the *barba amarillo,* pronounced "barba-ma-ree-yo." In Spanish, it means yellow chin or yellow whiskers.

The stories I heard about the barba amarillo! A close friend of mine had been in the jungle with a pack train a month before. One of the natives stopped to tighten his saddle girth. He put one foot back into the bush not more than six inches. The others heard him scream. By the time they got to him, he was dead.. The chicleros working out of Carmelita were losing an average of four mules a year to the barba amarillo. Just that season a mule had suddenly keeled over, and when they lifted it up the snake was still underneath. And yet one chiclero named Tomas Requena had been bitten four times and was still alive. He was just a freak in that respect. His last bite had occurred only three weeks before, when he was lying belly down at a waterhole, drinking. The snake bit him on the thumb, and he still had a blue rag wrapped around it. And just a few days before I arrived, a chiclero killed a barba amarillo not a hundred yards from the TACA radio shack. It lacked two inches of being seven feet long. Jeepers creepers and shades of William Wrigley.

A stranger was such a rarity at Carmelita that it looked for a while as though there wasn't an extra hammock or cot for me in the entire Petén jungle. But around six o'clock my first night Manuel showed up with a cot made of heavy canvas tacked onto a wooden sawhorse effect. They rummaged up three gunny sacks for me to lie on, and the chicle man sent over a blanket (I suspect it was his only one). The sawhorse, incidentally, was mahogany.

Ed Robinson, field engineer of the TACA Airlines, and the native radio operator and the gang foreman all slept in the same room, which was the dirt-floored "office" and radio room of TACA. My cot went in there too. We all turned in early and lay there in the darkness, three on cots, one in a hammock, all in mosquito nets. You could hear the monkeys chattering in the trees. Robinson said he heard baboons howl twice, but I couldn't hear them. Sometimes, they said, the monkeys would get on the roof and pound on it.

Only two things happened during the night. Manuel fell out of his hammock onto the hard dirt floor with an awful smash, and got back in without a word. The other thing was that Admiral Ernest Byrd Pyle froze to death right there in the heart of the jungle. They had warned me it got cold at night, but I couldn't believe it, for this was practically at sea level and the day heat was sticky and terrific. But I awakened at one o'clock so cold I felt like whimpering. Finally I reached out and got my clothes and put them on over my pajamas. I didn't get back to sleep until dawn.

And then there was the incident of the fried chicken. Over our lunch of rice and tortillas, Ed Robinson said we ought to have fried chicken for supper, except that he couldn't stand it the way Mercedes fried it. Mercedes was the native girl who did the cooking. So I said, "Well, now that you remind me, I was somewhat of a chicken frier in my younger days. Of course, I'm sort of out of practice—"

But Robinson was already out in the cook shack, telling Mercedes to have a chicken killed and dressed and awaiting His Highness the Frier by five-thirty that afternoon. He asked what I would need, and I said nothing but some flour if there was any. Of course there wasn't any, but it seemed some strange person about a mile back in the jungle was known to have a small can of flour. So a messenger was dispatched through the jungle to bring back a cupful.

That evening we lay in our hammocks and talked and talked till dark. It was six-thirty before food came to mind, and then we thought of the chicken. Everybody else had eaten. We beat it over to the cook shack, and sure enough, there was the bird, all cleaned. A kind of battlefield ecstasy seized us. I threw off my sweater, rolled up my sleeves, called for two pans of water and a butcher knife, and felt exactly like a surgeon preparing for a heroic emergency operation. Ed Robinson held the lantern and Mercedes poked up the fire while I dismembered the chicken into regulation Indiana frying pieces. Then I washed it twice

(Mercedes was aghast), salted it, and rolled each piece in the precious flour. The hut was dark, with only the glow of the burning wood and the dim flicker of the lantern, and I fried mainly by feel. The "stove" was a hard-mud trough about waist high, with steel sheets laid over it. The flames came up between the sheets, and that's where you set the skillet. There wasn't any stovepipe. The smoke just came out.

Mercedes stuck with us like a leech. She held the skillet handle for me, she kept putting in more wood, she fanned the smoke out of my eyes. The chicken began to sizzle and crackle and smell good. I thought Robinson would do a handspring. He hadn't eaten an honest-to-goodness meal in six weeks. Mercedes' skepticism passed, and her admiration grew. Along toward the end I said to Robinson, "What do you want to eat with it?" He said, "Nothing. Just chicken." And, do you know, I never fried a better chicken in my life. I guess I must have been inspired. Mercedes, not to be outdone, began frying tortillas like mad, and all through the meal she was running to us with them in her hand, one at a time, until she had a stack six inches high on the table. But we never touched them. We were ear-deep in *pollo frito,* done to a jungle turn by probably the greatest chicken frier this world has ever known.

I hopped all over the jungle with TACA's chicle freighters. We flew as high as eleven thousand three hundred feet, covered a thousand miles altogether, hauled terrific loads, and dropped into and pulled out of jungle fields with such casualness that finally, if you were in an exciting part of a detective story, you didn't even look up when the wheels touched. I flew clear over to Puerto Barrios, on the east coast, with a load of chicle. All the seats were taken out of the Lockheed, and heavy burlap sacks of chicle were piled over the cabin floor. The flying mechanic and I sat on the chicle bags—on the gum you would be chewing some day.

But the times I enjoyed most were at Carmelita, after Ed Robinson would knock off work in the afternoon and we would lie in our hammocks like tropical planters and just loaf and talk, with natives puttering about their chores around us. We lay in parallel hammocks, feet to head, so we could face each other. The hammocks sagged in the middle, and if we reached down, we could fish around till we found a glass sitting there on the ground.

Those talks in the late afternoon were the kind I liked best. We talked about tropical peoples and what the white man's place is; about how unreal the average person's mental picture of a jungle camp is, and how hard it is to describe. We talked about places we'd both been, and some of the things that had happened to me. We spoke of our ambitions, and of why we were both there where we were, and gradually we got off into the abstract, and then off onto romance—what is romance, and where is it, and why is it? And we decided that at that very minute we were the subjects the tropical novelists write romances about. Then we came to a thought that had never come to either of us before:

We suddenly realized, lying there in our hammocks, that there is no romance at all within one's own self. Romance must have an audience, or it doesn't exist. It is like the famous falling tree in the woods, when there's nobody there to hear it. Suppose you were to kill a tiger barehanded in the jungle. Would that be romantic to you if there was no one to see you do it, and if you knew that in your entire lifetime there would never be anyone to tell it to? I think it would not. And that was the way Ed Robinson felt about himself. He had all the intelligence and sense of drama to make his present circumstances seem romantic to him, and they were, in the sense that he knew how certain people elsewhere were thinking of him and picturing this kind of life. But he himself, living right there with the road scraper and the flabby tortillas and the pidgin English and the macaw that was after all just a pretty chicken, knew that it wasn't romantic at all.

You see, now, about the abstract? I'll bet that after a few weeks in the jungle with nobody to talk to, nine-tenths of you would abstract the hell out of the first visitor that showed up.

At San Salvador, the capital of El Salvador, I saw a boy who had wandered into the jungle when he was a baby, and for about three years lived alone like an animal.

· 45 ·

He was first heard of in the fall of 1933. When there were rumors that a humanlike animal had been seen sneaking through the bushes in the low-lying jungle country along the Pacific Coast, an expedition of farmers was organized. They hunted a good many months, and finally early one morning they saw the "monster" running through the trees, and captured him. He fought and bit and screamed. They took him to a farmhouse and shut him up in a room, but in a few minutes he was out and gone. He escaped three more times before they got him to the police station at Sonsonate. He was naked and filthy, and his hair and fingernails were long. He stared always at the floor. He was terrified of people, and would attack and bite without provocation. His only speech was a grunt or a scream.

No one knew for sure about the boy's origin. The theory was that the child lost his parents in a Communist uprising that occurred in that part of Salvador in the 1930s, and that he then wandered into the woods and went it alone. He was obviously a full-blooded Indian. During those years in the jungle he had probably slept in trees and caves. His arms were long, his chest thick, and he could swing through trees. He apparently had lived on live fish, tropical fruits, and herbs. When captured he had a handful of live fish, which he ate with delight. He had no fear of animals. He caught and killed poisonous snakes with his bare hands, even after he learned to talk.

After his capture he was kept for a month in the Sonsonate police station, where they studied him. He acted like an imbecile. His strange cries reminded people of an animal. He would not eat cooked food. They fed him raw meat, fruit, and tortillas— threw it in onto the floor—but he wouldn't touch it until the people had left. Then he'd crouch in a dark corner and tear at it. They watched him through slits in the wall.

Finally they took him to a government experimental farm a few miles from Sonsonate, where there was a school. And gradually they discovered he wasn't an idiot, but a very smart boy. His imitative instincts were acute. The first example they had was when a school official made a phone call; a few minutes later the boy was found ringing an imaginary phone and repeating the teacher's conversation.

After the teachers were sure the child wouldn't run away, they let him out at night by himself. Many times he went back into the jungle, swung through the trees, played on the riverbank, roamed alone throughout the night. But he always came back. He grew to prefer a bed to sleeping on the ground, and to prefer cleanliness, and he wanted to wear clothes. Slowly his sullenness vanished. And at last they knew for sure he was a genuine, living, breathing Tarzan. They were still calling him Tarzancita, which means "Little Tarzan."

He had now been six years in "captivity." He had become a part of our civilized world, and was going to public school. Doubtless his jungle years were growing dimmer and dimmer in his memory. He was in the fond and capable hands of Colonel Alfonso Marroquin of the Salvadorean army, and was living with the soldiers in the barracks of the First Regiment of Infantry, in the heart of San Salvador. The colonel had not legally adopted the child but had given him his own name—the boy was officially Ruben Marroquin. They did not know yet whether Tarzancita would go into the army when he grew up. He was excellent in mathematics. He loved football, and still had the strength and litheness of the jungle. He was fond of the cornet, and they planned to start teaching it to him soon.

When I saw him, he had on a neat khaki outfit, more like a mechanic's clothes than a uniform. I've never seen a boy more polite. He shook hands and smiled, and seemed to have a tremendous desire to be nice and do the right thing. You could see his respect and fondness for the colonel. But it was his voice that astonished me most. It was a frail little voice, of great gentleness, high but not sharp—rather, it was soft like a whisper. It seemed to express a great appreciation for everything.

One night at Managua, Nicaragua, we had an earthquake. That is earthquake country, and a little shake now and then doesn't impress the locals very much, but this one was severe enough to get into the newspapers next day.

I was sound asleep, as usual, having been all my life one of those individuals of pure conscience and simple mind who sleep like a log. But That Girl, tortured by her constant sins

· 47 ·

and thus accustomed to wakefulness at odd hours, was wide awake in an adjoining bed. In fact, she said later that she knew we were going to have an earthquake, because everything was deathly still and vacuum like. She said you could feel the terrible accumulation of quiet through your skin.

Well, anyway, the first thing I sensed through semiconsciousness was the bed squeaking to beat hell. I think that's what woke me up. And then I realized the whole bed was swinging back and forth, from side to side. Fast, too—about two round trips a second, it seemed. I heard a voice in the dark room say, "Wake up, we're having an earthquake!" Well, I already knew we were having an earthquake, and I was so sleepy I wasn't frightened. But when she said that out loud, it scared the daylights out of me and I got weak all over. So weak I never even raised up, and I'm not sure I opened my eyes.

We think it lasted six or eight seconds, but it seemed a very long time. Nothing in the room made any noise except the bedsprings. It was over before we got the light turned on, but somehow we sensed that the walls were swaying and the floor was rolling. In a few seconds lights began to go on in other rooms (we could see, for there was just a screen above the hall door). We could hear people talking all over the hotel, and then, about a half minute after the tremors, the most bloodcurdling female scream you ever heard. Then silence. We tried to figure out what it was, and came to the conclusion that some woman who had gone through the horrors of Managua's 1931 earthquake had awakened belatedly and, realizing she was in another quake, had let out this frantic war whoop. But we found out the facts next morning. She was an American traveler spending her first night in Nicaragua. The quake awakened her, but didn't frighten her in the least. She went to the bathroom, and when she took hold of the light chain she got a terrific shock from it. And she screamed. That's all.

Drought Bowl

Chapter IV I DROVE NEARLY TWO THOUSAND MILES AROUND the "drought bowl" in 1936. The whole United States seemed to be tortured and wounded in varying degrees with drought and heat, but in the bowl there was complete destruction. It started about a hundred miles from the eastern border of the Dakotas and extended all the way to western Montana, taking in both the Dakotas and a corner of Wyoming. It seemed to me that South Dakota had suffered most.

In that world of drought you finally arrived at a point where you looked and no longer said, "My God, this is awful!" You became accustomed to dried field and burned pasture. Day upon day of driving through that ruined country gradually made you accept it as a vast land that had been that way yesterday and would be tomorrow, and was that way a hundred miles back and would be a hundred miles ahead. The story was the same everywhere: the farmers said the same thing, the fields looked the same—it became like the drone of a bee, and after a while you hardly noticed it at all.

It was only at night, when you were alone in the heat and unable to sleep, that the thing came back to you like a living dream, and you once more realized the stupendousness of it. Then you could see something more than field after brown field, or a mere succession of dry water holes, or the matter-of-fact resignation on farm faces. You could see then the whole obliteration of a great land, and the destruction of a people and long years of calamity for those of the soil, and the emptiness of life that knows only struggle and ends in despair. I had seen a great deal of this in the past few years. Sometimes at night when I was thinking too hard I felt that there was nothing but leanness everywhere, that nobody had the privilege of a full life. Of course I was wrong about that.

I had just seen too much of the ruination of our great land. The beautiful valleys and hillsides of Tennessee washing away to the ocean, leaving a slashed and useless landscape. The raw windy plains of western Kansas, stripped of all life, a onetime paradise turned into a whirlpool of suffocation. And the vast rolling Dakotas, where huge herds once grazed with the freedom of birds, now parched and cramped and manhandled by man and the elements into a bed of coals.

Denver Williams had been sitting in my room at Miles City, Montana, for about two hours, chewing the fat, when who should walk in but Dr. Rexford G. Tugwell. Denver Williams was a cattleman and he was broke, and he had lots to tell. And Dr. Tugwell was the big works in the Resettlement Administration; he was out there seeing the drought, and he was a good listener. So for an hour Denver Williams talked and Rex Tugwell listened.

Fletcher Williams was born in Colorado; that's why they called him Denver. He was forty-six. He had been working and paying his own way in the world since he was eleven. He grew up as a cowboy. (He looked like a cowboy—tall and lean and brown. He wore a sweeping wide-brimmed hat, and when he was indoors he dropped his cigarette ashes in the cuff of his overalls. He talked slowly, and smiled a little all the time he talked.) Denver came to Montana's Powder River country in 1912, working as a cowboy. As the big outfits dwindled and the cowboys started setting up for themselves, he did likewise; he got a thousand acres. He raised from forty to a hundred cattle a year, and farmed enough to get winter feed. The years went on and he got himself in pretty good shape.

1919—drought. Denver went to the bank for a loan, and the banker said, "Well, the way I figure your assets you're worth about thirty-five thousand dollars."

1920—drought. When Denver sold his drought cattle and settled up, the banker said, "Well, the way I figure your assets now you're worth two hundred and fifty dollars."

So Denver left for the Colorado oil fields. He had never seen an oil rig. "But it's good for us to learn new things," he said. He got on as a tool dresser and sent for his wife. He drew eighteen dollars a day, and they saved thirty-five hundred dollars that year. They went back to Montana and staked themselves to a new start on the ranch. They got in pretty good shape again. Then 1924. Rain. Rain. Rain. His cows bogged down on the hillsides and died. His steers slid over banks and broke their necks. His little pigs huddled up in the rain and smothered to death.

Denver went to the oil fields again. Three times that happened. Twice it was drought, once it was rain. And now something was about to happen again.

His thousand-acre ranch had gone in 1934, the year of the big drought, but the bank let him stay on it, just for taxes. There had been six years of drought now. But this year things looked pretty good at the start. Denver had forty head of cattle and some crops. One morning about six weeks back he had seen some grasshoppers, and he'd had a hunch. "I'm letting the cattle go," he said. His wife said, "But maybe it'll rain." And he said, "And maybe it won't." He saddled the pinto ponies, and he and one of his little girls walked those cattle forty-five miles to a railroad. It took them four days and nights. And then he went with them on the train to Sioux City. He got a good price, because he sold early. But he owed it all to the bank.

All he had left now was three milk cows, his work horses, and a bunch of pigs. His horses and cows wouldn't last another two weeks, because the range was burned up and there was no feed. "I fin'lly gave away some pigs," he said, "but I can't even give away the rest. Nobody can feed them." He said the pine trees up in the hills were dying; the cones had fallen off. He had seen a man signing up for relief the day before; two months back the man had owned eight hundred head of cattle.

"We're the stayin'est fools in Powder River County I ever saw," Denver said. "We haven't got sense enough to know when we're licked." He never preached. He didn't appeal. He just happened to be there, chewing the fat with me, so he just told us how things were. He left after midnight, to drive in a friend's car the hundred twenty miles back to his ranch that wasn't his. When he had gone, Tugwell said, "Say, isn't he a swell fellow? He's the kind that's got to have help, and right now. He's worth helping."

The grasshopper is a ridiculous creature. His legs are out of joint and his eyes are funny. But in 1936 the grasshopper was to the Dakotas about the same thing as a hurricane to Miami or a tidal wave to Galveston. In the Northwest the grasshopper opened and closed every conversation. He held second place only to the great drought itself. You couldn't say the grasshoppers destroyed everything the drought left; rather, the two galloped down through the sun-parched summer nose and nose, and it would be hard to say whether the last blade of grass died of thirst or was gnawed down by a hopper.

Have you ever seen a freshly plowed field, just after the soil is turned, and it is all black and rich-looking, with no vegetation at all? Well, that's what a cornfield looks like after the hoppers are finished. They not only strip the blades—they eat the stalk and burrow down into the ground and nibble away the roots. They leave nothing whatever on the surface. They do the same with grain and grass and vegetables.

I wanted to take a picture of a hopper-devastated cornfield, but I didn't want a bare field, because you couldn't prove there had ever been any corn there. I wanted a field that had leafless cornstalks still standing like sticks, and I drove for a full half day through South Dakota before I could find a field that had even the stumps of cornstalks left. When I found one I took a picture. As usual, the picture didn't turn out, but that isn't the point. The point is that there was only one cornfield in about every hundred fifty miles that hadn't simply disappeared from the face of the earth.

The motorist's first engagement with a grasshopper horde gives him a queer feeling. They don't make a black cloud in the sky. They just sit thickly along the road, and you don't see them until your car stirs them up. Then all of a sudden they are streaking in all directions, like bullets on a war poster. They smack and hang all over the car. I was continually dodging and blinking. When you see one coming straight at you, you instinctively duck. And just as you do, he hits the windshield with a pop that sounds as if somebody had thrown a rock.

That first batch lasted for about three miles. I stopped at the next town and bought a grasshopper screen to go over the radiator. Nearly every car out there had one. If you didn't have one, the grasshoppers would stick in the radiator and the first thing you knew, the surface was solid with them and no air could get through, and your engine got hot.

The garageman swept the dead ones out of the radiator with a broom before he put on the screen. I was silly enough to count them: there were 284. After that I was running through grasshoppers at least a third of the time. There were never less than half a dozen in the car with me. About three times a day one would get up my pants leg, and I would have to stop and fish him out. You were liable to find them in your hotel room, or in your shirt in the morning, or hopping around the tables in the best restaurants.

The old-timers told me that grasshopper plagues ran in cycles. There was a bad one in 1902, and another in 1922. They usually last three or four years, and they are worse in dry years. This was the third and worst year of the current cycle. There wasn't much you could do about them, apparently. The government had used Paris green. That killed them, all right: But as one farmer said, "For every one that dies, a thousand come to his funeral." It was like trying to bore a hole in water.

What a magnificent place the Powder River country of southeastern Montana must have been fifty years ago. "It was the greatest grazing country that ever lay out of doors," said Ray Wilson. He was born on the range, and he rode it as cowman and operator for years, but in the summer of 1936 he was working in a lumber yard.

"This short thick grass was the richest in America," he said. "You could graze it the year around, except maybe for a month in the hardest winters. You could cut enough wild hay along the river bottoms to carry you through that coldest month. The government owned the land then. It was free range country. The cattle ranged at large and cowboys rode the way they ride in books. The great herds grazed by the thousands, always moving, always free—no fence lines, no property lines, no water restrictions. It was easy to borrow money and it was always paid back. A cattleman would go to the bank for a loan. The bank might ask how many cattle he owned, but no more questions were asked. It would have been an insult for a bank to send out to count his cattle. A total stranger could walk into a bank and cash a check and they wouldn't even look at him twice. In those days any rancher who went away and locked his house was blackballed. You could leave a gold watch and fifty dollars and a jug of whisky and a sack of tobacco on the table. When you came home the whisky and the tobacco might be gone, but the fifty dollars and the gold watch would always be there."

And this from a storekeeper: "In those days your customer came in only about twice a year. But how he bought! It wasn't anything for a cattleman to come in and buy eight hundred or a thousand dollars' worth of groceries in the fall. One man would often buy as much as a store keeps in stock nowadays. And maybe a man you'd never seen before would come in. He'd walk along the counter and pick out what he wanted—overalls, shirts, boots, and tobacco. It might total up to sixty or seventy dollars. You'd ask him who he was riding for. He'd say a certain outfit. That's all you needed to know. He'd take the stuff and you wouldn't see him again till fall and then he'd come in and pay. You never lost anything on those men. In the old days," the storekeeper told me, "cattlemen were worth from fifty thousand dollars on up into the millions. They lived in shacks out on the prairie and brought up their families on hard work. But they had money and they shot square.

"Today," the storekeeper said, "everybody in this Powder River country is broke. Probably nobody has more than fifteen hundred dollars in the bank, free of debt, and those are few. The banks wouldn't lend a dime on your life. The cattleman comes in for one cake of salt at a time, and the farmer takes a sack of potatoes and says he'll pay when he can."

The beautiful rolling green hills were bare, the color of the graveled road. Only now and then would you see a small bunch of cattle; the others had prematurely gone to market lest they wither away. The squat, treeless houses sat in the pitiless sun, far from the road, as always. Around them you saw long rows of rusty, motionless machinery. You saw the few work horses huddled along a dry creek, swishing the flies. There was no work for them in the fields. The farmers and cattlemen patched fences, or did chores, or just sat and waited.

It started in 1909, when the railroad came through. The government gave the railroad half the land—every other section— for fifty miles on each side. Then came homesteading; that brought in a new population. It brought the plow and the deadly constricting fence that barred off watering places. It destroyed the freedom of the range. Taxes were applied. Grazing land was cut down. The cattlemen had new overheads to meet, and less to meet them with. The farmers plowed up the great rolling plains, and they were scourged by drought, even in the beginning. The cattlemen, trying to keep above water, raised too many cattle on too little space. They themselves, denied the open range, were forced to do some farming for winter feed. The country was despoiled. It could not stand a seven-year drought.

True, the grass would come back in a year or two if they stopped farming, and springs would fill up again in a few years. But, as a mooner over times-gone-by told me: "It took character, and free money, and straight shooting, and we don't have the same things any more." All the old freedom, all the old bigness of the Montana range were gone. A rancher locked his house now when he went to town.

In Rapid City we happened to run into President Roosevelt's drought party, weekending there. We were in the same hotel, and our fourth-floor room looked right down upon the hotel entrance—a sort of grandstand seat for the President's arrivals and departures. It was Sunday, and a large crowd of Rapid Citians cheered as the President drove off to church. And after a while I was awakened from a nap by clapping in the street. The President was returning from church. The crowd was still there, and I watched from my grandstand window.

There had been, out of what I always felt to be a fine sense of consideration, few mentions in the press of the President's partial paralysis. But it seems to me there can be no violation of good taste in relating what happened at Rapid City that day. The crowd stopped clapping and stood silently watching as the car stopped at the hotel. It was a seven-passenger touring car with the top down. Two of the President's sons and a daughter-in-law got out ahead of him. While everybody waited, the President reached for the spare seat, and pulled it down in front of him. Then he reached to the robe rail, and with his powerful arms slid himself forward onto the spare seat. He turned a little and put his legs out the door and over the running board, with his feet almost to the curb. Gus Gennerich, his bodyguard, stood ready to help, but he was not needed. You could almost have heard a pin drop. The President put both hands on one leg, and pushed downward, locking the jointed steel brace at his knee. He slowly did the same with the other leg. Then he put his hands on the side of the car, and with his arms lifted his body out and up and onto his legs. He straightened up. I have never seen a man so straight. And at that moment the tenseness broke, and the crowd applauded. The President's back was to the crowd, and he did not look around. It was brief and restrained applause. I don't know, but I doubt if that had ever happened to the

President before. It was the tenderest, most admiring tribute to courage I have ever seen. It was such a poignant thing, so surprising, so spontaneous. It was as though they were saying with their hands, "We know we shouldn't, but we've got to." When I turned from the window there was a lump in my throat.

Rollo in the Rockies

Chapter V THE WRANGLERS AT BANFF, ALBERTA, ALL laughed when I stepped up to the horse. They thought I was a city dude. But they stayed to cheer when I leaped on and rode away with the grace of an Indian, rolling a cigarette behind my back with one hand as I disappeared into the forest. They didn't know that forty years ago I was a foreman of six hundred cowboys on Major Hoople's ranch, and that I always rode wild horses, and never the same one twice. After a wild horse has been ridden once he's too tame for me.

Well, I returned two hours later, having jogged over to Calgary and back, eighty-five miles each way. And then Dick Roberts, foreman of the Banff corral, and I sat down on the fence to talk. He said that, next to me, the funniest rider they'd ever had at this dude corral was a fellow named Yates, or Gates. He blew in one morning and said he didn't know how to ride, but wanted to try. He got on, and fell right off on the other side. The horse started going, and Yates somehow worked himself up under the horse's neck and twisted around into the saddle. By this time the horse was running wild, and the last they saw of Yates he had turned around in the saddle and was riding backward, yelling and waving his arms. It turned out he was a trick rider with Barnum & Bailey. He rode down the main street in Banff standing straight up on the saddle, waving his arms, his horse in a dead run. He almost drove the police crazy.

Dick Roberts was an Irishman who had never done anything but handle horses. He had run livery and riding stables in Ireland, England, Paris, the United States, and Canada. He had taken a shipload of horses to South Africa, and he had followed the horse business into Russia. Once he rode twenty-seven hundred miles through the wilderness of Canada, for the fun of it. He was still riding every day, though he was nearly sixty. In the summer he managed the pony corral at Banff, and in the winter he would go into the Calgary stockyards. He sent an average of a hundred people a day off over the mountain trails on horseback, most of them dudes.

"They all pretend," he said. "Good riders say they've never been on a horse before. And people who have never ridden are ashamed to say so, and ask for a fractious horse. But they don't fool me. I can tell by looking at them." The rich "horsy" people of the eastern cities could ride just as well as cowboys, he said. Most people rode only once there, but now and then some rich man with a party would stay for weeks, and run a horse bill of twenty-five or thirty dollars a day.

The dudes brought all kinds of tribulations to Dick Roberts. Women wanted to leave their husbands, husbands wanted to leave their wives, people came doped up with heroin, and whole parties of drunks showed up thinking a horseback ride would be nice. But they didn't ruffle Dick Roberts. "They're just ships that pass in the night to me," he said.

The corral was just across from the huge Banff Springs Hotel. It had thirty horses and seven guides, or dude wranglers, who were all ex-cowboys except one, a seventeen-year-old boy born in Banff. They said he was one of the best in the bunch. "A dude wrangler has to be born. You can't teach him," Roberts said. "The average cowhand wouldn't be worth a hoot. A wrangler has to have a sense of humor, be an awful liar, and have the patience of Job."

Roberts never smiled, but he always had a sharp, fast, Irish answer that kept people wondering after they'd ridden away. He had one of those freak mathematical memories. He knew the name and hotel-room number of every person who took out a horse. They had to tell him only once. While I was there, he knew the room numbers of two people who had forgotten the numbers themselves.

His only sin, he said, was reading. He said he didn't smoke or drink or eat. Oh, he took a nip of Irish whisky once in a while, and he pulled at a pipe (but never a cigarette), and he did take a little toast and tea now and then. But he didn't really drink or smoke or eat. And he felt great.

The white horse named Hawk was bored stiff. How many times, oh, how many times had he climbed this mountain? He didn't even look at the lovely lake below. He didn't feel, I am sure, the beauty of the drifting clouds of fog across the peaks. To him there was no freshness in the wet green of the forests after the night's rain. Didn't he know that he was carrying me, for the first time in my life, to a place you can't reach by auto or train or boat? No, he didn't know. He just climbed.

We topped the ridge and headed inland, you might say, up a long high valley. It was a good trail, cut through the forest, wide enough for two riders to pass, but full of rocks. The horse knew the way. We were headed for Lake O'Hara, high in the Canadian Rockies in British Columbia.

We wound and wound around, following small level spots. Even so, it was mostly up, the whole nine miles. Only a few times was it level enough to jog along. The rest was a hard, walking pull. We forded mountain streams—the leaping rocky kind you see in the newsreels, clear as glass and cold as ice. You could look up a quarter of a mile and see the glacier that bore the stream, or look down and see it rushing and falling away below you. Mountains were all around us. Across the valley one rose to the frightening height of ten thousand feet. It was as sheer as the Washington Monument, and solid rock. You believe it in a book or in a picture, but when you see it you can't.

What impressed me most was that death is constantly happening in the forest. I don't know why I had never thought of it before. Life comes, and stands a little while, and goes away again. Trees grow tall and die and fall over. The forest was a mass of leaning trees, of fallen trunks, of crumbling logs lying flat. I tied to a bush, and walked out through the trees. The ground was a sponge; it must have been inches deep with piled vegetation—long-rotted wood, leaves, needles, twigs, and bushes—moistened by rain and packed there layer upon layer for centuries. This forest had never been cut and never been burned. I must have been stepping upon earth that decades ago had been a growing tree. The tree had died naturally and fallen among its fellows, and returned again into the earth to bear a new tree.

I met only one person on the long ride—a wrangler, bringing a train of pack horses down the mountain. He said they belonged to a party of geologists who were hunting flora and fauna. It sounded funny to hear those words from a wrangler up in the mountains. I told him I'd seen a lot of flora on the way up, but nary a fauna except the one I was riding.

We stopped several times—to let Hawk get his breath, and to let me get off and on, to straighten out my sidewalk legs. It really was a short nine miles. I was surprised when the corral showed up in a clearing just before noon. Hawk and I had lunch, and I walked two miles to the other end of Lake O'Hara and back.

We went back down in the afternoon, the white horse and I. It was just as slow coming down as it had been going up, but the forest seemed darker, and even more silent. I liked it. We overtook a man walking down. He was from Chicago. He had been coming up there for years, and had walked and ridden all over the Canadian Rockies. He was a genuine wilderness lover, not just a dabbler in wilderness like me. I envied him. We met a one-eyed Indian guide on a horse, with a sour city fellow behind him. The Indian spoke pleasantly, but the tourist wouldn't speak, even when I spoke to him. Maybe his legs hurt, or maybe he was dead and just sitting on the horse. We met two women in hiking clothes, walking up. One was redheaded. They weren't young and they weren't pretty, but I liked them. One of the women said, "Here's your chance to make a wish—a white horse and a redheaded woman." So I pulled off my hat and said, "And also a redheaded man—or at least he was before the silver threads came among the gold." That made a hit. We talked for ten minutes.

Half an hour from home, we met the rain. It was a cold, gloomy rain that came close to being sleet. The wind blew it into our faces, and the horse kept trying to turn around. There was thunder off behind the mountains and the peaks slowly disappeared in mist. The wind through the fir trees made a sound like a human voice.

At the end of the day, after eighteen miles of riding, a lone rider and a white horse came out of the pass and down the trail to the lake. Their heads were low against the driving storm. The rain soaked through the rider's clothes, and ran into his shoes, and trickled coldly down his back. His saddle was wet where he sat. He had not been actually wet through from rain for many years. It made him feel kind of worth-while again.

The experiences of Rollo, the City Softie, hereinafter related, are in nowise to be considered remarkable. But since the world is full of City Softies like Rollo who have unremarkable experiences, it may be justifiable to record here for their benefit the slight adventures of our hero.

Rollo went alone into the high mountains of Glacier National Park, Montana, dressed only in his city clothes, with a new dollar-fifty canvas knapsack on his back. In two days he walked twenty-six miles, climbed with his own city muscles from three thousand feet to eight thousand feet, and back down and up again four times; walked along the shores of high hidden lakes; strode like a small boy in a fairy tale along narrow paths in the tall thick forest; learned not to jump at every crackle in the bush; learned to distinguish the high whistle of the marmot; saw shaggy white mountain goats standing on ledges at seven thousand feet; discovered what it was to toil upward until he was sick from exhaustion; felt the exhilaration of drinking pure cold snow water from a stream, on his hands and knees; and above all, experienced the powerful expansive inner glow that can come only to a tramper as, miles away from any other human being, he stands in the cold wind on an eight-thousand-foot pass and looks about him at the immensity of peak and chasm.

The sun was shining brightly and it was very warm at a quarter to nine when Rollo said goodbye and strode away from the sophisticated shores of Lake McDonald in Glacier Park. So tall was the forest that for two hours he did not see a mountainside, or hardly even the sky.

Like all men who do things for the first time alone, Rollo soon began to learn from experience. He learned that his city coat was too hot, so he took it off. He then learned that a walker of long distances cannot walk well if he is unbalanced, even by the small weight of a coat over one arm. Then he discovered quite by himself (as there was no other soul on the trail this day) that a coat can be carried quite simply by draping it over one's rear, wrapping the sleeves around the waist, and tying them together in front.

He learned to his amazement that tall trees in the forest, swaying slightly in the breeze, rub together and make exactly the same groaning noise as a ship makes in a heavy sea. He learned also that myriad little chipmunks, dashing about like lightning, will jump into the weeds and then peek back out, to watch the walker on his way. He learned too that though soft city hearts may have courage, soft city lungs are weak. He learned this from much gasping for breath, and many poundings in the head, and sudden incapacities in the joints.

It was a steep climb all the way. An auto would have had to go into second gear, though an auto could not have gone where Rollo went. Finally the timber began to get shorter and thinner and he could see the sun, and occasionally a mountainside across the valley. He was working through the timber line. When he came out above it, out among bare rock, he stopped to look around. Far below he could see the lake he had left. Mountain peaks were on each side of him, and ahead was a deep valley; up above, on a ledge at the end of the canyon (he had to hold his head back to look up at it), he discovered Sperry Chalet, which was his destination. Ah, good boy! thought Rollo. How fast I have come! There's the chalet and I'll be there in fifteen minutes. Six miles this morning. And they said it would be a tough pull. What Rollo didn't know didn't hurt him at the moment. He resumed.

The trail got steeper and made hairpin turns, and Rollo discovered that instead of just climbing up a mountain, he was walking back and forth across the side of a mountain—north a hundred yards, south a hundred yards, north a hundred yards. It was a switchback, designed for propelling oneself up a grade that was too steep for human legs to scale straight up. After infinite toiling and frequent resting, he gained a level space and sat down for a final look at his goal before the race up the stretch. You can imagine with what a shock he perceived that the chalet was still as far away as it had been half an hour before.

He reached the chalet an hour and fifteen minutes after he had caught the first glimpse of it. He stopped behind a tree for a final rest, a hundred feet from the door, so the people would not find him out of breath. He had come six miles (and risen thirty-five hundred feet) in three hours and fifteen minutes. His legs were sore. He told the woman at the chalet he was tired; he thought she would know anyway, and it would be better not to lie. She asked how long he had been on the way. "Why, that's good time," she said. "Lots of people take four hours, and one man took five and said he'd like to see anybody do it faster. You made good time."

"Yes, I guess it wasn't bad," said expanding Rollo. "And I'm not very tired either. Guess I'll have lunch now, and then run up to the glacier."

So, after lunch, he started out again. He thought they were lying when they showed him the trail. He followed it with his eye, around the valley, across the face of the immense slide, back and forth up the steep slope to the pass so very far up there, and then it disappeared. Rollo wanted to back out. But he was proud. He strode away.

The afternoon sun became hot as he toiled around the rim of the valley, climbing always. They said it cost fifteen thousand dollars just to build this narrow three-mile trail up to the glacier, and a trail crew was busy all summer keeping it clear of falling rocks. Rollo puffed and toiled and leaned far over and gave his arms long rhythmic swings to help him along. Every two or three minutes he stopped to rest. He kept his eye out for good-sized rocks along the trail, so he could sit down without the effort of sitting clear down to the ground. He looked up once or twice at the trail switching back and forth across the face of the frighteningly steep pass above him. He wanted to back out more than ever. But he went on.

At the turns he walked close to the inside. He felt sort of light-headed. A gale was blowing around him now. He grew cold. When he stopped to rest now, he could see the switchback trail below him, back and forth a dozen times, like an eternally diminishing letter Z, for a quarter of a mile down. He knelt down by a little lake and scooped out water with his hands and drank it. It was ice cold. Goats drank out of the lake too, Rollo supposed. But it tasted good.

Finally he came to a high straight wall of solid rock. There seemed no way out, and no glacier was in sight. Then suddenly he saw what he had to do. He had to go up over that wall. The trail builders had blasted an almost vertical stepladder up the stone. Rollo doesn't know yet how he had the courage; he would have shut his eyes if he had dared. It was fifty or sixty feet straight up. The wind blew upward through the cirque with a shriek. Rollo finally crawled out on top on his hands and knees. He stood up a little at a time. The wind whipped at him, and he felt light, and imagined he was swaying. He managed to look around. And there he stood, on top of the world, on a miniature plateau of rock scarcely a hundred feet wide—a sheer drop behind him, the long gradual slope of the glacier in front. He had sneaked up on it from behind.

Rollo had never before seen a glacier close up. He wasn't even sure it was the glacier—it looked just like a lot of dirty snow. He walked gingerly out on it. It was hard and slick, and he knew it was solid ice underneath. Its face was in thousands of gently round declivities, about the size of washpans. He stepped from one to the other. Once he slipped, and did a grotesque threshing of arms and legs in mid-air, trying to get a new footing, which he did. He probably wouldn't have slid more than a few feet anyway.

He did not go far out, for he was afraid; he had not asked just how dangerous the face of a glacier was. He could see deep crevasses not far over, and hear the trickle of melting snow water, and could even see small snow caves here and there. He thought of air holes in river ice. He eased back off the edge of the glacier, and onto the sheets of solid red rock that formed the mountaintop itself. Huge red rocks lay tumbled every which way, left like that by the glacier meltings of other years.

He stayed about half an hour around the edge of the glacier. It didn't seem real to him at all. He didn't seem real to himself. He knew he could never tell anybody just what the feeling was.

There was such lonesomeness up there, such a profound cold stillness, and no life whatever, except the movement of the little melting streams. There were no birds, no gophers, no little jumping things, no grass or trees or even air, it seemed. He lay on his back in the shadow of a red rock, and looked up into the blue sky. White clouds floated slowly, far above him. A few little white things, the size of ping-pong balls and the substance of snowflakes, drifted past above him. He did not know what they were.

He felt sleepy from the altitude. He was deathly weak and weary. He was cold, and he became very strange to himself in that high empty place. He got up to go, before they should come and find him dead.

Next morning his joints were stiff, and his whole left leg had the consistency of a fence post. And he was faced this day with a fourteen-mile walk right across the Great Divide of the Rockies, from Sperry Chalet to Sun Camp. It hardly seemed worth it. He pondered upon ditching this whole mountain-hiking business, and getting back to civilization—but only for a moment, because he was made of sterner stuff. And anyway, there was no way out except to walk. So he kicked his heels together, yelled a couple of times, and was off up the pass on the long climb toward the sun.

It is not necessary to give the details of the first two hours of Rollo's all-day amble. Suffice it to say that when he finally topped the first high ridge, the sun shone upon him and warmed him and the way led downhill, and the whole wide world seemed to roll out pleasantly below just for Rollo. He walked faster and squared his shoulders and beamed upon all the rocks and bushes by the wayside, and one or twice he could have been heard to mutter at a scampering chipmunk, "Hello there, you pretty little so-and-so, you."

This admirable condescension toward nature was further heightened when he came suddenly around the edge of a mountain, and there below him lay the weirdly beautiful Lake Ellen Wilson, looking up so greenly at him as if to say, "Surprise, surprise!" Rollo walked down. And then he started up, to Gunsight Pass. His pack became a scourge upon his back. The strap cut into his shoulder. He tried putting the strap across the top of his head, as he'd seen the Indians do in Mexico, but he couldn't find a spot on his head where it felt right. He put his hands on his knees, to brace himself for each climbing step. He learned to stop and rest before he was too far gone. He realized he was resting more than he was walking. He sat on rocks, and consoled himself with the immensity of rock and valley around him, and the great quietness, and his inflating pride in seeing and feeling something that many people would never even imagine.

The pass became an unattainable thing. Each time he looked hopefully upward it had receded by just as much as he had toilingly gained. He stopped looking upward. He climbed, rested. Climbed, rested. He was genuinely surprised when suddenly the trail leveled off, and he almost fell down from the suddenness of it. And when he looked up, there he was on top. The level space was no wider than a street.

He stood in the center of the most appalling panorama he had ever seen. To the west lay the valley from which he had come, with the walls of jagged rock rising mightily into the sky on each side, and the jade-green lake in the bottom. And turning to the east, he beheld exactly the same thing—beautiful Gunsight Lake, with only slightly varying details.

Sick with beauty, he rushed down the other side. The grade was precipitous. Rollo's body bore down upon his feet. With each step he landed with a great jolt. His knees began to go to pieces inside. The trail was of loose, sharp stone. It cut his shoes. There were sheer drops, hundreds of feet down. The trail had been blasted out of a perpendicular rock wall; it was just a ledge with a little ridge of loose stones on the outside.

He came upon a young man sitting on the trail, the only traveler he had seen in two days in the mountains. Rollo sat down, and the two got out their lunches and ate together, sitting there in the middle of the trail, looking straight down upon beautiful Gunsight Lake, hundreds of feet below.

Rollo went on down, through timber line again, and on past the lake and into the valley that seemed almost tropical. It became stiflingly hot. "Sun Camp—7.4 miles," said a sign. Seven miles! Why, he had thought it was only about three by now. He had been walking forever. The sun was far down the western sky. A great weariness came over Rollo, a weariness of legs and spirit. It was a torturing, endless anticlimax. Exhaustion, complete destroying exhaustion engulfed him. He knew he couldn't go on. But that, of course, was like a condemned man knowing he couldn't die.

The whole thing became automatic, without any feeling whatsoever. He didn't stop to rest any more. He just kept going. Nothing made any difference. He didn't even care when, ages later, he came round a bend and saw before him a beautiful lake, with a picturesque group of log chalets at the other end. Going-to-the-Sun Chalet. Fourteen miles he'd been crawling toward this. This was his goal. But it was too late. He didn't care.

Just outside camp he sat on a rock for one final blind rest. A dude cowboy, dressed fit to kill, came round the bend on a horse. Behind him rode three fat women in pants. The first horse shied a little as it passed. The cowboy spoke very courteously. "I'm afraid maybe you're going to scare those women's horses," he said. Rollo slowly raised his head. He looked up at the cowboy. "Aw, nuts to you!" said Rollo.

It is hard to find out exactly what is on a sheepherder's mind. A great deal of the time, I suspect, nothing is. A sheepherder is in solitary. He has hours and days and even weeks with only his dog and his horse and his thousand baa-baas for company. His actual work is snaillike, and infrequent. He has a large abundance of spare time. Should a man with that much time to himself be a smart man or a stupid one? If he's smart enough, he will have the capacity to endure himself, and pilot his thoughts about like an aviator, and be truly a great man. If he's stupid enough, devoid of imagination, not cursed with the delirium of introspection, then he will become one with the rock and the weed, moving about his shepherding duties with the blank passion of a machine. In either case, he'll be all right. But if he should be neither quite stupid enough nor smart enough, then he must eventually flee in terror before so much loneliness, and rage around in his vast valley of thoughts, and become in time what we slangily describe as coo-coo. It would not surprise me to find that a good percentage of the old sheepherders of the world are just a bit touched.

A sheepherder has company so seldom that when he does get a chance to talk he's liable to say almost anything. His conversation sort of flops around, like an old inner tube. For example, out near Castle Rock, South Dakota, Sheepherder Allen Bovey said to me, right in the middle of our conversation, and apparently apropos of nothing whatever, "When I was a little baby, my oldest brother ran away from home, and we never heard from him again. That was thirty years ago. He ran away with three Swedes, and we never knew what became of him." That was all there was of it.

I spent about an hour with Allen Bovey, out on the prairie. He loved his sheep, and his horse Red, and his little dog Tiddy, even though they didn't belong to him personally. He had been herding sheep for nine years. Before that he was a cowpuncher. Before that he was just a youth. He got forty-five dollars a month, and grub, and lived on the range alone. The "sheep wagon" was his home. It was like the covered wagon of frontier days. He slept in it, and cooked his meals in it. The rancher drove out about once a week with fresh supplies.

Every evening at sunset Allen Bovey's sheep came back to the wagon, even if not driven, and lay down and went to sleep. Bovey went to bed at sundown. He had trained himself to be alert to approaching storms. "If a storm comes up, I have to get out, and right now, too," he said. Sheep will stampede in a night storm.

Every flock has a born leader. Bovey's leader was a black sheep, the only one in the whole thousand. He said it was just a coincidence.

Bovey got up at dawn—which meant between three and four o'clock—up with his gun handy. Why? Because it's just after dawn that the coyotes come. That summer he had lost three sheep to coyotes. He had killed one coyote, but it's dangerous to shoot when they are among the sheep. Sometimes antelope got in among his sheep, too. This country was so empty and broad—not a tree as far as you could see—that you couldn't imagine that there were antelope around, but occasionally they would graze right with the sheep. Once in a while an old buck sheep would start a fight, and then the buck sheep always got killed.

Allen Bovey read magazines quite a bit, but he said his eyes were going bad from so much reading. His face was leathery brown, and wrinkled from squinting in the glaring Dakota sun. He didn't wear dark glasses, though he guessed he should. Once he went to Rapid City, the biggest town for hundreds of miles. He was walking down the main street, and two masked men with guns jumped out and took $175 away from him. His whole summer's work. He never went back to Rapid City.

I asked him what there was about herding sheep that anybody couldn't do—me, for instance. He said, "You'd go crazy in two days just from lonesomeness." I said no, I wouldn't. "Yes, you would," he said.

Cactus
Country

Chapter
VI

RUDY HALE AND HIS WIFE LIVED ALONE BACK OF their little store fifty miles east of Yuma, and there was no one else for miles. Three steps from their door and you were ankle deep in bare sand. The Hales caught live rattlesnakes for a living. To me that would be ten thousand times worse than death. But they enjoyed it.

The Arizona sands are filthy with rattlers. Rudy and his wife worked the desert for snakes as a farmer works his land for crops. Rattlers built them a place to live, rattlers kept them in food and clothing, rattlers provided the start for their little gas and grocery business. They loved rattlers.

Rudy Hale was born in Illinois of German parentage, and he still had an accent. He was brought up with the idea of being a surgeon. A relative sent him to school abroad and he studied medicine in Austria for years. When the relative died, his schooling stopped and his life turned.

He wound up in California, where he worked for twenty years as a master mechanic. Then carbon monoxide laid him out and he went to the Arizona desert for his health. It was after two years there that the Hales came right up against it and had to turn to snakes for a living.

They started out by advertising in a San Diego paper. Before they knew it they were swamped with orders. They sold snakes to zoos all over the country, to private collectors, to medical centers for serum, to state reptile farms, to the Mayo brothers. "They say there aren't any snakes in Ireland," said Mrs. Hale. "But I know there are, because we've shipped snakes to Ireland."

They didn't even use forked sticks to catch snakes—just picked them up with bare hands and put them in a box slung over the shoulder. They usually hunted snakes for an hour after daylight and an hour before dark. In eight years they had caught approximately twenty thousand rattlers. Rudy had caught as many as fifty sidewinders in one hour's hunting. They had the desert cleaned almost bare of snakes for twenty miles around.

There are twelve species of rattlers in that part of Arizona. The sidewinder is the most deadly, and the Hales specialized in sidewinders. They used to get fifty cents apiece for them. "I just wish I could get fifty cents again," Rudy said. "They're down to twenty cents now." The most he ever got for a snake was seven dollars; that was a rare Black Mountain rattler. He said the huge snakes didn't bring as much as medium-sized ones. They were harder to keep in captivity, and zoos didn't want them.

Hale had caught rattlers as big around as his leg. He had caught them so big that they'd overpower him and pull his arms together, and he'd have to throw them away from him and then pick them up and try again. "I'm careful not to hurt a snake," he said. "Any snake I ship is a good healthy snake."

Both Hale and his wife would let rattlers crawl all over them. She even carried them around in her pockets. Neither of them had ever been bitten, but her brother had. He was bitten five times, quick as a flash, by a nest of sidewinders. He didn't say a word—just went and lay down in the sand, flat on his back, stretched out his arms, shut his eyes, and lay there still as death for half an hour. Then he went back to work. Nothing ever happened. The Hales said that most people who died of snakebite really died of fright. Mrs. Hale's brother sat down on a rattler once. One time Rudy himself stepped right into the middle of a huge coiled rattler; his foot slipped and he fell down among the coils, but for some reason he wasn't bitten.

There's no danger if you watch your business, Hale said. You mustn't be thinking about anything else when you're picking up a sidewinder. He said the hand was quicker than a snake's strike, and if you missed him the first grab you could jerk back in time. Lots of times when they saw a rattler coiled they would just ease up and slide a hand through the sand under it, and lift it up right in the palm of the hand, still coiled.

Rudy had only one sidewinder on hand the day I was there. It was in a roofless concrete tank behind the house. He took me out for a look after dark and turned on a dim little electric light. He took a stick with a nail in it and got the sidewinder hooked over the nail, and had it lifted almost to the top of the tank. Just then his little red dog stuck its cold nose up my pants leg. I let out a yell and landed somewhere way over the other side of Gila Bend, and never did go back after the car.

I've noticed this: you can talk to a farmer or a cattleman or a desert man all day long and he'll talk freely and answer the most personal questions, but he'll never ask your name or your business, or where you're from.

Thirty miles south of Tacna, Arizona, on a desert hillside near the Mexican border, is a place called Tinajas Altas, meaning "High Tanks." It is a series of natural basins, one above the other, which catch and hold rain water. It was a favorite desert watering place in the early days.

On the slope above Tinajas Altas are countless graves of men. When I was there you could locate only a few, but when Ike Proebstal first arrived in that country he and his brother once counted a hundred sixty graves, all of men who had died of thirst —men who had groped across the deadly hot desert, hoped their last hope on finding water at Tinajas Altas and, not finding it, died. Proebstal said the tale was that in the 1849 gold-rush days a Mexican bandit named Blanco would sneak across the border and drain the tanks. Then when the thirsting gold seekers, California bound, had died their choking deaths, he would rob them.

Ike Proebstal knew about men who die of thirst. For thirty-three years he had been a prospector and a mining man among those snaky sands and bare mountains, and he had saved many a man from death. A fellow down the road said to me, "When Ike Proebstal tells you anything about this country you can bank on it being true."

· 73 ·

Proebstal was one of the handsomest human beings I ever laid eyes on. He carried his sixty-odd years like a lord. He had a little Continental goatee, and I'll bet there wasn't a man in Berlin who could so grace a silk hat and an opera cloak. He was born in Oregon, studied mining engineering, and then lit out. Was in the South African mines for years, spent a year on the Australian desert, four years in Hawaii, a year in China and Japan. He had been rich and he had been poor. Now he was living in a one-room shack, but he was no desert rat.

"I wish my brother was still alive to talk with you," he said. "He had a real reputation for finding missing men. But I've saved quite a few too. The first fifteen years we were here, my brother and I rescued at least two people a year, I guess. There isn't so much of it any more. The auto has changed that. People drive right out across the desert, and they can take plenty of water with them. But even so, there's somebody lost from around here about once a year.

"You know, a man dying of thirst always takes off all his clothes. I don't know why, but they do it every time. Years ago a man rode into my prospecting camp late in the afternoon. He was more dead than alive, and so was his horse. He said he had left his partner under a bush about five miles away. I started right out. I ran almost all the way, for I knew I could just barely make it by sundown. I knew that if I didn't get there before dark I'd never find him, because he'd get up at dusk and start traveling. They always do.

"Well, I found him. He was lying there on the sand, naked as a baby. A few feet away was a tripod made of short steel tubing about two feet long, with a kettle hanging on it. I kicked the tripod down and stood there and called to the fellow, 'I've got some water for you. Come and get it.' The fellow raised up. His face was black as coal and his tongue was swollen and sticking out of his mouth two inches. He jumped up and ran at me and tried to take the water away from me, but I handled him all right. I'd brought a canteen of water and a whisky glass. I gave him just one small glass of water. Then I made him put his clothes on and told him if he'd follow me I'd give him a drink every hundred and fifty yards. The boys back at the camp

· 74 ·

had built bonfires so I could find my way back. When we got about halfway I asked the fellow how he was feeling, and he said fine, that he was sweating. So I said, 'All right then, you can drink all you want now.'

"He told me later that he was crazy and yet he wasn't crazy. He said he saw me standing over those steel bars, and he knew why I was doing it. He said if it hadn't been for those bars he would have killed me to get at the water quicker."

Do you know that on a blistering hot summer day in the Arizona desert a man lives only three or four hours after the thirst craze hits him? That's what Ike Proebstal said. He himself almost got it once. He tried too long a hike between water holes, and the thirst craze set in. If he hadn't known the ways of the desert he'd be a dead one now.

"But there isn't much sense in dying of thirst nowadays," he said. "For instance, my wife and I are going on a little prospecting trip tomorrow. We'll take plenty of water in the car, and we'll leave word here where we're going, and if we're not back by ten o'clock tomorrow night they'll start looking for us.

"I don't know what it is about the desert. It's a godforsaken place, and yet it gets in your blood. I've lived all over the world, but I haven't been away from here now for thirty-three years. I couldn't live anywhere else."

In the thirties Sante Fe, New Mexico, had fifteen thousand people, of whom half were Spanish American. Of the rest about a hundred fifty were artists and writers. Which doesn't sound like many in figures, but it's an awful gob of genius. Then there were the governor and the politicians, whom the geniuses didn't recognize. Life among the upper crust centered by daytime in the La Fonda Hotel. (La Fonda is Spanish for "The Hotel," but people don't pay much attention to that. They just go on saying The-the Hotel-hotel.) You could go there any time of day and see a few artists in the bar, or an Indian that some white woman loved, or a goateed nobleman from Austria, or a maharaja from India, or a New York broker, or an archaeologist, or some local light in overalls and cowboy boots. You never met anybody anywhere except at the La Fonda. You never took anybody to lunch anywhere else. I couldn't see how some of the struggling geniuses afforded it. I stayed at the De Vargas.

Most of the artists seemed to be genuine people, living normal lives, though there were freaks and pretenders—people who liked to dress up like Indians and stare into fireplaces. Many people who go to Santa Fe stay sane. Some go to pot. Some go what you might call native, and don't take baths any more, and ride to cocktail parties on spotted ponies, and dress like Spaniards, and collect pink mice, and live in tents as the Indians used to do. There was one man who insulted every stranger at a party. And there was one woman who would go to parties, get bored, tie a string around her skirt, and then go and stand on her head in a corner the rest of the evening. But I regret to say that all the artists and writers I met were as fine people as you'd ever wish to see—intelligent, serious, good. I tried to find some of the freaks, so I could do stories about them, but they all must have been out picking huckleberries.

Just for my edification, some friends got to figuring up the people in Santa Fe that you could actually call interesting. I suspect they made the entrance requirements pretty stiff. Anyhow, as it wound up, they could think of only twenty people in Santa Fe who were downright interesting. Which, at that, is probably more than you'd find with a strict yardstick in any other American town of fifteen thousand.

Santa Fe is seven thousand feet up, and a newcomer has to gasp for breath the first few days. It gets very cold in winter and there is snow. But in summer it's cool, and people pay two hundred dollars a month for a house that goes for forty in winter. The climate is fine for tuberculars. Lots of people you meet, looking robust and full of vim, came out on stretchers. Yet you don't feel a sanitarium-town atmosphere.

It is the second oldest city in the United States, next to St. Augustine, Florida. Coronado came from Mexico and roamed all around there in 1540. The whole Rio Grande valley drips with history and with ancient Spanish and Indian culture. And I don't know of a town in America that has such astoundingly long unfoldings of nature as you see from just outside Santa Fe.

The town lies in a wide valley, close to mountains on the east. They are not the high, sinister mountains of the northern Rockies; they seem more like neighbors. But sometimes you can stand in the bright sunshine in Santa Fe and see not five miles away an ominous blackish-gray snowstorm swirling down upon the mountain ridge. Or if you visit a friend who lives a few miles out of town you can sit in his library and look northwest through the big window and see a vastness of valley and mesa and far-off mountain chain that almost drives you crazy with its immensity. In all the time I have spent in Santa Fe, I have never seen the surrounding country or sky look alike on any two days, and I have yet to see it when it was not fascinating. Boston for beans, Seattle for rain, San Francisco for bridges, and Santa Fe for long, far looks at what God made.

As for the town itself, there isn't anything else in America that looks like Santa Fe. The business section will disappoint you if you've heard too much about the beauties of Santa Fe. It has a lot of tasteless old 1890-type brick buildings. But scattered among them are the soft lines of warm gray stuccoed adobe in the new Santa Fe architecture, and the streets are narrow and twisty as of old. You hear as much Spanish on the street as you do English, and when you get out toward the edge of town among the poorer people the houses are a solid tan-gray wall, flush with the dirt sidewalk, and you're right down in old Mexico.

Most of the recent construction has been in this perfectly blended Santa Fe style—the art museum, the post office, the La Fonda Hotel—but some of the older buildings are hideously out of place—the red Scottish Rite temple, the state capitol, the Federal Building. Santa Fe architecture is simply a modernization and a softening of the age-old Pueblo Indian style. Outer walls slant slightly inward as they go up; corners are rounded; second stories (if any) are always set back; you don't see any roofs; the ends of vigas, or roof poles, stick out of the adobe. The houses are made of adobe bricks and covered with adobe mud or smooth mud-colored stucco. Fireplaces are in corners, shaped like one-fourth of an orange cut off at the bottom, and wood is set on end to burn, not laid flat. Inner walls are plain white, ceilings aren't quite level, many main rooms have old carved beams, hallways and stairways twist a little, nothing is square, nothing is sharp.

This architecture would look hideous in New York or Memphis or on an Iowa farm. It has to be in the southwestern desert, under bright sun and amid bare distances, blending with the earth and harmonizing with the mountainside, speaking in silent good manners with the personality of the Southwest. If I was dictator of Santa Fe I would not allow even a doghouse to be put up in any other style, and in fifty years we'd have the most charming city on the continent.

Any number of people in Santa Fe urged me to write something about Conrad, the chef at the La Fonda. "He is one of the main things in Santa Fe," they told me. I was reluctant to bother with Conrad, because I am not equipped for the fullest appreciation of chefs and food, so I listened politely to my friends and swore to do nothing about it. But—

When we were sitting in Tex Austin's place late one evening, a man came over to our table. He was slender and of medium height and had a gold tooth and a tiny goatee. My friends at the table jumped up and started yelling, "Conrad! Conrad!" and I knew I was lost. Introductions were made. When it came to me, Conrad said, "Ah, I wanted to see you. I've read your writings for a long time. Remember when you wrote about paying ninety cents for breakfast at the La Fonda?"

Sure, I remembered it. And I was sore when I wrote it, too. I'd paid ninety cents for orange juice, one egg, bacon, toast, and milk. The La Fonda people, Conrad said, had seen the column, and they sat right down and looked at the menu. They decided people shouldn't be paying ninety cents for a breakfast like that, and they changed the menu!

After Conrad told me that, we began to get along pretty well, and after a while he said, "You've got to come over tomorrow and let me fix a special luncheon for you. You come and bring your friends."

So next day we arrived in the beautiful dining room of the La Fonda. A table was reserved for four. Two waitresses knew all about it, and were hovering with service. We had six kinds of hors d'oeuvres, and turkey so tender you could cut it with a glance, and it had sauce and peanuts on top of it, and there were fancy vegetables and breads, and they wound it up with a handsome parfait. All of which was wonderful, except that I am a steak-and-mashed-potato man. Food means absolutely nothing to me; I often forget to eat lunch; when I do eat, it is merely to keep from getting weak. Meals are a task, like getting up in the morning. And here I was supposed to relish a luncheon prepared in my honor by the greatest chef in the Southwest.

The Santa Fe girl with me said it was undoubtedly the finest meal she had ever set tongue to, and that she knew food when she ate it. She cleaned her plate, clean as a Saint Bernard's tooth, and gave the waitress special instructions to take it back and show it to Conrad. Which put me in a spot—I'd never eaten a whole plate of anything in my life. So I did the best I could, and we went back to the kitchen and raved to Conrad about the marvelous meal, and he beamed and was satisfied. Then Conrad and I sat down and had a talk.

He came from Germany in 1922. He had been in the Kaiser's kitchen for six months. He saw the Kaiser often, and liked him. Every morning when the cooks came to work, he said, they had to have a shower and a physical examination.

Conrad started his apprenticeship at fifteen, and had been cooking thirty years. He said it took about six years to make a No. 1 chef. He had never had a request from the dining room that stumped him, though he could be stumped on Oriental dishes. He had cooked in Africa, Italy, France, England, and Sweden, but he said this business of having Pierre and Alphonse and Luigi and Conrad for chefs was a lot of hooey; any American could learn to cook just as well as a European.

And the funny part about him was that he didn't like all this fancy stuff he fixed up for people. What he enjoyed most, he said, was to get home and have his wife fix him something simple.

Irene Fisher lived in a boxcar four miles north of Albuquerque, New Mexico. Irene was no tramp, and she lived in a boxcar on purpose, because she was arty like the people at Santa Fe.

She bought an old refrigerator car from the railroad—paid forty dollars for it, and paid a trucker forty dollars to get it out there. Then she went to work. In one end she built a bunk, crosswise, the kind of bunk ship's officers have in their cabins. Beneath it, instead of drawers, was another bed which slid out. This was the "guest room." From this end of the car to beyond the big doors in the middle was one room. Then there was a partition, with a door. Next was the kitchen, with a coal stove for heating. And beyond that, in the far end, was the bathroom. The thing didn't seem cramped at all.

You'd be surprised how homey a boxcar can be. Irene had electric lights and running water. She had pictures on the walls, and bookshelves, and rugs, and a table and a chaise longue. She said the only thing wrong was that the railroad had carefully painted out all the bawdy poems that knights of the road always write on the inside of boxcars.

One of my friends in Albuquerque had a strange little affliction—he couldn't back into a parking place. That in itself wasn't so odd, but the strange part was that he had been driving for twenty-five years, and had always been able to back into a parking place all right, until all of a sudden one day he forgot how. And he was never able to do it again. Sometimes he had to go blocks from his office to find a place big enough to park head-on.

One evening I went down to the basement washroom of an Albuquerque hotel, and found it locked. After much inquiry I located the key at the cashier's desk in the cocktail room. I asked him why they kept it locked up.

"Because of the Indians," he said. "We can't keep them out of there. They're in there all day and all night. They even go in there and take baths."

And here I, being an old city cynic, had always supposed the Indians sitting in the lobby were paid by the hotel to sit there.

One afternoon we sat out in front of Pablo Abeyta's adobe house in the ancient Pueblo village of Isleta, New Mexico, while Pablo told me about Teddy Roosevelt.

Pablo had long hair, which kept blowing into his mouth, and he had two long braids behind. He wore a white lace shirt, like a woman's blouse, and a big gray hat. He had the biggest face I ever saw on a man, and it was all Indian. He was about sixty-five and he spoke better English than I do, and because he was smart and could talk he was always being sent to Washington as interpreter for Indian delegations. He had made eighteen trips to Washington, he said, and it was on one of these trips that the Teddy Roosevelt incident happened.

"We went into the White House," Pablo said, "and somebody introduced us one at a time, and the President shook hands and said a few words. Then when we left and were outside, a fellow pulled my sleeve and said the President wanted to see me alone. So I went back and he said, 'Pablo, sit down,' and he said, 'Pablo, I want to know all about your village and what the Indians need.' So we sat there talking and I knew he was busy and I kept rushing through so I could leave. But he kept telling me to go on. After a while some Cabinet men came in and sat down, and finally they got to fidgeting, and one of them took out his watch and pointed at it, and the President turned around and said, 'Gentlemen, I'm fully aware of the time we are spending here. Go on, Pablo.'

"Well, sir, I talked to him for two hours and twenty minutes, and when I left he said, 'Pablo, some day I'm coming to Isleta and I want to visit you in your own home.' So I came on back and didn't think much about it. Several months later I got a message that the President was at the main hotel in Albuquerque and wanted me to come right up. So I hitched up my horses and drove to Albuquerque and tied my horses outside the hotel. There were two men standing outside the door and they said, 'What do you want?' I said, 'The President wants to see me.' They said, 'What's your name?' I said, 'I haven't got any name. Tell the President an Indian wants to see him.' So they started an argument and we made so much noise the President heard us, and he recognized my voice and came and opened the door and pulled me in.

" 'Pablo, you didn't think I'd really come, did you?' the President said. And then he said, 'Pablo, how'll we get out to Isleta without all this crowd following us?'

"So I said, 'Mr. President, give me your hat and coat.' He handed them over without a word, and I put them under my blanket and went down and put them in my buggy, and got another blanket and went back up. I put the blanket around the President, clear up over his head, and then we pulled the blankets up around us and stooped over and shuffled down through the lobby and out across the street and got in my buggy, and everybody thought we were just a couple of old Indians. I galloped my horses all the way to Isleta, and we went into my house and the President said, 'Pablo, you didn't think I'd ever come, did you? Now I've fulfilled my promise.'

"So we had a bite to eat and sat and talked a few minutes, and then we got in the buggy and drove back to Albuquerque. When we walked into the hotel, the lobby was full of people and the Secret Service men were running around excited because they couldn't find the President. So I gave a big war whoop and jerked the blanket off the President's head, and you should have seen the people stare. The guards came running up and they were sore because the President had got away from them, but he turned around and said, 'Boys, I was just as safe in Pablo's hands as I am with anybody in the world.'

"And you know, he kept that blanket. I saw him again at the White House in 1915 and he showed me the blanket and said—"

"But Pablo," I interrupted, "Theodore Roosevelt wasn't president in 1915."

"Well, anyway," said Pablo, "he showed me the blanket and said . . ."

So that's Pablo's story. It doesn't make any difference to me whether you believe it or not. And it probably doesn't make any difference to Pablo either.

Tradition in southwestern Texas revolves around Judge Roy Bean, who was the self-styled "Law west of the Pecos" back in frontier days when horse stealing was worse than murder. Judge Bean held court on the porch of his saloon in Langtry. He always had two things on the bench in front of him—a lawbook, which he didn't know how to use, and a six-shooter, which he did. He died in 1903, but his saloon remained standing, empty now, and the big sign "Law west of the Pecos" stayed up in front.

I drove into Langtry, took a picture of the saloon, and asked a couple of loafers if anybody was still around who remembered Judge Bean. They said there was just one fellow—Ike Billings. He lived on a ranch four miles out, and maybe I'd find him there and maybe I wouldn't. So I drove out over the desert, across big washes and over rocks and through mesquite bushes raking the fenders, to Ike Billings' place.

He was there. He'd just come in from "pointing up" lambs, which means cutting off their tails and snipping their ears. He washed up and then we sat and talked. Billings was one of those hard-working, well-preserved desert men. He had a jovial, round, tanned face, and beautiful teeth, and white whiskers when he was needing a shave. He had turned fifty-nine the week before and he had a daughter thirty-seven years old, but he didn't look more than forty-five. He was born in mid-Texas, near San Antonio, and came to the Pecos country in '93. He settled in Langtry, and he knew Judge Bean well from then until the judge died.

"Sure, I used to play poker with him a couple of nights a week," Billings said. "He was a queer character, but people around here liked him. I think he was a Spaniard or something. He was a slick one. I remember once a cowboy fell or jumped off the railroad bridge up here a piece and was killed. They found forty dollars and a six-shooter on him. The judge convened court over the body, and took the six-shooter and fined the fellow forty dollars for committing suicide, and then had the county bury him because he was a pauper.

"There was a pile of rocks outside Bean's saloon, and he kept a big sign out there saying 'Ice Cold Beer.' In those days the railroad ran right through town, and in the summer tourists would get off here for a cold drink. They'd ask for beer, but it'd be hot when they got it. They'd say, 'How about that sign?' And old Bean would roar and yell, 'Who in hell ever heard of ice in this country in the summertime?' But he never took the sign down.

"He had another stunt. These tourists would get some beer and give him a ten- or twenty-dollar bill, and then he'd monkey around very busy and let on like he was having trouble making change, and the first thing you knew the train was pulling out and the tourists would have to run and jump on without their change."

Billings himself was "the law" in Langtry for six years. That was after Bean died, and old man Dodd was justice of the peace, and Billings was constable. His territory covered all the country west of the Pecos, and he had to do a lot of horseback riding. Everybody in those days carried a six-shooter.

"But I never did have any trouble," Billings said. "I never was shot at, and never shot at anybody but once, and then I missed him. It was a dark rainy night, and I was chasing a Mexican who had killed a fellow on the railroad. I shot at him when he ran around a building. We got him the next morning, though."

Billings moved out to the ranch in 1911. He had twenty-five hundred head of sheep, and some goats and a few cattle. He had twelve thousand acres of desert land, and thirty-five miles of fence around it. "Most people wouldn't give a cent an acre for it," he said, "but we like it here. We don't have things very fancy, but we get along. My wife wouldn't leave here for anything. I guess it's true I'm the only old-timer left around here. The others have died or moved away."

Ike Billings, like every person I ever met on the desert, was friendly and hospitable. "I sure wish you had been here last Wednesday," he said. "We had a big goat-fry down the crick here, celebrating my birthday, and people from all over this part of the country were here. You sure would have enjoyed it."

Gene Howe, the son of Ed Howe, the famous country editor, was owner and editor of Amarillo's two papers—the *Globe* and the *News*. He also owned the old family paper in Kansas, the Atchison *Globe,* and half a dozen smaller but prosperous papers in Texas and Kansas. He owned a big ranch, and a home. He was doing all right.

His father, the "Sage of Potato Hill," was eighty-three now, and spent his winters in Florida. He wrote from there to Gene: "A man is a fool who drinks before he is fifty. A man is a fool who doesn't drink after he is fifty. After you're fifty, one drink just before you go to bed makes you sleep better." So now his boy Gene could put on his pajamas every night, take a big swig, and topple into bed. He was fifty-one.

I was surprised when I saw him. I had seen his father's pictures—a thin, wise face, aloof, almost heavenly looking, very calm, and a little sad. Perhaps Ed Howe was not like that at all, but that's the way his pictures impressed me. I had supposed Gene would look like that too. But he didn't. He was medium heavy, was getting bald, wore fine clothes, talked easily and affably, had a business head, knew more people than anybody else in the Panhandle, and was always out and about.

Howe was a force in the Texas Panhandle. Before an election, readers by the hundreds would call up and ask whom to vote for, and Gene would tell them. His papers had never lost a local election. He ran them on that old Howe notion that if you put out a paper for the readers you can let the ads fall where they may, yet there was nothing "hick" about them. They had world news, and the same features you got in the big cities. But you found in them also the thing that makes a country paper —lots of news of the people at home.

The most important thing in Amarillo and the Panhandle was the hope for rain—they hadn't had any to speak of for five years. The second most important thing was Gene Howe's daily column. It was unsigned, headed merely "The Tactless Texan," with a picture of cross-eyed Ben Turpin at the top, but everybody knew who wrote it. The column was being read and talked about over an area six hundred miles wide—all through the vast flat Panhandle and in adjoining states. Its hold on the people was one of the most thrilling things I had ever encountered in journalism. It frequently ran three and four full-length columns, and as a scribbler myself I can testify that when you get anybody to read four columns of solid type you've got to be good.

A number of times Howe's columns had brought him national attention, for he didn't mince words. His greatest notice came from bawling out Mary Garden for not giving Amarillo a good opera performance. He and Mary made it up later. He had an autographed photo of her, and got a Christmas card from her every year. He bawled out Lindbergh for standing up a huge crowd that had turned out to see him after his Atlantic flight. Hundreds of people came in and congratulated Howe, but the civic bodies passed resolutions denouncing him for "besmirching the fair name of southern hospitality."

Howe was the culprit who started Mother-in-Law Day. He didn't realize what he was doing. He just threw the suggestion into his column lightly, to pacify a mother-in-law who had been hurt by something he said. The next day a hundred mothers-in-law were in the office, keen for the idea, and women started forming Mother-in-Law clubs. The first thing he knew Amarillo had a Mother-in-Law Day, with thousands of people and parades and forty bands and a hundred Mother-in-Law clubs from all over the Southwest. He took one look and went home.

He didn't go in for dramatic writing, or for the paragraphical philosophizing of his famous father. He wrote plain ordinary street talk. He would start the column every day with the weather, setting himself up as a sort of jovial Panhandle weather prophet. That's what the farmers wanted, so they ate it up. He talked about the local football teams, and sang a little song for people who had died, and asked why the taxi drivers weren't paid a living wage, and boosted a concert, or scooped his own staff on a coming wedding, and even commented on local suspected murderers. Then he'd run in Walter Winchell's entire column (he bought it from the syndicate), but he would run it right in his own column of shorts called "Interesting Facts," also bought from a syndicate.

He would print anything in his column, no matter what. He printed letters from people who wanted to get married. His column had been responsible for more than three hundred marriages in the Panhandle. He printed letters from women denouncing their neighbors by name, and then printed the neighbors' answers. He said it made wonderful reading. I should think it would. Once a week he published a couple of columns of letters from people wanting jobs, and he had placed hundreds. His column was getting around two thousand letters a month, but he didn't try to answer them all. Almost every day he asked everybody to go out and help find a lost dog or cat. He had given away hundreds of dollars in rewards for children's lost pets. He had turned down two offers to go to New York and write a syndicated column—said he'd rather live in Amarillo.

It was late at night, and the frogs were croaking alongside the road and the motor was purring. I was coming into Oklahoma City for the first time in my life. I knew by my map and speedometer that I wasn't far away now. I saw the reflection of light in the dark sky ahead. That was it—Oklahoma City. It looked good. The road came down out of complete flatness, and began to wind around a little. The glare in the sky vanished around a bend, and reappeared again at the next curve. I topped a little rise, and the fog of lights divided slowly into individualities. I saw tall buildings all lighted up, still far away. I thought, My, but Oklahoma City's a big place. Never knew it was so big. Lots of big office buildings, with people working in them this late at night, too. Why, it looked like the New York sky line, only the buildings all seemed about the same height. The tops made a ledge of light across the sky.

And then it suddenly hit me, right between the eyes: those weren't buildings all lighted up. They were oil derricks. Oil derricks right in the city.

I drove on in among the oil derricks. They were all around, hundreds of them, thick as trees. Some weren't twenty paces apart. Some were right on the highway, like filling stations. A string of bright lights went to the top of each one, and down below, on the ground, everything was brightly lighted.

First the sight, and then the sound. In among them there was a steady, heavy din. The whole field was alive with work. You heard deep, regular poundings; and a throbbing, rumbling, circular sound, like a grinding; and the clank of steel tubes and the whir of great pulleys; and steam shooting off. You saw men at work, and muddy autos dashing about, and the glare of flame in boilers. And the bright lights of the great derricks rose all around you. Immense activity, and it was nearly midnight.

I drove on and on. People's houses were all around the derricks —or rather, the derricks were wedged between houses, on open lots, on filling station aprons. That was the suburbs of Oklahoma City. And pretty soon I saw a sign: "City Limits, Oklahoma

City." I kept on driving, still amidst the oil wells, clear into town. They were all over the golf course. There was one on the side lawn of the state capitol. There was one up against the governor's mansion. The bases of some derricks were flush against the sides of beautiful residences.

Three months before this visit of mine, there had been only two oil wells in the northern part of Oklahoma City. Now there were at least three hundred, and new derricks were going up almost by the hour. Residential sections were being gutted. People were wild for oil. Of course, some were shocked by this glaring display of commercialism. Rearing an oil field right in the heart of a city. Ruining homes and fine residential sections. Where was the sanctity of the home? Putting oil wells on the capitol grounds. Where was the dignity of state? Greedy, greedy Oklahoma. Was nothing sacred?

Personally, I got a big wallop out of it. My vote for it was "yes." Put up a thousand more derricks! What if it did waste irrecoverable reserves of oil! Grind a thousand more holes in the ground! Who cares for the heartbreaks and the empty tomorrows? Tear down the statehouse. Throw up more silvery steel shafts. Fire up the black boilers. Drill in the gushers, boys. Cheat the poor folks. Ruin the homes. Squander gas. Throw away fortunes. Who cares? It's fun. Everybody's having fun, even the losers. It's a fever. Spread out your hands and catch the sparkling spray. Let oil reign unrefined. Let's all get rich. Boy, hand me that lease, before it's too late. God, it's exciting. It's a boom. It's a mania. It's great. Wheeee!

Oklahoma is one of the friendliest states in the Union. Taxi drivers open the front door, so you can ride up front. If there's just one passenger he always rides with the driver, and they talk.

Oklahoma City is an especially friendly town. People there have a pride about their town—not a silly civic pride, but that same feeling that exists in San Francisco and New Orleans. They just wouldn't live anywhere else, that's all. I too liked Oklahoma City, but I had a little bone to pick with it. In no other place had I ever seen the absolute wall of billboards that you got coming into Oklahoma City from the west. I could hardly believe

my eyes. After you looked a while it really got comical. In the
last ten miles I'll bet there were two thousand billboards.

"Alfalfa Bill" Murray let me down. I drove a hundred fifty
miles out of my way, over dusty gravel roads, to see the picturesque former governor of Oklahoma on his new farm, and
he acted just like any other ordinary human being. I had heard
such swell stories about him—how he had a big hole cut in the
living-room floor for ventilation; how he talked to one bunch
of hogs in English and the other in Choctaw because they were
Choctaw hogs and didn't understand English; and how he kept
an idiot down at the gate to gibber and scare away strangers.
But I spent the whole afternoon with Alfalfa Bill, and he didn't
talk to his hogs in Choctaw, and I couldn't see any hole in the
floor, and I guess it was the idiot's day off.

But Alfalfa Bill was a character, even if he didn't put on a
show for me. He was the hillbilliest-looking statesman you ever
saw—no shirt, winter underwear, plow shoes unlaced, handkerchief around his neck, an upper front tooth out, long hair, white
whiskers. He looked older than I had remembered him. He
cussed a lot, but his grammar was good and he was nobody's fool.

Alfalfa Bill had bought this farm, about a mile from the town
of Broken Bow, Oklahoma, a year before I dropped in. He went
there to recuperate from being governor. He said he was so all
in when he left the governorship that it was three months before
he could walk straight. He picked this location, down in the
corner where Oklahoma joins Arkansas and Texas, because it
was in the warmest part of Oklahoma and had the least dust.
Alfalfa Bill said he didn't have any money. Bought the farm with
what he saved out of his governor's salary and a purse some
friends gave him. His wife and daughter were living with him.
Mrs. Murray was hammering away at something in the kitchen.
I never did see her.

The place was a mess when he bought it, but he had cleaned
it up, made a nice flower garden, and built a couple of sheds
out behind the house. One of these was his office, where he had
a steel desk and two steel filing cabinets, and a big high-backed
swivel chair—the one they gave him when he was speaker of

Oklahoma's first legislature. The floor was thick with discarded papers and pamphlets and old envelopes. On the desk was a copy of Adams' *The Living Jefferson*.

Alfalfa Bill devoted every forenoon to what he called "intellectual" work; he had a secretary in town who came out and took dictation. He got a lot of letters—political letters, letters from people wanting things, crank letters. In the afternoon Murray would go around and boss the hired men a little, then come and sit in a rocking chair on his front porch. That's where he was when I walked up.

He took me way down to the back pasture to show me the spring where they got their drinking water. He showed me clover he'd planted, and all kinds of bushes and vines I'd never heard of. He showed me his hogs, his Italian chickens, and three chickens somebody sent him from the Himalaya Mountains. They had big white fluffs on their heads, and black faces. No combs.

I asked if he ever intended going back into public life. He said he didn't know. He said there was no sense in an honest and sincere man's being in public life these days. "I could run for Congress from this district and get nearly every vote," he said. "But what's the use of me going to Congress? I don't believe in a thing they're doing up there. And the way they run things all I could do is sit and vote 'no,' and look like an obstructionist."

Tennessee

Chapter VII THE MOST POWERFUL URGE I HAD EVER SEEN IN A human being was the determination of John Claybrook to make his son exactly like himself.

John Claybrook was a Negro. He was a self-made man, rich, proud, somewhat pious. He considered himself an outstanding example of what a hard-working, right-living Negro could do in this world. He owned twelve hundred acres of land in Arkansas, across the river from Memphis, and various logging contracting companies; he had a town house in Memphis and dealt with all the biggest banks there.

When he was a child he ran away from his home in Florence, Alabama, and started working on the docks. He knew then that he was going to succeed. He knew he was a better man than other men, that he worked harder and gave his employer more. And if he didn't get a raise, he quit and went elsewhere. Never in his life had he made a change for the worse.

He married when he was twenty. He had never been to school, so his wife taught him his ABC's. He still couldn't read or write very well, though he could spell out a piece in the paper if there was no one around to read it to him. But figures? Ah, figures are terms for money, and figures came easily for him; he could do them in his head. He never had to think twice as he tossed the numerals of a transaction around in his mind.

John Claybrook had always saved money; to him prodigality was a sin. His savings grew into a pile, and the pile into a fortune, yet his wealth put no flossy ideas in his head. He lived well, but without luxury or display.

Middle age approached, and his piety and his pride in his own success accumulated with the years. Then his wife died, and he married again. He was past forty-five when his only son was born of this second marriage. I don't know whether or not this determination to shape his son in his own image was an obsession right from the start, but it certainly was now. I would sure have hated to be in that boy's shoes.

John was sixty-six, still as sound as an oak tree, still able to do a day's cotton chopping in the field, though he seldom did. He devoted his time to supervising, and to the over-all task of making the son worthy of the father. The boy, now twenty, was inclined to be a little wild. He liked fun and didn't care for work. John had sent him away to school in Alabama when he was sixteen. He was made to wash his own clothes at school—a lesson in frugality. The other boys would say, "If my dad was as rich as yours, I wouldn't be washing my own clothes." John heard about it. So that's what a boy learns in school, eh? John took him out before it was too late, brought him back to the Arkansas farm, and put him to work in the fields. He paid him regular wages and made him drink out of the same water jug all the hired men used, so he wouldn't get the idea he was better than they were.

But, on the other hand, John evened things up. In school the boy had been crazy about athletics, so John built him a stadium on the farm and bought him a ball team. Yes, sir, actually bought him a baseball team. The whole thing cost him three or four thousand dollars. That pro ball team was known all over the South. Five of the players worked on John's farm; the others were just straight ball players hired by him.

That worked for a while. But the boy was wild. His father was always teaching him, always telling him, always exampling him, and they couldn't get along. Four times in four years they broke up and the boy left home, but each time he came back. When he was about nineteen he wanted to get married, and asked his father about it. John didn't know the girl and he told the boy to bring her over from Memphis. The three of them sat on the porch all evening talking about it. "If you're the right girl for John, it would make me happier than anything in the world," John Sr. told her. "But how do I know you're the right girl?" They talked and talked. Finally he gave his consent. "But remember this," he told her. "You're marrying John Claybrook, Jr., and not John

Claybrook, **Sr.** You won't live on my money. You'll have to live on what he makes."

It didn't pan out. John said he was getting his son a divorce soon; that was one of many blows he had had to take. But the boy was starting to come around. He was developing, and showing an interest in the farm. John had started to take him around to the banks in Memphis, introducing him to his bankers. And he was trying to teach him to think along business lines.

The fight wasn't over yet, but John Claybrook saw enough progress to encourage him. He told me about a meaningful little incident that had happened one day. He and his wife had left the plantation over Sunday for a short trip. They got back unexpectedly early, about two o'clock Sunday afternoon. All the hands, of course, had the day off. "We drove up in the driveway," he said. "We thought the boy would be dressed up and sitting on the porch, but he wasn't. I looked around, and finally I saw him. He was out in the field. He had on his overalls, and he was down on his knees, scratching the ground with his hands, to see how the cotton was coming up. It made me so happy I just had to shed tears, right there."

The job of being a roving reporter teaches you one thing: he who laughs too long and loud at other people is liable to get sand in his mouth. The more you travel around and see all sorts of people the less inclined you are to stand up on a dais and look down at anybody, and laugh at him. Because he may be looking up, laughing at you.

Take Frank Murphy, for instance. A few years ago, when I was a smart guy and knew everything, I could have written a mighty clever piece about Frank. But now I can't figure out whether it's Frank who was crazy, or me, or maybe both of us.

Frank Murphy was an old man. Seventy-six, he said. He was tall and thin and not very clean, and he had a bushy gray beard, and gray eyes that stared out through horn-rimmed spectacles. Frank had come from the "old country," from an island off the coast of Ireland. He thought he had a son, but hadn't heard of him in fifty years, since his wife died. He didn't have anybody in this world at all.

· 93 ·

He was a squatter. He lived just behind the Memphis city dump, right on the bank of the Mississippi. His home, everything he had—in fact, his whole livelihood—came out of the city dump. He had picked old auto hoods out of the dump, pounded them flat, and built himself a house. It wasn't one of these wobbly shantytown shacks, either; it was straight and solid. The doors closed snugly, the windows were tight, no rain or wind could get in. It had four small, fairly clean rooms, so full of homemade furniture and sundry trinkets you could hardly move around.

Murphy came pretty close to being self-sufficient. He had nobody to help him, and he made his own way. He got old tin pans and kettles out of the city dump and repaired them; he found steer horns and polished them up and mounted them; he filed down pieces of steel into butcher knives. All these things he peddled to housewives. "If they're too poor to buy them, I just give them away," he said. When he had enough for a few days' groceries, he didn't peddle any more, for he had many other things to do. He had a lot of painting and inventing to do, for instance.

He had something that was going to be a perpetual-motion machine—not exactly a machine, just a thing that would keep going all the time. And if you stopped it, it would start itself again and keep on going. He showed it to us. It was just the rim of an old Ford steering wheel hanging on a nail in the ceiling. He had it all figured out, except the one little item of how to keep it going. But things had a way of coming to him in the night, and he'd wake up with it some morning, he said. He'd let me know.

His house painting was what captivated him. His house was daubed all over—not solid, or striped, or patterned in any regular way, but just daubed, like a speckled chicken. And every color of the rainbow. I asked why he painted it that way. He said so strangers would think he was crazy and wouldn't come near. But it worked out just the other way; people came nosing around just to look at it. He did his painting at night. He used to paint in the daytime but then he stumbled onto this night painting idea. He did it in the dark—no light of any kind—so he couldn't see what he was doing. Then the next morning he would jump up and run out to see what it looked like. "And every time," he said, "I think it looks pretty." I thought it did too.

"Do you want to see my house change color?" he asked. We said we sure did. So he ran back into the house, and after a while the panel alongside the front door started sliding back and forth, and sure enough, it was changing color. You see, there were slats in front of the panel, and right behind the slats he had painted the panel a different color. He said he was going to put a little windmill on the roof, and hook it up to the panel through some Rube Goldberg arrangement, so that the wind would keep the panel going back and forth all the time—and wouldn't strangers think that was funny?

He had a picture of Joan Crawford hanging on his porch, and in the house a self-portrait that he had painted looking in the mirror. Up by the window were a couple of great big slingshots. He said that when people got to nosing around he let 'em have it, and they jumped and never knew where the rock came from.

There were a lot of laughs in Frank's place, but I didn't laugh any. After all, why not paint in the dark? It looked a lot better than some daytime painting I've seen in art galleries. And how many of us could make something, or paint something, and then when we sneaked in next morning to see how it looked, always have it look pretty to us? And am I laughing at the old Ford steering wheel that's going to be a perpetual-motion machine? I am not. There are a lot of things that would surprise me more than to find that wheel going around and around by itself some of these days. And what's wrong with making your house "change color"? I'll bet you can't make your house change color.

I wonder—yes, I wonder very much—if when I am seventy-six years old I will be able to build a house with my own hands, and paint pictures that look pretty to me, and have time pass pleasantly, and have to depend on no man in this world either for company or for the necessities of life? If I should find myself so blessed, I'll consider myself a hell of a long way from being crazy.

I suppose the most famous railroad engineer who ever pulled a throttle was John Luther Jones, better known as "Casey."

Nearly everybody in America has sung that song—how Casey "mounted to his cabin with his orders in his hand, and took his farewell trip to that promised land." But did you know that Casey Jones was a real person, who was actually killed in a railroad wreck? I had a long talk in Memphis with Casey's fireman, who went through the wreck with him. He was a colored man named Sim Webb. He was sixty-two, tall and slender, and his skin was light brown. His kinky hair was grayish, but his face was thin and young-looking.

The wreck happened at Vaughan Station, in Mississippi, just before daylight on the morning of May 1, 1900. Sim Webb could tell you the exact minute of nearly every mile of that last wild ride of Casey's. He had told it so many times that he reeled off stations and minutes and speeds with the sureness of a mental calculator.

Sim Webb was twenty-six at the time, and Casey Jones was thirty-two. Sim had been firing for Casey only four months. They were pulling a fast passenger train, on a run from Memphis to Canton, Mississippi. They were due out of Memphis at 11:30 P.M., but on the fatal night the connecting train was delayed and they were an hour and a half late getting out. But "Mr. Casey" was in high spirits, so Sim poured on the coal and Casey bent the throttle back and they boiled south through the night, making up time. They went so fast that when they hit the freight, with just twelve miles to go, they were running only two minutes behind time.

Somewhere around a quarter to four, with the cab a bedlam of noise and rushing air, and the miles clicking off every fifty seconds or so, Casey looked at his watch, and stood up and yelled across the boilertop to Sim: "Sim, the old girl's got her high-heeled slippers on tonight." Those were his last words.

The wreck wasn't Casey's fault; it was the fault of a freight train that had taken the siding, leaving several cars sticking out onto the main line.

"We were going around a double-S curve," Sim Webb said. "We had taken the curve on Mr. Casey's side, and then we swung around so the curve was on my side. All of a sudden I saw the caboose ahead of us. Mr. Casey couldn't see it from his side. I jumped up and yelled, 'Look out, we're gonna hit something.' I never heard him say anything. I just know he stood up, and I heard him kick the seat out from under him. I grabbed the hand-rail and swung myself down and out of the cab. I held to the rail till I was almost down to the ground, and then let go. Just missed a cattle gate by that far. I hit the ground at seventy-five miles an hour. When I woke up I was in a hospital. The engine went clear through the caboose, through a car of corn, through a car of hay, and stopped in a car of lumber, but it stayed on the track. It was stripped clean—cab and everything stripped off. They found Mr. Casey's body in the clear, lying on the ground by the back trucks. Every bone was broken. Mr. Casey was a fine man."

As soon as he was out of the hospital, Sim went back to firing on the same run. He went through another bad wreck during the flood time in 1918. A trestle gave way and the locomotive top-pled off and fell on its side into the river. The engineer was thrown clear, but Sim went under with the engine. Somehow he managed to fish his way out of the cab and get to the top. He had a cigar stub in his mouth when they left the tracks, and it was still in his mouth when he came up. His family kept at him to quit the railroad, so in 1919 he gave in and became a bricklayer. In his new, safe trade a wall caved in on him, covered him with six feet of rock, broke his leg, and put him in the hospital for two months.

Casey Jones's widow was living at Jackson, Tennessee. One day Sim happened to be up there, so he went around to see her. "I was just going to stay a minute," he said, "but we got to talking about railroads and old times and she kept me there two hours."

"I made a mistake quitting the railroad," Sim said, "but I'm too old now to get back on. I've done pretty well, though. I've seen hard times, but I never turn down anything honest, and we've managed to get along."

I asked Sim if he was a religious man. He misunderstood and thought I said a "careless" man. He said, "Well, no, I wouldn't say I was a careless man. I've got my faults—yes, sir, I've got my faults. I'll take a drink now and then, and I'm not perfect. But I go to church, and I've got three grown daughters and one of

· 97 ·

them has thirteen children, and I've still got the same wife I started out with. That's something to write about. We've never had but one quarrel. It was my fault. I was young and I got to liking some of the girls at the other end of the line, and she found out about it. But that's the only time we've ever had a sharp word. And it's going on thirty-nine years now."

William Andrew Johnson was a happy old man with a distinction; he was, so far as he knew, the only living ex-slave of a president, and he was mighty proud of it. William was seventy-nine. He was freed when he was still a boy, yet his whole attitude toward life was shaped by the fact that he had been born into slavery.

I sat in the back end of a restaurant in Knoxville, Tennessee, and had a long chat with him. Despite his age, he had all his faculties; he heard well and saw well, and his mind worked quickly. He was good-humored and felt kindly toward everything.

"My mother was a good-looking woman," he said. "Her owner sold her at a big auction at Greeneville, Tennessee. She looked around the crowd of buyers before the auction started, and she saw Andrew Johnson and liked his looks. So she went up to him and asked him if he wouldn't buy her. He bid her in for five hundred dollars. And he bought my uncle (her brother) for five hundred and forty dollars.

"So I was born into slavery under Andrew Johnson. When I was little, Mr. Andrew used to hold me on one knee and my sister on the other, and he'd rub our heads and laugh." William chuckled to himself. "One day Mrs. Johnson called us all in and said we were free now. She said we were free to go, or we could stay if we wanted to. We all stayed.

"I was only seven when Mr. Andrew was president, and I never went to Washington with him. But after he came back from Washington I was with him all the time. He was elected senator, but he died before he could get back to Washington. He died in '75, when I was seventeen. I used to sit by the side of his bed day and night. He was paralyzed on one side. He would reach over with his good arm and take hold of his wrist and say, 'Is that your hand, William?' And I'd say, 'No, Mr. Andrew, that's your own hand.' You see, he couldn't feel his own hand."

When Andrew Johnson died, he left a house and some land to his ex-slaves, and there they lived until William's mother died. William moved to Knoxville many years ago. He had never married, and he had no kinfolks at all now. He had made his living mostly as a cook, and even at seventy-nine he was cooking in this Knoxville restaurant.

Andrew Johnson's granddaughter, Mrs. Margaret Johnson Patterson, would come down from Greeneville occasionally. The very first thing, she always came to the restaurant to see him, and he would cook her a meal just the way she wanted it and serve it to her himself.

William had seen some hard times. Once a Knoxville reporter who knew him well wrote a story saying it looked as if William would have to go to the poorhouse. The woman who owned the restaurant threw a fit. William quoted her: "Do you think I'd ever let that old man go to the poorhouse? William needn't worry about the poorhouse as long as I'm here."

"White folks have been awful good to me," William said. I asked him if he was better off when Andrew Johnson owned him. He said, "Yes, we were mighty well off then. But any man would rather be free than be a slave. Some of us had fine masters, and we were better off. But some had awful bad masters."

William had a keen disappointment in the spring of 1936. President Roosevelt came to Knoxville to dedicate Norris Dam. William got it into his head he wanted to shake hands and tell him he once was a slave of a president. So he went to some of his white friends—big men in the Chamber of Commerce—and asked if they would fix it up. They told William they would try, but they didn't think anything could be done. Later they reported back that such a thing was impossible. William was mighty upset about it.

Of course, it wasn't impossible at all. William had just used poor judgment in picking his fixer-uppers. He should have known better than to ask a Chamber of Commerce man; he should have asked a newspaperman. If my idea of President

Roosevelt was correct, the whole thing would have been as simple as this: a reporter would have told him that William wanted to shake hands, and the President would have said, "Sure," and they would have brought William up, and the President would have pumped his old brown hand and given him a big smile, and in all this world there wouldn't have been a happier or prouder mortal than William Andrew Johnson.*

The way the government interferes with private business is enough to drive a fellow crazy. That old government moved into Tennessee and bought a lot of hilly land. Then they signed a proclamation making this land into the Greak Smokies National Park. And thereby ruined the finest settlement of moonshiners in the U.S.A.

Cocke County, in southeastern Tennessee, had for twenty years been producing more moonshine than any other county in America. Even with this newfangled government interference, they said Washington still listed it as the moonshiningest spot in the country. We didn't see any stills in operation, for naturally nobody knows where they are when a stranger's around, but at least they didn't consider us important enough to start setting off the dynamite. That had been the old signal system in prohibition days, and it still was. A watcher along the one road that led into the moonshining hills jerked out his dynamite and set it off when a suspicious car went past. You could hear the boom for miles around—much farther than you could hear a gunshot. A minute or two after the first explosion, dynamite blasts would start going off one after another in the timbered hills, until the air was so full of noise you couldn't talk. The sound carried to the farthest ridge of the highest mountain, and it meant "Look out! The revenooers are coming."

Newport, the county seat, is a modern little city much like any other modern little city in America. But only fifteen miles away, in the foothills of the Great Smokies, lies what they call the "Cosby Section." Cosby was just a few houses strung along several miles of road, with a country store or two and a post office

* Editor's note: See page 467 for the ending to this story.

in an old one-room board shack, but it had the honor of being the moonshine capital of America. The day we were there we were told that thirty-six stills were in operation. During prohibition, hundreds of them were hidden around the mountain slopes; the agents sometimes captured as many as thirty stills and seventy-five men in one day. Moonshine sold for twenty dollars a gallon. A thousand gallons went over the mountains in trucks every night to Asheville, and Asheville was the small end of the market. Even more than that went to Knoxville, and on up to Kentucky. But the old days were gone now; repeal, and the new national park, and tighter restrictions on moonshiners' supplies had pretty well shot the business. Moonshine was down to two dollars a gallon.

The moonshine distilled in the mountains when I was there was made mostly from sugar, and it would knock your head off. In Knoxville the Negroes and poor whites drank it almost exclusively. The Negroes called it "splo," which was undoubtedly short for "explosive," and you could get a half pint for fifteen cents. The famous old mountain corn whisky, which many a connoisseur still says is better drinking liquor than your bonded stuff, had almost gone out of existence. It took too long to make, and there was no market for such a high-class product.

I went into the Cosby Section with a man who had sent scores of its residents to the penitentiary. He was J. Carroll Cate, who until recently had been high sheriff of Knoxville, and before that had been an agent of the Internal Revenue Bureau in the Cosby area—in other words, a revenuer. You'd think a man who had put a lot of people behind the bars wouldn't be coming back to his old haunts without a little shaking of the knees, but I rode all day with Cate, and his visit was like a homecoming.

We spent most of the day with a former moonshiner whom Cate had run down and wrecked at seventy miles an hour on a gravel road. Both of them were hurt, and the moonshine runner served two terms in the pen. He was one of the nicest fellows you ever met, and he and Cate were good friends and always had been. We stopped at the home of a woman who had once been known as "Queen of the Moonshiners." She insisted that we stay for lunch, and said she'd scare up a chicken. She hadn't seen Cate for a long time, and they had always been on opposite sides of the legal fence, but I heard her say to him, "Everybody always liked you up here. You played square with us."

That day in the moonshining country gave me a new idea of honor. For one thing, most of the moonshiners weren't criminals at all. They were violating a law, of course, but, as they said, how else could you make a living up there? And you don't find vicious criminals having genuine respect and friendship for the men who are sending them to the penitentiary right and left. When I asked Cate about this, he said it was partly their sense of the inevitability of things, and partly because he had never double-crossed them. In the old days, he'd know a fellow was running moonshine, but of course he had to catch him at it. And the fellow took the attitude, "Well, catching me is your job, and if you can catch me then it's just my tough luck and your good luck, and no hard feelings." But the main thing, according to Cate, was to tell the truth when the case came to court. If, just to get a conviction, you testified to something the men knew was a lie, then your name was mud.

We sat alongside the road in the Cosby for an hour, talking with people who had been moonshiners or liquor runners. They were complaining that the Cosby was almost dried up. "Practically everybody's in the penitentiary," they said. So-and-so had just come back from "down there." So-and-so had just got fifteen months, and he wasn't any more guilty than you are.

There were three federal agents stationed in the district now and the people referred to them by their first names. "They're pretty nice fellows," they said. There had been only one agent who was really hated. He was one of their own who turned deputy against them, and it was said that he killed a man. He didn't live around there now. The people said, in their gentle way, "We don't like him very well around here." Boy, I'd hate the mountain people to say gently of me that they just didn't like me very well. I'd spend the rest of my life in California.

Most of the moonshiners had started poor, and were still poor. There were only a few people in Cocke County who had made big money in moonshine and were among the county's richest people. Repeal, of course, had dealt a tough blow to the industry, but of late the law had dealt further blows. The storekeepers were scared into making everybody who bought an excessive amount of sugar sign up for it, and the moonshiners wouldn't put their names down in that book where the revenuers would see it. So they couldn't get sugar. So they didn't make so much moonshine. See, it's simple. You don't even have to shoot anybody.

I also found out that Cocke County, the moonshine capital of the world, had just voted to keep the county dry!

Uncle Steve Cole lived in the Great Smokies National Park, in Tennessee. He was a typical mountain man of the old school. I dropped in one afternoon to talk to him. He lit a fire, and sat down beside it and began spitting into the fireplace. He wasn't chewing tobacco, but he spit into the fireplace all the time anyhow.

Uncle Steve had killed more bears than any other man in those mountains. He hadn't the remotest idea how many, but he had killed them with muzzle-loaders, modern rifles, deadfalls, clubs, and axes, and he even choked one to death with his bare hands. I got him to tell me that story.

He and a neighbor went out one night. The dogs treed a bear. Uncle Steve's story of it took half an hour to tell, but the gist of it is that they built a fire and the bear finally came down the tree. Uncle Steve stood there until the bear's body was pressing on the muzzle of the gun and then he pulled the trigger. "I figured I couldn't miss that way," Uncle Steve said. He didn't miss, but the shot didn't kill the bear. It ran fifty yards or so, and then the dogs were on it. And the first thing Uncle Steve knew, the bear had clenched his great jaws right down on a dog's snout and was crushing it to pieces.

Now, Uncle Steve's gun was an old-fashioned, sawed-off, muzzle-loading hog rifle, and he didn't have time to reload it. So, to save the dog, he rushed up to the bear from behind, put his legs around it, and started prying the dog's snout out of the bear's mouth. "And before I knew what happened," said Uncle Steve, "the bear let go of the dog and got my right hand in his mouth, and began a-crunchin' and a-growlin' and a-eatin' on my

· 103 ·

hand. One long tooth went right through the palm of my hand and another went through the back of my hand. There wasn't nothin' for me to do but reach round with my left hand for the bear's throat. I got him by the goozle and started clampin' down. Pretty soon he let go. Then I just choked him till he was deader'n four o'clock." Uncle Steve spit into the fireplace.

Mrs. Cole was sitting on the bed, listening. Nobody said anything for a minute. Then Mrs. Cole chuckled and said, "Four o'clock ain't dead." Uncle Steve didn't dignify her quibble with an answer. He just spit into the fireplace again.

Leadville and Points West

Chapter VIII   Big Jim McDonald, of Leadville, Colorado, was seventy-two when I met him in 1936, and he had never had an ache or pain in his life.

He had left Halifax, Nova Scotia, and come to that romantic old silver camp, two miles above sea level, when both he and Leadville were young—fifty-two years before. At first he worked for wages in the silver mines and socked every penny back into leases of his own. For ten years nothing came of them, and then he hit. He didn't have to worry about money now—hadn't had to for forty years. They said he was worth a hundred thousand dollars. But he still liked to see new mines coming in; mining was his whole life. And he loved Leadville.

Big Jim was a Scotsman. He had never married, and had no regrets. He lived all alone in a small but comfortable house. He wore a cap all the time, even indoors. He kept a loaded rifle by his bedside, and nobody bothered him. In fact, nobody ever had bothered him—he was too big. He was a whopper of a man— six feet three. A year before he had weighed 335 pounds, but he had dieted and was down to 265. He ate meat only once a day, and kept a bag of oranges around to nibble on. He slept like a log. He never worried, he said.

Big Jim's main strength stunt was tug-of-war. He used to pull eight men down as easy as pie. When he was fifty-two they put on a big tug at a celebration one night. "It was all I could do to hold five men," he said. "That's the first time I realized I was going down the other side of life. I've never pulled tug-of-war since then." When he was young, he used to dance all night in

Leadville's Wild West dance halls, and then work in the mine all day without going to bed. He could do that till he was fifty, he said.

For thirty years Big Jim was in the mines; he was everything from mucker to superintendent. Then he ran smelters and managed mine properties for eighteen years more. He had quit work four years before I met him, and he enjoyed not doing anything. He had considerable property to look after, and he would sit around town and chat, and read the papers and the *National Geographic,* and sit in his front door and look out at the mountains. He was happy.

Once a year he took a trip. "I can stick a thousand dollars in my pocket and start out," he said, "and have a thousand dollars' worth of fun." He used to go back to Nova Scotia every seven years, but his mother died and he hadn't gone now for twenty years. One year he did the West Coast, clear from Tia Juana to Seattle. At seventy-one he took his first airplane flight; said he'd done everything else—now he wanted to try that. His friends were terrified and said he'd be killed. "A man born to be hung never gets drowned," said Big Jim, and flew away to Albuquerque.

"Maybe I missed a lot by not getting married," he said, "but I was independent. I had to have my own way." But that isn't all of the story. He took in two orphan girls when they were five years old. Their parents had worked in the same camp with him. People said to him, "You don't want to do that. They'll cost so much money." "What the hell of it?" said Big Jim. "It's my money." People said, "They'll grow up and sass you." Big Jim said to me, later on, "They've never spoken a sassy word to me." The girls worshiped him. He put them both through college. They were married now. One lived in Seattle, and the other lived next door to Big Jim. "They were good for me," he said. "They softened me. I'd come home from the mine out of sorts and mad, and they'd crawl all over me and I'd forget about being mad."

Big Jim drank hardly at all; he swore a lot. "Once in a while, like on Bobby Burns's birthday, I may take a drink, or I may take a dozen," he said. "But I've never let it get the best of me."

He was a Republican until the Republicans took twenty-two thousand dollars away from him in income taxes that he said he didn't owe. He'd been a Democrat ever since. And he said Roosevelt was the only president who ever did anything for the West.

"I've been lucky all my life," said Big Jim. "Anybody who works thirty years in the mines without getting hurt is just plain lucky. If I get sick or die tomorrow, I've beat the game. I'm well fixed and I'm comfortable. I've never been sick a day in my life. I've been lucky all the way through. I've lived my threescore and ten, and two years more, and I've come out ahead. From here on in everything is velvet, no matter what happens."

As we drove across the state line from Colorado into Utah, I abruptly abandoned my natural dignified reserve, let out a bloodcurdling yell, gave the steering wheel a couple of jerks, and wound up with a wild cowboy "Yippee!" Rattlesnakes took to their holes for twenty miles around, and That Girl who rides with me slumped away in a dead faint. The reason for this unparalleled behavior on my part was that I had just crossed my last state line; I had now been in every state in the Union. Forty-eight states. That, of course, wouldn't get me into *Who's Who*, but it was a distinction, and I don't think anyone should begrudge it to me.

For weeks I had been wondering just what my feelings would be when I crossed that final frontier. I was watching myself closely as we hummed along at fifty miles an hour and kept looking for the Utah boundary marker. Finally we saw it in the distance—a fine stone monument—the goal, drawing nearer and nearer. Utah, the last state. And it was then that I suddenly realized I wasn't having any feelings about it at all. That's when I decided to yell. It was purely artificial—merely a manufactured sound to cover up my emptiness of emotion—but it had a strange effect. In addition to frightening That Girl nigh unto death, it also gave me quite a start, and did finally open up a spring of genuine feeling about conquering the last state barrier. In fact, after driving a couple of miles into Utah I turned around and went back. I took a picture of the monument and fooled around for fifteen minutes, walking back and forth across the line, and I really did then have a sense of accomplishment and, if you'll pardon me, superiority. Also, I might add, I did considerable gloating over That Girl, because she was just a homebody and had been in only forty-five states.

No state ever presented its visitor with a more desolate front yard then did Utah at that point. It was desert—complete, unabridged desert. There was just a little sage, and all the rest was long brown emptiness, with ragged buttes rising to the horizon far away. I had no doubt that Utah would some day erect a monument there on the desert, commemorating the exact spot of my great achievement. They would, of course, if they hewed strictly to the line, have to put it right in the middle of the highway. But I figured people wouldn't mind driving around it, when they learned its significance.

In Salt Lake City I found to my surprise that Mormons were people. I had innocently assumed that they were a strange race you couldn't talk with—cold, bluenosed, mystic, and belligerent. They're nothing of the sort; they're just like anybody else. And contrary to popular belief, the Mormons do not control Salt Lake City. The city itself is only thirty per cent Mormon, though Utah as a whole is seventy per cent Mormon. The Mormons are important in the business of the city, but they do not dominate it.

There are more than 750,000 Mormons, and their numbers are increasing slowly. They live in a north-and-south strip, from Arizona right up the mountains into Idaho and Canada. There are scattered churches elsewhere—in the East and a few foreign countries—but the bulk of the Mormons are there in the desert. They are mainly a farming people—always have been, ever since the church was founded more than a hundred years ago. The Mormons are conscientiously law-abiding. They are proud of the fact that they have never questioned any law of the land. They think more of the Constitution than most of us do. When the Supreme Court ruled against polygamy, half a century ago, the Mormons immediately abandoned it. Polygamy is, of course, the first thing anybody thinks of when you mention Mormons, but it has been half a century since the last "plural marriage," as they call it. And another thing: a learned Mormon historian told me that he went back into the records and found that polygamy had never been practiced by more than three per cent of the

Mormons. Brigham Young, however, had nineteen wives and fifty-five children. The upper-crust Mormons seemed to swarm around the dining room of the Z.C.M.I., a department store built by Brigham Young. At noon one day I stood in the entrance to the dining room with Professor Levi Edgar Young, and within five minutes was introduced to six granddaughters of Brigham Young. Practically everybody who came by was Brigham Young's granddaughter.

The Mormons were eager to explain and justify their church. I doubt that the following incident would happen in any other city in America. We were walking down the street near Temple Square on a Sunday afternoon. An elderly man came up along side and said pleasantly, "Lot of out-of-state tags, aren't there?" We said yes and the conversation went on, and it wound up with his showing us all over the Temple grounds, taking us to the famous Mormon Choir recital in the Tabernacle, and then up to the top of the big Hotel Utah for a look over the city. He was a delightful man, and he told us a great deal about Mormonism and the early history of the church. When we parted I asked him who he was. He turned out to be one of Salt Lake City's leading bankers.

I had a friend in the city who was a Mormon, and I asked him to tell me man-to-man just how Mormons differed from other people in their personal and business lives. He said they didn't differ at all. "We have some of the orneriest bastards alive, and some of the finest people on earth," he said. "As far as their conduct and attitude outside the church are concerned, I can't see a bit of difference. Why, I worked seven years at the same desk with a fellow before I happened to learn that he was a Mormon too."

On a train once, coming back from the East, he got into a conversation with a Chicago woman who knew he was from Salt Lake City, but didn't know he was a Mormon. She told him she wanted to get off and see the city, but was afraid to go on account of the Mormons. My friend assured her that he knew the city well, and that she would be perfectly safe. Then she said, "How can I tell a Mormon when I see one?" And he said, "That's easy. Just look up under the brims of their hats, and if you see a red spot above each eye where the horns have been pulled out, that will be a Mormon." He said she believed every word of it.

The Mormon church is said to be one of the most perfectly organized institutions in the world. I believe that must be true; they get things done. At the head is a president. Under him is the Council of Twelve Apostles, called "The Twelve." Under them are various "Quorums of Seventies," each ruling over a certain district. Mormon territory is divided into stakes, and the stakes into wards. In Salt Lake City, for instance, a ward is four blocks square. In conversation, people say that So-and-so lives in such-and-such a ward. Each ward has a bishop and two assistants. Each has its chapel for services and its entertainment hall. The Mormons are strong on entertainment. They foster the drama and they are great dancers. They say they hold more of their young people than any other church because they provide amusement for them. Also, they keep the children busy in the church by giving them duties. A child can be a deacon at twelve, a teacher at fourteen, and a priest at sixteen. One of the child's first important jobs is to go around to the houses in his ward and see how things are going. If he scents domestic trouble, he tries to smooth things over. (I could not learn how many fourteen-year-olds got kicked in the pants and told to mind their own business.) If the child sees poverty, he reports it to the bishop and something is done about it. No Mormon is ever supposed to be in want.

The church is exceedingly wealthy. Every Mormon is supposed to give ten per cent of his income to the church. A Mormon friend of mine said he thought the rule of tithing was not more than fifty per cent observed, but a church official told me it was nearly a hundred per cent.

The Mormons don't believe in too much preaching; they don't have hundreds of paid preachers, like other churches. Even the ward bishops are laymen who run their business and do their bishoping on the side. The ward bishop presides over the services, but he usually has an invited speaker; if he can't find one, he calls on somebody in the audience. No one in the Mormon church wears a special vestment of any kind.

The Mormon missionary system is interesting. Missionaries are youngsters, from eighteen to twenty-two. They pay their own expenses—or, rather, parents or friends usually pay them. The church itself pays nothing but carfare home. These missionaries go all over America and to foreign countries. They usually stay two years, and then come home and go into ordinary careers. The result is that the Mormons are a widely traveled people. There were two thousand missionaries out that year, I was told. Their work, as I understood it, was more to explain and spread knowledge about the church than to save souls.

I have never seen finer school buildings anywhere than in Salt Lake City. What they taught inside, I didn't know. I had a futile little conversation about that with one man. We were standing in front of a statue of Joseph Smith, on which were carved some of his teachings. One of them was: "It is impossible for a man to be saved in ignorance." I asked if that meant that some poor hillbilly who never had a chance at learning couldn't possibly be saved. The man said that the hillbilly had as much chance to learn as anybody else, that intelligence was in learning the truth about God. I started to ask how you knew what truth was, but I suddenly realized we were puffing up different tracks, so I let it go.

Mormons believe their church is the only one clothed with authority direct from God. Other churches are merely organizations. This is not a quarreling point, however. One of the main points of their creed is freedom of worship, and they never utter a word against any other church. They believe that Joseph Smith, the founder, was the first person since the Twelve Apostles to receive a direct commission from God. It is hardly fair for me to say it just that way, however. The church history does say it, and some people in the church say it. But the gentler members hold that God is constantly sending messages to people everywhere, and that He did not allow seventeen centuries to pass without getting in touch with somebody on earth. All members, however, believe that God gave Joseph Smith a divine authority to form the Mormon church, and that Smith was a prophet. They also hold that each president of the church is a prophet, though not the long-haired, gleamy-eyed kind—just a superior man. The Mormons believe that everybody will eventually be "saved." If you're not saved while you're alive, you still have a chance after you die. They believe that every human being is a continuing personality—that each of us has lived somewhere before, in the same body we are in now, and will live somewhere else after we're dead. They don't know where, but it's a real, material place. They believe that this continuing personality is constantly developing and being improved through the ages, and that someday it will reach a state of perfection wherein we will all be gods. That seems to me a rather beautiful way of looking at us.

The *Book of Mormon* is not, as some people believe, the Mormon Bible. They use the same Bible other churches do. The *Book of Mormon* is simply a supposedly divine history of the North American Indian. It was written by Mormon, the father of the angel Moroni, who was the messenger between God and Joseph Smith. I tried to read the *Book of Mormon,* but I couldn't make anything out of it. The Mormons hold that the American Indians are descendants of the ancient Hebrews, that they got over here somehow a long time ago, and that the only true history of them is the one written by Mormon, which was buried on a hill in New York State thirteen centuries ago and dug up and translated by Joseph Smith.

The Mormons are not supposed to drink or smoke or use rouge or eat too much meat, and so on, but, taken as a whole, they are not bluenoses. The fanatics are, of course, but so are the fanatics in any church. All those "don't" rules are contained in what the Mormons call the Word of Wisdom. Although it came in one of God's messages to Joseph Smith, it is considered less a religious rule than just good common sense for keeping healthy. A Mormon told me that the Word of Wisdom was observed today by only about half the Mormons. There had been quite a letdown in the past fifteen years, especially among the women, who had taken up smoking and drinking. They said that if a person from Utah went to the Mayo hospital in Minnesota with stomach trouble, and if one of the Mayo brothers himself happened to treat the patient, he would say to him, "Uh-huh, if you had kept the Word of Wisdom you wouldn't be here."

The Mormons have a creed, called the Articles of Faith. The thirteenth and last seems to me worth quoting: "We believe in being honest, true, chaste, benevolent, virtuous, and in doing good to all men; indeed, we may say that we follow the admonition of Paul, we believe all things, we hope all things, we have endured many things, and hope to be able to endure all things. If there is anything virtuous, lovely, or of good report or praiseworthy, we seek after these things."

Mizzoo Townsend, even at seventy, called himself the champion poker player of Idaho. For years he had a sign on the front door of his gambling place in Pocatello: "I'll play any man from any land, any game he can name, for any amount he can count." Mizzoo said it was more of a joke than anything else. Traveling salesmen used to take him up, and sometimes they'd win, but usually he would. If somebody had come in with a lot of dough, Mizzoo would have had to swallow his words, for he never had any really big dough.

Mizzoo had been a gambler in Pocatello for forty-seven years. He wasn't the kind of old-time gambler you see in the movies. He looked more like a gold-prospecting "pocket hunter." He looked as though he should have a burro walking behind him.

He came out about 1885, from Missouri—that's why they called him Mizzoo. His real name was John. He tarried four years on a ranch in Wyoming. The rancher ran a saloon and gambling house for the cowboys and wagon freighters, and that's where Mizzoo learned to gamble. He wandered into Pocatello in 1889. There he ran gambling houses when gambling was legal in the state—and afterward too. He was fined several times, but never went to jail. He ran saloons, and even secondhand shops. He accumulated a lot of worn-out real estate—houses that nobody lived in, full of dust and old junk. His own house, where he lived with his son and daughter-in-law, was a small frame cottage, with no grass around it. I guess he made about the same financial progress over the years as a grocery-store keeper would.

Mizzoo used to have a blackboard in front of his gambling house. Every morning he'd write something new on it, and people would stand around waiting to see what it would be. It might be something like this: "For rent—four-room house. Plenty of ventilation. Windows all out. No extra charge for the bedbugs. I still think I can beat any man in the state playing poker." He was running a lottery game now. It didn't amount to much, he said, but he was trying to build it up so he could leave his son a little business when he died.

Mizzoo was a gentle sort of fellow to be a gambler. His eyes puffed up and twinkled when he laughed, and you couldn't imagine his ever getting tough. He said there had been rows in his places, but he personally had never had any trouble. He laid that to the fact that he was a big man, and that he never drank. He said he never forgot anything. He could read a name or a date in the newspaper, and it was just as if it was carved in his head. He had never had much education, but he read quite a bit. He didn't talk much about old-men things; he liked to talk about current events. Gambling wasn't what it used to be, he said; people spent their money on other things now.

He puttered around his bedroom, trying to find some pictures to give me, with his daughter-in-law helping him. I kept asking him questions.

I said, "What was the biggest amount you ever played for?"
He chuckled and said, "Oh, not very big."
I said, "How long has it been since you played poker?"
He said, "Oh, quite a while."
I said, "What did you do when you found people cheating on you?"
He said, "Oh, just quit playing."
Said his daughter-in-law, "He shoots 'em."

I wish that every state historical society in America would send a delegation to Montana. They might also invite a few writers of history textbooks to go along. And if they would then practice what they had learned, I'll bet that twenty years from now we Americans would know a lot more about American history. Montana makes its history a thing of joy, instead of a stodgy sermon. Every so often along the highways—maybe twenty miles apart, sometimes fifty miles—you'll see a neat little sign: "Historical Point—1000 feet." You coast along and pull over to a wide graveled area, and there is a handsome signboard consisting of two logs set upright in the ground, with a third laid across the top, from which hangs a neat wooden placard about six feet square. On this board the historical message is painted in black letters a couple of inches high. The message is not only easy to read; it says something—for instance, this one a few miles east of Shelby:

THE OILY BOID GETS THE WOIM!

A narrow-gauge railroad track nicknamed the "Turkey Track" used to connect Great Falls, Montana, and Lethbridge, Alberta. When the main line of the Great Northern crossed it in 1891, Shelby Junction came into existence. The hills and plains around here were cow country. The Junction became an oasis where parched cowpunchers cauterized their tonsils with forty-rod and grew plumb irresponsible and exuberant.

In 1910 the dry landers began homesteading, they built fences and plowed under the native grass. The days of open range were gone. Shelby quit her swaggering frontier ways and became concrete-sidewalk and sewer-system conscious.

Dry-land farming didn't turn out to be such a profitable endeavor, but in 1922 geologists discovered that this country had an ace in the hole. Oil was struck between here and the Canadian border, and they all lived happy ever after.

In other states you never see a car in front of those stone monuments with their dull bronze inscriptions. But in Montana you hardly ever pull up to a historical sign without finding a car or two already there, with people out copying down the inscription, and chuckling. One grave fellow got up in the Malta Lions Club and introduced a resolution asking the state highway department to tear the signs down and replace them with something "dignified." Unfortunately, the Lions didn't string him to a tree, but they did shout him down.

Speaking of signs, there was one at a fence corner on a back road several miles east of Crawford, Nebraska, which said: "NOTICE— Hunt & Fish all you d—— please. When the bell rings, come to dinner. B. G. Pinney."

The Pinneys settled in Nebraska in the 1880s, when it was open country. By 1900 the homesteaders were getting things pretty well fenced in, and they were full of a great possessive feeling, and they put up "No Hunting" and "No Trespassing" signs all over. One day when B. G. Pinney was in a saloon in Crawford, a rancher said to him, "Pinney, when are you going to put up a sign?" Pinney replied, "Just as soon as I can get one painted." There was a fellow around town whose occupation was drinking liquor, but who painted a few signs in his spare time. Pinney bought this fellow a pint of whisky, and told him to paint the sign quoted above. It was put up about 1901. After twenty-five years it just wore out, so they had a new one painted, exactly like it.

Quite a few strangers came to the house and asked if the sign meant what it said. They were told it did, and the Pinneys even told them where to find the ducks down along the creek. Nobody ever came to dinner, though, except neighboring ranchers who would have come anyway.

Not one in ten thousand of us jobholding mortals would dare do what the Partridge family did. E. Harve Partridge had always lived in Spokane. He married young, he never went to college, and by the time he was twenty-five he had two daughters. At forty-one he had been a reporter on the Spokane *Chronicle* for eighteen years. His daughters were sixteen and seventeen.

Each year the Partridge family would take its little vacation. But early in the spring of 1936 a bigger vacation dream began to stir in the Partridge breasts. They decided to take a steamer trip to Alaska. Then one evening at supper Harve Partridge said, "Why don't we buy a boat and sail it to Alaska ourselves?" The kids were wild about the idea, but Mrs. Partridge said, "Don't be foolish. You've never been in anything bigger than a rowboat. We couldn't sail it by ourselves."

One weekend Harve Partridge took a bus to Seattle—three hundred miles away—and saw a small cabin cruiser for nine hundred dollars. He steered it for an hour around the bay, wrote a check, and took the next bus home. The Partridges were going to sail to Alaska.

The three months of preparation were as much fun as the trip itself. They bought twelve dollars' worth of nautical charts, and a parallel rule, and a compass that cost two and a half. Every evening the whole family got down on the living-room floor and, using a footstool for a boat, with the compass on top of it, worked

· 116 ·

out nautical courses and steered them. The upshot was that they went to Alaska and back, all by themselves. When they started, Skipper Partridge had steered a boat exactly four hours; the others, never.

Not one of the landlubbers was seasick, though they wallowed through waves ten feet high. Sometimes it was so rough they couldn't cook. They chugged within sixty feet of whales. The girls went out in the little lifeboat and with axes chopped off hunks of floating icebergs for their refrigerator. They drove ahead for hours through thick fog, and hit their destination right on the nose, like Lindbergh. They were tossed around in terrific tide rips. So innocent were they that they didn't know what a tide rip was till after they'd been through one. They navigated the swirling currents of dangerous, rocky narrows. Partridge learned to fix a broken clutch at sea. Frequently they sailed all night, through rain and darkness. They put faith in their nautical book-learning and it brought them through.

On the way back the eldest daughter, Jean, was ordered by the skipper to take the wheel at night, lay out her own course, take them through a narrows in pitch darkness, and wake her father when they got safely on the other side. She did.

The Partridges sailed twenty-five hundred miles in three weeks, spending three hundred dollars. When they returned they sold the boat for as much as they'd paid for it.

Rufus Woods was a big frog in a small puddle. They told me at Grand Coulee that I ought to stop in at Wenatchee, Washington, and see him. I found him the oddest combination of opposite instincts I have ever seen. He was a typical small-city civic leader, and he was also a nervous searcher of the world.

In appearance and action, he was the booster, glad-to-see-everybody, great-little-old-town-we've-got-here type of citizen. He was a little heavy, and wore a gold watch chain. He had a wife and three children, a house and a car, and owned a very prosperous newspaper. He was a Republican because his father was. He liked to speak at luncheons, and he had ten "calls," as he put it, on his desk right then.

But, on the other hand, he was a fiend for wandering. He knew people all over the world, and enough odd bits of history to make a book. One day he said to his wife, "I think I'll go to Russia this afternoon." He did. And when he had been back just ten days he hopped a boat for Alaska. He wrote up his trips for his newspaper—and what a reporter! If I had his inquisitiveness plus my good looks I'd be another Richard Harding Davis.

The reason I'm writing about Rufus Woods is that he was a sort of hero in those parts. He was one of the parents of Grand Coulee Dam. In the summer of 1918 he carried the first story on the idea of damming the wild Columbia River at Grand Coulee, and from that day on he plugged the idea to the tune of nearly a page a day in his newspaper, the Wenatchee *World*. For thirteen years his was the only daily paper in America supporting the dam. And he didn't support it mildly; he roared and screamed about it. He spent his own money, and his time. He was made fun of, scoffed at, actually abused by some civic leaders. But after the dam started going up, people fell over themselves to shower honors on persistent Rufus Woods.

And the funny part of it was, the dam wasn't going to benefit him a bit. He wouldn't make any money out of it. The dam was a hundred miles away, and his paper and his town were already in a rich, irrigated section. It was just stubbornness, I guess. He got started on the idea, and so many people opposed it that it finally became a hobby; but it was a dramatic story at that.

Whitman College gave him a Doctor of Letters degree. A thousand of the state's most prominent men gave him a testimonial dinner. He was praised and written up and presented with desk sets and this and that. He was mentioned for Congress. But he said, "No, not for me. You know, we newspapermen have the greatest job in the world. I go to Washington and sit in the gallery and see those senators and congressmen and I say to myself, 'I wouldn't trade jobs with one of you.' "

Woods came from Nebraska. He started on the adventure trail by following the gold seekers to Alaska in 1900. He spent three summers up there, on surveying gangs. On his return from the third trip in 1903, he stopped in Wenatchee. He was broke, and Wenatchee was just a dump on the desert, but it became a thriving little city, and Rufus Woods published the paper and got rich. His wife said she had to learn to run a big house—Rufus was always bringing somebody home for dinner. In just one month they set a hundred extra dinner plates. Occasionally Rufus would show up at home with a bunch of Indians.

He was a bug on searching out historical facts. One of his hot ideas was that John Wilkes Booth, the assassin of Lincoln, was not killed. He said Booth escaped and somebody else was killed, and that Booth lived for forty years and took poison in Oklahoma in the early 1900s. He traveled all over America digging up evidence.

He had been to Russia twice. Though a Republican, he thought we could do with some of the Russian ideas. He thought hospitals and dairies should be government-owned. He had been to New York seven times in the last year and a half. He used the airlines a lot. He was hardly ever home more than a week at a time. If it wasn't a long trip, it was a dash to Seattle or an auto tour over the state. When he would drive through small eastern Washington towns people would yell, "Howdy, Rufus." He was a success, and he loved it, and I didn't blame him.

The prairies are all right. The mountains are all right. The forests and the deserts and the clear clean air of the heights, they're all right. But what a bewitching thing is a city of the sea. It was good to be in Seattle—to hear the foghorns on the Sound, and the deep bellow of departing steamers; to feel the creeping fog all around you, the fog that softens things and makes a velvet trance out of nighttime. It was good to say to yourself, "Out there through the mist is China. Out there the dirty freighters go, and the fishermen for Alaska." And it was good to hear the tall and slyly outlandish tales that float up and down Puget Sound . . .

Once upon a time there was a tugboat on the Sound, dragging behind it a long tow of logs. There was no special hurry, so the tugboat was hardly moving at all. Furthermore, it was using its leisure time to run some oil tests on its new diesel engines. The engineer had several five-gallon cans of different brands of oil. He would let the engine run until it exhausted one can, then cut in a different brand, start the engine, and plow ahead again.

All this left the captain bored, and with nothing at all to do. Furthermore, his feet hurt. He stood sadly on the deck, watching the shore which hardly moved at all, and now and then taking a jealous look at the water around him. It looked so cool. If he could only put his aching dogs into it. Finally he took off his shoes and socks, sat down on the low rail, and hung his feet over the side. Lordy, it felt good!

The water kept on feeling good, and the old captain was enjoying it immensely, until a seal popped up and swam past (or do they have seals in Puget Sound?). Anyway, the captain thought it was a dog. He leaned far out for a better look and fell overboard. By the time he had come up and had rid himself of that portion of Puget Sound which he had imbibed, his favorite tugboat had drawn away from him. But all was not lost, for the tow of logs was still coming along. So the old man drifted back and h'isted himself up.

A bunch of logs on the end of a towline is no place for a dignified shipmaster to be, so our captain kept running up and down, yelling to the engineer on the tugboat. But the engineer couldn't hear him for the engine noise, and wouldn't have heard him anyway, for he was asleep.

At this interval we must leave the captain a moment and switch to the shore. Somewhere along the Sound lived one of those delightful people whose sole profession is watching the boats go by. Every harbor has one. A lot of them are wavers-at-the-captains, but this one was just a looker. He stood on the shore, pulled up his telescope, leveled it first on the tug, and then on the tow, and finally on the captain. Aha! thought the watcher. Poor Captain Blank has gone off his nut. So he phoned the tug company's office that the captain had gone crazy, that he was back on the tow of logs, barefoot, running up and down and screaming like a wild man.

Now we shift back to the tugboat. One of those five-gallon cans of oil ran out. The engine stopped. The engineer woke up and went about his business of cutting in a new can and getting the engines started again. This gave the captain his chance. He jumped into the water, half swam and half pulled himself along the towline up to the tug, climbed aboard, sneaked into his cabin without anybody's seeing him, changed his clothes, and was out on deck by the time they got going.

That evening they pulled into Port Angeles. The company officials were all down at the dock. So were an ambulance and the sheriff and a couple of policemen, just in case the old man should be really violent.

The captain stepped out on deck and greeted them. The company president began to fade slightly beneath his skin. "Why, Captain, I understood you were . . . ah . . . sick."

"Fit as a fiddle," boomed the captain. "Never been sick a day in my life."

I don't know how the company president explained to the sheriff. Anyway, he never said another word to the captain about the matter.

A lot of people in Seattle hated Dave Beck just as the bankers hated Roosevelt. He knew it, of course. But he said, "They may hate me, but any businessman in this town will tell you that my word is as good as gold, and that the teamsters never violate a contract."

Dave Beck was head of the teamsters' union in Washington State. But that wasn't all—not by a long shot. He was the No. 1 man in Seattle. Bigger than the mayor. Bigger than anybody. So of course I had to go out and see what he was like. "I'm glad you came," he said, "so you can see I haven't got any horns."

Seattle was one of the most thoroughly unionized cities in America. You heard a lot of discussion about it, in Seattle and outside. You heard that Seattle was stifling under the union grip. You heard that business was fleeing, because of union czardom. You heard, on the other hand, that the unions were helping business, because there was more money in workers' pockets to be spent. You heard that the standard of living in Seattle had been raised immensely by the unions. I don't pretend to know the answer.

Dave Beck was forty-one when I saw him. He was slightly on the heavy side. His hands were freckled, his face was red and smooth, his brown hair was almost gone, and you could hardly see any eyebrows. He looked like a laborer who had been dressed up for ten years—which was correct. He knew how to be pleasant, though a ferocious earnestness kept creeping into his conversation. He talked very loud. He was thoroughly patriotic, and was against all "isms."

"My parents were miserably poor," he said. "I can remember how my sister and I used to sit on the curb at ten and eleven at night, waiting for my mother to come out of the laundry. And she had gone to work at six in the morning. I really think it was that first impression that put it into my head that something had to be done for labor."

At sixteen Dave Beck quit high school and followed his mother into the laundry. Soon he was driving a delivery wagon. The laundry drivers' union was formed a couple of years after he went to work. He was one of the leading spirits in the organizing.

When the war came in 1917, he joined the aviation service. When he came home on furlough he got married and two days later he was on his way to France. After the war he went back to his laundry wagon, and became very active in the union. In 1926 one of the national officers was in Seattle and asked him how he'd like to devote his full time to labor work. He said he'd like it fine. So he went to work as an organizer for the International Brotherhood of Teamsters. That is what he still was in 1936. His territory covered the whole Northwest, and he had organized everybody who even slightly resembled a teamster. There were eight thousand members in Seattle alone.

Just how Beck gradually rose to be the kingpin of Seattle is too long a story to tell, but he was. He was "the man" who spoke for labor, and labor was the big thing in Seattle. I know that Mayor Johnny Dore had to come and beg before Beck would bother with him. And when Beck said the word, Johnny Dore was in.

Dave Beck, like most serious men in the grip of a "cause," did almost nothing but work. He was at it all day, and at least five nights a week he was attending labor meetings or making speeches. He had to travel a great deal. He went always by air, said he was United Airlines' best customer. Once he flew to Washington, D.C., three times within a month.

He did not smoke. He had never taken a drink or played a game of cards or a game of pool. It was all right with him if others did so—but not in excess. He was a Presbyterian, but rather a passive one. He uttered a mild oath occasionally.

He had one child, a boy, then sixteen. He wasn't trying to steer him into labor work. Wanted the boy to make up his own mind. The Becks lived in a five-room bungalow, the same house he had built years ago when he was a laundry driver. His mother lived with them. Beck used to read when he got home at night. He loved biographies; he worshiped Shakespeare, and could quote him. He was one of the few men in the world who read the *Congressional Record* through every day. His speaking English was good, although he did say "attackted" for "attacked." He was a past-exalted-something of the Elks, and had been active in the American Legion.

He said the secret of the teamsters' success in Seattle was in always being fair. "The teamsters have never broken a contract," he said. "We will never go out on a sympathy strike if we have to break a contract to do it. There hasn't been a teamster strike in Seattle since 1913. There never has been a laundry drivers' strike. We don't like strikes."

Do you know what Portland is? It's Paradise on earth. At least, that's what people in Portland said. Personally, I had never thought so, and I'll tell you why. In 1926 I came through Portland, wearing overalls and driving a Model T Ford, with a tent and blanket roll tied onto the fender—a young man seeing America. I stopped at a roadside stand in the suburbs to eat some watermelon, and I was eating along, minding my business, when up came an old codger and started bawling me out. He gave me a long lecture, and wound up by yelling that if I didn't stop smoking cigarettes and eating watermelon on Sunday I would undoubtedly land in hell. I'd never had any use for Portland after that.

Of course the incident was on my mind as we drew near Portland this time. But I said, "No, let's be fair. We'll start all over again with Portland and see what happens." About that instant we came around a bend, and there staring us in the face was an expensive signboard, as big as the side of a house, saying in huge letters: "ALL HATH SINNED." That's all it said. Now, I don't know whether all hath sinned or not. But supposing all hath, why put up a signboard about it? After that, it took my friends five days to convince me that I was wrong about Portland.

And incidentally, I stumbled onto a fine formula for getting treated like a visiting lion. Just say to somebody, "Describe to me the character of Portland, will you, so I can write a piece about it. You know—its personality, its spirit." How they went to bat! People started giving parties so I could hear about the spirit of Portland. They'd run to the phone and say, "Come right over, quick! And on your way be thinking up how to describe the spirit of Portland." It was marvelous. I went to five parties, and two luncheons, and to two dinners in one evening. And another evening we went to dinner and forgot to eat, all because people were trying to get across to me the spirit of Portland. Maybe that's it, right there.

Well, anyway, here is what I put together out of all the scramble: everybody in Portland is crazy about Portland. They rave about it. They don't talk like chamber of commerce folders; they don't talk about their industries and their schools and their crops; they roar about what a wonderful place Portland is, just to live in, and people do live well in Portland. That whole Northwest country is beautiful, and the climate is gentle, and existence is pleasant.

Portland is a place, they told me, where money doesn't get you anywhere. They meant socially, I guess. So I tried to find out what would get you anywhere—what was the standard for social admittance in Portland. Definitely, they said, it wasn't money. And definitely, too, it wasn't blue blood. "What is it, then?" I asked. "Intelligence?" They hadn't thought what it might be. So they thought. No, it wasn't intelligence. Some of the social elite were both as poor and as stupid as myself. They thought and thought. They finally decided that it was merely an ability to contribute something—usually agreeableness and interest.

Portland is, on the whole, a conservative place. It is a city of homes—a place to raise your children. It was settled originally by "down-Easters" who came around the Horn. They made the money and became the backbone, and they kept on being the backbone. But somehow they mixed their New England sound-ness with a capacity for living the freer, milder Northwest way, and it made a pretty high-class combination.

As for the physical appearance of the city, the downtown sec-tion is neither unattractive nor distinctive. The nice thing about Portland is that it rises into hills, and they're the most livable hills you ever saw. Thousands of people live up there in fine houses, among trees, looking hundreds of feet down onto the city. All about Portland there are small rivers and green fir trees, and not far away are the mountains themselves. A friend of mine, searching for the reason he loved the Northwest, finally decided that the sense of having everywhere around him these clear, cold, tumbling streams had a great deal to do with it.

The Saxton kids are cousins of mine, born in a log house about a mile and a half from our farm in western Indiana. We were poor and they were poorer. I played with them all through my childhood. I always liked them, all six of them. We used to ride the running gears of an old buggy down the slope and through the creek, making a sputter with our lips and pretending we were race drivers at Indianapolis. And sometimes, after spe-cial pleading at home, I could stay all night with them, and we'd sleep in the attic among the rafters of the log house, four or five of us in one bed. We had fun in those days. But we all grew up, and most of us left home. Some of the Saxton kids I hadn't seen for nearly twenty years. Paul was one of them. The last time we rode downhill on the buggy running gear was probably around 1914.

I asked for Paul Saxton at the main office of the Pacific Lumber Company in Scotia, California. They gave me a pass card and told me how to find him, and said I'd have to leave the car and walk across the railroad trestle to the camp. And to be careful.

A train of flatcars was backed up a temporary track in a gulch among tall trees. At the rear, a steam derrick with an "ice hook" on the end of a cable was lifting huge redwood logs off a pile and laying them on the flatcars. I asked for my cousin. They said he was one of three "cat" drivers dragging logs down from the woods, and that each driver got down once an hour. So I waited. After a while a big yellow caterpillar poked its nose over a hill and started down. Behind it were three of the biggest logs I ever saw. I looked the driver over, and decided he wasn't my man. But just as he got even with me and stopped, I recognized something. I don't know what it was, for he certainly didn't look like anybody I'd ever seen before, but there was something. I started forward to shake hands. He jumped off the cat with a big grin on his face. "I wouldn't have known you," he said, "except you look like Uncle Will." That's my father.

I made the next trip with him on the cat. It was an immense machine, with a cat trailer behind it, bearing a big derrick which lifted up one end of the logs for dragging. It made so much noise we had to yell at each other. What a ride that was! We climbed up a worn lane through the forest, rising more than a thousand feet in half a mile. No auto could have pulled the grades we took. We went up so slowly that the dust rose around us in a cloud, and my topcoat was ruined from the oil and dirt.

Paul had come west eight years earlier, and had never been back to Indiana; he seldom heard from home, or wrote. He didn't know his oldest brother was married. He had been in the logging woods all this time, and he liked it in California. "This is the worst job in the woods," he said, "because it's so dirty— we have to wear masks on account of the dust. But it's about the best paid. I high-climbed for three years. That's climbing up and cutting out the top and getting the tree ready to fall. I never got hurt. That's a good job."

Some of those redwoods were more than three hundred feet high. They're beautiful, and yet they are not the most valuable lumber by any means. It seems a shame to cut them. They're very brittle; if they don't fall right, they splinter all to pieces. My cousin said they sometimes worked for a week just preparing a bed for a tree to fall in.

Coming back, we nosed down grades so steep you had to brace yourself and hold on to keep from falling out. It was like a nose dive in an airplane. But nothing makes any difference to a cat; up or down, it's all the same. Finally we came back to the railroad. My cousin hated it because I couldn't stay all night so we could talk longer. I hated it too. Just an hour, after a lifetime, and then goodbye. A couple of cousins that pass in the dusk of the tall redwood forests.

Two o'clock in the morning, and Fisherman's Wharf at San Francisco is a bedlam of crabmen—three hundred little boats ready to go to sea, one man to a boat.

Loud language split the night air. Italian, profanity, and English—in the order named. All but five of San Francisco's three hundred crab fishermen were Italian. Among the five was one Negro. They say a plain American couldn't stand the life. I believe it.

I went with Emile Barbara, a young man who was born a fisherman. His tongue was equally at home with Italian or English. We were on our way by three o'clock, in a thick procession, seaward bound. Chug, chug, everywhere in the darkness. Little lights gliding. Voices across the water. Silhouettes on patches of moonlight. Out under the Golden Gate Bridge, black and mighty against the moon. Out over "the bar," where the waves leap and twist. Then into wide-open water, the boats falling into a long string. Ahead for miles they flowed in the darkness, like runners after the bunched start. Their lights made a sky line across the dark Pacific.

By daylight we were fifteen miles west of the Golden Gate, and crab fisherman Pyle was sick at his stomach. The sun was rising very red. "It'll blow like hell about ten o'clock," Emile said. He stood up and looked all around, picking an empty spot. We were on the grounds. He decided, and throttled down. We were ready for the day's work.

Emile put on boots and a rubber apron. On deck was a pile of traps, each consisting of a steel hoop about three feet across, from which hung a net a couple of feet deep. In the bottom was a wire bait cage. Emile took three sardines from a box (they were big sardines, six inches long), split them open with his thumb, turned them inside out, crammed them into the cage, and threw the trap overboard. A small buoy, fastened to it by a stout line, marked the spot.

Emile started the boat going slowly forward. He laid a trap about every block, in as straight a line as you can make in wallowing water. There were twenty-four traps.

The traps all laid, we beat it back to the starting end. Emile grabbed the first buoy with a boat hook. He pulled up some line with his hands, then hooked it over a winch (funny little winch, size of a tomato can), put his foot on a pedal, and the winch started pulling up the trap. All the time we were moving ahead.

Thrills of a fisherman—the trap came out of the water. Two small scrambling crabs. Emile swore and threw them back. He put in new bait and tossed the trap over again. By now we were right on the next buoy. The crab fisherman has no rest. All day it's like that. His boat is never stopped. The fisherman works fast, and hard.

"Blankety blank dash blank!" Emile said. Only three crabs from the first "drift." That's what they call running the line of traps. "We're going to move." So we pulled up all the traps. It took nearly an hour.

We chugged southward. Porpoises leaped gracefully around us, some not twenty feet away. Far to the left we saw the mountainous bare shore, and one tower of the Golden Gate Bridge. The sun was bright now, but it was chilly. We ate some lunch from a sack. (Yeah, I felt fine now.) The tide was changing, and it wasn't so rough. We went south for an hour.

All over again the traps were laid. It was ten o'clock by then. We started our drift. The first trap brought up half a dozen big crabs. "Blankety blank!" Emile swore. "What's the matter?" I said. "This looks good." That was the trouble. "I had a hunch to come over here first," he said, "and I didn't. We've lost four hours and ten or twelve dollars."

Four times we made our drift on that line. I got so I could hardly wait for each trap to come up. It was like seeing what's in a Christmas box. Sometimes we had as many as a dozen crabs in a trap, but you could keep only the ones of seven inches or more. Emile had a ruler to measure the doubtful ones. We threw back four for every one we saved, it seemed to me. Emile handled them with his bare hands. A few wanted to fight. "That means bad weather's coming, when the crabs are wild," Emile said.

I got to counting the crabs. We took thirty-one in one drift. On the next drift Emile said, "Could you count the crabs and the traps at the same time?" He had an idea some other fisherman had stolen a trap. They do that. But we still had our twenty-four.

At two o'clock the sea began to roll heavily again, but I liked it by then. We started our last drift, stacking the traps on deck as we pulled them in. It was hard to control the boat, and it took us much longer than usual.

When we were through, the floor of the crab box was covered solid. They are beautiful when their shells have dried—brown and cream-colored. Not one moved, though they were all alive. We had a hundred and eight—nine dozen, at two dollars and a half a dozen. Not bad.

We left the grounds at three o'clock, and it took two hours to twist and roll our way home. We had been at sea fourteen hours. On the way, Emile took off his boots and lay on the deck, steering with his foot. "How would you like to make your living this way?" he asked. Not I.

Construction engineers are great fellows, and they are smart. They know all about stresses and strains. You admire them a great deal while sitting around a table looking at their blueprints. But just wait till you are seven hundred fifty feet up in thin air, standing rigid and paralyzed in a rickety little cage, suspended only by a piece of wire. At that moment you wish all construction engineers were in hell, and you know very well, figures or no figures, that a one-inch steel cable isn't strong enough to support a big guy like you who weighs a hundred and fifteen.

On the south shore there was a little frame building which served as field office for the great Golden Gate Bridge. We went in there to get our safety helmets. When we came out we couldn't see any bridge at all, because the fog was so thick. "Well, we'll go up anyway," the bridgeman said. "Maybe it won't be so thick up above." We walked out along the temporary pier under the bridge, to the immense south tower, three blocks out in the water. We got into a wire cage and started up.

This cage was like an elevator, except that it didn't go up anything. No shaft at all. It just went up through empty air, like a bucket on the end of a rope, and the top of the ride was nearly two hundred feet higher than the Washington Monument. As long as we were in the fog I was all right, because I couldn't see. But pretty soon we came out above it, and then the fright closed in over me. We went up and up and up. The fog and snatches of bridge and shore and city widened out below us. The elevator began to swing up and down. I knew instantly what that was: it was the cable fraying, and only a strand or two was left holding us. At two places on the way up we passed little shelves where the elevator sometimes stopped to let workmen out. When you came to one of these shelves the top of the elevator would hit it, and the cage would bump and jiggle around. It was enough to make a man want to lie down on the floor and cry.

Finally we were up there. Then we had to step across an open slice of sky about a foot wide (wide enough to fall through, all right), and then climb a steel ladder for twenty feet, cross a catwalk, climb another ladder fifteen feet, and then we were out on top of the world. Oh, God, who ever talked me into this?

The top of the tower was as big as eight or ten rooms. There were little shops and control houses, and men in helmets were sitting around eating lunch. The view was wonderful, if you dared look. The fog was vanishing now, and the whole immense bridge was there below us, in both directions, and there was the Golden Gate with little ships going through it, and over yonder was Sausalito, and back here was San Francisco, and out there was the ocean.

Around the edge of the top was a strong wooden railing. Sense told me I could pound on it all day with a sledge and not make a dent, and yet I knew that if I leaned on it, as the bridgeman was doing, it would collapse. Furthermore, I knew that if I stumbled I wouldn't fall to the floor. No, I'd fall up about five feet, and then out about five feet over the rail, and then seven hundred fifty feet down. That's the way I fall at the top of a high tower. Consequently, I stayed about six feet from the edge, with one arm wrapped around the doorway of one of the control houses.

The bridgeman said I was doing all right; a lot of people kept their eyes shut all the way up in the elevator, and a lot backed out when the elevator stopped—they just couldn't step across that foot of open space. And others who had gone on up would get so scared they would lie down on the floor and turn white and sweat and tremble. I was doing all right, he said. I was very careful, however, to step rhythmically and like a cat, so as not to set up any vibration that would collapse the tower. He said it was built so that an earthquake wouldn't collapse it, but you never can tell.

He asked if I wanted to walk down the catwalk that ran beneath the two cables, from the tower clear down to the bridge floor in the center. I sure would have liked to, but unfortunately I had an appointment with my music teacher and couldn't wait. So we climbed down the ladders and waited for the cage, and went swinging and jerking down to sea level again, me getting braver with every foot of the descent.

There was a young fellow in workmen's clothes on the elevator. I said to him, "How long did it take you to get used to these high places?" He said, "When I started I was on the graveyard shift, from midnight till eight. It was so dark I couldn't see what was under me. By the time it got daylight I was all right. But I was so damn glad to get a job I'd of clumb the Eiffel Tower." Personally, I would joyously starve to death before I'd work one hour at the top of the Golden Gate Bridge.

A newspaper friend of mine in San Francisco named Bob Elliott (he's a Hoosier too—they're everywhere) was the first man ever to walk from San Francisco to Oakland—the first to walk across the Oakland Bay Bridge. It took him all day. The bridge was then nothing but bare steel framework. In places he had to walk hundreds of feet on six-inch girders, twenty stories above the water, or on rounded cables, with only a thin wire guide rope to hold to. In places he had to climb right up over the top of great steel arches, slick with fresh paint, with no handholds at all. A hundred times he thought he would die. He wanted to quit and go back, but that was just as bad as going on. He was terribly shaken. He couldn't sleep the night after he made the trip, and it was three days before he became composed again.

I had the privilege of being one of the few outsiders to cross the finished bridge before it was opened. But it didn't scare me. No, sir. We rode across in an automobile.

Detour
by Water

Chapter
IX IT WAS DUSK WHEN WE CAST LOOSE FROM THE PIER
at Buffalo. They tried hard to make it romantic; quite a few
people were at the dock to see friends off, and there was considerable kissing and weeping. The gangplank was pulled up,
the whistle blew, and the ship eased out into the river. People
started waving handkerchiefs, and somebody tore up paper and
let it drift down from an upper deck like confetti, and then—this is
God's truth—a three-piece band on deck swung into "Aloha Oe."
You'd have thought we were pulling out of Pangopango.

I was talking with the captain about it later. If I thought that
was funny, he said, just wait until we got to Houghton, Michigan,
the last stop before Duluth. He said two hundred people would
come down to see one passenger off, and there would be more
weeping and wailing and kissing goodbye than you ever saw in
your life, and the passenger would just be going to Duluth, coming back day after tomorrow.

The captain had been leaving home all his life, he said, and
nobody ever cried about him.

Alex McPherson, our skipper aboard the *Octorara,* was half
Scot and half Irish. He had been sailing the Great Lakes for
thirty-seven years, and looked good for another thirty-seven. He
was a big man, full of dry wit, and I'm afraid he was capable of
playing a practical joke. But I'd pity the poor sailors on a night
like this if Captain McPherson got sore about something.

Passengers sometimes drive ship captains completely crazy,
but McPherson got a lot of fun out of his passengers. He was
telling me about a crowd of women he had on board once—mem-

bers of a women's club. All of them wanted to cut loose, but each one had about half a dozen neighbors watching her, each of whom in turn was being watched by half a dozen others. He said they'd dodge behind posts and sneak into the bar, and have drinks sent up to their rooms after the others had gone to bed. He got so he'd go around and whisper to each one, "I see you got your drink all right." And she'd look startled and say, "How did you know I had a drink, captain?" "I smell it," he'd say. "You can smell it all over the ship." He had those women nuts.

People on ships are always complaining or wanting something done or undone, and they think their ticket entitles them to take up everything with the captain. McPherson said most ship's officers take the passengers too seriously and get upset when they go on the loose. You've got to realize, he said, that most passengers are on a vacation, and they're out to blow off steam.

Sometimes McPherson would go back to the dock to pick up passengers who were late, though it was against regulations. He just felt sorry for them. He said Mr. and Mrs. John D. Rockefeller, Jr., were about the most agreeable people he had ever had aboard. The bigger they come, he said, the more decent they are. Sinclair Lewis was aboard once. The captain soon found out that the easiest way to get along with Lewis was to be just as tough as he was. Lewis said to him, "Have you read any of my books?" The captain said, "Only *Main Street,* and I can't remember whether I ever finished that or not." Lewis said, "Well, at least you're honest about it."

Fundamentally, I objected to Moxo the Magician. I objected because he was master of ceremonies aboard the *Octorara*. He would say to the passengers, "Now we'll have fun at 8:35 this evening if everybody is on time." With Kipling, I prefer my fun where I find it, and not organized, charted, and preordained by any Moxo the Magician. I would much rather sit alone and watch the wide dark water than win the ship's masquerade-ball contest.

But Moxo said I didn't know what I wanted. He claimed that only three people out of every five hundred want to be left alone; the rest are eager, willing, even hungry to have somebody round them up, get them together, tell them what to do, lead them in fun. And he almost proved it to me. He was the damnedest guy I ever ran on to. He was like war music—infectious.

Moxo was a gifted man. God had showered on him the following qualifications: he was a full-fledged magician; he could hypnotize people; he read people's minds; he was a ventriloquist; he was an excellent clown; he could dance like a fool; he could make an after-dinner speech on any subject whatever without preparation; he was a supersalesman; he could land in a town broke and by afternoon make sixty dollars just putting on a show or speaking before the advertising club or organizing a grocery-store treasure hunt. And on top of all this, he was a nice fellow. It burned me up. I couldn't even do a card trick.

Moxo's real name was M. E. Barker. He was a tall, thin New Englander about thirty, who lived with his mother in Buffalo. He had been master of ceremonies on the *Octorara* for two years. He would sleep only about three hours a day. Every morning till three o'clock he worked getting out his little mimeographed ship's newspaper. And then he was up at six to sell it to the passengers. The rest of the day he spent organizing bridge tournaments, golf contests, bingo games, introducing people, getting afternoon tea under way, putting on his magic show or leading the masquerade ball in the evening, cheering up the sad, consoling the angry, mending broken hearts, and doing individual tricks for people. He had a way of getting on with the passengers. For instance, he would tell them that anybody who didn't come to the masked ball would be put out in a lifeboat without oars, and that the Great Lakes sharks would eat them up. Some of them believed it, and all of them liked it.

He took a lot of kidding from the officers; they razzed him about the way he acted with the passengers. But they should have been thankful he was aboard for all the grief he took off their shoulders. Moxo was the fixer; the passengers came to him for everything, and some funny things had happened in his two years of being father confessor. A wife left her husband because her name was omitted from the passenger list in the ship's newspaper. It took Moxo a whole day to fix that. Another time, a passenger reported that his pocketbook with ninety dollars in it had been stolen. After the magic show that night, the man went to the purser and accused Moxo of stealing it. "His fingers are so nimble," the man said.

Once there was a crazy woman on board. She wanted to sing all the time. He let her sing on the ship's program, and she was terrible. Then, to save her feelings, he had to get up and make a fool of himself, so the passengers could laugh at him and not at her. One time a country girl's feelings were hurt by an innocent poem about "big feet," which she drew out of the ship's grab bag of presents. She went to her cabin crying, and Moxo had to talk to her for an hour through the door before he could calm her. There was a fellow on board once who had a letter to the captain, and he thought this practically gave him command of the ship. Moxo got so mad he was going to kill him, but he looked up the ship's regulations, and they said the master of ceremonies wasn't allowed to kill the passengers, so he had to let it go.

One passenger invited Moxo on a year's free trip around the world on a yacht. He couldn't go, because he had to support his mother.

The ship stopped at Mackinac Island for two hours. This was my second visit there. The first one was in June of 1921, during the time I was a member of the Naval Reserve. That summer, having nothing else to do, I dug my sailor pants out of the attic and went to Chicago for a three weeks' Naval Reserve training cruise.

We sailed on the USS *Wilmette,* formerly known as the *Eastland.* It was the ship that turned over in the Chicago River in 1915 and drowned eight hundred twelve people. When it was raised, the Navy bought it and painted it gray and filled it full of innocent farm boys who wanted to be sailors. It was still in a sinking condition, I assure you. It constantly shied to the right, and once in a while felt as though it wanted to lie down in the water.

But anyhow, it did carry us to Mackinac Island where we tied up for a full day. By this time I had rapidly risen in the ranks from mere seaman to the exalted position of second-class cook. That entitled me to stay on board all the time we were at Mackinac, frying pork chops. I had to start at two in the afternoon, to get all the pork chops fried for the evening chow. I would fry two huge skillets full at a time, and when they were done I would dump them in a washtub. I had two tubs full by evening. It was hotter than a Kansas prairie fire on board the *Wilmette* that afternoon, and the galley was twice as hot as that. I was working without a shirt, and a dirty apron was tied around my waist. Grease kept popping on my arms and face. I looked like a pork chop.

The Navy loves a show, so it had thrown the ship open to visitors that afternoon and hundreds of vacationists at Mackinac came aboard. All afternoon they filed around the decks. The galley happened to be on the main deck, and visitors could stop and look right in the galley door at the funny man frying pork chops. A lot of them did. It gave them, I am sure, a great deal of entertainment. But I didn't care. They would look and pass on, right out of the cook's life.

But gradually I became aware that somebody had been standing in the door a long time without moving on with the rest of the crowd. I turned around and looked. And who do you suppose it was? Admiral Farragut? No. Mrs. Roosevelt? No. The governor of Michigan? No.

It was a girl friend of mine from college, and she was standing there laughing at me.

That's all there is to the story. I'm sorry I started it. It would have been a much better story if I had been in love with her, but I wasn't. I think we just talked for a while, and then she got off the ship, and I saw her in school that fall and we probably never spoke of it again.

In the village of Baudette, Minnesota, there was a trio of great friends, three men who had been pals for thirty years. They were Jack and John and Bill. Jack Collins kept the hardware store. John Kennedy was a United States customs man. Bill Noonan was editor of the weekly newspaper. They were not "characters." They were intelligent, kindly men, the same as you might find in any town, except—there was something about them, a quality that seems to me to exist only in people who have lived the raw life of the frontier.

Jack and John were getting close to seventy. Bill was a little younger. What they really lived for was to hunt and fish. Every one of them said he would want to be dead if he couldn't hunt and fish any more. Jack and John were natural outdoor men, woodsmen as well as sportsmen. But Bill was a little different. He would go on all the hunting and fishing expeditions but he wasn't domestic, even in an outdoor way, and he couldn't learn to do anything around a camp on a bet. The other two got awfully mad at him sometimes. Once they had a little portable cookstove with them up in Canada. The first night out they pitched camp, and while Jack and John went out to see what they could scare up, Bill was to get the fire going. They even gathered the wood for him. But when they got back Bill was sitting peacefully in the middle of a great cloud of smoke, reading a book. He had not only kindled up a blaze in the firebox, but he had built a fire in the oven too. He didn't know the difference.

Another time, they camped in a lodge that belonged to a doctor friend. It was a very modern affair, with a gasoline stove that had six burners and a big oven. They had brought a ham with them, so they explained to Bill just how to start the stove, and just how to put the ham in, and everything. Then they went out for a couple of hours' shooting. It was cold and raw—late fall and late evening—and their blood was like ice and their stomachs were empty when they got back. Their minds were on that beautiful ham Bill would have ready. When they walked in, he was sitting at the jug, reading a book. "How's the ham, Bill?" "It ought to be about done by now," he said. "I put it in a couple of hours ago." So John Kennedy went out to see. He was back in a minute. "You blankety-blank so-and-so. I'm going to shoot you." Jack Collins took a look at the stove, and said, "No, please don't shoot him. I want to shoot him."

Well, Bill had put the ham in and just turned on the pilot light. He thought that would cook the ham. It was still sitting there in the oven, cold as a chunk of ice.

Jack Collins and John Kennedy were laughing as they told me these stories about Bill Noonan. "But say," they went on, "he is a wonderful man. He's the wittiest man in this part of the country.

And I don't suppose he ever thought a bad thought about anybody in his life."

Bill used to do more than his share of drinking. And Jack wasn't averse to taking a number of nips now and then himself. But a year or so ago the two of them decided it was going too far, and they would stop. "It was a good idea," said John Kennedy, "and I wanted to help them along. So I told them that every time they felt like taking a drink, just to call me up, and I'd take it instead. They kept me pretty busy for a while. But now it's got so I have to call them up and ask if they don't want me to take a drink for them."

John Kennedy had had fun all his life. I'm sure he drove everybody almost crazy in the days when Baudette was a frontier settlement. Just one example, out of hundreds:

There was an old man, the town drunk, who finally died of alcoholism on the floor of the hotel lobby. They carried him down to the little clapboard church, took the door off the hinges, and laid the corpse on the door inside the church. They set another old man to watch the body. To keep up courage for his grim task, the old fellow had to run back to the hotel about every hour and get a drink. After a few he got to waving his gun around and saying nobody would steal the corpse while he was on guard.

So Kennedy and a friend slipped over to the church, ran some twine through cracks in the wall from each side, and tied the twine around the corpse's wrists. Then they hid outside the church. When the old watchman came back from his tippling, Kennedy and his friend started pulling the cords back and forth. The corpse's arms started flying. The old man screamed and dropped his lantern and ran. The lantern started to set the church afire, so Kennedy ran in and threw it out the door. That scared the departing watchman even worse. Kennedy cut off the twine and beat it.

The old man spread the alarm. In a couple of minutes the whole town, Kennedy among them, came surging down to the church. They decided the old man was having visions. They wanted to hang him, but somebody talked them out of it. Maybe it was Kennedy. He didn't dare tell the truth of that story for years afterward.

Jack Collins said it was a lie that he told lies. He said he never told anything but the truth. He said he was hunting deer one fall, and a beauty came out of the woods toward him four hundred yards away, so he pulled up and let him have it. Just as he shot, he said, the deer made a lightning reverse turn, and started back for the woods, but dropped dead after a step or two.

Well, they went down and started cutting up the deer. They saw that the bullet had hit the deer in the eye. Suddenly one of the fellows said, "Hey, what's this?" He pointed to a small tree nearby that had been freshly splintered, apparently by a bullet. So they looked around, and traced the splinters over the snow for about fifteen feet, and there lay the bullet. It came from John Collins' gun all right, and he had fired only one shot. Then they examined the deer more closely, but found no place where the bullet had come out. So, the bullet had gone into the deer, and apparently had not come out, and yet there it was on the ground. How would you explain that?

Well, here's the way John Collins explained it. "Remember," he said, "the deer made a fast reverse turn just as I shot. Well, what happened was that the bullet went into the deer's eye but the deer changed ends so fast that the bullet, still traveling in the same direction, came right out of the deer's eye the same place it went in, and then hit the tree and bounced off. It was the damnedest thing I ever saw."

One summer afternoon in 1910, a little dog came trotting a bunch of cows down the main street of Baudette. The dog had been trained by his owner to bring in the family's cows every evening. But this day the little dog got the cows in early, and he rounded up not only his own cows but a couple of dozen more. He herded them in a bunch right down the traveled main street, and on through town to the river. People didn't think much about it at the time, though they remembered it later.

All was peaceful that late afternoon when the dog brought in the cows. Then just about dusk the people heard a faint sound, and looked to the west. And what they saw would drive many a brave man into the horrors. A vast forest fire was coming like a hurricane, roaring with the deafening roar of a thousand furnaces. It was 7:45 when they first heard the fire, ten miles away. It traveled in from the great green forests at forty miles an hour, whipped along by a terrific wind. By 8:05 every building in Baudette was afire. The town was burned off the map and thirty-five lives were lost. The little dog had known what he was about, all right.

One afternoon I stood on a rock that is the northernmost foot of land in the United States. It is in what is called the Northwest Angle, in Minnesota—that little spot of the United States that lies illogically over in Canada, forty miles across the Lake of the Woods from the northern Minnesota mainland. It is not connected with any part of the United States except by water. It has Canada on the west side, and water on the three other sides. There are no roads into Northwest Angle. The only way you get there is by boat in summer, or across the ice in winter. Or, now that we're in the twentieth century, by airplane.

Northwest Angle is in two parts—the mainland and the islands. The islands are the more attractive; there are about a hundred of them, ranging from mere rocks to one island of thirteen hundred acres. They extend eastward into Lake of the Woods for about ten miles, to where the unseen international boundary cuts them off from their fellow islands in Canadian waters. The Angle mainland is about ten by twelve miles, and it is all muskeg, or swamp, and nobody lives in it except along the shore.

The Angle has a total permanent population of fewer than a hundred. About half live on the mainland, half on the islands. There is no town, but there are two post offices, both on islands, with two or three families living around them. People come by canoe to get their mail. There are two fishing camps in the Angle, where tourists may come to rest or fish. But it would be stretching a point to call it a resort country; the tourists come in dribbles instead of droves.

I have never been any place where the inhabitants know so little about their own history as the people of Northwest Angle. Not a person I talked with knew why the United States-Canadian boundary was so ludicrously drawn around this isolated spot. One story is that the British surveyors got the Americans drunk, and they drew a line; and then the Americans got the British drunk, and they drew a line. But from the best information I could gather it was this: a treaty to settle the boundary between the United States and Canada was made shortly after the War of 1812 and at that time they didn't know the exact location of Lake of the Woods. According to the treaty, the boundary was to run east and west along the middle of Rainy River until it emptied into Lake of the Woods, then across water to the northwestern corner of the lake, and thence either north or south, whichever it might be, to the forty-fifth parallel. And when they surveyed it, Lake of the Woods turned out to be farther north than they had thought, and the northwest corner was way up in Canada. When they drew the line back down to the forty-fifth parallel, it left Northwest Angle as United States territory.

I had heard that a strange kind of people inhabited this isolated spot, but that is not exactly correct. They are strange only in that they lack ambition. They are satisfied, most of them, just barely to exist, and that's all most of them do. They raise a little hay in the summer for a couple of cows. They do a little commercial fishing. In winter they trap muskrat and mink. Most of them don't get into Warroad, Minnesota, fifty miles away, more than once a year.

But the kids do get to school. There are two schools in Northwest Angle: one on Oak Island, the other on American Point, also an island. Each one has about six pupils. The kids on Flag Island, for instance, are three miles away, and they have to get to Oak Island. In early fall and late spring they go by outboard canoe. But during the two-week freeze-up in November it's too icy for boats, so the children stay on Oak Island those two weeks. The same thing happens during the spring thaw-out.

And all winter they walk the three miles across the ice. A grownup always goes with them, for there are treacherous air holes in the lake. "The kids never missed a day last winter," says Papa McKeever of Flag Island. "They usually started about eight. But a few mornings it was fifty-six below zero, and we waited till about ten o'clock. It had warmed up to forty below by that time."

Middle West Again

Chapter X ONE NIGHT MORE THAN HALF A CENTURY AGO, IN Corning, Iowa, a young lawyer named Howard Russell was burning the midnight oil preparing a defense in a murder case. His father had been an Episcopal preacher, but Howard didn't want any preaching in his life. He wasn't wild and he wasn't bad, but he professed no formal religion. His wife, Lillian, the daughter of the man who fathered him into the law business, did not share her husband's apathy toward religion. Her mind was made up that Howard was going to become a Christian. She had mentioned it to him a number of times, but he used to turn her aside with a bit of his conversational German: *"Das ist verboten"*—don't talk about that. And she would stop.

But this certain night when Attorney Russell came home about eleven o'clock he saw a light in an upstairs bay window. Lillian is still up, he thought to himself. She is going to talk to me about religion again. He went upstairs and found her sitting in the bay window. When he greeted her, she got up and came toward him.

"Howard, I'm worried about you," she said. He knew what she meant, but he said, "Why, I've never been in better health in my life."

"It isn't your health I'm worried about," she said. "It's your soul."

"Das ist verboten," laughed Howard, but his laugh was a little dry, for he was getting annoyed beyond his patience.

"Howard," she persisted, "will you kneel down and let me pray for you?"

That was too much. Lawyer Russell didn't say another word.

He went to a hotel and got a room and went to bed. And he slept too. Never had a better night's sleep in his life.

Next morning he went to his office. He did not go home for breakfast, or dinner, or supper. He worked all day without going home to see his young wife. He was punishing her for her impudence. Late that night, after his work was done, he went back home. Again the light was burning in the upper bay window. He began to feel a little badly—like a brute, in fact. He went into the house. Lillian rose from the window seat and came toward him, smiling and happy. She put her arms around him and kissed him. She got their baby from the crib, and snuggled it up to him. She kissed him again.

"Howard," she said, "you went away last night. But I knew you were all right, for I was awake all night, and till after daylight, praying for you. Howard, will you kneel down now and let me pray for you?"

"Why, yes, I reckon," said Howard, thinking it wouldn't do any harm.

And so they knelt, and Lillian started to pray. She had taken a leaf from her husband's profession, and her prayer was a listed series of indictments against his character. She prayed on and on. ". . . and, dear God, Howard drinks," she said. Howard Russell listened. And suddenly he felt chains of heavy thorns around him, binding his arms to his chest, crippling him, stifling him. And then as she prayed on and on, he became conscious that they were breaking. He could feel them give, one by one. Finally he was free. Like a great light in the sky it came. He knew he had broken the fetters of unselfishness and stubbornness and willfulness that bound him.

He turned jubilantly to Lillian. "I am giving up," he said. "Giving up what?" she asked. And he shouted back, "I AM GIVING UP SIN! I AM FREE!"

"Will you go in the morning and tell the preacher about it?" she asked.

"I certainly intend to, before breakfast," he said.

"And will you get up and tell the congregation about it?" she asked.

"You couldn't keep me from it. I want everybody in the world to be as happy as I am."

And that was how in a little town in Iowa God and man were brought together into a driving force that gave America the Anti-Saloon League, the Eighteenth Amendment, and fourteen years of prohibition. Many years later, at Westerville, Ohio, the Rev. Howard Hyde Russell, LL.D., D.D., L.H.D., founder of the Anti-Saloon League, the dauntless spirit of prohibition, choked up and his voice broke with happiness when he told about that night.

The boys on the newspaper at Akron, Ohio, said they'd like me to call on the Akron widow who had been advertising for a husband, to see if I could figure out people like that.

There wasn't a telephone, so I just drove out and rang the bell. "Is this Mrs. Cunningham?" I said, she being the one who was looking for a husband. She said yes, and to come on in. There were three people in the living room—Mrs. Cunningham, her sister Mrs. Keener, and a man named Jimmy. When I introduced myself they all laughed. They had thought I was a prospective husband. (And a mighty fine one I'd have made too, with my new Borsalino hat and my smooth city-slicker tongue.)

Mrs. Cunningham was in her early thirties, and had two boys twelve and ten. She had lost her husband three years before in an accident. This Mr. Jimmy, on the davenport, said practically nothing. Mrs. Cunningham wasn't averse to saying a few words now and then, but she didn't have much chance while Mrs. Keener was around.

"This was all my doings," Mrs. Keener said. "We read in the papers about somebody advertising for a husband, so I said to Sis, sort of kidding like, I said, 'Why don't you do that, Sis?' So just more for a joke than anything else she sat down and wrote a letter to the *Times-Press,* giving her qualifications and what she'd expect of a husband. Well, next morning the reporters and photographers were out here." (Mrs. Cunningham here got in a word—said she wouldn't have done it if she'd known how the paper would play it up.) And Mrs. Keener continued: "But we're people that don't start anything unless we finish it. And we're Irish and like a joke."

I got there about a week after the first announcement, and already ten men had applied in person, and letters had come from four more. They were having a lot of fun, but Mrs. Keener was getting worried too. They'd had some nasty letters from Akronites who didn't approve of such goings-on. "But I say that if any of our friends don't take it in the right spirit they're not the kind we want for friends anyway," Mrs. Keener said. "We're open and aboveboard about this. A girl like Sis doesn't have a chance to meet many new people, and maybe this way she might meet some nice man she wouldn't meet otherwise. As I tell Sis, she wouldn't take any beauty prizes, but beauty isn't everything and after you get to know a person you never think about how they look." Mrs. Cunningham laughed.

I asked Mrs. Cunningham how many of the ten men she would even consider as husband material. She said only three, but Mrs. Keener said all of them except one were all right. She called them by their first names. She said they all came in about the same spirit they were received with—partly in fun, and out of curiosity. This one fellow, though, was a sort of clotheshorse, and kept saying he wasn't in the habit of answering ads like this—in other words, trying to lord it over them a little.

I said that I could never answer such an ad because if I didn't want to marry the gal I wouldn't know how to get away. And at that point this Mr. Jimmy, on the couch, sort of raised up and said, "That's just what I was wondering all the way out here." I had thought he was one of the family all the time, but here he turned out to be one of the applicants! Everybody laughed.

Mrs. Keener said, well, no matter how it turned out, they'd met a lot of nice people. Mrs. Cunningham laughed and said that even if she didn't get a husband she'd sure met a lot of newspapermen. Mrs. Keener said that they'd never known any newspapermen before, and they sure did like that bunch down at the *Times-Press*. She was referring to them all by their first names. And she said to me, "Why, I feel like I'd known you all my life."

And then I suddenly realized how nice people could advertise for a husband. It was just because they were so friendly—the friendliest people you ever saw, and the minute you stepped into their house you were welcome. They came from down in West Virginia (everybody in Akron is from West Virginia), where the people don't have so many inhibitions, and their private affairs don't seem very private to them. They just aren't self-conscious.

I went to lunch with some fellows in Toledo, Ohio. The restaurant was a big one—there must have been a hundred fifty men and women eating lunch. A waiter came up and said to me, "What'll you have?" I didn't say anything for a couple of seconds, of course, and then suddenly the waiter turned toward the kitchen and yelled so loud you could hear him all over the place: "Hey, this rube won't order. Come here."

Waiters all over the place threw down their dishes and came running, and those apes grabbed me fore and aft and on each side and underneath, and dragged me clear across the restaurant, kicked open the front doors, and whisshhh—there I was right on the sidewalk, thrown out of the place!

That's the way things went in that restaurant all the time. It was a madhouse. Something was always happening. The whole business—and a prosperous business it was—had been built up on the policy of insulting the customers. The waiters all wore galluses and kept their hats on and talked all the time. If you were getting bald, they called you "Curly." If you were completely bald, they would polish your head with a rag. If you spilled something, they'd bring a big baby bib and tie it around your neck. To set the table they just brought an armload of silver and threw it at you. If you ate left-handed, as I do, a waiter would stop dead in his tracks and point at you and yell to the whole house, "Hey, look at this rube, he don't even know which hand to eat with. Haw! Haw! Haw!"

The head man said to me, "A new customer always gets rolls and a cup on his first visit here." And just then a waiter came running and yelling, "Rolls and a cup for the new customer." He had an empty cup and two rolls of toilet paper on a plate. Everybody laughed, including me, although I didn't see anything funny about it. During our soup course the waiter came around and said solicitously, "Is there enough water in that soup, or would you like me to put my thumb in it?" Once in a while a waiter got up and walked on the tables. And from the kitchen there was a constant bedlam of dishes breaking, pots falling, women screaming, bells and whistles going off, moans, shouts, and thumpings. All during the meal a waiter kept going around the restaurant like a newsboy, yelling, "Here ya are—*News-Bee, World-Telegram, Daily News*—read Ernie Pyle's column—read all about it!" He was holding high in the air a big roll of toilet paper.

When we started to leave, I could hardly lift my topcoat from the rack, it was so heavy. Waiters came running from everywhere. They felt in the pockets and yelled, "We've caught a thief! We've caught a thief!" And then they started unloading the pockets. They took out enough knives and forks to set up the whole restaurant. They took out salt and pepper shakers, and jars of sugar, and bottles of ketchup—I didn't know my pockets could hold so much—and all the time yelling, "Boy, did he try to make a getaway!" Everybody in the place was howling.

By that time I decided, aw, to hell with it, I might as well get in the spirit of the thing too, so when they had all finished I picked up a handful of knives and forks and put them back in my pocket, and at the counter I took three cigars and two chocolate bars and walked on out the front door.

The place was known as Bud & Luke's. It was run by two brothers, Eugene and Glenn Fowler. They had started it as a side line eleven years before, when they were auto salesmen and not doing very well. At first they were too busy to do a decent job of waiting on people, and had to cover up their poor service with a little kidding. The kidding seemed to take hold, and now it had grown into this colossal buffoonery.

People were always saying to Bud and Luke, "Say, I know a fellow who would be a wow as a waiter." But these wows never seemed to turn out. It worked better just to hire some casual applicant; in a couple of weeks he would get in the swing of the thing and be crazier than anybody.

I asked Bud (or maybe it was Luke) if anybody ever really got sore. He said, yes, once in a while. They would always try to smooth things over, but if the guy didn't warm up, then they would really let him have it. Nobody had ever got sore enough to fight, however. More people got sore because they came for a ribbing and didn't get it.

They threw a customer into the street only about once a week. These throwouts were generally arranged ahead of time (as mine was, I learned later). I think the funniest one was when a couple of boys from the *News-Bee* called up and arranged to have an out-of-town guest thrown out, and the waiters got mixed up and threw out one of the arrangers.

Those strange men in screaming cars that tear around the Indianapolis Speedway on Memorial Day—how different are they from us common mortals who drive down the road at fifty miles an hour? Off the track, you couldn't tell a race driver from anybody else; some are dapper and keen, and some are plodders—just human beings. But on the track? Well, they have to be different from us. For five hours out there they live in a world we can hardly conceive of. I spent some time among the drivers, asking them schoolboy questions about this other world and getting the answers. Here are some of them:

Can the driver and mechanic hear each other talk during the race? Yes, but not very well. They shout back and forth a little, though not much. They talk mostly by pointing.

Can they hear that dramatic, momentous, mile-long yell of the crowd as the winner comes down the stretch on the last lap? No. The rushing wind and the roaring motor make too much noise, and anyway, by the end of the race they're almost deaf.

Are the boys in the cars conscious of the crowd? Yes. I hadn't supposed they even know the crowd was there, but they see quite a few things. Wilbur Shaw said he could actually see the crowd getting drunk as the day wore away. One year he saw a woman standing on top of a car in the infield. She threw up her hands and fell off backward, drunk as the moon—he saw it all while taking a turn at a hundred miles an hour.

Does the driver ever take his eyes off a straight line right ahead of him? Yes. Once in a while, when the cars aren't bunched, he gawks about a bit just to relax. But in the two-man cars the driver seldom looks behind him.

Does the race ever get monotonous to the driver? Yes. Sometimes they drone along for a hundred miles with the cars well scattered and no change in position, and it is then like monotonous driving anywhere else. Can the driver squirm around in his seat for a new position when he gets tired? Hardly at all. The seats are very narrow. Do they ride on air cushions? Some do, but most of them don't. Some of the cars ride as smoothly as our touring cars. Others ride like log wagons.

Does a driver ever get sore at another one for the way he's driving? Yes. A driver sometimes gets mad at his best friend for blocking him off.

How much does the driver depend on the riding mechanic? A great deal. The mechanic has to watch behind for cars trying to pass; he helps read the pit signals; he watches the outside tires for dangerous wear. And to me one of his most interesting little duties is this: going into every turn, he looks to the left, clear across the turn, to see if there are any pile-ups on the far corner.

How do the drivers feel about the danger of racing? Their attitude toward death is exactly the same as it is among aviators. It's a simple philosophy—it can happen to the other fellow, but never to me. A friend who is close to the game told me that after one of the boys has been killed, the drivers say, "Well, Jim was a swell fellow, but he never should have been allowed to drive," or "Well, Bob was a great driver, but he should have had more sense than to take that old pile of junk out on the track."

If a car really gets into wide and handsome slides, the boys say there isn't anything you can do. You just "take to the cellar and ride it out." Taking to the cellar means ducking way down low, so your head won't stick out.

Do drivers get scared during a race? Well, yes and no. Naturally you couldn't see a car pile up and people get killed without being affected, but the drivers seldom slow down. The hardest part is being flagged down to sixty or eighty miles an hour for several laps because of rain or a wreck. When you drive four hundred miles at real speed you're in a state of nervous tension that will carry you on through nearly anything. But have that spell broken, and the fine tight wire of your senses goes slack. Drivers almost go crazy during the "flagdowns." They want to get going again.

They yell at the race officials as they go by, pleading with them to "let us go."

And then when they do get the green flag and everybody guns it and they go slamming around faster and faster than ever, wild over lost time, their armor of rigid tenseness all shot, their nerves frazzled—right there is the most dangerous part of your five-hundred-mile auto race.

Nearly every car in the race is an individually made job. No car even faintly approaches being a stock car, and the drivers say there isn't any such thing as a speedway car's having a certain make of engine. Maybe it was to start with, but the mechanics and engineers so alter and rebuild these engines that by the time the race starts you couldn't call them anything.

Race cars have no speedometers. At their speed, a speedometer wouldn't be accurate within many miles, and it would be just one more gadget to cause trouble. Most of the cars do have tachometers, which register the engine revolutions per minute.

Each car has two sets of brakes, hydraulic on the foot brake, mechanical on the lever. They all have electric starters. The motor itself is often a better brake—and a more dangerous one—than the brake itself. On some of the high-compression four-cylinder jobs a driver would be committing suicide if he suddenly lifted his foot off the throttle at a hundred forty miles an hour. It would be like slamming on the brakes, and the car would go into a wild skid. Letting up on the throttle is called "backing off." Instead of slowing up for a turn, you back off from it. But because of the danger of your engine's overbraking your car, you must back off slowly and easily.

Taped onto one spoke of the steering wheel is a little push button just like the button on the hotel wall that you use to ring for ice water. This is a cutout for the whole ignition system. In case of a skid, if it looks to the driver like a bad pile-up, he presses this button and the ignition is cut off, so there won't be a fire after the crash. There might not be time to reach down to the dash and turn the switch.

The drivers and mechanics take an awful beating on the rough Indianapolis track. Wilbur Shaw said he happened to look down into the cockpit once on the back stretch, and there were four legs jiggling and shaking all around the car like jellyfish. It tickled him so he punched his mechanic and made him look.

You're mighty tired at the end of five hundred miles—if you haven't won. There is an old saying around the speedway: "The winner is never tired."

Harold Korb, of Evansville, was the champion soda jerker of the United States, and he didn't take the honor lightly. He was proud and serious about it. It was more as though he had been given a medal by a scientific society in recognition of years of research. And the funny part about it was that Harold Korb wasn't a soda jerker at all, and never had been. He was an ice-cream salesman. But he sure knew how to make a chocolate soda— only I shouldn't say it that way. You never make a soda, or jerk a soda, or mix a soda. What you do is "build" a soda. Korb's great distinction came at Cincinnati, at a convention of sixty-six ice-cream salesmen from all over America. These salesmen have to be better soda jerkers (builders) than the jerkers themselves, because it is part of their job to tell the jerkers how to do it. Well, at this convention, every salesman had to build a soda. The judges didn't sample the sodas; they just watched the building process. And it was such a beautiful sight to watch Harold Korb build a chocolate soda that even before he had finished they told him he was the winner.

His prize number was called the Mellow-Cream Chocolate Soda. Here's how he built it: he put in an ounce and a half of chocolate syrup, then two soda spoons of stiffly whipped cream; he stirred them up very thoroughly and discarded the spoon; he shot a very fine stream of carbonated water into the glass until it was three-quarters of an inch from the top (didn't dare stir it any more); then he plied (yes, plied) two No. 24 dips of ice cream, one gently on top of the other, so it would stick up on top of the soda and the customer would see it and say, "Oh, goody!"

Harold Korb wasn't a smooth-tongued man, but the confectioners must have sensed that he was very honest and very thorough. His years of close attention had been rewarded. At thirty-five he was a white-collar man in the dairy's promotion department, and he owned two homes and had a wife and children.

I laughed and said, "Well, you're really a big shot now, aren't you?" Korb laughed too, but he said, "I've never been anything but a big little shot to Harold Korb." Success had not turned the head of the man who built a better Mellow-Cream Chocolate Soda. And if I was in the soda-fountain business, and Harold Korb told me to stick a corncob in every chocolate soda—boy, I'd stick a corncob in every chocolate soda.

In recent years we had heard a lot about the "good neighbor" policy among nations. But to me, and I suspect to most of us, "good neighbor" had become a mere academic term; city dwellers had almost forgotten what a good neighbor is. But the country people still knew.

My mother had a second stroke and became paralyzed on a Thursday night. By Friday morning the whole countryside knew about it; word travels fast among the neighbors of western Indiana. Help began to roll in instantly. The strongest men in the neighborhood came, without being asked, to help lift my mother in her bed. The women came to help Aunt Mary with the washing and housework. Others came, and others called, to see what they could do. Mrs. Goforth baked two butterscotch pies and sent them over. Lou Webster sent up an angel-food cake and came twice to help us with the work. Hattie Brown cooked a roast, with dressing and everything, and sent it up steaming hot for our Sunday dinner. Cousin Jediah Frist, who would be eighty his next birthday, drove down from town in a sleet storm to see if he could do anything. Nellie Potts brought flowers clear down from Newport.

Mrs. Bird Malone brought a beautiful hyacinth. When my mother had had her first stroke a year earlier, Bird and Mrs. Malone started over to see her. On the way, the car door came open and Mrs. Malone fell out and broke her arm at the shoulder. She was in a cast for three months, and still couldn't close her hand. I told her she was pretty brave to start the same trip over again.

Oll Potter's mother sent a whole basketful of fresh sausage and pork tenderloin, and a peck of apples. When I was a little boy, the Potters were the poorest people in all our neighborhood. They were just up from the Kentucky hills, and they never smiled. We thought they talked funny. Dan Potter worked for farmers by the day. But the Potters toiled and saved their money, and all their boys grew up to be workers. Now they lived in a nice house and had a fleet of cattle trucks, and the whole country admired them for the way they'd raised themselves by the bootstraps.

Mrs. Frank Davis, the new neighbor just up the road, brought over freshly butchered pork ribs. My Aunt Mary said it was good of her, she not knowing us very well. Mrs. Davis said that once when she was sick over in Parke County people were mighty good to her; and when she told them she didn't know how she could ever repay them, they told her she didn't need to repay them personally, just so she did things for other folks when they needed it. And that's what she was doing.

My Uncle Oat Saxton brought over a freshly butchered side of a hog. Uncle Oat kept batch, and he was the laughingest man in Vermillion County. He laughed at everything, and especially himself, and when he laughed it was like the melodious peal of a cathedral bell. It helped ease the strain to have him come and sit in our kitchen, and take off the lid and spit into the stove, and tell stories and laugh at them.

On Sunday there were thirty-eight people at our house. We couldn't get them all in the front room, and at one time the kitchen and dining room were so full that half of them had to stand up. Anna Kerns was one of the thirty-eight, and when she left she didn't say, "Now, if there's anything at all I can do . . ." She said, "Mary, I'll be here at seven-thirty in the morning to do the washing for you." And she was too, and stayed all day, and got down on her knees and oiled the linoleum, and then sat all afternoon with Mother while we rested.

Bertha and Iva Jordan came twice for half a day each. They brought two pies the first time and a cake the second time, and they did the washing and ironing. Iva Jordan was my first schoolteacher. We talked about my first year in school, and we both hated to realize it was more than thirty years ago. She was gray-haired now, but she was still pleasant and soft-spoken.

Jennie Hooker, the mother of my closest childhood chum, came and stayed all day. Bill and Beatrice Bales came and sat up all night, and ran innumerable errands for us in their car. Rema Myers, the doctor's wife, came one afternoon and did the ironing. She was the prettiest girl in our town. When we were of high-school age, Rema and I never dared to go anywhere together, because we always got the giggles so bad. Rema was still getting 'em.

Uncle John Taylor, my mother's brother, came and sat up two nights, and would have stayed every night if we had let him. Claude Lockeridge got out his truck and drove nearly twenty miles on a snowy day to get a hospital bed from Earl White's, north of town. Other people did things, and brought things, and called up, but I can't remember them all now.

For forty years my mother was the one who went to all these people when they needed help. They hadn't forgotten, and now they were coming to her in droves. Indiana farmers know what a "good neighbor" policy is. It's born in them.

It isn't everybody who has three hats. It isn't everybody who has even one. For many years I never had more than one. Now I had three.

The story began nearly twenty years before, when I first went out into the world and bought a hat of my own choosing. Somehow I got started wearing wide-brimmed Borsalino hats imported from Italy. It wasn't that I went in for fancy imported stuff, but I got started on these hats so I kept wearing them.

Now, I am easy on clothes. Shoes last me four and five years, and so do suits. I never do get rid of an overcoat. And some of my hats have seen generations come and go. My last Borsalino had been bought in Washington, years ago. Even at that time they were getting hard to find. (That is, my wide-brimmed model was hard to find.) So I wore it, and I wore it, and I wore it. It turned from gray to cat-colored, and from there it turned to no color at all. It took on an exotic shape, which neither wind nor fire nor mud puddles could change or destroy. It had holes in the crown that people thought were bullet holes. It was refused a cleaning and blocking by a hatter, because he said it would fall to pieces if he touched it. It was worn with full soup and fish to a Gridiron dinner in Washington. It was hissed by a hat-check girl. One night in San Francisco it went under a hind wheel of my car, to give traction in a mud puddle. A few weeks later, in Hollywood, the end came. I was watching Joan Crawford make a movie, and I left it hanging on a studio light bracket when I went to lunch. When I came back the hat was gone. I always felt that Joan fell in love with me at first sight, and took the hat as something to remember me by. At any rate, I never saw it again, and I was very lonely without it. Not only lonely—my head got cold. I had to have another hat. I looked in Los Angeles, and in San Diego, and in Tia Juana, but they didn't have my kind of hat. Finally I had to buy an American hat. It was the nearest thing I could find to my wide-brimmed Borsalino, but I didn't like it.

So when I got to New York, I said I'd get me another Borsalino or I'd blow the joint clear off the map. I went to eight places. They said they had Borsalinos, but not that style. They said people didn't wear them any more. They said the duty was too high. They said this and they said that. They raised their eyebrows and advised me to try somewhere else. But finally I found a sympathetic soul. He didn't have one, but he thought he could get one. Just wait a few days—he'd see. Well, one morning the phone rang. It was my hat man. You'd have thought he had just struck gold, he was that enthusiastic. He had my hat! Just what I wanted! Come right down and get it! So I beat it down and there, sure enough, was the hat I wanted. I bought it, and that made me two hats, and I was very happy.

And then it seems a guy in Hollywood named Fredric March read about my losing my hat in Hollywood. So he wrote to me as follows: "Since you lost your hat, I am sending you a beautiful old brown one which has a cigarette burn in the brim, and can be knocked into practically any shape you wish. It will probably prove much too large for you—requiring several strips of toilet paper around the inside band. You must have discovered on your visit here what big-heads most of us 'big shots' have, but I hope that even though it doesn't prove serviceable you will keep it for a laugh."

Well, the much-forwarded hat, cigarette burn and all, caught up with me in Indianapolis. March was right; it did need toilet paper in the brim, and that's what it got. It fitted all right after that, but somehow it wasn't a success. Every evening I would put it on and look at myself in the mirror. I didn't look like anybody I ever saw before, least of all like Fredric March. But I kept it, you bet.

So now I had three hats. I carried them all with me, and took turns wearing them, and they were a nuisance.

I'm ashamed to get as attached to an automobile as I do. It had been like a death in the family to give up the old one a year ago. And now it was goodbye to the new one for a long time; she was going into dead storage in Clarence Russell's garage in Dana. My last glimpse of her was at midnight, sitting there all alone in the darkness on the graveled drive of my old home. The rain was pouring down on her. We had been a long way together, and now she was to stay, and I was to go on alone. She didn't look back, and neither did I.

The man in 1021 hasn't been out of his room all day. Why has not the man in 1021 been out of his room all day? Because the man hurts. The man's head hurts. His eyes hurt. His back aches. There are knots in the back of his neck. His throat is sore. His nose is stopped up. His ears ring. And his stomach—oh, Lord, don't mention his stomach. The man is also cold.

I know all these things about the man in 1021 because the man is me. (Or is it I? Let's see. Turn it around, "I is the man. Me is the man." Neither one sounds right. It must be "I am the man." "The man am I." That's it—"Because the man am I"? Or am I the man? When you hurt the way I do how can you expect to know who you are?) Anyway, I'm sick; and I'm plenty sick of being sick. Here I am sick in Chicago. Not long ago it was sick in New York. Before that sick in Memphis. Sick in Phoenix. Sick in Mexico City. Sick in Jacksonville. Sick in, sick 'em, stickem, stick 'em up . . . What nutty things go through a guy's head when he lies all alone in a hotel room in a strange city and hurts.

I'm going to quit my job. If I'm going to be sick all the time I might as well drop all outside interests and devote my career to being sick. Probably could be a lot sicker than this if I worked at it a while. Might study and learn and work long hours at being sick, and maybe in time I could become the sickest man in America.

Feel sort of lank again, but what's the use of eating? Just makes me sick. Not a bite since last night, and it didn't stay. Have to have something to eat pretty soon, though. Wish I wasn't so cold. And my topcoat that I've got wrapped around my shoulders—the cloth is rough and hurts my chin.

Somebody trying to get into the room. The key is turning in the lock. Probably the maid. Guess it's late in the afternoon. Wonder where she's been all day? Yes, it's the maid. There are two of them. I hear them talking. The maids walk into the room. Two of them. They see the man in bed. "Oh!" says one maid. And "Oh!" says the other maid. They are startled. I reassure them. "Ladies, do not be alarmed. It is only I. I mean it's only me. I'm sick again. Sick in Chicago this time." I tell them they needn't bother about the room. Except I wish they'd get me another blanket, for I'm cold. So they hurry off, and pretty soon they both come back. "We've got you two blankets," said one of them. "It's no fun being sick away from home."

And I said, "Ladies, I'm just a poor orphant boy. I have no home. Might as well be sick here as anywhere else. It hurts no matter where you are. The blankets, please." So the two maids (both of whom had broken-down feet but were very nice women just the same) put on the two blankets. And one got on one side of the bed, and the other on the other side, and they tucked the covers around me as though I were a little boy.

The day went by and I never knew where it went. And the night too. And the next day. I slept, and daydreamed, and was sick, and dozed jumpily from hour to hour, as though I was leaping across time on stones. On the second day I decided the time had come to eat. So I phoned downstairs and ordered prunes and cream, and an egg and bacon, dry toast and tea. I waited half an hour and phoned again. "Has my order started up yet?" I asked. The man at the other end said, "Guess so. Don't see any orders around the kitchen."

I waited twenty minutes and phoned again. "Now tell me honestly, do you intend to send up my food or not?"

"Coming right up," said the voice. "Well, it better, for I've

· 158 ·

waited three-quarters of an hour and I'm . . ." Bang! The brute had hung up on a sick man.

Finally the food came. "I'm sorry you had to wait," said the boy.

"Well, it wasn't your fault. But I hope you'll give those apes downstairs my kind regards." Instead of prunes, there was pine-apple juice. Instead of one egg, there were two. Instead of tea, it was coffee. The boy was sorry. "I'll change it for you," he said. But I told him it didn't matter, that I was eating merely to observe the conventions, and that I wouldn't keep it long anyhow. And I never said anything truer.

Land of the
Sourdoughs

***Chapter
XI*** WHEN I ARRIVED IN JUNEAU THE PAPERS WERE
full of stories about John S. Bugas, the new G-man who had been
sent up by the Department of Justice to establish a permanent
Alaska office. It turned out that he and I had been fellow passengers part of the way on the ship from Seattle, and he told me about
something that happened when he first got to Juneau. An old
trapper on one of the islands had been missing for months. Occasionally someone would think he saw him in the woods, and it
was generally believed he had gone off his nut. The newspapers
called him a "wild man." Somebody thought he saw him on an
island one day, and a posse went after him. They brought him
back, all right, but it wasn't the right man. He was an old prospector whose boat had gone dead on him, and he had been
marooned. He was pretty well done in.

He wasn't a criminal, but as a matter of routine the authorities
put him on the pan to get his story. Bugas sat in on the questioning. It seems the prospector had got all his gear ashore from the
boat and set up camp and built a fire, and then a spark caught
his mattress and everything he had was burned. He wandered
around the island, and couldn't find much to eat. After a week in
the woods he ran onto a lighthouse tender's cabin, and the tender
asked him in for supper. They sat down to eat, but after a few
moments the light tender excused himself and said he had to go
outside. That made our refugee mad; he thought the light tender
was insulting him because he was so dirty. He jumped up and
yelled and ran into the woods again, and it was a couple of days
later that the posse found him.

Bugas, the new G-man, said to him, "Weren't you a little too sensitive to get mad and run away from your food?" The still unkempt "wild man" glared at him and yelled, "Shut up, you cheechako!" That's the Alaskan term for greenhorn or tenderfoot. The new G-man said he shut up, all right.

The Lady Known as Lou didn't put in an appearance, but I did sit on the deck of a Yukon River boat and hear the story of Klondike Kate from her own lips. The Lady Known as Lou was fiction, but Klondike Kate was real. She went to the North in 1900 to perform in the dance halls of the new Eldorado. She went through White Horse rapids dressed as a boy.

She was a genuine sourdough, but she was no crude nugget—wasn't now and never had been, despite that nickname. She was tall and straight and stately—almost regal. Her table steward told me she had the finest manners and was the most considerate of all the people at his table. He said her manner was that of a queen. Even when she was rolling a cigarette.

In 1900 her name was Kate Rothrock. She was young and beautiful and good. It isn't true that every Klondike dance-hall girl was a prostitute. Kate had her man, all right, and lived with him. But she was a one-man woman; she was in love with him. Everybody in the Klondike, even today, knows the story of Klondike Kate and her man. They lived in Dawson for three years during the boom days—Kate dancing, her man tending bar, working in stores, finally going into a little business. You would know the name of the man if I told it. He became rich and famous, known throughout the United States. And it was Klondike Kate who staked him—shelled out her poke for him, because she loved him, to give him his big chance "outside." And he took it and made good, and then he threw her down.

She didn't cry or squeal. She went to work like a man. She stayed in show business until a knee injury put her out of professional dancing for good. And then she took in washing. Finally she homesteaded a place back in Oregon, and proved up on it. She traded that for a house in Bend, and that one for another. She built herself a beautiful garden, and a fireplace with rocks all of different kinds.

Somehow she could never learn to hate him, even in later years, when she went to him appealingly and was turned away. Even that didn't teach her how to hate him. She stayed in love, and the years passed to ten, and to twenty, and to thirty—and still she couldn't hate him. During all that time she never went back to Dawson. The Klondike was far, far behind her. And then a funny thing happened. She got a letter from a prospector somewhere up on one of the Yukon tributaries. He had seen her name in the paper, and said he remembered her from the dance-hall days of 1900 and wanted to correspond with her. So they corresponded. Finally the prospector went all the way from the Yukon frontier down into Oregon to see Kate Rothrock. And they were married.

It was one of those unbelievable things that sound like fiction. Johnny Matson had fallen in love with Kate Rothrock when she was a Dawson dance-hall girl. But he was a rough, backward man and she was taken anyhow, so he said nothing. And then she disappeared—where, he didn't know. He stayed on in the hills, panning a little gold. Not much—just a little. Through all those years he lived out on the creek alone. And then he found her.

Kate Rothrock was still living in Bend most of the year. But every summer, on the first Yukon boat, she would go north all the way to Dawson to see "her Johnny." They saw each other only twice a year. He would come in from "the crick" for a few days after she got to Dawson. And again for a few days just before she left in the fall, on the last boat out. That's all Kate Rothrock saw of her Johnny. She'd go out on the crick and live, gladly, but he wouldn't let her. "No, he says he waited thirty years for me, and now he's not going to have me living in a cabin up some crick," she said. "This is what he wants me to do, and I want to do it for him." All summer she stayed in Dawson, living in a room in the home of a friend, strolling the dead boardwalks of the town that once roared and fumed to the touch of gold.

"Doesn't it make you sad," I said, "to be in Dawson again, after all that happened to you there? And to see Dawson so quiet and still now, remembering how it used to be?"

She said, "No, I love it. I've learned long, long ago to live within myself. I had to. Memories of the old Dawson are still there, but they don't hurt me. It's beautiful to be back."

A little later my friend Albert Moss said, "I saw you talking to Klondike Kate. I don't expect she told you the real lowdown on her life."

"No, I expect not," I said. "What was the real lowdown?"

And then Mr. Moss told me, from his own memory, slowly and rememberingly as though it was a great epic, the very same story that Klondike Kate had told me. So it was all true. And more so . . .

"I haven't talked to her on the boat," Mr. Moss said, "for I know she wouldn't remember me. But I knew her well in the old days in Dawson. She was a wonderful woman. The man she lived with was a skunk. But I guess she was in love with him. She staked him to everything she had—forty thousand dollars. And then he absolutely repudiated her."

So Klondike Kate Rothrock, who couldn't learn to hate, and her Johnny, who waited thirty years, were going into the sunset together. It was too late now, but they did find each other in time to snatch something—a quality of unusual tenderness, and a beauty surely, the beauty of brown autumn leaves along the northern rivers. Leaves that the frost can't hurt, because the frosts have already touched them.

I had met Mr. Moss at White Horse. He was white-haired, and wore horn glasses, and had a pipe in his mouth all the time. He was the kind of man you could talk with. It turned out that he had gone over the pass to the Klondike, on foot, not once but twice. He made it first in '97, went back outside, and came again in '98. He went through the whole Klondike rush and was one of the thousands who didn't make a million, though I suspect he developed character. He knew eastern Alaska and the Klondike region by heart. He had mushed over it with a dog team, ridden through it on river scows, "siwashed" it on bitter arctic nights, and mellowed it all in his memory like a pleasant summer. He lived now in Seattle, but every spring he went back to Alaska. He had built a fine log cabin up on Porcupine Creek, out of Circle. He had considerable property up there, and a big dredging outfit was turning his land into gold-in-the-pocket at last.

At Dawson we hired a car—Mr. Moss and his friends Mr. and

Mrs. Duane Bush and I—and drove out along Bonanza Creek. The road was just a trail, and sometimes we could hardly get along it. Less than a mile out of town we were in the heart of the golden ground of '98. As far as you could see, the earth was thrown up in raw gravelly ridges—the trail left by electric dredges that gouge and devour the earth and sift out its wealth and spill out the long dikes of goldless gravel behind them. It was a no man's land, without trees or grass or life—the work of the machines that followed the men into the Klondike. All around Dawson, up every creek, the earth was like that. And dredges were still working.

Mr. Moss never found a dime in Dawson ground. His three years of gouging were a complete failure. But he could look back and laugh about it now. It was toward the scene of his last and biggest failure—where Boulder Creek runs into Bonanza—that we headed now. Mr. Moss had never seen the spot since he left it in disgust nearly forty years before. We passed snipers' sluice boxes. We drove across vast washes of white gravel, smooth and slanting, big as farms. They were the hydraulic washings—whole mountains slowly washed away for the gold that was there. We forded creeks. We looked across valleys at green ridges, where Mr. Moss and our driver said there was gold, but nobody had ever found it. Once a prospector, always a prospector. We passed a spot, twenty feet or so below the trail, which they said was the richest small piece of ground in the whole Klondike. From a "fraction"—just a small part of a claim—only a hundred feet square and eight feet deep one man took between two and three million dollars. A few years later he was wandering the streets of Fairbanks, ragged and penniless and crazy for drink.

We came finally to a cabin, beyond which the road was not passable. The valley of Bonanza Creek was half a mile wide there, and filled with the glacierlike washings of the hydraulic lines. And just across, on the other side, was Mr. Moss's monument of failure—the mouth of Boulder Creek. We stood on the bank and looked. Mr. Moss stood, as usual, with his old pipe hanging straight down from the middle of his mouth.

"Nothing looks familiar," he said. "It isn't the way I remembered it. But I know it was right over there.

"The third winter we were here my partner and I sunk everything we had in that spot. We worked all winter thawing ground with open fires, and sinking holes. We put down holes all around that spot. It was hard work. But every place we tried, we hit bedrock. We spent every cent we had and got nothing. A little later a company came in and put down holes not eighty feet away, and went on down. We just happened to pick the biggest rock in the Klondike to work on top of. If we'd gone eighty feet in any direction we'd have hit good stuff."

Mr. Moss chuckled. His final, crowning humiliation was a gem in his memory. He had gone into Dawson without even the price of a meal, and asked a fellow for a job, doing anything.

"Will you cut wood?" the fellow said.

"Sure, I'll cut wood," Mr. Moss said.

So he cut a cord of wood. And then the fellow asked him to carry it into the house and stack it. Inside, he noticed the place was curtained off into a dozen or so little cubicles, and then he noticed several girls and realized what it was. He said he just had to stop and laugh. The girls got the point, and laughed with him. The great prospector—the man who thought he'd find a million, the man who had worked like a dog for three years and spent every penny hunting the Eldorado—finally brought to cutting firewood for a bawdyhouse. He laughed and laughed, and so did the girls.

But he finished the job. The fellow paid him off in gold dust. In the dust he found a little nugget, worth about four dollars. He sent the nugget to his family in the States, and a letter with it saying, "This is the first gold I mined in the Klondike."

"They've still got that nugget, and they don't know the difference, even today," he said. "I never did tell them."

Adolph Biederman was the sort of man we in the States think of when we think of Alaska. He was sixty-eight and tough as nails. He was a small man, brown as leather, and wiry, and he walked with a thump-thump. He spoke with an accent, and with that jumpy, hard-to-follow manner that you frequently find in transplanted foreigners. Biederman was the winter mailman between

Circle and Eagle. For thirty-five years he had driven the dog-team mail routes of bitter central Alaska.

Biederman was born in Bohemia and came to this country when he was thirteen. He wound up in Alaska at the turn of the century and had never been out since—and never intended to go. He married an Indian woman, and had seven or eight children. He lived in a log cabin at Eagle, and always stayed up all night when the boat was in. Biederman loved Alaska. He said he loved it because you were so free. That's what they all said, and I was trying to find out: free from what, free to do what? I couldn't get it, but that doesn't matter. They were free.

The things Biederman had been through would fill a book. I suppose no man knew more about sled dogs, or winter weather, or making his way alone in wild country. He walked with that thump-thump because he had lost the front half of each foot twelve years before. He had let himself get caught—after twenty-five years of knowing better. It happened because he lost his regular dogs. Captain McCann, the skipper of our boat, accused himself of causing Biederman to lose his feet. Biederman's dogs were coming up river on a barge which Captain McCann's boat was pushing. They hit a rock and the barge upset and drowned all the dogs. So Biederman had to borrow a team and start the winter mail run with green dogs. His sled got stuck in an overflow spot. His regular dogs would have circled it, but the new ones didn't, and Biederman's feet got wet. It was forty-two below, and his moccasins were frozen on him before he could cut them off.

He knew he was in for it. He had frozen his feet before, but this time he knew it was for good. He got to an empty cabin not far away, built a fire, and got his boots and moccasins off. And then he went outside, at forty-two below, and walked around in the snow in his bare feet. But it was too late; he couldn't feel anything. He sat down and pulled his big toe away over to one side. It stayed there. Then blisters came on his feet. And the flesh was all black. He was in the cabin four days. When they found him, they sledded him back to Eagle, and later into Circle, where a doctor amputated the foreparts of his feet, a little at a time. The next winter he was running the mail again.

He wore regular shoes in summer, and had phonograph springs

in them to keep the toes from flying up. In winter he wore three pairs of socks, and stuffed the toes full of rabbit fur. Over these he wore moccasins.

It is a hundred sixty-two miles from Eagle to Circle. The winter mail makes the round trip every two weeks—thirteen round trips during the winter—forty-two hundred miles of mushing behind Huskies every winter. Biederman had cabins strung along the route, twenty-five to twenty-eight miles apart. Sometimes he would make it from one cabin to another in four hours; sometimes it took as long as eighteen hours, depending on the weather. When it got under forty below it was almost impossible to go on; dogs perspire through their tongues, and if a dog sticks out its tongue at fifty or sixty below the tongue freezes. Also, the sled's runners seem to stick at that temperature, and it's like pulling a sled over bare ground.

Biederman's boys had grown up now, and they ran the mail most of the time. They were steely, brown, half-breed boys, wiry and bashful and strong. I asked Biederman whether he rode the sleds or mushed behind all the way. He laughed and said, "Well, I never ride the sled, but I'll have to say my boys do. I don't know whether they're lazier or smarter than I am, but they ride the runners most of the time."

Biederman had a great deal of humor, and talked a lot, though there was a northern grimness about him too. He cussed mightily, but he didn't drink or smoke. Quit drinking twenty-eight years ago, because he got drunk and missed collecting $190 somebody owed him. He quit smoking because it was hurting his wind. He used to wear a mustache to cover up his bad teeth. Now that he had false teeth he still wore it. He said it frosted over in wintertime and protected his mouth.

All the way from Seattle I'd been hearing about Nimrod. According to the story, Nimrod was an Alaskan woodsman who lost his teeth, killed a bear, took the bear's teeth and fashioned a crude false plate for himself, and then ate the bear with its own teeth. So, at Eagle, I went to sit at the feet of the great Nimrod and hear the epic yarn in his own words.

I found the story true in its larger elements, but its purveyors had neglected a number of small facts. They neglected, for instance, to state that Nimrod was not an uncouth creature of the wilds, but a cultured gentleman from Maine who still spoke with a Boston drawing-room accent after thirty-nine years in northern isolation. And they didn't mention the fact that Nimrod was an experienced artisan, who could do any sort of minute mechanical work with his hands. Making a set of false teeth was no great task for him.

Nimrod was living way up the creek out of Eagle, and he and his partner were working at a little gold and cutting some wood. The year was 1905. That winter the wolves got in and destroyed all the cache of meat, leaving them with nothing but vegetables and canned foods. Nimrod got scurvy. Within a few months there wasn't a tooth in his head, so he decided to make himself some teeth. He knew how.

For the four front ones he used mountain-sheep teeth. He said they were almost like human teeth, except longer, so he just filed them down. Back of these, four on each side, he used caribou teeth. And for the grinding molars, bear's teeth. Just one on each side—a bear's back tooth is so large it takes the place of two human teeth.

He made his plate of aluminum, drilled out holes for the teeth, set them in, and then worked the warm aluminum back over to hold them tight. It took him a month. He made both uppers and lowers. And he wore them for nearly twenty-five years. He told me he ate a lot of bear meat with them, but not the bear the teeth came from. Eventually a Seattle dentist offered to make him a set of real teeth in exchange for those homemade ones. Nimrod sent in his specifications, and back came the store teeth. He was still wearing them now, after seven years, and the "teeth of the wild" were on display in a Seattle dental shop.

Nimrod's real name was Ervin Robertson. He got the nickname when he was a boy in New England. He was a jeweler by trade for fifteen years in the East before he made the break for Alaska in the '98 days. For more than a third of a century he lived in a cabin "up the crick" from Eagle. He hunted and fished and cut wood and played at gold, but nothing much ever came of anything. Now he was living in a tiny old log cabin in Eagle, a streetless riverbank village of eighty-five people, not more than a dozen of them whites.

Nimrod was one of those perplexing human question marks you find now and then in far spots of isolation. Buried, by choice. But he had never let himself slip into shoddy ways, as most self-exiles do. His speech was professorially precise. He wore a neatly laundered gray shirt with long collar points, and blue trousers with belt and suspenders. He was freshly shaved, and meticulously clean. He apologized for his appearance, said he hadn't cleaned up today, and he kept standing while he talked.

His ancestral tree went back to Scotland, and he still had the family crest between tissues in a cardboard folder. He had scads of relatives in New England, and corresponded with them regularly. I asked why he went to Alaska in the first place, and he said he joined the gold stampede in the hope of making a thousand dollars. He needed that much to develop his ideas for an airplane. "If I had had a thousand dollars I'd have flown long before the other fellows," he said. "But I'm not much nearer to my accomplishment than I was forty years ago." He laughed as he said it, but the note of failure in his voice made it a poignant thing.

Nimrod made his living now by creating small things. He fashioned beautiful hunting knives, and fine gold-wire puzzle rings, and he repaired watches. He was a crack rifle shot, and an ardent hunter. He said he hadn't hunted much in the last year because he had been so busy in the shop. The truth was, he hadn't been able. Constantly he made those little excuses. They were perfectly plain to you as he made them, but you wouldn't let on for anything.

Nimrod had been outside only once in forty years. He probably would never go again. But forty years of isolation had not corroded him. He was still just as polite, just as gay, just as neat, just as gentle as the day he arrived to make a thousand dollars.

The Yukon had very nearly killed Heinie Miller a few months before I met him in 1937, and yet you couldn't get him out of that wilderness of his, there where Sheep Creek runs into the Yukon. He lived alone in a cabin, with nothing around but trees and Indians and wild animals and the big outdoors. And him originally a city feller too—born and raised in Chicago. He had never been outside since the day he came, thirty-seven years ago. "Hell, no, and I ain't goin' out," he said. "I didn't lose nothin' down in the States I have to go back after."

Our boat stopped at Heinie's woodpile early in the morning. We had heard about his catastrophe before we got there. The ice breakup had played havoc with his home and his woodpile. They were still a mess.

Heinie and the Indians who worked for him would cut about seven hundred cords of wood each winter. They stacked it on the riverbank to feed the fireboxes of the Yukon steamers during the summer. By spring their year's work was done—piled in beautiful rows along the riverbank. But this year nature had taken a hand. The breaking ice was pushed far up the bank, and then flood-waters came rushing out on top of it and crushed everything before them.

Heinie saw the flood break and started running. He had got less than a hundred yards when it was up to his waist, so he climbed a tree. He stayed in the tree two hours. Then the tree started to go. Heinie got down and waded in water up to his shoulders, toward the woodpile. "By the jumping —— —— ——, but it was cold," said Heinie. He made the top of the wood-pile, and there he was marooned for sixteen hours. It was just above freezing, and pouring rain. Ten feet of water all around him, and the wood liable to go floating down the river any minute.

The water suddenly went down, as fast as it had risen, and Heinie got off the woodpile at 4:00 A.M. He started walking to a trapper's cabin, two and a half miles away. He was so done up it took him six hours. He thought sure he'd catch pneumonia and die. He dried out and stayed with the trapper two days. "And damned if I even got a cough out of it," he said.

But even so, nature served Heinie pretty badly. He lost around a hundred cords of wood (at eight dollars a cord). And his new log house, which he had just finished a year before, was swept off its foundation and tipped over. His radio was ruined, and his ice-box and stove and all his tools. He said he never would find lots of his stuff. It would take all summer to rebuild the cabin.

One of the pilots on our boat said, "You better move out and go to California to live." And Heinie said, "By —— ——, no. I love this country and I'm gonna stay right here and die right here."

Heinie was getting along in years. His clothes were old and not too clean, which could be said of almost everybody who lived in the woods. He needed a shave, and a large brown string of tobacco juice trickled down each side of his whiskery chin. His eyes were as blue as the sky. I had noticed that about so many of those men in the Yukon country. But Heinie's eyes were going bad. He had a cataract, and he was scared to death he would have to go to Seattle for an operation.

One morning a couple of years ago Heinie had dreamed he was back in Chicago. He woke up and sat up in bed, still thinking he was in Chicago, and thought, What the hell am I doing here? And then he realized he wasn't in Chicago at all. "Damn, but I was glad," he said. And yet he subscribed to the Chicago *Tribune*. He had been a newsboy on the *Tribune* when he was a kid. He said he couldn't read it any more, but he still took it.

There were trappers and Indians scattered through this country, and they got around a lot, by snowshoe and boat. Whenever anybody showed up, it was food and drink time. "The Indians eat me out of house and home," Heinie said. "They always show up at mealtime, and I can't say no. I've been trying to say no for twenty years but I can't do it." An Indian named Willie drove Heinie's caterpillar tractor, dragging the logs down from the hills. "Hell, them Indians come all the way from Dawson, a hundred miles, just to watch Willie drive the cat," Heinie said, "and I have to feed 'em."

Every couple of years Heinie would take the boat up to Dawson, and three days later he would have shed about nine hundred dollars and would be weak and weary from too much celebrating, and ready to go back to his cabin on the riverbank among the trees and the mosquitoes.

At Fort Yukon, Alaska, I met a remarkable woman. Nine years before, her world had come to an end in that mosquito-infested village; she had had more than she could take. Two of her boys had just been buried—mysteriously drowned in the Yukon. Her husband had quit cold on the family. Everything was on her shoulders, and they had grown too weary after fifteen years of half-living and scraping and scratching in the arctic woods and villages. It was time to quit. Nobody cared anyhow.

She led her four children down to the riverbank. "Come on, let's go for a little ride in the canoe," she said. It would be easy. Over the side with them, and herself over last. You live only a minute in the Yukon River; the cold water stops your heart. They were ready to step into the boat when an old man with long whiskers came and tapped the woman on the shoulder. "Come walk up to my cabin," he said. "I want to talk to you." She barely knew the man, but she went. And the man said, "I know you don't want to go onto charity. You can make a living on the trap line. It won't be easy, but it will be an opportunity for you to support yourself and the children."

So Mrs. Maud Berglund turned trapper. She bundled her four children into a gasoline boat, and the old man went with them. For two weeks they chugged up the Porcupine and its tributaries. The baby died on the way. They buried him, and went on. They chugged up the Black River, and up a river that runs into the Black. Fort Yukon is north of the Arctic Circle and approximately three-quarters of a mile beyond the end of the earth; but they didn't stop until they were two hundred eighty miles beyond Fort Yukon. Then they camped on the bank of a river, under a mountain slope. They built a log house and fixed it up with stuff they had bought on two thousand borrowed dollars.

When I met them, the three little girls were young women. The two thousand dollars had been paid back. There was a little in the bank. And they were still trapping.

Only nine times in the nine years had Mrs. Maud Berglund and her three daughters been back to the "metropolis" of Fort Yukon. Eleven months of the year they did not see a living soul. They lived alone among snow and wolves and moose and mountains. Just after the spring ice-break they would come down river with their pelts, on a combined vacation and business trip. They sold their furs at auction, and loaded their boats with a year's supply of staples. The round trip took two weeks and they tarried in

Fort Yukon a couple of weeks. They were gone from home just a month.

They made the trip to Fort Yukon in two open motorboats, with a small scow that they pushed ahead of them. At night they camped in tents. Besides the winter's catch of furs, the boats carried bedding and personal belongings, also seven rifles. And twenty-two Husky dogs. They had to bring the dogs and guns and clothing with them, for nobody lived in Berglundville but themselves.

Mrs. Berglund had a one-room log cabin in Fort Yukon, which was occupied only those two weeks out of the year. The twenty-two dogs were staked out behind the hut, and what a howling they set up when strangers came around! I was lucky enough to catch the Berglunds there, and I spent an evening in the log cabin and a forenoon with them. I shot their guns at targets. And they told me about themselves, as helpfully and as simply as people can talk.

"This is just a stopping place," said Mrs. Berglund, apologizing for the cabin. "So we don't try to keep it nice. Our home is 'up there.' I wish you could see it. We have made a real home of it."

Mrs. Berglund was a handsome gray-haired woman—fine of feature, refined in speech, easy and gentle in her manner. I did not learn her early story, but once long ago she had painted in oils, and she had come to Alaska from Oregon twenty-five years before. The rough life seemed not to have touched her personality at all.

But her three daughters were children of nature. They were deeply tanned; their hands showed hard work; their shoulders and legs were strong like a man's. They were Marion Hazel, Evelyn Maud, and Elsie May, and their ages were fourteen to twenty-one. These girls grew up in the woods. Elsie May was carried over the trap line by dog sled for two years before she was big enough to make it herself. All their education was given them by their mother. They knew no life but that of the trapper. They had never been south of Fort Yukon—never seen a village with real streets or brick buildings. They had no conception of what a city is like. They didn't know much about men. They had never drunk or smoked, or danced or played cards. They wouldn't know what the words "automat" or "salon" meant. But they had to shoot only once at a running moose, and they could freeze their feet without crying.

Their hobby, their amusement, their recreation, their joy, were all in one thing: their dog teams. Each girl had her own team, her own sled, her own rifles. They would talk dog to you until you were black in the face. They loved their dogs above all else.

Although they did not know our world, the girls were smart, and they were zestful and eager. Their conversation flowed out like a torrent, and their eyes shone. They accepted new acquaintances at face value; after the first few minutes of bashfulness, they talked enthusiastically; out came guns and wolfskins to show you, and moose antlers, and stories of little incidents in excited snatches. Those three girls were the freshest in spirit of any women I had ever seen.

I asked them, "Do you ever look at pictures of people or scenes in the cities?" One of them said, "Yes, we've seen pictures of New York and places like that. But we don't know anything about what it's like, and I don't think we'd ever want to go there. We've got too much freedom up here."

"Are you so busy that you don't have time to get lonesome?" I asked Mrs. Berglund.

"Well, we're busy all right, and we don't get lonesome much any more. But when we first went up, I would get in these black sloughs and I couldn't see daylight for days. The girls are a reflection of my mood, and when I got down we'd all get down. The radio has helped that a lot. We've got two radios now, and when we get low we go turn on the radio and we're soon out of it."

In their cabin at home they had gasoline lamps, which make good lights for reading. They picked up books and magazines on their annual visits to town. But the girls didn't care much for reading; they turned on the radio instead. They had a camera, and on this trip out they had brought four rolls of films to be developed.

Every year as soon as they returned from Fort Yukon to their cabin, they started a busy season of picking and canning berries and wild fruit. And they caught salmon with a fish wheel, and dried it and stored it for winter feed for the dogs. They repaired their dog sleds and the harness, and got the traps in order, and stored and packed the four tons of supplies they had purchased in Fort Yukon. When the fall freeze-up came they cut ice from the river and stored it in the ice well. They would kill a moose apiece and fry the steaks and then freeze them.

In the late fall, when the snow was on and the season opened, they started their real winter's work—five months of lonely running of trap lines. They had more than two hundred miles of lines, along which were scattered some four hundred traps. They ran the lines with a dog team apiece, hitched to a sled carrying traps, bait, guns, dog feed, tents and sleeping bags, and frozen food.

John Roberts and one of the girls started out together. Mr. Roberts was the long-whiskered old man who had tapped Mrs. Berglund on the shoulder and given her the opportunity to do something besides jump into the Yukon River. He had trapped with them ever since, and though he was now aged and shaky he could still shoot as straight as a G-man and tramp behind the dogs all day. Mrs. Berglund and the two other girls went in the opposite direction, setting traps as they went. Only a trapper could tell you why they set them where they did—but they knew the right places, by tracks and trails and gnawed bark and little things.

Every fifteen miles or so they had a log cabin about ten feet square, with a door so low you had to crawl in. They tried to reach a cabin each night, but sometimes they didn't. Every cabin had a stove and a couple of bunks. Candles were used for light.

Frequently a branch line of traps was laid at right angles to the main line. In following the branches they would separate, so a good part of their winter was spent in traveling absolutely alone. They were away from home four to ten days each trip, and on the return visits at home they stayed only a day or two. So the majority of their winter nights were spent in tiny candle-lit way cabins scores of miles from home, hundreds of miles from other human beings.

They would get to some of the traps once a week, but a month might go by between visits to the others. "Don't you lose a lot of fur, waiting so long?" I asked. "Don't wolves and things eat the trapped animals?"

"No, not much," Mrs. Berglund said. "They die pretty quickly, and the fresh snow covers them. We couldn't find the traps ourselves if we didn't know the country so well."

"How do you kill the ones that aren't already dead?" I asked.

"We have to shoot the wolves, lynx, and wolverine," she said. "The others are smaller, and we rap them on the head with a club."

The Berglund girls hated wolverines. They said they were mean and vicious, and would fight you to the last breath. But it was the marten that got under Mrs. Berglund's skin. "They cross their little paws above their heads, and look up at you so pitifully, it's all I can do to hit one of them," she said. "When I first went up, I said I was going to save pelts and have myself a fine marten coat. But I don't want one now."

The Berglunds never went out unarmed, yet they had never been injured by a wild animal, except for little things like squirrel bites. Wolves had never bothered them, though they had had narrow escapes from charging moose. All four of them seemed to be in awe of a moose's killing powers.

"One jumped right over my sled and hit me with his hoof," said Evelyn, the middle girl. "The gun was lashed to the sled and I couldn't get at it in time to stop him, so I just ducked. Believe me, I had it out by the time he came back."

"And you ought to see a moose strike with his foreleg," said Hazel. "Why, a moose could reach clear across this room. You'd think he had India-rubber legs."

Home from the trap line late one night after ten days' absence, the Berglunds walked up to the cabin and found a bear inside. He had upset things pretty badly, enjoyed a good meal, and then lain down on Mrs. Berglund's bed to rest. They made a gasoline torch, and one of the girls held it while Mrs. Berglund shot Mr. Bear.

The girls said bears would attack you if surprised; a moose would attack you any time; a wolverine would fight you in the trap; wolves were cowards, and had never made any show at getting ferocious with them. They hated wolves anyhow.

Mother and daughters liked to tell funny stories about their experiences. Mrs. Berglund told one on herself, to get it out before the girls told it. There is a bird known as the "camp robber." He is a huge nuisance, because he gets into the cabin and eats up your grub. The Berglunds had a persistent one, so Mrs. Berglund decided to shoot him right into the Happy Hunting Ground. She got out the .22 rifle. Every time the camp robber would light she'd start to get a sight on him, but just before she could shoot he would jump. That happened half a dozen times, and she was getting exasperated. She knelt and waited, the gun to her shoulder, ready to shoot quick the next time. And what did the camp robber do but fly around the cabin, up over Mrs. Berglund's shoulder, and light right on the barrel of her gun. She went in the house and shut the door in disgust.

The Berglund women wore men's clothing all year except when they came down to Fort Yukon. Then they dressed in calico prints. Up at the camp they'd have frozen to death in dresses. They had all frozen their hands and feet many times, but had never had any serious aftereffects. Fortunately, they had never had any critical illnesses or injuries up there. If they had, it would have taken two weeks of hard sledding to get word out to a doctor. And Mrs. Berglund wouldn't have had a doctor in the house anyhow. She knew all the home remedies, including castor oil. She said that even if one of them was to break an arm or leg they could handle it all right.

Mrs. Berglund gave me a little jar of cottonwood salve for my mosquito bites. They made it by crushing the green buds of cottonwood trees and boiling them with moose grease. The salve had a woodsy smell, and it stopped the itching within five minutes. They also used it for cuts and sores.

The Berglunds got mail only by chance. If an Indian was traveling north from Fort Yukon, the postmaster would give him any mail for the Berglunds. He would take it as far as he was going, but it might lie there for a month before another Indian happened to be going on. It was two days by dog sled from the Berglunds' cabin to their mailbox, which was on a tripod stuck in the river ice. They would get there about every two weeks, but usually nothing was in the box. A letter received in Fort Yukon in September might not reach them until April.

Despite such isolation the Berglund women could take care of themselves. The first year they were up there they caught an Indian robbing their trap line. Mrs. Berglund told him to get out of that country, and said that if she ever saw him around there again she'd put a bullet through him. "And I would too," she said. It's hard to realize that so soft-spoken and refined a woman could stand alone in the deep snow at forty below, two hundred eighty miles from nowhere, holding a rifle in her arm, and tell a man she'd kill him—and mean it.

I said to Mrs. Berglund, "You speak so often of the cabin up there as your real home. Do you expect to stay there forever?"

"No," she said, "we'll stay till the price of furs or the run of pelts drops so that we can't break even. Then we'll come out. I expect we'll live on the south coast somewhere. But we'll never leave Alaska. We've been here too long. Sometimes I like it up there, and sometimes I feel I can't bear it another minute. My health hasn't been good for the last two years—I've lost thirty pounds. We all have too much meat in our diet. And I've got so I suffer from the cold."

Living in the arctic isn't any bed of feather mattresses, no matter what some people say. In summer the mosquitoes buzz in poisonous, tormenting clouds. The Berglund women said that sometimes they were so thick you couldn't see to build a campfire, and that you could run your cupped hand along the side of your face and come away with hundreds of them in your fist. In the fall, when the mosquitoes die, the gnats come to life. Mrs. Berglund said they are worse than mosquitoes—they get in your eyes, and up your nose, they burrow in your hair, they make life a misery. And when the gnats go, then comes the winter.

You may read in the booklets that the winters in Alaska aren't so bad because they're dry. But just talk to some of the people who have been through them. At sixty below, your fingers freeze while you're unhitching a dog. You must move with the caution of a man with a bad heart; to breathe hard is to frost your lungs. You dare not perspire; your clothes would freeze on you. To get your feet wet is to lose your feet. To touch a piece of metal is worse than a bad burn. The Berglund women have seen it seventy-eight below, and they don't know how much more, for that was the last mark before the mercury went on down into the bulb. And don't think you don't feel the cold, either. "You shiver," said Evelyn, who was born to it, "until you just can't shiver any more."

But they kept on trapping. Nine years in the Far North, alone. Four women and an old man. Fighting, as we all do, for life. And what did the four women trappers make from all this work? Well, here was that last winter's catch—twelve mink, fifteen lynx cats, eleven wolves, two ermine, thirty-one marten, and one wolverine. These brought about sixteen hundred dollars. Their supplies for the coming year would run them about six hundred dollars. That left a profit of one thousand dollars. Some years they did a little better; other years they barely made "grubstake," as they called it. But on the whole they were keeping well ahead of the game.

Just before our boat left, Mrs. Berglund told me a secret. "Mr. Roberts and I are going to be married," she said. "He'll just be in his overalls and me in a calico dress. There won't be any fuss. And in a couple of weeks we'll be on our way back in again. Nobody will ever know how big his heart is, or what he's done for us. He was the only one who sensed what I had come to that day nine years ago down by the river bank."

You don't burn up with this thing called love, I guess, when you're knocking at the gates of threescore and more. But there is a deep thing called gratitude, and there is another thing known as human companionship, and the two put together sometimes do just as well as love, I guess, or maybe even a little better.

I had always been skeptical about this all-night-daylight business. It was my belief that it would be an inferior brand, pumped up by the Chamber of Commerce, and not really what an honest man would call daylight at all. But, as usual, I was wrong. We had actual daylight all night long. (This was in June.) True, it wasn't so light at midnight as at noon. But you could stand out in the open at midnight, anywhere on the whole mainland of Alaska, and read a newspaper with ease. The light would be about the way it is in the Midwest a half hour after sunset, or on a very cloudy day. Not bright, but you could see. If you were inside a house you couldn't quite see to read a paper, but it was light enough for you to see everything in the room.

I had heard that this daylight upset your sleeping schedule, so that you couldn't sleep in the summer. Well, I could sleep all right when I went to bed, but I would monkey around and not think about going to bed. It didn't look like bedtime, and the first thing you knew it would be one o'clock. You would turn in, feeling a little silly about going to bed in broad daylight. And then an hour later you'd wake up with the sun blazing through the window. That was the biggest kick of the all-night light to me.

I'm an eight-hour-sleep man. If I don't get eight hours I bite off people's heads the next day. But for weeks in Alaska I didn't have more than five hours any night and seemed to think nothing of it. And didn't get sleepy in the daytime, either. People in Fairbanks laughed and said that in the summer people set their alarm clocks to go to bed by, instead of to get up by.

Certain of my helpful friends thought that I should live life more in the raw, instead of just going around and passively looking at things. Well, the cup of those dear friends should run over like a waterfall; I had twenty-four hours of the rawest living I could take. It consisted of riding over Richardson Highway from Fairbanks to Valdez—three hundred seventy-two miles, all night and all day over a mountainous gravel road—standing up in the back end of a truck. I went in a truck because the bus ran only on Thursdays and I had to go on a Tuesday.

When I arranged passage with the truck company I was under the impression that there would be just the driver and myself. But when we highballed it out of Fairbanks in a cloud of dust at high noon there were a white woman and a half-breed girl up front with the driver, and two Swedes and myself third-classing it among the bedrolls and spare tires in the back.

The driver was hurrying, and he crowded every curve to the skidding point. He took a gambling chance that what appeared to be a hole in the road ahead wasn't a hole—and ninety-nine times out of a hundred he lost. For three hundred seventy miles he pushed that truck for every inch it was worth, and we took the result back there in the bounding truck bed.

It was so rough you could neither sit down nor stand up. You couldn't keep a cigarette lighted. My shoes wouldn't stay laced. When we got to Valdez our shins and knees were barked and our shoulders were black and blue; our eyes were bloodshot, our faces wind-burned. For the first few miles we tried sitting on rolls of canvas and duffel bags, but there wasn't anything to hold to, and you couldn't see the bumps coming. So we stood up. That was better; you could hold to the side and watch for bumps ahead and stand on your toes like a dancer, giving yourself a spring cushion when the shock came. We stood for six hours. Then we were in the mountains amidst snow, the sun was behind a mountain, and the thermometer stood just at freezing. We had no overcoats. And the wind—when you stand up and face the world at forty and forty-five miles an hour without a windshield on a night like that you've bitten off more than you can chew. It was impossible. We had to sit down out of the wind.

For the next six hours we sprawled over the floor of that truck like epileptics. We rolled in canvas. We came unrolled. We were thrown, jerked, propelled, shot, upended, somersaulted, from one wall of that truck to the other—up and down, sideways, scrambled. Once I was thrown from the back of the truck clear to the front, leaving a piece of my knee on the corner of a box as I went. And once, just after hitting a whopper of a bump, I looked around and there was the oldest of the Swedes—he must have been seventy—lying in the corner flat on his back, his arms and legs sticking straight up, like a dead rabbit. I had to laugh, and he saw me and laughed too.

After that it rained, and then it poured. We tried to cover up with canvas. We shivered; we shook; the chill ate in and through us, and it seemed that we were suffering beyond endurance. And we couldn't curl up and shiver in a rigid civilized manner, because we couldn't keep our balance long enough.

I don't know what might have happened if the driver hadn't decided to stop, along about midnight. We went into Paxson's roadhouse, a rustic log affair up among the mountains and lakes. The midnight light was a deep, ominous dusk. We warmed around the tin stove for half an hour, ate the hot supper they fixed for us, and then piled in for a three-hour nap. By 3:00 A.M. we were up and away again. The sun was shining brightly by then, but it gave off the same amount of heat as that generated by a hundred-pound cake of ice. The road was still astoundingly rough. I never closed my eyes, but the rest of the journey I remember hardly at all.

I do recall that about 5:00 A.M. the old Swede's hat blew off. By the time he could pound on the cab roof and get the driver stopped, the hat was a quarter of a mile back. I ran back and got it, but I don't deserve any credit, for I didn't know what I was doing.

Some time around noon the truck stopped and the driver said we were in Valdez. I went to a hotel and right to bed.

The Bering and
the Aleutians

Chapter
XII Our takeoff from Anchorage, Alaska, was auspicious and certainly boded no ill. We flew in a cabin monoplane on pontoons, headed for faraway Good News Bay on the Bering Sea. Six hundred miles, and we started at three-thirty in the afternoon and expected to be there that night.

Pilot Ralph Savory wore hip boots and overalls, a leather jacket, and a canvas hat around which was draped a mosquito net, and the airplane was typical of Alaskan workaday flying. Hooked onto the cabin walls were a rifle and an oar. In the emergency kit was concentrated grub for three weeks. One seat had been taken out to make room for sacks of mail, boxes tied with rope, boots, bed rolls, a coil of cable, and other paraphernalia of the frontier. The floor was covered with dried mud.

We flew right across the great Alaska Range, dog-legging between the peaks, with snow-topped mountains on either side. We saw so many moose I lost count, and I got so I could pick out a lone moose in a clearing as quickly as the rest. We saw half a dozen black bears waddling through the brush, and one mother bear with two cubs. Up among the mountain peaks we saw small herds of caribou traveling on the more level fields of snow. And we saw white mountain sheep by the dozen, running along paths so narrow and precipitous that it made you dizzy to look down at them.

We made McGrath, Alaska, a log-cabin town, at six in the evening, feeling fine. We landed in the Kuskokwim River and taxied up to the bank. Two natives in overalls came out to catch our lines. Each was drinking a can of beer and each took time to drain the last drop before he bothered with the lines.

"Well, guess we'll stay here all night," the pilot said. We didn't know why, and don't know yet, but that's what he said. So we stayed. Everything seemed to be going fine till about eleven o'clock that night, when somebody yelled that the steamboat was coming. It came, all right, full blast around the bend, and smacked right into the tail of our airplane tied up at the bank. I could hear the frail canvas ripping, and it was like a rip in my heart. The thought passed through my mind, we're stuck here forever.

And we were—or so it seemed. Two days passed, while the pilot patched and fixed and doped up holes, and I got close to the paper-doll-cutting stage. We fought mosquitoes the whole time. Inside the cabin, you dashed around like a fool with the spray gun. Outside, you didn't dare lift your face net or take off your gloves. And cold—we were chilled to the bone. And there was nothing to do. You were too miserable to read. You loafed in the store, but it was cold there too, and all you heard was a bedlam of senseless filth from the drunken loafers. A good big part of the population, both native and white, was drunk. The whites would shake their heads and say how awful it was to see the natives drunk, but I couldn't see that color made much difference.

We took off from McGrath into the late sun and droned to the westward toward the Bering Sea. I sat beside Pilot Savory and felt big. In an hour we landed in Sleitmut, just long enough to throw out a mailsack to two men in mosquito nets on the riverbank. Sleitmut wasn't on the map, but it had a niche in Alaskan history because the post office had been held up the preceding winter, and the robbers had got away. Now, it's almost impossible for robbers to get away in Alaska. A man could hardly camp anywhere in all Alaska without being seen very shortly by someone—a wandering prospector, an Indian hunting moose, a dog-team driver, or a mere traveler between villages. Everybody knows everybody. A stranger in Alaska sticks out like a red flag. That's what made it so remarkable that the Sleitmut robbers got away. But, you see, they weren't strangers. The people knew who did it, but just couldn't prove it.

Good News Bay is in far southwestern Alaska, a long way from anywhere else. It is in a country that is bleak and without trees— a country that has bitter, blowy winters, and summers that aren't much better than a gusty March morning. If the sun shines for a total of three days in summer, it sets a weather record. Yet tiny vivid flowers were blooming among the rocks on the mountain-tops. If you walked across the tundra a gaunt red fox might go loping off ahead of you. Reindeer roamed the tundra in herds of thousands. An occasional walrus came onto the beach. Beautiful white swans rested on the swampy lakes of the flat land. It was a weird country. And in it lay Platinum, the new, the great, the fabulous city of metal—Alaska's latest "strike," the place they were stampeding to, the Dawson of 1937.

It could not rightly be called a city, a town, or even a village. It would have done well to muster a population of one hundred, counting Eskimos and a dog or two. Crowded up close together, it wouldn't have covered a city block. As it was, it didn't cover more than four. It had fifteen buildings, including the four Chic Sales. It had fifteen tents. The fabulous city of Platinum!

On the strength of what I'd heard, I had spent good money to fly there in order to gather a little blood and thunder. And here is what I found:

There wasn't a gambling hall in Platinum. There wasn't a beer parlor. There wasn't a dance hall. There were eight white women, and not one of them was a floozy. One storekeeper had been to law school. Many of the test drillers were recent college graduates. You saw mining engineers in green uniforms, and government men making surveys, and honest Swedes going seriously about their jobs. One store sold beer and hard liquor, but I saw only two cans of beer drunk there. I didn't see a drink of whisky taken. I didn't see anybody drunk. You couldn't spend even twelve hours in any other town in Alaska and say that. Everybody was working hard and making good money. Wages out at the placer diggings ran from seven to fifteen dollars a day with keep. But you had to make good money; it cost two hundred dollars to fly to Platinum and back to Anchorage, and your working season lasted only five months, from late May to late October.

It was a bleak place. And yet I felt more at home with the people of Platinum and felt less bleakness of spirit than in any other place I visited in Alaska.

I was the first man ever to be shaved in the city of Platinum by Alaska's famous lady barber. Her name was Alice Forsgren. She had just thrown up the sponge in Bethel, where she first won fame, and migrated to fresher fields. She got to Platinum only two days ahead of me, and wasn't even set up for business yet when I dropped in out of the sky, my whiskers undulating in the slipstream. I approached and said, "Madam, shave me." She was baking a pie, and she said all right, if I'd wait till she got through with the pie. So I waited, and then she got a pitcher of hot water off the stove and we walked to her sister's tent, by which time the water had practically turned to ice. In the tent we got a camp chair for me to sit on, then piled empty boxes behind it till they were up to my shoulders, and put a pillow on them, and I sat down and leaned back and heaved a great sigh of farewell.

But everything went off all right. I hadn't been shaved by a barber more than half a dozen times in my life, so I don't know whether it was a good shave. At least I came out alive.

I asked how she happened to become a barber. She said that her sister, Mrs. Bill Hurst, who used to live at Bethel, wrote to her in North Dakota, suggesting that maybe a woman could make a good living in Alaska at barbering. So Alice went to barber college in Fargo, and a few months previous to my historic shave she blew into Bethel, at the mouth of the Kuskokwim, lather flying and blade flashing in the fog.

Her first customers were two prospectors who paid her five dollars each for a shave, just as a stunt. Things went pretty well for a while, and then I guess the novelty of having a lady barber wore off. As one fellow told me in Bethel: "We've been shaving and cutting our own hair here for fifty years, so we don't really need a barber. And although we make money, a dollar for a hair-cut and fifty cents for a shave is pretty steep."

Then Alice's sister and her husband moved to Platinum and

started a restaurant. The sister sent word to Alice to come down, so Alice packed her clippers and hair lotion and hopped the first plane. In addition to barbering, she baked pies and stuff for her sister's lunchroom, and did washing and ironing which they took in from the citizens.

You couldn't see any mining by sitting in the village of Platinum, so Pilot Savory and I decided to walk out to the diggings on the other side of Red Mountain—a mere ten miles. We started very bravely, but mosquitoes followed us in a swarm and walking was tough. The western Alaska tundra is full of what they call "niggerheads," which are tufts of grass-covered soil about the size of a bucket, sticking up a couple of feet. In some places they shiver like jello when you step on them, but here they were hard, and we jumped from one to the other. Finally we made the foothill slope and started up. As we climbed, the wind off the Bering Sea grew stronger and blew the mosquitoes away, and when we stopped to rest we were quickly chilled. We seemed to be far, far away from anywhere. We felt a great isolation, and a genuine closeness to the natural earth.

After two hours and a half we made Dave Strandberg's platinum camp on Clara Creek. On one slope sat half a dozen frame cabins where the men slept and ate. The creek bed was all torn and eroded where the dragline had dug up the gravel and the sluices had spilled it out again, minus its platinum. Draglining for platinum is exactly the same as draglining for gold. The shovel gets a mouthful of gravel from the creek bed, lifts it up, swings around, and dumps it into a large box set up twenty feet or so on wooden pilings. Up there stands a man directing a hydraulic "giant," from which gushes a three-inch stream of muddy water. The water shoots onto the newly dumped gravel and washes it down into the sluice box, a slanting trough about two feet wide and fifty yards long, with steel riffles in the bottom. The dirt and water go on out the other end, and the platinum, which is even heavier than gold, settles to the bottom.

The pilot and I stood around for about an hour talking to the men and watching the stream of water making the dirt fly, but we didn't see any platinum, and we couldn't see any romance about it. So we hoisted our packs and started plowing across the next mountain to Olsen's camp, three miles away.

Olsen's was on Squirrel Creek, a couple of miles from the sea. There were half a dozen bunkhouses, a big cookhouse, a couple of small homes for the owners, an office, a radio shack, warehouses, and repair shops, and there were electric lights. Savory and I dragged into camp just a little before 6:00 P.M. Our feet hurt and our stomachs were gaunt. We knew they would put us up and feed us and not charge a cent, for that is the etiquette of mining camps, but we didn't know just what the standard of living might be. You can imagine our surprise when we walked up to the cookhouse, some six thousand miles from Broadway, and saw standing on the steps a handsome woman in a green smock-uniform, ready to ring the dinner triangle.

It was Mrs. Pearl Gustafson, wife of the welder at the Olsen camp. She took us back and introduced us to Mrs. Brown, the chief cook, and Mrs. Ed Olsen, wife of the camp owner. Savory and I were flabbergasted to see so many women around. They got us hot water to wash up in. And then we ate with the men at a long table. And, boy, the grub they put out for those miners! We had chowder, red fresh salmon and dressing, baked potatoes, string beans, carrots and peas, cake and peaches, and all kinds of jellies and sauces. Hors d'oeuvres and finger bowls wouldn't have surprised me, but I guess they forgot them.

After supper we went down to where the dragline was working on Platinum Creek, half a mile from camp. They worked two ten-hour shifts, so the dragline was idle twice daily, for two hours each time. This was one of those periods, so we saw the sluice box when it wasn't flooded with water. That was another disillusionment. They were to have the "cleanup" next day, which meant that in the box right there before our eyes was probably fifteen thousand dollars' worth of platinum. But do you think we could find a single little grain? Nope. Not a one. The superintendent and I got down on our knees and dug around in the fine black sand behind the riffles with the point of a knife. Of course, I wouldn't have known platinum if I'd seen it, but the superintendent couldn't find any either. He said that was always the way

—when you wanted to find a nugget to show somebody, there never were any.

When we got back to camp, Mrs. Olsen said Savory and I were to sleep in the back end of the office building. So we went back, and there we were in a little apartment with twin beds and electric lights and extra blankets, and even an alarm clock. Roughing it.

When the alarm clock went off it was six o'clock in the morning, and it was cold. Savory and I yelled when we pulled our cold overalls over our bare legs. The water from the washpan was like a slap in the face. It didn't take us long to get outside into the early sunshine. They told us to climb straight up over the mountain and down the other side to the sea, and then walk the beach back to Platinum. It was only nine miles this way, they said. There was a preposterous springiness in our muscles, and we were glad to be alive. By seven o'clock we were halfway up the mountain, though sagging a little. The ground began to level off near the top and we almost ran the last few steps. Suddenly a thousand feet below us lay the beach and beyond it, as far as you could see, the blue of the Bering, immobile and silent. And peaceful. We sat on a rock for a long time.

After a while we started down. The slope was steep, and plungingly hard on our knees. We passed a claim stake with a tobacco can tacked to it. We lifted the lid and took out the claim papers, and saw it had been staked by a man I'd met in Seward. No matter where you go in Alaska, you know somebody. Finally we came down to the beach, where the gentle surging surf beat a rhythm for us to march by. And so we marched northward along the shore of the Bering Sea. Gradually we grew weary. Our feet sank into the sand where the ebbing tide had left it soft; our heels began to blister, and our knees to creak. Twenty miles in two half days is a lot of activity for a couple of cheechakos.

We passed a tent, and a pretty young girl hailed us. She wore riding pants and boots, and a blue turtleneck sweater, and was carrying a red leather jacket and an aluminum double boiler. She was Margaret Culver, and she had walked out to her father's drilling camp before breakfast, and was now starting back. She could walk much faster than we could, but she stayed with us. At first I tried to swagger a little to make an impression on her, but my knees hurt so I decided to hell with it, and fell back into my natural plowman's waddle.

And so we plodded painfully on, aching legs building mile upon weary mile. And somehow, at some vague point in our pilgrimage, we attained the oasis of Platinum and fell blindly into our airplane, and lay there.

Later, while we were waiting for the tide to float our plane off the beach, Savory and I decided to kill time by doing a little shooting. He got his emergency .22 rifle out of the plane, and we stood on the beach and threw tin cans into the water and shot at them. Not only shot at them—we hit them.

All this cannonading soon attracted all the Eskimo children in town. They came and stood behind us, and admired our wizardry with the flintlock so much that they began throwing in cans for us to shoot at. We sank them so fast it kept the kids busy running after more. They gathered them from all over the village, and I think we pretty well cleaned up the town's rubbish that afternoon. Naturally tin cans disappear pretty fast when a rifleman sinks twelve cans with twelve shots. (That was me!)

Once when it was Savory's turn to shoot, I sat down on the beach to watch him. A friendly Eskimo dog came up and nosed and pawed all over me, and I petted him a while. Then I happened to remember—or rather was startled into remembering—that Eskimo dogs live on dead fish. And by dead fish I don't mean fish that are just a little dead. I mean fish that are awfully dead. So I yelled "mush," and the dog scrammed. But it was too late. I had already become saturated with an odor which could scarcely be described as *toujours l'amour,* whatever that means. I beat it back to the roadhouse and hunted up Frances Berg, who was a very beautiful girl. I was embarrassed, but I finally asked her if she had any perfume. She dug up a bottle and poured it all over my sweater. After that you could detect me from a quarter of a mile away, and Savory said he didn't know whether it was worse to smell like a dead fish or a beauty parlor. Only he didn't say beauty parlor.

After a few days in Nome, I boarded the Coast Guard cutter *Northland*, bound for St. Lawrence Island. (Up in those waters the Coast Guard will carry citizens who can convince them they have a purpose.) The skipper was Captain Frederick Zeusler, whom I had met in both Washington and Seattle. This was his ninth cruise in the Bering Sea.

We were far out of sight of land when suddenly the clattering diesel engines in the *Northland*'s bottom stopped their commotion. The ship rolled as the waves caught us broadside. I lay on my bunk and heard the engines start again, to reverse the propeller and bring us to a dead stop. Then silence again.

I waited. Pretty soon I heard the high whining grind of an electric winch on deck. We were "taking stations." We did it every twenty miles, which meant about every two hours. No matter where we were going, or where we were in the Bering Sea, or whether it was day or night, we stopped every twenty miles to take stations. This was scientific business. It was part of that nebulous government work which to most of us is as vague as the scientists' reason for chasing butterflies.

Four groups of sailors jumped to their tasks the minute the ship stopped. One group threw overboard a long two-by-four, weighted at one end and attached to a line. They measured the distance it drifted in a certain time—they were checking the speed of the ocean's surface current. Another group threw over a canvas-covered hoop apparatus that looked like a half-opened parachute. In the bottom of it was a milk bottle, with an apparatus to keep the mouth closed until it got way down. At a certain depth the bottle mouth opened, and then they pulled the whole thing back up, took off the bottle, and looked at it. They were taking specimens of marine life. You wouldn't think the ordinary sailor would care two hoots whether they pulled up a bottle full of tadpoles or bath salts. But they crowded around that bottle. One time they got a lot of good specimens, for one sailor was going around saying, "Boy, when I go after bugs, do I get bugs!" I looked, and the water in the bottle was full of silly little things without any shape.

Another group let down a thin steel cable that ran over a

pulley on a davit. Every few feet they stopped the cable and clamped onto it a steel can about a foot long. They let the cable down some more, and then stopped it to clamp on another steel can, until they had half a dozen cans on it at intervals. When the cable reached the ocean floor, they stopped. The fellow at the rail took a weight out of his pocket, slipped it onto the cable, and tightened a screw so it wouldn't come off but would still slide up and down the cable. This weight, falling down the cable, hit a tripper on top of each can, which opened it so that the can would fill with water at a certain depth. When the cans were pulled up, they were taken off one by one and the water was poured into bottles, each labeled with the exact location, the depth, and so on. The bottles were stored away.

Still another group let down a "clamshell" on a long steel cable, and brought up a mouthful of mud from the ocean floor. This also was labeled and stored away. Wouldn't it have been awful if we'd run into pirates and they had taken all this mud away from us?

The last group took soundings, and the temperature of the water, not only on top but at various levels clear down to the bottom. The water, I might say, was cold.

It took about twenty minutes to go through all this rigmarole, and then the diesels started their clatter and we were off again. The *Northland* would have taken about 275 stations by the end of summer. It seems that the sounding figures, the current measurements, and the temperatures go to the Coast and Geodetic Survey, to be transferred onto mariner's charts of the Bering. The water specimens go to various universities (chiefly the University of Washington) and to the Scripps Oceanographic Institute. They show, for example, what kind of animal lives in that area, and thus they can figure out where the feeding grounds of various fish are.

That's about all I can tell you about taking stations. The only thing I'm sure of is that they've found that the water runs out of the Pacific Ocean and up through Bering Strait, and then around the top of North America, and comes down past Greenland into the North Atlantic, full of icebergs.

It was ten-thirty at night when we dropped the hook off St. Lawrence Island. The sun had just set, but there was still some daylight, and a faint ribbon of red lay low on the western horizon. A wind was blowing, and the lonely sea rolled in long deep swells; the cold twilight was thick with an acute sense of great remoteness. Davits swung and pulleys creaked, and down into the water went one of the *Northland*'s surfboats. They lowered a bag of mail and the doctor's black kit, and then down the ladder went the nine of us. Every man was in hip boots and heavy-weather clothing. Some of us wore sheepskins and wool stocking caps. Some wore parkas, with hoods drawn tightly over heads. Our little boat rose high, and fell deep, and a cold spray filled the twilight and whipped our faces as we tossed across the mile of Bering Sea to St. Lawrence Island.

On St. Lawrence I had an Eskimo friend dressed in a reindeer parka, whose name was John Apangalook. I knew he was my friend because, as we were walking along, an Eskimo voice apparently asked him who I was, and I heard him answer in English, "My friend." John took me about the village of Gambell, through the late dusk. He took me into his house, and the houses of his friends. "There are only two of the old-time Siberian-type houses left," he said. "Nowadays we buy lumber and windowpanes and build our houses like you do. Maybe you'd like to see inside one of the old houses."

We stepped through a hole about two feet square, doubling up as we skinned through, and found ourselves in a sort of shed. It was darkish in there, and smelled strongly of walrus. Old gasoline barrels, full of mukluks in brine, stood on the graveled floor. There were pieces of walrus and seal meat hanging around; there were walrus hides that hadn't been dried, and reindeer blankets rolled up. The rafter poles were loaded with furry winter clothes.

John went to the back end of the shed, where there was a doorless wall, and knelt down and said something in Eskimo. An answer came from beyond. John reached down and pulled up the bottom of the wall, and then I realized it was made of hide— reindeer hide—which fell from the ceiling like a stage curtain, making a separate room beyond. On hands and knees we crawled under, and the curtain dropped behind us.

We were enfolded, encompassed tightly, by windowless walls of thick hide. The light was very dim, and for a couple of seconds I could not see. Then the scene grew slowly before my eyes. A thin old man sat cross-legged, Gandhi-like, on the floor. He was naked to the waist. A reindeer blanket lay spread across his lap. He was just sitting there, alone.

I said, "Good evening. I'm sorry we woke you up." He smiled and said something in Eskimo. His face was very friendly. "He wasn't asleep," my friend John said. "He is just resting. He is very old."

The ceiling was too low for me, so I squatted in front of the old man, and John squatted too. There was no furniture—no beds, no chairs, no stools. Along the walls, in a thin line like surf on a beach, were stacked the few trappings of an Eskimo's household life. The floor was of walrus hide, dark and smooth like linoleum, and slightly oily. But the walrus smell was faint in here, and after a minute or two you were conscious of only a vague oiliness in the air. The dim light came from a small flame on top of an empty tin can. It was a seal-oil "stove." The flame wasn't much bigger than that from a kitchen match, but it was cookstove, lamp, and heating plant. The old man sat close to it. He stuck some paper in the little flame, and lighted his pipe with it. I asked how old he was. He smiled and said (through John the interpreter) that he didn't know; they didn't keep records back when he was born.

John and I talked a little, though not much. We just sat and said nothing for quite a while, but there was friendliness and a feeling of welcome in the room. And I thought to myself, How far this is from my world, that I always thought was the whole world. It is a vast world and I don't understand it. And I thought, If we could all come and sit in each other's houses for a minute, maybe it would be better. No, I don't know what it's all about. But the old man smiles and welcomes me—he doesn't even know my name, but he smiles—the brown old man who has lived out his days and is soon to die in this little world of his, in the faraway Bering Sea.

There is an involved ritual of courtship and marriage among the Eskimos on St. Lawrence Island. When a young fellow likes a girl, he goes and tells his papa, who goes to the girl's papa and says how about it? Then that papa asks his daughter how about it, and if she agrees, it is arranged that the young man shall come and live with his prospective in-laws. They all live in one room, of course—parents, all the kids, and the shy young lovers. The boy lives on one side of the room and the girl on the other, with the whole family between. The idea is for him, through dignified advances, finally to get over and live on the girl's side of the room.

Now, I guess it's sort of hard for even an Eskimo to bill and coo with a whole roomful of people staring at him. Often the young fellow is so bashful it takes him months to get started. Also, it is possible for the girl to change her mind, and not have anything more to do with the young fellow. That's what this business is for, anyhow—a trial period.

Even after the young fellow gets accepted by the girl and things are getting pretty well along, it isn't over. The young man now starts to build a house. And not until the day it is finished and the young couple move into their own home are they considered married. There isn't any actual ceremony.

It is a long process. Sometimes the young man lives with the girl's family for two years before he gets to the point. There is plenty of time for deliberation on both sides. But once it is done, it is final. An Eskimo knows he is taking on a wife for life, and there's no getting out of it later on.

The Eskimos are a gentle people. I like gentle people, because there are so many in the world who are not gentle. Sometimes in a big city I just sit all day in my room, with my head down, afraid to go out and talk to tough people. I expect Eskimos have spells like that too.

Except for a few strays, Alaska's Eskimos live only along the west and north coasts, and on the islands of the Bering Sea. They do not live inland. They live in everything from grass-covered cellars to shacks built of Standard Oil gasoline cans, but they do not live in ice houses in Alaska. They do, I understand, have these up on the Siberian arctic coast.

Eskimos are short, and usually well built. I've seen some pretty hefty Eskimo women, but I don't remember seeing a fat man. Most of them don't keep their noses very clean. Some of them are very ugly, some are fine-looking specimens in an Eskimo way, and once in a great while you see one that is good-looking even to our Occidental eyes. I saw only one I would call beautiful. She was a girl on St. Lawrence Island, who had definitely Oriental features. She was so beautiful in her bright red calico dress that I got fluttery and didn't have the nerve to ask her to let me take her picture. Later I asked the doctor if she was married, and he said, no, she was only fourteen years old.

Most Eskimos are bowlegged, some of them ludicrously so. This is caused, maybe, by being carried piggyback when they're babies. Little Eskimo babies are the cutest things in the world. Mothers still carry them on their backs, often completely hidden under parkas. The Eskimos have a good deal of eye trouble, and Dr. Wolcott thinks possibly it's because the hairs of the fur parka get in the babies' eyes and start an infection.

I do not believe Eskimos are, or ever have been, a brilliant people. They are easily led, too easily swayed, just as easily swayed back again. Eskimos like to imitate whites, and they are pushovers for gadgets. They are mail-order fiends, and get some weird things. They buy electric irons, when there isn't any electricity within two hundred miles. And so far as I can see, an Eskimo needs nothing in the world less than an alarm clock. But almost any Eskimo hut you go into has from one to four alarm clocks. I love Eskimos.

For forty-eight hours we lay at anchor a mile and a half from the Pribilofs, with the wind blowing fifty miles an hour and the rain pouring down so fiercely and so cold it seemed like sleet. We never did get ashore. Captain Zeusler was very patient with the weather, but finally he said nuts to it, and at four in the morning we pulled anchor and made a run for Dutch Harbor, farther south.

I was asleep when we upped anchor, but I soon woke up. The old *Northland* was rolling up as high as forty-seven degrees by the official rollometer, and when you roll forty-seven degrees, let me tell you, baby, you're rollin'. A deck at that slant is more than halfway to being straight up and down. My two chairs went slamming across the cabin floor into the door; a traveling bag piled on top of them; six drawers beneath my bunk flew open and whammed out their full length; the bottles in the toilet shelves stacked up with a great glassy bedlam; I reached out just in time to save the typewriter as it was going off the table; and down on my head from the shelf tumbled an assortment of pictures, carbon paper, chocolate bars, Bull Durham, carved ivory elephants, playing cards, and magazines. And to top it off, I looked up and there was my bath towel, hanging straight out from the wall.

I got down there amidst that prowling furniture in a hurry. You had to keep dodging, to keep from getting hurt. I got the drawers shut first, and found that each one had a little catch to hold it. Then I got some twine out of my bag, backed the chairs up against the bunk, and tied each one tightly to a drawer handle. Then I tied the traveling bag to the leg of one chair, and my wrapped bundle of sealskins to the other chair.

At the bottom of each roll the waves were slamming against the port windows. Years ago, off Cape Hatteras, I was under a port when it was smashed by a wave, and I didn't get the ground glass out of my hair for a week. So I clamped down the steel covers over my ports, taking no chances. Then I went back to bed.

I stayed in bed most of the way to Dutch Harbor, largely because there simply wasn't any sense in being up. If you got up, you couldn't stand up. You couldn't sit in a chair. You couldn't walk without being hurled against something. You couldn't read, because your eyes bulged every time the book moved. We ate only sandwiches for lunch and salads for supper—ate them standing up. It was utterly impossible to sit at a table. If you were eating in a restaurant, and the fellow across from you got up and upset the whole table right in your lap, could you eat? Also, you can't sleep in a sea like that. No matter how you lie, your position changes about every five seconds, no matter how rigidly you hold yourself. Could you sleep if some fellow kept lifting the side of your bed about four feet and then letting it drop and running around and lifting the other side?

When we passed the headland and eased into the smooth waters of Dutch Harbor, I never saw a hundred men so relieved as was this crew. They were worn out. And so was I. In fact, I was worn out twice—once from rolling around for twenty-four hours and once from pretending, every time anybody looked at me, that I still felt all right.

My athletic prowess was demonstrated during our stay in Unalaska. There was some kind of accident in the weather, and it turned out to be a warm, sunshiny day, so we went out to play tennis on the concrete court the Coast Guard had built. Doc White, who ran the government hospital, and I teamed against Doc Wolcott and Lieutenant Stephens, of the *Northland*. We were all pretty good, but I was the best because I won the game.

We had arrived at the very dramatic moment of set point (at least, we'll say it was) and I was playing net. Lieutenant Stephens caught one and sent it back across like a cannon ball. It was unquestionably my ball (practically between the eyes), so I squared off and took a magnificent swipe at it, and the ball hit the wood at the end of the racket and went fifty feet straight up in the air. When it came down it landed just about two inches on the other side of the net, and it was our game.

It was one of the prettiest and most difficult shots I ever saw. I was elated. I thought Doc White would surely yell "Nice shot, pardner," but instead he just said "Good God!" and walked off the court and sat down on the grass and put both hands up to his head.

Idyl in
the West

Tʜᴀᴛ Gɪʀʟ ᴀɴᴅ I ᴅʀᴏᴠᴇ ᴜᴘ ɪɴ ғʀᴏɴᴛ ᴏғ ᴛʜᴇ ʙɪɢ
Sun Valley Lodge in Idaho, where the rich people stay, and I got
out of the car all wind-burned and bareheaded like a sportsman,
and sauntered in through the lobby, and asked the man what he
was gettin' these days for a room with twin beds and bath. The
man looked up at the rate card, as if he didn't already know, and
came back with the calm information that the least he was gettin'
was twenty-six dollars a day. Well, I didn't make a single one of
the smart retorts I thought of half an hour later. I simply said,
"I guess that's a little more than I want to pay," and marched
sadly out of the lobby, just a hatless tourist covered with dust.
Then we drove down into Ketchum, a mile from the lodge, and
found a place where we could live very scrumptiously a whole
week for just a little more than one day at the lodge.

Ketchum lies in a mile-wide valley nearly six thousand feet
above sea level. The mountains, which look like an unbroken
circle around the valley, are mostly bare, except for a foot-high
growth of bluish-brown sagebrush. From a distance you can't
even see this, and the slopes look clean and smooth. That's the
reason the Union Pacific Railroad picked this spot for building
up a skiing resort—on account of the smooth slopes.

Forty years before, Ketchum had been a town of several thousands, booming because there were big lead and silver mines
around. But about 1900 the bottom dropped out, and Ketchum
dwindled and dried up until its population numbered only two
hundred fifty-two. Then came skiing. People around Ketchum
had always used skis to get around on, but that isn't really con-

sidered skiing, I guess. Before it's really skiing, you have to dress up like a New York store window, and pay a lot of money, and go bareheaded and be gay. That's what the Union Pacific brought. So Ketchum changed; it became in a small way a boom town again. Hundreds of workers who came in to build the Sun Valley development were living now in trailers, tents, cardboard cabins, frame huts, slab-pine lean-tos. There were five times as many temporary shacks as there were permanent homes. The population must have been more than a thousand.

There were two small hotels in Ketchum, and a group of nice cabins built around a hot-water pool. The business section consisted of one block: two grocery stores, three restaurants, one drugstore, and twelve combination saloons and gambling halls. These were called "clubs." Gambling was not legal in Idaho, and neither was liquor by the drink, but nobody in Ketchum paid any attention. Everything was wide open.

Sun Valley at the moment was almost completely empty of tourists. The crowds had left two months before, and wouldn't be back till mid-December. And it was grand, with nobody around but us old Westerners. We lazed along through Indian summer, with the sun like a ball of white fire in the valley and everything quiet and still. When I woke up in the morning I would just lie there for about an hour before I really moved. Sometimes I would get up around eight o'clock, and sometimes around eleven. On the eight-o'clock days I would put on my overalls and big shoes and go out and climb a mountain.

Down from the mountain, I would get a bite of lunch and then take a bath in steaming water that came out of a natural hot spring right into the hotel, and that would make me feel so listless I would have to nap for an hour or two. Then we would take an armload of books and drive out four or five miles along a shady creek that we'd found, way off the road, and spread out a horse blanket we always carried in the car in case we should run onto a cold horse, and we would take the cushion out of the car and prop our heads on it, and then lie there and read all afternoon.

Pretty soon it would be five o'clock; the sun would be getting down behind the mountains, and we would stop reading and sit up. The most wonderful long shadows would creep down all over the bare country and a great softness would come with the twilight. We would feel an awesome gentleness about everything, and we wouldn't have wanted anybody to speak very loud, or say anything funny.

Before I started climbing any mountains around Ketchum I asked about snakes, and people assured me there were no snakes in those parts—it was too high for them. When I started out to climb Bald Mountain I found I had to wade a rocky little river along the foot of the mountain. So I looked for a rock to sit on while taking off my shoes and socks. I saw a nice round one about four feet away, and just as I had taken one step toward it, there went a big green snake slither-slither right around the rock.

Always when I see a snake I jump backward and an idiot scream comes from somewhere way down in my neck. I have no control over it. It's a shameful thing, and fortunately nobody was around to hear it except a few brook trout and the snake itself. I stood in that one spot for ten minutes, turning round and round, before I got nerve enough to wade the river and go on with my mountain climbing.

Back in town that evening I told people about the snake. And they said, oh, they meant no poisonous snakes. As if that made any difference to me. I'm not afraid of being bitten by a snake. I'm afraid of SEEING a snake.

For nearly twenty years I had rolled my own cigarettes. I did this because (1) I liked them better than ready-mades, and (2) people, especially in the East, admired this strange ability, and the distinction made me somewhat more of a drawing-room attraction than I would have been otherwise. My friends all knew that I could roll a cigarette in the dark, or in the wind, or behind my back, or riding a horse, or with my eyes shut. But that wasn't enough. What I really wanted to do was roll 'em with one hand. I'd rather roll a cigarette with one hand than be president. In the West I was always watching for a cowboy who might teach me to roll 'em with one hand. But I'd never seen a cowboy rolling a cigarette with one hand. Most of them couldn't even do it with two hands.

One night, sitting in one of the Ketchum "clubs" watching a 21 game, I found my man. He wasn't a cowboy; he was just a nice-looking young fellow in overalls, and he had only one arm. And I sat speechless as he laid the paper on a crease in his pants, filled it with tobacco, and twirled as neat a cigarette as you ever saw. So I walked over to him and said, "Would you step outside a minute? I want to talk to you." In the East you'd probably get hit if you said that to a stranger, but this wasn't the East, so the young man said, "I certainly will," and followed me out.

"I saw you rolling that cigarette," I said. "I've always wanted to roll them with one hand, and I thought maybe you could teach me."

"Well," he said, "I don't know whether I can teach you, but I'll show you how I do it."

So I sat on the bumper of a car, and he squatted on the sidewalk in front of me and pulled out his tobacco sack. "To begin with," he said, "you crease the paper way up high, like this."

I said, "Oh, I never thought of that. How long ago did you lose your arm?"

He said, "Eight years ago. Then you slide it down along your second and third fingers, and then joggle it with your thumb till the tobacco's even."

I said, "Did you roll your cigarettes before you lost your arm?"

He said, "No, I never smoked at all till after I'd lost my arm. When you get it all even, then you slip your first finger over across it like this, and then press down hard."

I said, "That's where I get stuck. My finger's too stiff. How did you lose your arm?"

He said, "A runaway team of horses."

I said, "They must have broken your arm a dozen times, to have to have it amputated."

He said, "It got caught between the wagon tongue and the singletree and they just beat it to pieces. There wasn't hardly anything left of it."

I said, "Are you working here in Ketchum?"

He said, "I'm not doing anything right now. Last year I worked up at the construction job carrying water. But they won't give me anything this year. A big outfit like that don't give a damn for one man."

I said, "Here's my trouble. I never can keep the edge of the paper turned under."

He said, "That's the hard part. You have to press real hard. It's easier with that ribbed paper you get with cans of Prince Albert. It takes a lot of practice."

I said, "I'd think there'd be lots of jobs you could do with one arm as well as two."

He said, "Sure there is, but they won't give me nothing on account of it."

I said, "Are you gonna stay around here if you can't find anything?"

He said, "No, I'll go down below and get a little work diggin' spuds. After that I don't know what I'll do. I'd like to go over close to Portland and rent a farm, but it takes a little money and I can't make any money."

I said, "I did pretty good on the first one, but this second one keeps slipping." Then I said, "Are they just indifferent, or have they got something against you?"

He said, "It really looks like they've got something against me. I can't get on nowhere. Sometimes I get so blue and disgusted I feel like gettin' me a gun and just go shootin' up and down the street. You're gettin' onto it now, but it takes practice."

I said, "Will you be around tomorrow night?" He said, "Sure, I'll be along here somewhere." I said, "All right, I'll practice and let you know tomorrow how I get along."

I went back to the hotel and sat over a wastebasket and practiced. I had to keep my right hand in my pocket, so it wouldn't always be jumping up to help my left hand. And as I sat there it came to me that rolling a cigarette with one hand was a very trivial thing in the awful pilgrimage we were all making across the hard years to the goal of final sleep—just a little whim that didn't have to be humored at all. And yet I sat there and tried and tried and tried, till I got so damn mad and disgusted I felt like gettin' me a gun and shootin' at the floor or something.

At the gambling casinos in Ketchum they took the big beautiful wheels off the roulette tables at the end of play every night and locked them up. Why? Because if they didn't people would come in and paste numbers on the wheel—say three of four 27s—and then play that number the following night, and it would be quite a while before the dealer realized what had happened. It was done three times in one club before the proprietors caught on.

There was a pleasant and jovial drunk in one of the clubs. He wasn't any bum, either. Just a fellow taking the day off and being mellow. He had to leave for Boise or someplace right away, but he didn't get started till after dark. Every few minutes he'd look at his watch and say, "My God, it's Monday, and I haven't had anything to eat since September 5, 1908."

"Red" Wood, a husky young fellow from Boise, was working behind the desk at the little Casino Hotel in Ketchum. After work one night he went up to his room, and in the room above him he heard a guitar going and some cowboy warbling, and the heavy tap-tap-tap of a rhythmic boot. If there was anything Red loved it was music, and when he couldn't stand it any longer he went up and joined the party. The two fellows up there were Ted Terry and Vic Lusk, onetime cowboys out of work. They all played and sang a while, and found they were pretty good harmonizers. And then they sat around and talked, and one word led to another till they got off onto an idea—why not be singing cowboys, and ride a bull clear from Ketchum to New York City? "It's so preposterous," Red said, "that it couldn't help be a success."

There were drawbacks, the chief of which was that they didn't have a bull, or money to buy one. Next day they went around to the few merchants of Ketchum, and explained their idea. They got ten dollars here and five there, and finally raised about one hundred thirty dollars. They spent a month getting their outfit together—three ten-gallon hats, checkered shirts, flowing bow ties, overalls, bright gloves, and high-heeled cowboy boots. They looked just the way New Yorkers think cowboys look. And in addition to this royal regalia, they had a two-year-old Durham-Here-ford bull named Ohadi, which is Idaho spelled backwards. (Ohadi was a mean bull, and every morning he had to be broken to ride all over again.) Also one ten-year-old white saddle horse named Silver Bell. (She did tricks, like playing sick and pawing seven times when you asked her how many days there were in the week.) Also one beautiful bay saddle horse named Laddie Boy. Also one coal-black mule named Josephine. (Josie was to be loaded down with a hundred seventy-five pounds of camping equipment—tarpaulin, sleeping bags, and kitchen outfit, with a big guitar case flopping up and down on top of the whole thing.)

The boys called themselves the "Sawtooth Range Riders." They were all under twenty-five, I'd say, and all nice-looking. All three could play the guitar, all three could play French harps, all three sang cowboy songs. Silver Bell could do twenty-five minutes of horse tricks. They would put on shows in every town, and take up collections. At big towns they would try for radio and tavern engagements. And then in New York, because of the novelty of their stunt, they expected to smack the big-time radio.

They would camp out all the way, even through the bitter Wyoming winter, they said. They would take turns riding the bull. He was shod with a special set of shoes—funny-shaped shoes, two for each foot, on account of his being cleft-footed. The boys counted on only about six miles a day, because a bull can't—or at least won't—go very fast. They figured the trip would take two years.

Ten-thirty in the morning was the hour set for the great departure, but a lot of time was spent in dawdling. Finally around two-thirty you could feel a trend toward a climax. Red began packing the mule—the last act. He slung one big box on each side of the forked saddle, then the three sleeping bags and the new white tarpaulin on top. Then came the final lashing down. The great white pack at last lay high and wide on the mule's back, and seemed like a caravan all in itself. All was ready. The crowd was large now, and tense. And just then from the other side of town came the sound of a band playing. One of the town's pranksters had got together an eight-piece band to serenade the boys out of town.

By now there must have been two hundred people around the

little yard where the caravan stood, almost ready to go. The sun was mercilessly white, pouring down blindingly into the dry valley. A nail in a sapling fence gave way, and twenty kids went sprawling onto the ground. The band arrived, playing and laughing, and everybody took pictures.

There wasn't really any official start. About 3:45 in the afternoon the boys untied the bull from the telephone pole, and Vic got on him. There were no farewell handshakes. The band started to play again and marched off with the Sawtooth Range Riders falling in behind. They bowed from their saddles and smiled and waved their ten-gallon hats in true Madison Square Garden style. "Goodbye, Ketchum. Goodbye for three years. Goodbye, Jack. Goodbye, Slats. Goodbye, Idaho."

The band played exceptionally well, and it was all in the spirit of fun, but there was a pull in it too. The musicians dropped to the side, and they played "Bury Me Not on the Lone Praireee" as the Range Riders passed. And then just as the little pilgrimage turned the bend, down behind the trees, the band stood still and erect in the middle of the road, and slowly and sweetly came the frail notes of "Farewell to Thee," and under the hot sun the band leader stood still with one arm aloft in a silent gesture of hail and farewell. And it was all a joke, but I'll be damned if people weren't crying.

It had always been my ambition not to have to work for a living. It was in Denver that I decided I had hit upon the right scheme: just go around from city to city, get invited to a nice party in each city, and then write a story about the party. No effort at all.

The party in Denver was a dandy. It was given by Mrs. William H. Downs. She and Mr. Downs were rich, but you didn't have to be rich to be invited to their parties. You just had to be interesting. How I got in is a trade secret between Mrs. Downs and me. There must have been fifty people there—artists and poets and architects and sculptors and doctors and literary people. In fact, Anne Downs herself was one of Denver's best painters. Ordinarily I'm a round peg in a square hole at a literary party, but these people were different. They would listen to something besides art. And when the word got around that I was the only person in the house who had been to certain parts of Alaska, I was practically the hero of the evening. People were asking me all kinds of questions all through dinner.

And then after dinner Polly Abbe said she'd take me upstairs to see her kids—the ones who wrote *Around the World in Eleven Years*. Richard and Johnny were asleep, so I didn't get to see them, but Patience was still awake. We went up to the little den where she was bedded down on a couch, and we sat around on the floor among sweaters and leather boots and things and kept her awake for half an hour.

Patience had grown up a lot—she was past fourteen—and her face was beautiful and frail. I couldn't think of much to say to her. But I noticed she kept looking at me and laughing as though she would split, and finally I said, "What are you laughing at?" And she said, "You. You look so funny." So I said, "Well, you don't look any too hot to me. And since you're so smart and don't have any ash trays around here, I'll just put my ashes in your shoe, and then in the morning you'll have something to remember me by." Which I did. After that we got on a nice basis of sarcasm with each other and had a good time.

The Abbes had bought a ranch about fifty miles south of Denver. Jimmy Abbe, the photographer father, was back from the Spanish war. And the reason he wasn't at the party was that he stayed home to get out the sheriff to run dudes or something off their new ranch.

Finally we decided to let Pattie go to sleep, and we went downstairs. All was confusion and din. You know how big parties are—some people in one room, and some in another. Some stand up and some sit down. Lots of talk and chatter and milling. The hours passed.

But at last everybody seemed to wind up in the basement, an elegant place, full of clubrooms with fireplaces and immense chairs and divans all in white leather, and beautiful paintings all around, and very cozy. And then, down there, we got Gilda Gray to dance for us. She was a friend of the Downs or the Abbes or somebody. When we were introduced I was sort of taken aback. It had been close to fifteen years since I had seen her in the *Fol-*

lies, and I had supposed she would be old and fat by now, but she wasn't. She looked just as I remembered her.

It was getting late by then, and things began taking on a sentimentality, and her dances carried us back to romantic days. Between dances I would sit on the floor beside her chair and talk to her. I liked her very much. And then, far late in the evening, she sang for us. Stood at the piano—dramatically, it seemed to me—and sang "St. Louis Blues" and all the others in that throaty voice just as she used to, and I thought I would go nuts—it was so beautiful.

When the others started leaving I don't know. But the first thing I knew it was 3:00 A. M. and everybody had gone, and a friend of mine named Tom Ferril, who is a poet, was trying to coax me out the front door with some raw hamburger. So I finally left, though I didn't want to.

Nevada Old
and New

JOSIE PEARL LIVED THIRTY-FIVE MILES FROM THE town of Winnemucca, Nevada. Lived all alone in a little tar-paper cabin, surrounded by nothing but desert. From a mile away you could hardly see the cabin amidst the knee-high sagebrush. But when you got there it seemed almost like a community—it was such a contrast in a place filled with only white sun and empty distance.

There really wasn't any road to Josie Pearl's cabin—merely a trail across space. Your creeping car was the center of an appalling cloud of dust, and the sage scratched long streaks on the fenders.

Josie Pearl was a woman of the West. She was robust, medium-sized, happy-looking, and much younger than her years, which were sixty-some; there was no gray in her hair. Her dress was calico, with an apron over it; on her head was a farmer's straw hat, on her feet a mismated pair of men's shoes, and on her left hand and wrist—six thousand dollars' worth of diamonds! That was Josie—contradiction all over, and a sort of Tugboat Annie of the desert. Her whole life had been spent in that weirdest of all professions, hunting for gold in the ground. She was a prospector. She had been at it since she was nine, playing a man's part in a man's game.

She was what I like to think of as the Old West—one day worth one hundred thousand dollars, and the next day flat broke, cooking in a mining camp at thirty dollars a month. She had packed grub on her back through twenty-below Nevada blizzards, and had spent years as the only woman among men in mining camps, yet there was nothing rough about her—she didn't drink, smoke, or swear, and her personality was that of a Middle-western farm woman.

She had been broke as much as she'd been rich; but she could walk into any bank in that part of the country and borrow five thousand dollars on five minutes' notice. She had run mining-camp boardinghouses all over the West. She had made as much as thirty-five thousand dollars in the boardinghouse business and put every cent of it into some hole in the ground. She had been married twice, but both husbands were dead now. She never depended on men, anyhow.

She had lived as long as nine years at a stretch at one of her lonely mines. She had found her first mine when she was thirteen, and sold it for five thousand dollars. She had recently sold her latest mine and was well off again, but she was staying on in the desert.

Her cabin was the wildest hodgepodge of riches and rubbish I'd ever seen. The walls were thick with pinned-up letters from friends, assay receipts on ore, receipts from Montgomery Ward. Letters and boxes and clothing and pans were just thrown—everywhere. And in the middle of it all sat an expensive ward-robe trunk, with a seven-hundred-dollar sealskin coat inside.

She slept with a 30-30 rifle beside her bed, and she knew how to use it. In the next room were a pump gun and a double-barreled shotgun. And a dog. But Josie Pearl was no desert hermit, and she was not an eccentric. Far from it. She had a Ford pickup truck, and when she got lonesome she would go and see somebody. She had a big Buick in town, but didn't drive it much because it made her look rich. She would put on her good clothes and take fre-quent trips to Reno and San Francisco. She knew the cities well, and was no rube when she got there.

She talked constantly, and liked people to like her. Her favorite word was "elegant." She would say, "I have elegant friends all over the West." And, "I may tear down this cabin and build an elegant house here." Nobody could deny that Josie Pearl was elegant toward the human race. She had educated three girls, and grubstaked scores of boys and found them jobs. She had nursed half the sick people in northern Nevada. She was known all over the western mining country.

She said gold brought you nothing but trouble and yet you couldn't stop looking for it. The minute you had gold, somebody started cheating you, or suing you, or cutting your throat. She couldn't even count the lawsuits she'd been in. She had lost fifteen thousand dollars, and sixty thousand, and eight thousand, and ten thousand, and I don't know how much more. "But what's eight thousand dollars?" she said. "Why, eight thousand doesn't amount to a hill of beans. What's eight thousand?" Scornfully.

People had been doing her dirt for forty years. But here's a strange thing: every person who had ever done Josie Pearl dirt had died within a couple of years. She wasn't dramatic or spooky about it when she told you, but she thought she had put the hex on them. She had been trimmed out of fortune after fortune by crooked lawyers, greedy partners, and drunken helpers. Yet she still trusted everybody. Anybody was her friend, till proved otherwise. On one hour's acquaintance she said to me, "You get your girl friend and come out and stay with me two days and I'll take you to a place where you can pick nuggets up in your hand. I'll make you rich."

Which I consider exceedingly elegant of Josie Pearl. But if I got rich I'd have lawsuits, and even one lawsuit would put me in my grave, so I started back to town—goldless and untroubled. But on the way, a stinging little flame of yellow-metal fever started burning in my head. Me? Rich? Maybe just one little old lawsuit wouldn't kill anybody.

All the people you saw on the streets in Reno were obviously there to get divorces. You could tell by the look in their eyes. You felt like stopping each one and asking, "Why couldn't you get along with him?" And yet, when you checked up, you found that was just the way they looked.

There was a fairly constant year-round population of around three hundred people putting in their six weeks' residence. Many of these stayed at dude ranches outside of town, so there were maybe no more than two hundred actually living in Reno at a given time. Reno's population was twenty thousand. That would make only one divorce seeker for every hundred inhabitants.

Our hotel in Reno had paper-thin walls, and you could hear everything in the next room. One evening some new customers checked into the adjoining room and I could tell from their conversation that they were an elderly couple on a vacation trip. They retired early. I was trying to write, and the typewriter went bang-bang-bang like a little cannon, there in the stillness of the room. I knew it must bother them, and I got self-conscious about it, so I quit early and went to bed.

But next morning I was up early, as were also the old couple, and I started writing again about 7:30 A.M. Up to that time they had made no remarks about the noise in my room. But as I started pecking away the man's voice came plainly through the wall—not annoyed, but just making conversation with his wife. He said, "There goes Charles Dickens again!"

You can read that Nevada is the most sparsely settled state in the Union, but it takes an example to make you really feel it. There was just one telephone book for the whole state! Every phone in Nevada was listed in it, plus four counties of adjoining California. And the whole thing made a thin little volume that you could stick in your topcoat pocket.

I asked a dealer in a Reno gambling house how many times he had seen the same number hit in succession on the roulette wheel. I had seen a number hit twice on several occasions, and a fellow told me he once saw one hit three times. But this dealer said he had seen the same number hit five times in a row.

I don't know what the odds are against such a thing's happening, but it must be in the millions. I know that if you played a dollar on the number the first time, and kept all your winnings on that number clear through, you would theoretically come out with better than fifty-two million dollars on the fifth whirl—but the house would have closed its doors on the third whirl—when you made forty-two thousand dollars—and the owner would have gone home in a barrel.

Virginia City, Nevada, sits right on top of the famous Comstock Lode, the richest vein of ore ever found in America. By the late 1930s, the Comstock had produced more than seven hundred million dollars in silver and gold. It was so rich it was ridiculous. It had ore running as high as five thousand dollars a ton—while all over the West they were mining five-dollar ore at a profit.

The Comstock was discovered in 1859, when Nevada was merely a territory and there were no more than a few dozen people in it. Within a couple of eyewinks Virginia City had a population of thirty thousand. It went wild; it splattered money in its Civil War type of splendor; the great actors of the world came to perform; there was a man for breakfast every morning, as the saying goes, and in the first seventy-two murders there were but two convictions; it was in Virginia City that a Samuel Clemens started reporting on a newspaper, and assumed the pen name of Mark Twain.

For nearly twenty years Virginia City was the hottest thing between Chicago and San Francisco. And then exhaustion came to the Comstock Lode; it had given its all and could give no more, they thought. The tycoons moved out in '78.

Virginia City didn't show until we came around the last bend on the twenty-mile drive from Reno and looked straight upon it. There it clung, six thousand feet high, plastered to the side of a steep hill—a little old town surrounded and impregnated with countless old shaft houses and long gray piles of dirt and rocks from the tunnel depths. An old town set amid rolling hills and deserts.

I wanted to be impressed and excited when I came round the bend and saw this sight of my grandfather's day. But I couldn't even have that privilege. The skeleton was there, but progress had slipped inside the bones and made a mundane stirring. There was life in Virginia City again—not the old riotous life of bonanza times, but twentieth-century life, flowing just as it flowed in countless hundreds of other American towns.

Virginia City could not truthfully be called a ghost town. True, it had withered and dwindled. Where it used to sprawl for blocks up the mountainside and spill over the divide for more blocks and blocks into Gold Hill, now the slope was bare and the houses stretched a mere two blocks from "C" street. But the houses were full. You couldn't rent a house in Virginia City. The mines were working again, since Roosevelt had raised the price of gold.

Why, I wonder, can't an old place really die? Why can't it lie down amid its old drama and pose there, ghostlike, for the trembling contemplation of us late-comers?

There was an old whitish house on a sort of ledge in the hillside on the upper edge of Virginia City. There was a white fence around it, and a gate with an old-fashioned latch. An oldish man, small, a little stooped, and wearing overalls, came out and shook hands. This was Jimmy Stoddard, the Comstock's only living bridge between the distant past and the present. He had been on the Comstock for seventy-five years.

"I guess you go back further than anybody else in Virginia City, don't you?" I asked. People had told me that.

"I think you called the turn on that one, son," he said. "I think you called that one right. I guess I'm the oldest, all right."

Jimmy Stoddard arrived in Virginia City with his parents from New York in 1864. He went to work in the bowels of the Comstock when he was thirteen, and there he worked until he was seventy-one—fifty-eight years in the mines, right beneath Virginia City. Jimmy Stoddard was eighty-four, but he was still going out into the hills and prospecting around.

He was a truthful man, and admitted he didn't remember awfully much about the early days. He didn't recall that he ever saw Mark Twain; he did remember seeing many a man hanging from the beams of the shaft houses in the old days; he said he ran the cage that brought General U. S. Grant up from the mines on his visit there in '78; he said that in the boom days miners on their way to work would slip an order for stock under the bank door, and when they came out of the earth that evening they'd be five hundred dollars richer, just by speculation; and then they'd go to San Francisco and spend it all. He was one of them. His memory was clear but not spectacular. Seventy-five years is a long time to recall details and keep things straight in your head.

Not all the old-timers remembered as unspectacularly as Jimmy Stoddard. The most remarkable remembering was done by those who would tell you all about Mark Twain. It was truly amazing how sharp their recollections were. One old fellow told me that although Twain came to be known as a humorist nobody around Virginia City ever saw him smile. This old man remembered him well, even referred to him as "Sam."

He said Twain used to stand all the time in the doorway of the *Enterprise* building and spit tobacco juice onto the steps of the adjoining doctor's office, which happened to belong to this old man's uncle. So this old man—just a boy then, of course—called his uncle's attention to it, and the uncle put up a sign not to spit there. After that Twain stood in the doorway and instead of spitting on the steps he spit on the new sign.

I thought that was a grand little story, and I had a sort of thrill from talking with a man who had actually known Mark Twain in those far days when they called him "Sam." Before parting, I asked the old man his age, and he told me. When I got home I figured back on the dates, and discovered that this old man wasn't even born till a year after Mark Twain left Virginia City forever. That's the kind of memory I admire.

Not a single descendant of the Comstock's great bonanza kings had any financial holdings in the remnants of the Comstock. Some of the first-generation descendants were still interested in Virginia City, sentimentally. Some of them would make occasional visits, to talk and look over old spots. Clarence Mackay, of Postal Telegraph, whose father was the king of kings of the Comstock, used to come back every few years. He would always go into the Catholic church and say a prayer in memory of his parents.

But the second generation, people said, had no interest in Virginia City. In fact, some of them were quite, quite ashamed of the roughness of their grandfathers. One day the grandson of one of the bonanza kings showed up with his bride. A pleased old-timer volunteered to show them around. He steered the couple out past the edge of town, up a little gulch a hundred yards or so, and then he stopped and said, with an emotion that was filling him, "Right there is the spot where your grandfather staked his first claim."

And the rich grandson said, "Isn't the view gorgeous from here?"

The old-timer thought he hadn't been heard. So he said again, "There, right in front of you, is the very ground where your grandfather made his great strike."

And the rich grandson said, "Aren't the clouds over there magnificent?"

And the old-timer replied, with what seems to me exactly the proper answer: "Well, you can go straight to hell."

And he turned and went back down the gulch, leaving them there.

Pacific
Paradise

Chapter
XV
THE NIGHT THE *Lurline* SAILED FROM SAN FRAN-
cisco I stood on the rolling deck in the cold wind and listened to
the wash of the ocean against our sides, and saw the moonlight
make a boiling strip across the flaky waters, and felt a great isolation from the good earth. By morning we would be hundreds of
miles from our native soil—a white speck alone on the endless
blue of the Pacific.

And so at seven in the morning I came awake and got up on
my knees in bed for a look out the porthole, thinking maybe I
might see a whale—and what do you think I gazed upon? A string
of dirty freighters and pier sheds and oil derricks and old warehouses as far as I could see. We were tied up at the pier in Wilmington, California. Wilmington is a part of that conglomera-
tion of docks and small cities known to sailormen the world over
as "Pedro," and referred to in the steamship folders as "Los
Angeles Harbor," though it's thirty miles from Los Angeles. Well,
I didn't know we were going down to Los Angeles. Nobody told
me anything about it. I thought we were going to Hawaii. But
it seems the *Lurline* always went to Los Angeles first, to pick
up the Hollywood folks, and if I had read the steamship folders
I would have known it.

Since we weren't to sail again till ten at night, most of the passengers gulped breakfast and hotfooted it off for a day of touring
about Los Angeles. But I had seen Los Angeles, so that left nothing
to do but go call up Paige Cavanaugh and tell him to come down
to the boat. Which he did.

Cavanaugh was a very witty fellow who used to make many funny remarks about southern California. He had lived out there ten years now, but hated it worse every day, and was dying to go back to Indiana and raise hogs. I was always glad to see Cavanaugh, despite his being so witty, because we were old schoolmates from way back when, and I didn't have a better friend in the world, and we saw each other only about once in two or three years. So as soon as he got aboard, Cavanaugh took off his shoes and curled up on one bed and I curled on the other, and we both slept nearly all day, leaving the two chairs to the womenfolks. They were very witty also.

Along about dark we woke up, and as we had invited the Cavanaughs to have dinner with us on the ship, I went down to the purser's office to buy the guest tickets. What I found out there would have embarrassed many people, but it didn't embarrass me—it merely changed my plans. The steamship people wanted three dollars apiece for those guest tickets—six dollars to feed a man and a woman who weren't very hungry anyhow. So, since Cavanaugh was very witty and sometimes I was too, I went back to the cabin and explained the situation and we all laughed loud and long, so the steamship people could hear us. And then we went out into town and bought a dollar's worth of sandwiches, and came back to our cabin and ate them, right there on our luxury liner.

I noticed there was always a little crowd at the back rail, looking down onto the afterdeck below. Finally I went to see what the attraction was. You wouldn't guess. It was the rich passengers in first class, standing at the rail and watching the passengers down in cabin class having a good time. The cabin class paid no attention. They went ahead with their shuffleboard and walking their dogs around, and sunning themselves.

Cabin class wasn't steerage, by any means. Cabin class had a fine dining room, and social halls and a swimming tank, and a lot of nice things. It was merely a little cheaper, and it permitted a sharp line of distinction to be drawn—something that Americans decry but most certainly demand.

With a slight salaam in the direction of Captain Cook's ghost, I inserted in my journal the following:

Dawn broke upon a lifeless sea. The atmosphere was seamy and breathless. I awoke parched. The water carafe was empty. The flying fish were suspended motionless above the water. Under the heat the universe stood still. We were a painted ship upon a painted ocean. I was a little sick at my stomach from all the fresh paint. The water carafe was empty. I raised myself feebly, and made a mark on the calendar. This was our 108th hour at sea, without a sight of land. There seemed little hope. How I cursed myself for ever leaving my native shores. The water carafe was empty. The ship's stores were gone. Nothing left for breakfast but orange juice, bacon, eggs over well, buttered toast, and coffee. Hunger shook me. For a while I lay chewing on my finger for sustenance. Then I wrenched myself from bed and crawled wretchedly up on deck.

All was silent. Men lay sprawled in deck chairs, gazing at the sea. At last I forced myself to look. You could not believe what I saw. A miracle—land. Land! It was pure delirium, of course. But I crawled to where the mate was lying and whispered, in a parched voice, "Do you see land ahead?" He said, in a parched voice, "No, because I'm looking aft. But what you see is Koko Head. The Waialae golf course is just behind there." So, on this, the 108th hour, we sighted land. We had found the long-sought Sandwich Islands of the Pacific. Oh, glory be. We nailed a seagull to the mast and ran up the pennant of the Honolulu Golf Club.

For the benefit of future historians, I will set down what the sight was like. At a distance, the island seemed to be of earth and rock. It was quite mountainous and green. Apparently the island was uninhabited, for we could see no sign of life ashore. That might have been due, however, to the fact that we were still too far away. Later we did make out little white habitations stuck on the mountainside. But apparently the natives had taken to the jungle, for we could see no movement in the village. But presently, through the glasses, we saw a big war canoe put out from shore. Also, the natives released great savage birds which came charging through the air with incredible speed and made maddening swoops around us, turning on their sides and roaring hideously.

By this time we had passed Diamond Head, and the main village lay before us only a few miles away. We could see signal smoke coming out of great tall concrete poles that protruded above the village. Spreading the word to other villages, no doubt. The war canoe approached rapidly, belching smoke. It must have carried at lease two hundred savages, all brandishing native weapons known as leis. They were obviously a vicious lot, all baring their teeth and screaming and making threatening gestures. I could understand only a few words of their jargon, except occasionally some nonsensical phrase such as "Hi-ya there, Harry. When dja git back?" And then they came swarming aboard. In a few seconds they were all over the decks. Each one picked out his victim, and went running and yelling at him, throwing leis around his neck, and subduing him. A few were put through even more horrible tortures. The natives seemed to work in gangs, and while one would lasso the victim with flower ropes, another would point at him with a peculiar black instrument, which went "click," and the victim knew he had been shot. He blushed and looked silly.

I saw all this as if in a dream, yet the savages did not touch me. In fact, they seemed totally unaware of my presence, despite the fact that with remarkable bravery I strode up and down the deck amidst the mob, trying to sacrifice myself and intercept leis aimed at my fellow explorers. But somehow the barbarians seemed uninterested in me. It began to look as though I might escape capture altogether, when suddenly round the fo'c'sle head loomed a great swarm of two savages, named Jane and Charlie, who rushed at us and strangled us with their leis and screamed, "We've been looking all over for you." And then all went black.

When consciousness came again we had moved up to shore, where thousands of savages stood on the high concrete bank eying us. And then, from a large group of picked warriors, dressed in white uniforms with brass buttons, came the ominous notes of a war song. It sounded so much like "Aloha Oe" that I could hardly believe my ears.

At last the pagan ceremony was over and we were permitted to go ashore, only to be set upon instantly by another crew of brown warriors with badges who kept saying, "I take you for seventy-five cents. Them others charge a dollar and a half. I take you, huh?" Whereupon, thoroughly captured, we said "yes" and climbed into a green La Salle sedan, and were whisked along between rows of great six-story native stone huts, fringed with high coconut palms, to one of the chief's houses.

Here we registered, something was said about eight dollars a day, and then two of the chief's servants, Nos. 9 and 17, took our gear up to a large cell with wide windows, and we lay down exhausted and gave ourselves up utterly to the Sandwich Islands, which we have discovered this day, and which some day in the future—or is it past—are to be known as Hawaii.

It seems doubtful that I shall ever return to my native land. I am very happy.

There are a few little quirks about any new country that a stranger picks up in the first day or so. The one thing you must be particularly careful about out in Hawaii is always to refer to the States as "the mainland." Most first-time visitors are liable to drop in some such phrase as "now, back in the United States . . ." That makes the local people sore, because Hawaii is a part of the United States, and they don't care to be left out of it.

I don't believe I could ever learn the Hawaiian language. As one fellow who had lived there fifteen years and couldn't speak it said, "It's just too damn simple. Everything sounds alike." There are only twelve letters in the Hawaiian alphabet—all the vowels, and the consonants H, K, L, M, N, P, W. When you make a whole language out of twelve letters, things are bound to sound pretty much alike.

For instance, up on the north side of the island, within a few miles of each other, were places named Waialua, Waialee, and Haleiwa. I just shut my eyes and drove on through.

There was something almost of reverence in Hawaii's attitude toward its great swimmer, Duke Kahanamoku. His character and his conduct had been so near perfection that he had become almost symbolic of the greatness of old Hawaii.

Duke Kahanamoku had been one of the greatest swimmers ever known. At twenty he was a world-wide hero of sports. He was in the Olympic games of 1912, 1920, 1924, and 1932. At one time he held practically all the world swimming records in existence. His house was full of cups he had won, and others were scattered around town in the offices of friends.

For a quarter of a century he traveled and was acclaimed, but he kept his balance. He never made a fool of himself. He never stooped or lost his dignity. And of the many types of dignity, I believe none can surpass the simple serenity of the pure Hawaiian. Duke's face had an utter calm about it.

Duke Kahanamoku had not married. When I met him he was forty-seven—big and well-kept and handsome. He towered above you, and in his 210 pounds there was no fat. Although his once coal-black hair was now a steely gray, he could say "pooh" to middle age, and he still swam or went surfboarding at Waikiki almost every afternoon.

Duke was sheriff of Honolulu at that time. I had luncheon with him at the county jail. He was quietly cordial, and once he got started he reminisced enthusiastically. Although his schooling had not been extensive, his English was good.

At Waikiki the tourists pestered him, always wanting to take his picture. He usually obliged. If you went up and introduced yourself and asked if he minded your taking his picture, he would pose every time. But he said too many yelled at him, "Hey, you. Get up there. Want your picture." To those people he would say, "I'm sorry. I'm not in the mood for pictures today."

Duke hadn't any money to speak of. Before his election he had some filling stations around Honolulu. Now he had only his sheriff's salary and a little change from royalties here and there. He was called upon to spend far more than he made. There was a constant stream of people hitting him for jobs, or favors, or a handout of a dollar or two. "I just had to stop it," he said. "I didn't have the money."

He had friends all over the world, and they were always cabling him to meet some friend of theirs at the boat. He had to spend his own money to be a sort of unofficial host for the islands. Honolulu tried to get him to take a paid job as official greeter, but he wouldn't do it. He had never capitalized on his fame. That's one reason he was still poor—and also why Hawaii regarded him so highly. I suppose there wasn't a man in Honolulu—white, brown, or yellow—who wouldn't have been proud to walk down the street with Duke Kahanamoku.

A few days after he and I had lunch together the midafternoon sun was hot on the beach at Waikiki. On the sands and under the umbrellas of the Outrigger Club there was a rich laziness. Men, deeply tanned, lay in the heat. Women in bright bathing suits dug toes into the sand. Somewhere behind the palms Hawaiians were singing. Doris Duke was there. And a princess or two. It was a beach scene out of *Esquire*—correct tan, dark glasses, bright trunks, leisurely ease, poise.

Suddenly people sat up and stared. Look! What fantasy is this? Four dark Hawaiians carried a yellow outrigger canoe toward the water. Behind them strode a huge Hawaiian, six feet and then some with a great chest and muscled arms and legs, darkly brown—a figure as natural on Waikiki as the surf itself. And behind this magnificent specimen minced an embarrassed, spindly ghost, a veritable Milquetoast of the beach. He couldn't see over the Hawaiian's shoulder. His skin was as white as writing paper. His knees didn't come together, and his arms were muscleless. He wore a common white undershirt where other men wore big raw chests. And around him dangled borrowed red trunks, far too big. He stepped awkwardly in the deep sand. The rich beach crowd sniggered. Funny little man. Funny little hothouse man—no chest, no tan, no muscle, probably couldn't even swim. What a sight.

The big Hawaiian was Duke Kahanamoku. And the awful contrast trailing behind him was—as you may have guessed—me, in person. Me, wanting desperately to get under water and drown.

The canoe was built for four. Duke called to a beautiful girl on the beach, and she came running with a little child. They piled in, for ballast and the ride. I never did know who they were. He put me right in the nose. He sat in the stern. We paddled out against the surf and into the sun. Crossing the rollers, the prow of the canoe was left high, and would fall to the water with a smack. It was good to get way out, away from the beach crowd. We must have been half a mile out when finally Duke turned the canoe around.

"Now we'll wait for one," he said. "And when I say paddle, you paddle hard." We sat there for many minutes in the sun, talking idly. A few canoeists and surfboard riders lay waiting also, but not very close.

Suddenly Duke dug in excitedly and yelled "Paddle!" We did, and the canoe started to move. "Paddle! Paddle hard!" Duke yelled. We clawed at the water. "Paddle hard!" Duke yelled. We labored, the girl and I. There was a roar of rushing water behind us. "Paddle harder!" yelled Duke.

Then suddenly I could feel the stern lifted. The prow dug into the water with a showering splash and the little boat trembled all over. And then we were off, as though someone had pulled a trigger and shot us out of a gun, going like the wind, riding shoreward on a roaring downhill of white water. No need for oars now.

"Lean over toward the outrigger," yelled Duke. We were already leaning. It was a thrill. The air whistled past. The white comb of surf under our stern raced to overwhelm us, but bore us ahead of itself, just out of reach.

Duke sat hugely in the stern, his paddle dug edgewise into the water alongside, making a sort of rudder. The ride lasted maybe a minute, maybe less. Gradually we slowed. Duke hunched the canoe onward; you could feel the jerks when he humped forward. Finally the wave died and passed beneath us and the canoe floated quietly again, a hundred yards from shore. We paddled seaward again.

Half a dozen times we made the round trip. Sometimes we'd have to wait five or ten minutes for the surf to break. Once all four of us got out of the canoe and played around in water over our heads. We hung onto the outrigger, for only Duke could swim.

Every time I'd try to judge in advance just when Duke, watching seaward, would yell "Paddle!" But I never could tell. Always, when we started stroking, the water behind us seemed smooth and motionless. But we'd paddle frantically for five or ten seconds and then I'd see the wave break on the reef, yards back of us, and start piling up its white crest, and in a few seconds it would be half under us, shooting us along before it.

I'm not sure whether the afternoon of riding the nose of an outrigger on the roaring surf was worth that awful outward march through the lounging society of Waikiki or not. I guess maybe it was. For when it was over, and we strode wetly back across the sands, I had somehow grown an inch or two and possibly gained a few pounds, and I couldn't hear anybody laughing. I even helped Duke carry the canoe. And I guessed that in just a couple of days now I could be a cat on a surfboard and stand up all alone, graceful and bold, waving my thin white arms.

The Leper Colony

Chapter XVI YOU MIGHT NOT RECOGNIZE THE NAME OF KALAU-papa, but you must have heard of Molokai—the dreaded leper colony, the martyring place of Father Damien who died a leper's death. In Hawaii the colony is called only Kalaupapa (just pretend the "u" isn't there, then go ahead and say it). It is a rare thing for a layman to get to Kalaupapa. Those who do are usually there only a few hours. But by an odd series of circumstances I was permitted to go there for as much time as I wished.

The leper colony has been dramatized and fictionized until it is known over the world as a spot of veiled mystery, a cursed place where cursed men are banished to await death, a place where martyrs sacrifice their lives in a beautiful attenuation of human suffering. Many of the things that have been written about Kalaupapa are not true. There is drama there—intense, awful drama. But it is not quite the sinister place that fiction gives us. It is a human place. Once you are there, there is no mystery about it.

Molokai is the first island south of Oahu, about thirty-five minutes from Honolulu by plane. The leper colony occupies only ten square miles out of Molokai's total area of two hundred and sixty. The island is long and narrow. Suppose you set a shoe box on the table; that would represent Molokai. And then put a tiddlywink up against the shoe box, along about the center. That would be Kalaupapa—both in relative size and in relative altitude below the rest of the island.

Kalaupapa is a triangular spit, like an arrowhead, about two miles across the base and a mile and a half from base to point. It is flattish and rocky, except for an old blown-out crater rising not very high in the center. The spit is surrounded on two sides by ocean, and on the third side rises an appallingly sheer rocky cliff, or *pali*, nearly two thousand feet high. It is one of the world's finest natural barriers. It cannot be ascended in any form, shape, or fashion except by one narrow horse trail, over a switchback path ascending like needlework up the face of this frightening wall. Near the top of the trail is a high padlocked gate with barbed wire stretched around it. If you tried to climb around the outer edge of the gate and lost your grip, you would fall eight hundred feet before you hit the first rock. There is a cabin on top, just above the gate, and a watchman stays there all the time —more to keep curiosity seekers out of the colony than to keep patients in.

Our plane's course took us right down the center of Molokai. Symmetrical pineapple fields lay spread below us. To the right the land slanted downward to the sea, and we could see the rollers breaking on the beach. To the left it slanted upward into a long mountain ridge, and we could not see beyond. The pilot swung to the left. We climbed toward the ridge, skimming just over the trees. We topped the ridge. Ahead appeared the ocean—and nothing else. There wasn't any other side to the ridge! It was as though the mountain range had been sliced vertically in two, and half of it thrown away. From the peak it was practically straight down to the water's edge—two thousand feet. It was a sickening sensation.

And there far below, sticking out from the base of the cliff, lay the promontory, Kalaupapa. The airport runway at the far point, the lighthouse on a rise behind it, and underneath us, right on the shore and snug up at the base of the cliff, lay the unreachable, the untouchable leper colony.

The day was misty, and air currents banged us as we dropped over the cliff and roared down upon the earth. It was as though we were suddenly flying over the remote Tibetan monastery of *Lost Horizon*. We bounced on the rough runway. Only one person was in sight when we climbed out—a Hawaiian in overalls, who stood by the side of an old Ford a hundred yards away and looked at us. He was a leper—a word that is in disfavor at Kalaupapa. In the local phraseology, he was a "patient." He merely stood and watched.

In a few minutes a car came speeding over the dirt trail from the settlement. It was "Doc" Cooke, the settlement's superintendent, come to take us in. He wasn't a doctor; they just called him that. We rode in a new Chevrolet sedan, and talked about things in Honolulu. But my thoughts were not on Honolulu. I was peering ahead, filled with an eager but fearful anticipation.

The first thing I saw was symbolic. It was the rusted hulk of an old freighter lying in the surf just off the rocky shore. It had gone aground six years before, and now lay there close to the other dead. These—the other dead—lay on a rise a few feet above the rocky shore line. There was cemetery after cemetery. They adjoined, and they stretched on and on until they beat upon my consciousness like a funeral drum.

We began to pass cottages along the beach. Then we met cars. I felt ashamed to look, yet could not help it. Some of the occupants seemed perfectly normal. But beside them sat others horrible to look upon.

We drove into the staff compound in the center of the settlement, and carried my bags into my room. Then we went for a first trip through the settlement, and visited one of the dormitory "homes." As we stepped onto the porch I raised my arm to embellish something I was saying. One of the officials apparently thought I was going to touch a post, and he pushed my arm down. Later I learned that it was nothing to touch a post. The official's action was merely a first lesson in extra precaution, and it sank in.

The patients had had their supper and were sitting around on their cots, smoking or talking. The whole dormitory seemed hushed. The patients looked at us, and we looked at them and passed on. But it seemed wrong to be there staring, and I was uncomfortable.

Outside again, just at twilight, we walked down a bower lane of arched flowers and vines. The director grabbed my arm and pulled me back. "Look," he whispered, "isn't that a picture?" Framed by a gap in the flowering foliage, a hundred feet or so away, was an old man. His wide black hat was on his head, his cane on his arm, his gray beard a contrast against his black clothing. He was standing there alone on the green grass of the lawn, absorbed, unaware of this world—an old priest, intently reading his breviary.

Darkness came on, and we returned to the staff house. The director went into my bathroom and took down a bottle of alcohol solution and said, "After we've prowled around we always use some of this on our hands." I did likewise.

I felt no fear. I was keenly conscious of the necessity for precaution, but it was not fear, though I did have a weird feeling of inability to become placed. So quick had been our transition from cosmopolitan Honolulu to the serene yet stern strangeness of this fabled spot that I could not adjust myself. It seemed to me there was contamination everywhere. In the air, in everything I touched, in mere sight and thought. Not uncleanness, not foulness, not even danger—but an invisible and innocent evil everywhere.

Bedtime came. The freshly laundered sheets smelled of disinfectant. I knew they had never been seen or touched by leprous patients, but the odor of precaution was there, remindful. I couldn't sleep. The darkness was terribly still. The only sounds were the roar of the ocean on the rocks and the occasional crow of a patient's rooster. The pali was darker than the night. There I lay in the center of a group of four hundred human beings cursed with a disease. What were they like? What were they thinking tonight, this very minute? I could not believe I was really there. My brain whirled, and all night I tossed and rolled, sleeping as little as I had slept in many years. And still I was not afraid.

After the first night I did not feel that way at all. I came to be easily at home in this community of people who, like most of us, took things as they came and were not extraordinarily unhappy, and who, like all of us, were going to die some day. True, everywhere I turned I saw suffering and disease in piteous and repulsive forms. I didn't really get used to that—but I did come to accept it, and then I gradually came to see that the place was far more "natural" than I had ever dreamed.

Kalaupapa was not regimented in appearance, like most institutions. You saw no rows of cottages all alike, and no great prison-like dormitories. Nothing was crowded together. There were gardens and shrubbery and space everywhere. About half the patients were housed in private cottages on good-sized plots of land. The others, those least able to take care of themselves, lived in the four "homes." Kalaupapa was almost like any small town of five hundred people, except that there was not much of a business block. You wouldn't even recognize as a hospital the one-story building with its tropical architecture.

The staff compound was simply an area with three private homes and one fairly large U-shaped building, enclosed by an unobtrusive picket fence. Great coconut trees towered over the whole compound, and the homes were almost hidden behind banana trees and banks of flowers. The superintendent and each of the two doctors had a home. The rest of the staff lived in the general building, which had private rooms and a small general dining room. The servants, who were Japanese, were quartered behind the staff homes.

The hardest thing for me to realize about Kalaupapa was that, within the confines of the settlement, the patients were free men and women. Nobody had to do anything. You could lie in bed all day if you wanted to. You could read all night. You could go to another fellow's house and stay the night. Even going to the hospital or receiving medical treatment was absolutely voluntary. You could lie in your cottage and die without anybody's bothering you, if you wanted it that way.

There used to be "Lepers Keep Out" signs all over the place. There wasn't a one in the settlement when I was there. The patients knew where they mustn't go; why flaunt it at them? The whole attitude was one of kindness and gentleness. The superintendent and the doctors and the nurses all impressed me with their compassion and understanding.

Of course, the patients had to obey the territorial laws. Fire-arms were forbidden. There was a jail, and now and then somebody was in it. The usual offenses were fights, profanity on the streets, and petty thieving from one another. In the whole year preceding my visit there had been only four court cases, all minor. The settlement had a sheriff and five policemen who were patients or ex-patients. A community of five hundred pretty peaceful people didn't need six officers, of course, but it gave them something to do.

In 1936 a Filipino girl shot and killed her sweetie, another Filipino patient. They had quarreled, and it seems he was going to stab her, so she plugged him. They didn't know how she got the gun. The case was taken to Honolulu and they finally decided, "Oh, well, insufficient evidence." The girl was still at Kalaupapa. Once a Filipino stabbed his wife and then stabbed himself to death. The wife recovered. Suicides were few and far between. Right now there was only one fellow in jail, and he hadn't done anything wrong. He was crazy, and too violent for the mental ward.

A large proportion of the patients worked. They didn't have to, but they liked to be busy and to get the extra money. Six were cowboys, tending the settlement's three hundred cattle (the meat went only to the patients). Some of them grouped together and fished, and sold their catch to the settlement. Some did carpentry work. Some acted as nurses' assistants. Four or five ran little stores of their own. Any patient could set up in business if he wanted to; in fact, it was encouraged. One ran a garage. One sold radios and had a repair shop. In the last year more than fifty thousand dollars had been paid out in wages to patients for work done.

Each patient got twenty dollars a year from the government, in quarterly installments. This was just jingling money, to make them feel they were not completely indigent. Those in the "homes" were housed, clothed, and fed. Those in private cottages got ration allowances. If you think leprous patients aren't human, just listen to this partial list of the electrical appliances bought for their homes by patients in a single year: ninety radios; fifty-eight washing machines; twenty-two vacuum cleaners; twenty-two toasters; forty-two refrigerators; eighteen waffle irons; and, bless their hearts, four electric cocktail shakers! Beer and wine were sold at the settlement store. Patients could get hard liquor over the superintendent's signature. He said the requests probably hadn't come to a gallon in three months. But liquor was smuggled in to some of the patients.

There were about a hundred autos among the patients, ranging from old Ford trucks to brand-new Plymouth convertibles.

It startled you to see a car go by, glistening with newness, and at the wheel a maimed and bandaged driver. Patients didn't have to buy license plates. You saw tags of several years back—whatever had been on a secondhand car when they bought it and had it sent over. And Kalaupapa was the only place under the United States flag, I was told, where people could buy gasoline without a tax.

And to top it all off, some of the patients who got money from their families outside had beach cottages a mile or two away from the village. They spent weekends in them.

The leper population of the settlement was four hundred and fourteen when I was there. In addition there were ninety-one well persons—officials, nurses and gardeners, and electricians, carpenters, and so on who lived in special construction barracks and did not come in contact with the patients. There was also a group in between—*kokuas* and parolers. A kokua (helper) is the husband or wife of a patient, who has elected to go along in voluntary exile to Kalaupapa. It was the custom for a long time to permit this, but in more recent years the practice had been done away with except in the rare cases where the kokua had nursing ability or could perform some useful task in the settlement. There were now fourteen kokuas. As long as tests showed them nonleprous, they could leave any time they wished.

A paroler is a person whose leprosy has been arrested to the point where it is safe for him to go out into the world again. That does not necessarily mean he is cured. Many of them relapse. But for the time being he is not considered hazardous to other people. There were about a hundred forty parolers in Hawaii in 1937. They had to report every so often for inspection. Nineteen of the parolers lived on at Kalaupapa—people who were free to go any time but preferred to stay there.

A number of times Hawaiians had tried to palm themselves off as lepers in order to live in Kalaupapa and be with their friends. The Hawaiians do not have the feeling of disgrace about leprosy that most people have. They will keep a leper in the family without any apparent fear or concern, just because they don't want to be parted.

The average life of a patient after arriving at the settlement was eight years. Most of those who came to Kalaupapa had already had leprosy for many years. Some died right away. On the other hand, there were patients—three of them, I believe—who had been there more than fifty years. There is no consistency about leprosy.

The truth is that few of Kalaupapa's patients die of leprosy. Some other disease jumps in—tuberculosis, pneumonia, syphilis —and, since they are already weakened by leprosy, it carries them off. Dr. G. B. Tuttle, the head physician, said about ninety-eight out of a hundred die of something else.

Statistics on Kalaupapa vary from year to year of course, but the yearly average had been running like this: sixty deaths, fifty admissions, fifteen to twenty-five paroled. So you see the population was slightly decreasing. It was now only about one-third of what it had been in 1890, the peak year.

About half the patients were pure Hawaiian, though pure Hawaiians accounted for only one-twentieth of the population of Hawaii. Part-Hawaiians formed another fourth of the settlement population. Hawaiians seem especially susceptible to leprosy. The remaining fourth at Kalaupapa were Japanese, Portuguese, Chinese, Koreans, Puerto Ricans, and so on. There were six white patients, five men and a woman. The woman was Spanish-Portuguese. One of the men was an old German sea captain. Only one of the six whites was born on the United States mainland. He was a soldier. The whites took it much harder than the Hawaiians, it was said.

There was almost no attempting to escape. The patients either wanted to stay because they liked it or else knew it was best and were resigned. There had been only two escape attempts in the past decade. One Hawaiian boy, a fine swimmer but demented, started to swim to Honolulu, forty miles away. Hours later the waves washed his body back onto the rocks of Kalaupapa. Another one went up over the pali, but he was back the next day.

Many of the patients were feeble-minded. Leprosy does not necessarily attack the brain, but it seems that a good percentage of leprous cases are mentally below par when they arrive.

I was shocked at one thing: leprous patients—even those

scourged to the very doors of death—were permitted to reproduce themselves. The officials could do nothing. It was the law. Patients married, and remarried, and didn't marry at all—and babies kept on coming. True, indications are that children do not inherit leprosy—that they are born nonleprous. Yet some 7.6 per cent do develop leprosy later, and an overwhelming proportion of them are born feeble-minded. What is the use? What is the gain? There can be no parental affection, for the babies are taken away at the very moment of birth, and the parents usually never see them again. And even though they may avoid leprosy, the children are doomed to either imbecility or unnatural loneliness. They are taken to the Kapiolani Home in Honolulu and kept there as wards of the territory. Those who do come out fairly natural are placed out in families.

All the world fears a leper. Nearly all the world believes that those who work in a leper settlement are doomed sooner or later to contract the dread disease. That is nonsense. Leprosy is less infectious than tuberculosis. Scores of well people had worked at Kalaupapa in its seventy years of existence, as nurses, executives, and emissaries of the church. And out of those scores only four contracted the disease. Father Damien, who died in 1889, was the first. Brother Van Lyl was the second. He died in 1925. The third was a doctor who had served there for many years. He left the settlement in 1925 and set up in private practice on leeward Molokai. After a short time he left—disappeared from Hawaii, in fact. It was believed that he had discovered he had the disease. They did not know whether he was still alive or not. Father Peter, who was still there, was the fourth, and he had apparently been cured.

Brother Dutton, one of the most beloved of the many who had served the settlement, worked and lived among the lepers for forty-four years and never got leprosy. Some of the nuns had been there even longer. Superintendent Cooke had been there twelve years, and Dr. Tuttle ten years, and they were not afraid of leprosy. Perhaps "afraid" isn't the right term. They were afraid of it to the extent that they took precautions—which some of the four victims had not done. They knew that if they were careful the chances of getting leprosy were infinitesimal.

It has been written that houses are always burned at Kalaupapa after a patient's death. Preposterous. It has been written that a doctor always kicks open a door, so as not to touch it with his hands. That is not true. In the first place, you can't kick open a door that is latched. In the second place, it would not be smart psychology for the patients.

The people who work at Kalaupapa touch leprous things daily. How would they nurse the patients without touching them? All the clerks in the main office are patients. All day long Superintendent Cooke handled papers that had been in the hands of patients; all these papers were fumigated, of course, before leaving the settlement. All mail goes through eighteen hours of fumigation. And nothing that has been in patients' hands, except mail, ever leaves the settlement.

Employes are not timid about touching, but they are alert about sterilizing. Superintendent Cooke carried a bottle of antiseptic solution on the floor of his car. When he got back into the car after a leprous contact, he would reach down and pour the stuff onto his hands before touching the steering wheel. At home in his bathroom there was a large jar of antiseptic solution. It had a rubber bulb and a glass spout, and he pumped some onto his hands every evening and washed in it. Every day he took a shower as soon as he got home. His clothes were cleaned with a fumigating solution. The great danger lay among those who became so accustomed to being there that they thought, "Oh, nothing will happen," and became careless about contacts and lax in sterilizing.

The medical tests of new leper suspects are usually made by taking a little strip off the ball of the forefinger. It is often hard to find the leprous germ, even when it's there. Dr. Tuttle said the one sure way to tell was by making a test from just inside the nose.

Chaulmoogra oil—which for a time in the twenties was believed to be the long-sought cure for leprosy—had since been proved ineffectual. They still gave it if a patient requested it, but, like giving a sugar pill to a dope fiend, it was for the psychological effect. The oil is injected with a hypodermic needle, and sometimes swallowed in capsules.

The patients themselves were self-disciplined about protecting well people. They would never think of offering to shake hands with you, or of leaning on a gate that well people used, or of going into the staff compound.

Children used to be permitted at the settlement, but they hadn't been for several years. One day Superintendent Cooke's baby girl got outside the compound and was crawling around under the feet of a horse. A number of patients saw the peril the baby was in. The natural impulse, of course, was to run up and snatch her away, but they knew they must not touch her—must not rescue her from one danger and subject her to another. They were panicky; they ran frantically in all directions around the settlement, yelling for some well person to come and get her. Superintendent Cooke said the horse was so old and docile it wouldn't have stepped on her anyhow, but the patients didn't know that. He was deeply touched by the incident.

The settlement was rife with dogs and cats, which helped keep the rats down. (I didn't see any rats, but I did see a mongoose run across the trail outside of town.) Many of the patients had horses. The first thing you thought was: would the animals catch leprosy? The answer was no. There was no known case of an animal catching leprosy from a patient.

It has been written that visitors to the settlement are put through an examination before they enter. Well, they aren't. And it has been written that their clothes are burned when they leave. If that was true I'd have had to go out wrapped in a banana leaf.

As a matter of fact, with the necessity for constant precaution drilled into your mind until it becomes second nature, you're probably safer at Kalaupapa than you are out in the world licking stamps, handling money, buying vegetables.

One of the most universally believed myths about Kalaupapa is that those who serve there are inspired martyrs who have doomed themselves to a lifetime of exile. Actually a person with a martyr complex would be worse than useless there. Except for those assigned to the settlement by the Catholic Church, every person who works for the colony does so simply because it gives him a job. Employes can quit any time they want to. The key people on the staff—superintendent, doctors, head nurse, and so on—get one week off the settlement every three months. And once a year, in addition, they have three weeks' vacation.

Another myth is that there is an atmosphere of despair and impending doom in the settlement. It struck me, as a matter of fact, as a rather happy community. Not exactly hilarious, but there was gaiety. The patients had their clubs, they played games, they had dances, they went to the movies three times a week, they even had cocktail parties.

I would be misleading you if I gave the impression that all the people who worked at the settlement liked it, and that they were not depressed by the place and the contact with the patients. The turnover of nurses was rapid. A new nurse came the day before I arrived. She was there only two nights, and never slept a wink. It was not so much revulsion as pity for the patients that drove her away. She was a middle-aged woman. Dr. Tuttle, who had been there ten years, told me that on his first day in the hospital he had to go home in midforenoon and go to bed. He was thoroughly sick.

Nobody knows how or when leprosy came to Hawaii. The first vague knowledge of its existence in the islands was recorded between 1820 and 1835. Once started, it spread like wildfire. A law for segregating lepers was passed in 1865, and the next year— January of 1866—the first twenty-five were sent to Kalaupapa. The government simply dumped them there, made no provision for them at all, abandoned them. They lived in caves and grass houses, and under trees. They ate fish and birds, whatever they could get.

It wasn't until twelve years later that a doctor was sent over; Father Damien had arrived five years ahead of him. Things improved steadily after that, but you might say that only in the past half dozen years had a social consciousness stepped into Kalaupapa. That came about during the administration of Governor Judd. He appointed a former army engineer to make a survey of the leper settlement. The engineer's report started things rolling.

In 1931 a board of citizens was set up to direct the leper institutions. The board appointed as director the man who had made the survey, Harry A. Kluegel. Vast improvements followed. Before 1931 there were no electric lights. No paved streets. No paid nurses. No movies. Now Kalaupapa was in the midst of a continuing program of improvement. Many streets were already paved, and the paving was going on. A new hospital had been built, and a mental ward added. Old cottages were being torn down and new ones put up. A breakwater had been built, and an airport. Trees and flowers had been planted everywhere. Someday there was to be either a private room or a private cottage for every person in the settlement. There were to be more nurses and greater hospital facilities. And there was to be a crematory, to end that mental and actual hazard of thousands of graves at the edge of town.

Father Damien, the Belgian priest who gave his life to the lepers, arrived at Kalaupapa in 1873 and died in 1889, still in his forties. He became an almost legendary figure, and many books were written about his life. When I was there, the man who was wearing Father Damien's mantle among the lepers was Father Peter d'Orgeval-Dubouchet. He was a Frenchman who had been in Kalaupapa twelve years. You never saw a more lovable character. He was nearly seventy and had a steel-gray beard, and he weighed less than a hundred pounds. When he talked he talked all over; it took at least six square feet for Father Peter to talk in. He jumped, struck attitudes, and laughed loudly and frequently.

He lived alone in a cottage behind the church. At night you could see him flitting about the dark streets of Kalaupapa, cane in one hand, flashlight in the other. He must have carried the cane from habit, for he didn't need it any more than a flea would. He could climb the steep pali trail in sixty-five minutes, which is only five minutes slower than a horse does it.

Ordinarily Father Peter didn't smoke. But during my visits—purely out of courtesy, I assume—he smoked cigarette for cigarette with me. And he puffed and waved his arms so furiously that he scattered ashes all over himself, and I became seriously alarmed about his beard.

Father Peter entered the priesthood when he was twenty-five. In his youth he had wanted to be a musician. He started on the piano at eight, and later studied in the Conservatoire at Paris. "Ah, I love music," he said. "I love it too much. I could not serve two masters. It had to be either God or music. I gave up music." But he was still a fine pianist. You should have seen him at the old upright piano in the rectory—bent over, intent, fingers flying, hands crossing, and the piano shaking with the classical thundering it gave forth. Then Father Peter would get up and say, "Ah, very poor. Fingers too stiff." But his hands were tiny —the hands of a boy—and they showed no age whatever. They were sensitive, frail hands; his whole character could be read in his delicate fingers.

Father Peter served as a chaplain throughout World War I. He said bullets went through his clothes but never touched him. He was gassed many times. After the war he had what he called his "nervous years." He went into semiseclusion for two years. Then, well once more, he decided to apply for transfer to Kalaupapa.

"What put it into your head to come to Kalaupapa?" I asked.

"Ah!" Father Peter jumped, sat on the edge of his chair, gesticulated. "Ah, it came to me in one sec-OND! In one sec-OND it came to me, like that. Twice in my life things have come to me in one sec-OND. First, to enter the priesthood. Sec-OND, to come to Kalaupapa. I do not know why. Just came, like that." And then, as if anticipating my next question, he said, "And I had never read a single book on Father Damien. I had heard of him, but never the details had I read."

Father Peter was fifty-three when he applied for Kalaupapa. He had never been out of France, and knew neither English nor Hawaiian. Before they would let him come he had to learn both languages and serve an apprenticeship at the leper colony in Tahiti in the South Seas. He reached Kalaupapa in 1925.

Within two years after his arrival he contracted leprosy. It was generally agreed that he had been indifferent to the usual precautions. Some even said he *wanted* to contract leprosy, to follow literally in the footsteps of Father Damien. There is some truth in this theory, though perhaps it should not be put so flatly. I asked Father Peter himself about it. He gave me the answer: "I could not serve until I had made the sacrifice of putting myself in a position to become a leper." Those weren't his exact words —there is no way of putting Father Peter's machine-gunned crazy-quilt English down on paper. But what he said, in substance, was that he felt that in order to serve God among the lepers he must go through the leveling spiritual experience of attaining that same "other world" in which the lepers lived.

His condition was noticed immediately by settlement physicians. It showed itself as a dark spot high on his forehead. He was operated on at once—the scar on his high forehead was still visible after ten years—and the spot was removed; it was definitely leprous. It is most unusual for the disease to be discovered so quickly; Father Peter said the doctors told him his case was one in a million. He was more careful afterward, and there seemed little likelihood of his contracting leprosy again.

Conditions had changed enormously since Father Damien's day, and the priest now did no manual toil among the stricken people. His work was solely spiritual—he visited the patients in their homes, preached his sermons, conducted funerals. His days were busy.

He preached in Hawaiian, and he said he thought the Hawaiians understood about half of what he said. He would write out his sermons in Hawaiian, then have a Hawaiian boy come in and correct them. One day the boy played a joke on him. Father Peter had wanted to use the phrase "fallen woman," but the boy put in a word that meant something else. It wasn't dirty, but it was very funny. When Father Peter came to it, the whole churchful of people howled.

Father Peter frequently went over the pali to leeward Molokai, and at least once a year went to Honolulu for a week or more.

"Father Peter," I asked, "have you been happy here?" He wasn't sure. He loved Kalaupapa—the scenery, the climate, the people—but those things didn't matter. It was how well a man served his God. He tried, but he didn't know how well satisfied God was, to put it mundanely. That's the reason he couldn't say he had been fully happy. "Let's say I have not been unhappy," he said.

I loved Father Peter, as did everyone else in Kalaupapa. He would undoubtedly spend the rest of his days there. And spend them, I was sure, "not unhappily."

Shizuo Harada and I became friends, through the simple process of sitting down and talking with each other. Our subject was leprosy. We talked about how it affects people—their minds, their attitude, their whole remaining lives. Shizuo Harada could tell me these things because he was a very intelligent man—and because he was a leper.

Harada managed the settlement's general store for patients. I was introduced to him over the counter. He was a small but well-built man in his early thirties, and he was wearing a blue work shirt and blue dungarees. His hands were bandaged. He did not, of course, offer to shake hands. I knew he couldn't do that, but still I felt that he resented my wishing to talk with him. For privacy we stepped into the warehouse back of the store, and I asked some questions about the volume of sales and so on. It took only a few words to show that Harada was a mentally keen man. Our conversation drifted from the store to Harada himself, which was what I wanted.

I asked if he was a full-blooded Hawaiian. He said, "I don't know what I must look like to you, Mr. Pyle, but I am a full-blooded Japanese." I could see then that he was Japanese. He was born in Hawaii, however—had been to Japan only once, and then he was so little he couldn't remember it. He spoke perfect English with no accent. He went through high school in Honolulu, and then on to the University of Hawaii. He graduated on June 5, 1925, and on June 21 they found he had leprosy. It started as a numbness in his little finger.

"What were your feelings when you knew what it was?" I asked.

"I just couldn't believe it," he said. "I thought the doctors were wrong. I thought for years they were wrong." Like most of the patients at Kalaupapa, he had no idea how he contracted the disease. There had never been leprosy in his family.

It had been nearly thirteen years now since he discovered he had leprosy. "Up until three years ago," he said, "you couldn't have told by looking at me that anything was wrong. But three years ago it broke out, and once it started it came on fast. In a few weeks I became as you see me now. There is a possibility that some day I may have what they call a 'reaction,' and be very sick and have a high fever, and then come out 'clean' and be almost normal again."

Later I asked Dr. Tuttle about it, and he said that was right. He said that if Harada did go through the reaction and came out clean—by which they mean that sores would heal up, enlargements would diminish, and the appearance would return nearly to normal—he might live for many, many years, and might never have another flare-up. But some patients never get this reaction. A visiting Johns Hopkins specialist had suggested the possibility of using the machine for artificially inducing fever in an attempt to bring on the reaction in leprous patients. But there was not sufficient personnel at Kalaupapa to handle such work.

Harada said he imagined there wasn't a leprosarium in the world where the patients were treated better than at Kalaupapa. But he felt that lepers had not had a fair break from the medical world. "The doctors don't know any more about it than they did thousands of years ago," he said. "So few doctors go into deep research on leprosy. Of course you can't blame the individuals; a doctor has to make a living, and there isn't any living in doing research on leprosy. Lots of my classmates in the university were studying medicine, and some of them have already made names for themselves and are well off. But not a one has gone into the study of leprosy. I don't blame them. They'd starve. There should be pay that would induce doctors to go into it."

We talked in the forenoon and we weren't through, so we talked again in the afternoon. I said: "I had always thought of Kalaupapa as a place of great gloom and dejection. But they tell me it is really a happy community, and it seems so to me."

Harada said: "Well, I guess it depends on the individual. Most of the patients are Hawaiians, you know, and they are by nature a happy people. They take things as they come. They aren't so much affected by being here as some of us. As for me, sometimes I feel in good spirits and sometimes I get way down in the dumps. We get down in the mouth, and then see somebody in worse shape than ourselves, and then pick up a little and say, 'It could be worse.' And with me, I feel so often that if I could just sit down and talk about it—just get it off my chest, as they say, like talking to you here—then I'd feel better. It does something to you after a few years here. I can tell it has done something to me, but I fight against it. You lose the spirit of—I don't know what you'd call it—the spirit of fraternity, I guess. That's the reason I've tried to keep busy and keep little activities going among the others. In school I was active in athletics, and in organizing things. Here I've got several leagues going—handball and things like that. I can't play myself any more, on account of my hands. But it's hard to keep an organization going. There isn't enough permanence about it. You get some good key men, and the first thing you know they're gone. It takes the spirit out."

Harada had not suffered any extreme pain from his disease. There are two types of leprosy and his was the less painful type. In most cases the disease seems to deaden some of the nerves. "I could break off my fingers and never even feel it," he said. Sometimes he hadn't felt very well and couldn't sleep, but he was proud of the fact that he hadn't missed a day's work in the four years since he took over the store. He was glad of the opportunity to manage the store, for it gave him some slight way to use the knowledge acquired in the university. He had majored in economics, and had read widely on political science and commerce.

"Do you do much reading now?" I asked. His answer was one of the really sad notes in our long conversation. "I used to," he said. "For a long time I kept on reading in economics and agriculture, which is a sort of hobby of mine. But now I've got so I just read light stuff whenever I get hold of a magazine. There isn't much point in trying to keep on learning . . ."

He was lonely, because there was no one in Kalaupapa that he could really talk with as he was capable of talking. He apologized for saying what he did, and explained that he didn't feel himself any better than the rest, but there was a difference. He felt that he was stagnating mentally. He told me of a former teacher of his who came down to the settlement to see him one visiting day. The teacher told him she could notice that his grammar, which had been perfect, now had many errors in it. He hated to think of things like that happening to him.

I had completely lost the feeling that Harada resented my wanting to talk with him. As we sat and chatted and the hours passed, I realized that his facial expression was merely a result of the disease.

He was as interested in talking of the psychology of lepers as I was. He was eager and kind. He said several times that if there was anything personal about the patients I could think of to ask, he would try his best to give me the answer. But I ran out of questions, and then we talked about general things. He was interested in my job, and I told him of things I had seen in Alaska and other places. I shall always have a mental picture, to the end of my days, of us sitting there talking. Sitting in chairs, face to face, not three feet apart—one "clean" and one "unclean," as Harada would put it. The truth would be: one lucky and one unlucky. But whatever our appearances, we talked and talked and talked. Thoughts are wonderful things, that they can bring two people, so far apart, into harmony and understanding for even a little while.

When I got ready to go, Harada asked for my address, so he could write to me some time. And as I handed him the paper, and told him how grateful I was for the talk with him, he paid me the most touching compliment I had ever received—a compliment of such poignancy that I could barely acknowledge it. He said, with eagerness and deep feeling: "You have given me the happiest day I have ever had since I came to Kalaupapa. Thank you. Thank you."

My stay on Kalaupapa was one of the most powerful adventures in my life. There is something I need to say about it, and I cannot say it very well. It was a feeling something like this: out of the defilement and abuse that nature had heaped upon those people, there had arisen over Kalaupapa an atmosphere that was surely spiritual, almost heavenly. It was a strange atmosphere of calm—a calm that was invitational, and almost irresistible.

I am sure it was true that there were no martyrs serving there, and yet I don't see how they kept martyrs from pounding down

the gates to get in. I myself wandered into the foothills of martyr-
dom. Roaming Kalaupapa, I felt a kind of unrighteousness at
being whole and "clean"; I experienced an acute spiritual need
to be no better off than the leper. It wasn't romantic, it wasn't
drama; it was something akin to that urge that lures people standing on high places to leap downward.

My feeling will likely seem ridiculous. But I did experience it.
The emotion itself was an adventure in desire, and I am glad I
had it. But I am glad also that I had to go on, for I know that in
real life I am a sprint martyr; the long steady pull is not for me.
I tire of too much goodness, and wish to dart off and chase a
rabbit.

No man dare say that he has advanced through the curriculum
of all emotions until he has had sung to him the beautiful "Aloha
Oe," Hawaii's song of greeting and farewell, by the leper singers
of Kalaupapa.

There were ten of them, all men, some with *leis* around their
hats. They sang in a harmony of high pitches, yet infinitely soulful and soft. They sang in Hawaiian, which is the only way the
song can be really sung. They sang slowly and with love—for a
Hawaiian, no matter where he is, loves everything. The ten voices
intermingled, and swept in harmonies to a perfect blend. There
were modulations and graceful interweavings of tones that I
had never dreamed existed in this or any other song. The sound
fell at times almost to a sweet whisper; it never rose above the
level of graciousness.

The night was dark, and even the nervous palm fronds were
still. I stood while they sang. Aloha oe . . . farewell to thee . . .
farewell to thee forever. . . . And any man, going away, who can
stand and hear the last fragile notes fade from the throats of the
leper singers of Kalaupapa without tears in his eyes—well, he
would be better off dead.

Over the Pali

Chapter **I** WAS SUPPOSED TO LEAVE THE LEPER SETTLEMENT
XVII by horseback before 7:00 A.M. and get to the top of the two-thou-
sand-foot pali by eight. Kikukawa, the mayor of Kaunakakai,
would be waiting to drive me to the airport to meet a friend coming from Honolulu. But it was all done in the Hawaiian way,
which meant that the Hawaiian who furnished the horse and
donkey couldn't catch them till nearly eight o'clock. So it was
time for us to be at the top before we even started.

The Hawaiian rode the donkey with my traveling bag balanced
on his saddle horn. I rode the horse with my typewriter slung
from the saddle horn. Well, my horse was dead. I don't know how
long he had been dead, but it must have been a long time. It was
only the pull of the moon on him, like a tide, and the fact that
occasionally I got off and lifted one of his legs ahead of the other,
that gave us any progress at all.

In the meantime, my Hawaiian friend was having trouble too.
His donkey was too much alive. It would go lickety-split up
the trail for a hundred yards, then suddenly wheel and come
charging back down, bucking and jumping. Each time my traveling bag would go flying off into the weeds, and the Hawaiian
would act scared to death, and it would take us ten minutes or
so to get the donkey turned around and my bag balanced on
the saddle horn again.

About 8:45, when we were only halfway up the pali, we heard
the plane roaring across the island on its way south. The Hawaiian turned around and said, "Are you trying to catch the
plane?" He didn't say, "Were you?" He said, "Are you?" Isn't
that beautiful?

The ride up the pali is along a switchback trail, very rocky and just wide enough for two horses to pass. From the bottom it looks like a zigzag line painted on the side of the steep cliff. The upper half of the trail is just sort of glued to the cliff, like a stamp. I don't see how they ever got it built in the first place. There are places where you can look straight down eight hundred feet, as though it was the side of a building. At such moments I prefer stereopticon slides. But we did make it, and Kikukawa the mayor was there waiting.

The real name of the place was Puuohoku, which I can't pronounce, so let's just call it Fagan's ranch. I don't know what a Wyoming cattleman would do if he saw a ranch like that. Probably just think it was a mirage, and take another chaw.

Six or seven years before I was there, Paul Fagan had had a little spare cash so he up and bought one whole end of the island of Molokai—twenty-five or thirty or forty thousand acres. Bought mountains and rivers and beaches and wild goats and pineapple fields and whole Hawaiian villages. Then he started redecorating the scenery. He put hundreds of men to work. They tore up the pineapple fields. Terraced the hillsides for miles. Planted fresh grass. Threw away old houses and built new ones. For Fagan himself, a lodge on the hillside looking downward across a mile of beautiful slopes to the sea. You could have played tennis in the living room. There was a swimming pool in the shape of a teardrop, and a bar, and guest rooms and—well, you know, like Hollywood.

A quarter mile down the hill, on another knoll, he built a home for Fred Schattaeur, his ranch manager. Even this house would be dandy for any run-of-the-mine millionaire. And there was another beautiful home for the head cowboy, and a cottage for the ranch bookkeeper. The bunkhouse looked like a weekend guest house—which is not to imply it was not in good taste.

There were about eighty laborers on the place now, mostly Filipinos. Only a few of them tended cattle; the rest were chopping and burning and planting—still making a park out of hillsides and valleys. Hundreds of silver pheasants had been turned loose. Peacocks strutted all around the place. Soon they would high-fence a couple of valleys and fill them with Japanese deer. There were forty riding horses, and in the saddle room were two dozen fancy saddles for Fagan's guests. The gun case had thousands of dollars' worth of shooting irons. There was a special airplane landing field, and the place had its own waterworks and even an intra-ranch telephone system. Fagan wouldn't have a regular phone in his house, because he didn't want to be bothered when he was there. There was a dairy, all sanitary and everything. And they were building up a blue-ribbon herd of thoroughbred beef cattle. Ranch Manager Schattaeur had just returned from the mainland with six bulls worth twenty thousand dollars.

Fagan himself wasn't due out from San Francisco for a month yet, so I didn't get to see him, but Molokai was full of stories about him. His main pleasure in life, according to the stories, was giving away money and being lavishly good to people. If the town of Kaunakakai wanted anything, Fagan built it. If the village of Halawa needed something, Fagan whipped out a few hundred dollars. If a church at Kalaupapa needed a pipe organ, Fagan would say, "All right. Why not?"

Fagan was in his forties, and a democratic guy. He had a good time. He'd sit all afternoon in a beer joint in Kaunakakai hypnotizing natives. (He really could hypnotize people.) After he had brought them to life again he would slip them twenty dollars. His generosity was almost a problem. He would give a Hawaiian kid a two-hundred-dollar rifle, and offer a Hawaiian five hundred dollars for a hundred-dollar horse. He would give the schoolteacher a hundred. He would throw a party at his mansion for a whole native village. Everybody could see very plainly that he had more money than he needed, and that he liked to share it. So the natives at the party would slip quarts of liquor under their shirts before they left, and next night they would come back and clean out his flock of a thousand turkeys. No, it wasn't stealing. Mr. Fagan would undoubtedly wish them to have the turkeys, for he had so many more than he needed. It almost drove Fred Schattaeur nuts.

Everything flowed freely when Fagan was there. But after he was gone, a Hawaiian would come to Fred Schattaeur and ask for money for a gallon of whisky, and Schattaeur, who was practical and didn't like Hawaiians anyway because they wouldn't work, would say, "Get the hell out of here and stay out." And then the Hawaiian would go back home and his feelings would be hurt, and nobody understood anybody else, and it was awful. So maybe it's better just to be pore and not have no half-million-dollar ranch at all.

It seems that all visitors to Maui must go up to the top of the volcano Haleakala and see the sunrise across the crater. Well, the Rotarians were having a Saturday-night blowout in Wailuku, with a lot of visiting Rotarians from the other islands, and they were to polish it off by going up to see the sunrise on Haleakala. I was invited to go along.

I went to bed fairly unexcited, but for some perverse reason couldn't sleep till about two-thirty. So, when the phone rang at three-thirty and they said they were ready to start, I felt sort of like an active volcano myself.

It's forty miles over a good macadam road from Wailuku to Haleakala crater. You go from sea level to ten thousand feet. And as we climbed, the lights of Wailuku and Kahului and Paia spread out far below us; above were the myriad tropical stars, and far down we could see the dim beach line on both sides of the island. It was a wonderfully impressive sight. And our host, who was driving, said it would be an almost perfect morning to see the sunrise.

And so it would have been, I guess—except that it began to mist and fog up, and when we finally got to the top the wind was blowing forty miles an hour, the rain was a horizontal deluge driving into you like a sandblast, and you couldn't see five feet. If we'd been sitting on top of Mendenhall glacier it couldn't have felt any colder.

We ducked into the shelter house, built a fire, had hot coffee and sandwiches, dried out our clothes, and got slightly warm. The sun never did come up, and it was nine-thirty before we got back downtown and into bed. The Maui people felt terrible about it.

Live volcanoes are probably the main tourist attraction in Hawaii, but volcanoes aren't spectacular to look at, except during the few weeks every three or four years when one of them is throwing fire. And when I was there they were exactly as alive as a stone dog on a gatepost.

The two largest volcanoes are about twenty miles apart, in the center of the island of Hawaii. They rise nearly fourteen thousand feet, and the "saddle" between them must be ten or twelve thousand feet high. The taller of the two, Mauna Kea, hasn't streamed lava in our time. The other, Mauna Loa, is still active. Very few people ever get up to look into the crater on top of Mauna Loa. They say it's a weird world up there amidst that fantastic formation of solid lava. But it's a terrific three-day journey on horseback, even after you've driven a third of the way up in a car; you mustn't eat on the trip up, or you'll have altitude sickness; some horses can make it clear to the top, but the Army won't allow its horses above the ten-thousand-foot rest-house; the trail is so jagged you'll wear out a pair of heavy new boots, and often come back with your feet cut and bleeding. So I didn't go.

But I did see the crater of Kilauea, a small volcano four thousand feet up on the slopes of Mauna Loa—a sort of subsidiary, you might say. Kilauea isn't a peak. In fact, the mountainside for many miles is fairly flat, and Kilauea crater is just a big hole in level ground. It's about seven miles across, the floor is hard and barren, and you can drive clear around the rim. At one point you can look down into the "firepit," which is a crater within the crater. This is the hole where Kilauea spouts and surges whenever she spouts and surges. The pit is a horrible thing to look into —270 feet deep and about three thousand feet across, roughly circular. The walls are absolutely perpendicular. The park service has built an iron railing, which you can lean on while looking over. They warn you not to throw anything in, for fear of starting a landslide down the crater wall.

I asked if anybody had ever jumped into the firepit. A Ranger said, yes, just a couple of years back a young Portuguese shot his sweetheart, threw her in, and jumped in after her. It took twelve days to get the bodies out. There is no possible way to descend the firepit's walls, so they had to stretch a cable clear across, then run a little wheeled apparatus out on the cable, and let a volunteer rescuer down from this cable. I wouldn't have done it for ten thousand dollars.

The floor of the pit was hard lava rock and looked as dead as a desert, though in a couple of places you could see a little sulphur fume seeping out. She was long overdue for another flare-up. The volcano people were hoping, and so was I, that she'd fly off the handle during my stay. But she just slept on.

Not far from Kilauea is what they call the "Chain of Craters." It consists of nine old craters in a row. Mostly they are just deep holes in the ground, completely inactive and grown up with vegetation. But in one very old crater, about seven hundred feet deep and half a mile or so across, a lot of wild goats were living. They had first been noticed about fifteen years before, and the Park Rangers had no idea how they got there. The sides were perpendicular, and even a sure-footed goat can't walk like a fly up and down a wall. And at the point where the crater floor slants up closest to the top, there were still about two hundred feet of straight-up-and-down wall. The only way the Rangers could figure it was that a couple of goats must have fallen in, somehow survived the two-hundred-foot tumble, and set up a new little goat world of their own from which there was no escape.

Flowing lava on the island of Hawaii does some mighty funny things. The flow of 1926, which was a very rapid one, went clear into the sea, wiping out a small native village and covering up the highway. But it left an oasis that you could see from the highway—a spot as big as three or four city blocks. And on this oasis fifteen head of cattle were left stranded. It was nine months before cowboys could ride over and bring them out. And when they got them out, the cattle were fatter and healthier than when they were trapped. They had lived on trees and bushes, and got water from the rain that fell on the bushes.

And speaking of cattle on Hawaii, here's another funny thing. There are spots on the islands where you see vast expanses of prickly-pear cactus, which the cattle eat. They know how to knock off a "leaf," paw it open with their hoofs, scrape back the spines so they won't get pricked, and then eat the inside. Cactus has a great deal of water in it—enough, they say, for animals to live on it without any other water. And some of these cattle born and raised up the mountainside among the cactus don't know how to drink regular water. When they're brought down to a creek or a water trough they just plunge their heads clear in and nearly drown, I was told. I don't believe it, but that's what they said.

Boat day in Honolulu is famous the world over. The way people come down to see the boat off, and stand there and weep and scream and wave, is an internationally celebrated phenomenon. J. P. McEvoy once wrote a funny piece about it—how everybody with friends comes down to see them leave, and they weep and take on, and those who don't have any friends come down anyway just to have a good cry. Funny or not, that's what happens, and it's genuine and sincere. People at both ends of the gangplank have an almost hysterical feeling that you cannot, must not, dare not say goodbye to Hawaii.

We knew, before it ever started, that we would break under it. We knew people would come, and it would be colorful and gay for a while, and then we would be overwhelmed at the moment of parting. We had read how it is to sail from Hawaii. But we never really dreamed.

Our friends came in a stream for an hour. They came until the cabin was full, and the beds and chairs and suitcases were covered, and friends overflowed into the companionway. They brought books, and candy, and orchids, and lei upon lei for our shoulders. Leis stacked up to our chins, and on up till we could barely see over them. You could feel the cool petals on your face. I don't know where the last hour went, or who was in it, or what anybody did. I just remember people swarming off at last, and then our crowd starting to say goodbye, and people crying and kissing. And I remember that I, being very hardhearted and cruel, didn't cry, but I sure did kiss everybody in sight.

And then they were all gone, and we were standing at the rail holding colored streamers and waving at those same friends through a sort of haze. The streamers broke and suddenly we were far away and couldn't make out our friends. A woman standing behind us was screaming as though it had just suddenly come to her, "I'll never see you again. Do you hear, I'll never see you again in my life!"

Brown boys in trunks swarmed over the upper decks as the tug pulled us out into the harbor. They were making collections for the high dive off the top deck. I gave one boy some change, and he said he'd let us know when he got ready to dive. We stood waiting at the rail, overwhelmed with flowers, just looking down into the water, thinking or not thinking—I don't know.

The ship moved forward. The muddy water became blue water. I heard a voice and saw our diving boy waving to us that he was about to go over. Head down, he went like a dark bullet. The distance was terrific, for the *Lurline* is an immense ship. We grimaced when he hit. But he went in like an arrow, and in a second popped up again. He shook the water from his eyes, lay on his back and looked along the rail till he saw us, and then with a great smile he waved, and we could hear from far down his "aloha." And then he turned and swam for Honolulu.

The ship straightened out, and sailed past Diamond Head, a couple of miles offshore. It's here that you toss your leis into the water, and they float ashore, forming a bond that irresistibly draws you back again some day. Standing at the rail, we could see bright flashes along the Waikiki shore—people flashing mirrors in the sun to their friends now far out at sea. A last goodbye. We couldn't make out any people, but with glasses we did pick out our beautiful lawn on Waikiki. Had our friends had time to get home, we wondered. And as we watched, a blinding mirror flash came from the center of our own Hawaiian lawn.

Then we threw our leis . . . the wind caught them and carried them along for a little, and then they fell on the water in pure, beautiful circles, and started their little journey back to Hawaii . . . while we sailed away. We turned and went below, and did not look back until Hawaii was far beyond the horizon.

The Movies

Chapter XVIII   ON YOUR FIRST DAY IN HOLLYWOOD YOU THINK everybody you see walking along Hollywood Boulevard is in the movies. They all look the part. You feel like stopping people and asking, "What do you do?" There are lots of women in slacks and sweaters, and men without neckties, and scores of amazingly beautiful girls, so beautiful they all look alike. And the ugly people you suppose are character actors, and the rich-looking men—no doubt they're film executives.

Hollywood is immense. You can't tell where it ends and such unimportant places as Los Angeles, Beverly Hills, Burbank, Santa Monica, and Culver City begin. It's all the same place, with different names. Hollywood itself is a city of common people. The dazzling ones live apart, up in the hills, walled off from the world by secretaries and butlers and unlisted phone numbers. The pee-pul, they just live off each other and bask in sunshine and proximity to glory.

There is a lot of here-today-and-gone-tomorrow about Hollywood. People come, and fail, and hang on a while, and some go away. If they stay too long they're licked. They buy an old wreck of a car, and borrow gasoline money from each other, and mooch on from year to year—pretending. Hollywood the glamorous is sad under the skin—though always hopeful.

Walt Disney was my kind of folks. His brother Roy said, "We're just common ordinary people. Walt is one swell guy, and he hasn't changed a bit since he was a kid." Walt was somewhat "Hollywood," though. He wore sport shirts and zippy coats; he had a home with the inevitable Hollywood swimming pool; he drove big cars; he went often to the Santa Anita race track and mingled with the big Hollywood names in the clubhouse. But it stopped at that. He didn't go to the night spots, and you wouldn't find him at the cocktail parties.

When you sat and talked with him, he was not in the least retiring. He talked with enthusiasm and ease, and made you feel he was interested in you. He had a habit of saying "you know" very often, and of nodding at you as if to say "sure you know, don't you." Yet he had a feeling that he made a bad impression on people, owing partly to his lack of formal education. He was uncomfortable in crowds, or in the presence of stuffed shirts. He told me that Mickey Mouse, not Walt Disney, was the thing, and that if he didn't come up to people's expectations it would hurt Mickey's reputation.

He had to make a speech once in a while, but usually it was just to do some friend a favor. He was asked to accept an honorary degree from a California college. "I sort of liked the idea," he said. "I only went through the first year of high school, and I thought it would be sort of nice to have a degree. But I got to thinking I'd have to get up and say nice things that I didn't feel, so I called it off."

All the time I was with Disney I was trying to find something that would explain his ability (or even his desire) to create beautiful, fanciful, fairylandish things. But I couldn't catch anything. He was just people, with a sense of theater showmanship.

I remarked that I was tremendously impressed with the whole studio's dissatisfaction with the work they'd done, even with *Snow White*. "That's the spirit now," he said, "and that's what we want. But it wasn't always that way. After *Three Little Pigs* the praise began rolling in, and some of us sat back and rested on our oars. That won't happen again."

Disney was thirty-six when I met him. He had been in Hollywood since 1923—fifteen years of long, hard plugging. He had had a couple of breakdowns from overwork, and that started him reading up on the human mechanism. He told me things about the "chemistry of the body"—he knew the intricacies of digestion and all that. He used to think he was awfully sick—even thought he had infantile paralysis once, and was sore when the doctor said he hadn't. But he wasn't a faddist.

Walt's fame had not affected his personal life, mainly because he wouldn't let it. He had been married twelve years, and had two little girls, one adopted. He saw practically all the movies made, because he enjoyed them—they relaxed him—and because he got ideas from other pictures. He played badminton with friends some evenings. Other evenings he read or played with the kids. His closest friends outside the family were at the studio. He still knew most of his seven hundred employes, and they all called him Walt. (That's his name, by the way—not Walter.)

I knew that he had long since stopped doing any of the actual drawings for the Disney pictures, but I supposed that he still sketched out his ideas. He said he did not. "I just talk a new character," he said, "and the other boys draw it from that."

"But surely," I said, "you draw some, don't you?"

Walt seemed sort of embarrassed. He laughed and said, "Well, yes, but I never let anybody see what I do. You have to keep in practice, and the other boys have gone beyond me now. But, by God, I could animate again if I had to."

His spirit was still very much in every quack of Donald Duck and every squeak of Mickey Mouse. In fact, the voice of Mickey Mouse was Disney's voice. Nobody else had ever voiced Mickey for the films. They were trying to work him out of that role, his men told me, because he shouldn't waste his time on it. And anyhow, they said, his voice was no good for the part!

As the organization built up, he'd had to pull further and further away from the details. Yet there was hardly a movement in any Disney film that he hadn't personally seen and discussed half a dozen times with his men. And at least half the ideas and the suggestions for changes came from him.

I wanted to find out how his animated cartoons were made. Roy Disney, Walt's business manager and brother, said, "If you do find out, I wish you'd come and tell the boys around here. We don't know." Bill Garity, head technical engineer, said, "My mother was out here for six months last year. We talked animated movies day and night. The day she left she said, 'But, Bill, what makes them move?'"

Well, they work like a child's "flip book." You remember how you flipped through with your thumb in a couple of seconds and saw the characters move, because each picture was a little further along in the action than the preceding one. Animated cartoons are nothing more than that. It took about fifteen thousand pictures to make a Mickey Mouse short which would run seven or eight minutes. In successive drawings the artists moved their characters anywhere from a sixty-fourth of an inch to an inch and a half, depending on the type of action. If Mickey was moved an inch and a half in each picture, he would go so fast you could barely recognize him, and it would take only about ten drawings to get him across the screen. But if the interval was a sixty-fourth of an inch it would take him nearly a minute to cross the screen, and would require hundreds of pictures. This very fine interval was used only for very slow body movement, or for a close-up change of facial expression. If the cartoon character was a soldier walking in regular march time, it would take twelve pictures to make him take one step. That gives you an idea how much work goes into an animated picture.

Most of Walt Disney's office time was spent with the story department, which consisted of artists, not writers. They sketched out their ideas for the characters and the action, but it was Disney who made the decisions. Through continual conferences he molded and shaped the yarns until he was absolutely satisfied, down to the last tone of a voice and turn of a face.

Then the picture was ready to go into production. It was recorded first in sound—the music and the dialogue—and then it was broken down into scenes and assigned to artists for the final drawings. Disney employed four hundred artists, from the highly paid "animators" who created the characters and drew the high spots of the action, down to less experienced men who did the in-between drawings and added the details, such as buttons, neckties, and shoes. Every figure and every background was drawn separately, and they didn't come together until it was time to combine them on movie film.

The whole business looked like a jumble. You could see just one little Mickey Mouse scene being drawn on thousands of sheets of paper and traced and colored on tens of thousands of sheets of clear celluloid. I couldn't imagine how on earth they kept track of things and got them all together in the end. The secret was simple—bookkeeping. Everything had a number on it. In the end you just lined up the numbers and there you had a movie. But I couldn't help wondering if all seven hundred employes didn't sometimes have to get down on their hands and knees and hunt for the scene of Mickey falling into the pie.

One blistering night during the big drought of 1936 I went to a movie in Miles City, Montana, just to get out of the heat. The leading man was a young fellow named Gene Autry. I had never heard of him. Yet it turned out he was the hero of heroes to millions of children. He was getting more fan mail than Clark Gable and his phonograph records were outselling Bing Crosby's.

Autry was twenty-nine when I met him in 1938. Even though he was a crooning cowboy, he wasn't synthetic. He was western, all right, and regular. Hollywood hadn't fazed him. He had an Oklahoma drawl, and his grammar wasn't any too hot. And he said he'd rather make phonograph records than act in movies.

He was born on a farm in northern Texas and raised on another farm in southern Oklahoma. He could ride horses long before he could play a guitar. The steps in his career had been as follows: from farm to telegraph operator on the Frisco Railroad; then to singing on a radio station in Tulsa; then to New York to make phonograph records; then to Chicago on the "Barn Dance" program for five years. And then to Hollywood in 1935.

His movie rise had been spectacular. The year before I met him he became the first cowboy hero ever to sweep the board as No. 1 favorite in the United States, Australia, South America, and England. His popularity had risen so fast that his pay hadn't kept up with it, and he was in a legal quarrel with his studio. His contract had three more years to run, and he was getting only forty thousand dollars a year, plus a few thousand for personal-appearance tours between pictures. Some of the Western stars whom he far outranked in box-office appeal were making two to three times as much. "If it was just one year, I wouldn't open my trap about it," he said. "But a movie career is so short and things change so fast that you can't tell where you'll be three years from now. You've got to get it while you can."

He lived fairly simply, but it did take money. He had the inevitable agent, who took, I assume, ten per cent. He had a "public affairs" man. He had a two-room office in downtown Hollywood. He had a secretary. The photos he sent out cost twenty-five dollars a thousand. Count the stamps, envelopes, extra help, and so on, and his fan mail alone cost him close to ten thousand dollars a year out of his own pocket. He owned seven horses, and had to keep stables and several acres of ground in Burbank, with three men to care for the horses. The feed bill wasn't tiny, either. Like all stars, he had to take ads in the trade magazines. Charity organizations would send him ten tickets to a dance. They didn't say, "Will you buy?" They said, "Sign here . . ." Old friends would drop in for a sawbuck or two, and he also supported a good many people. "A man who wouldn't help his folks ought to be shot," he said.

I asked him how it felt to jump from a poor boy, making a few dollars a week, way up to a thousand a week. "Well, I honestly can't see much difference," he said. "I've got a Cadillac now, where I used to have a Buick. Before that it was a Ford. The main thing is that you don't have to stop and think it over if you see something you want to buy. Outside of that, I don't see much difference." He still hadn't bought himself a fancy house with an estate—he just lived in an apartment. "I'm not a glamour guy," he said. "This Hollywood stuff don't mean anything to me. I do sort of like it out here, and I don't mind getting up in front of a camera any more. But I don't pretend to be an actor. Bill Boyd's the best actor among the Westerns. Sure, I like to get all this fan mail, and it makes me feel good that I can entertain people all over the world. But I'm telling you, it hasn't got me to the point where I couldn't stop every bit of it right now. I'd like to get me a radio station in a medium-sized southwestern town, or else two or three good theaters. Just something I'd enjoy, and enough to insure me a good living. And then I'd have me a ranch out in the country not far away, and live out there. Somewhere around Santa Fe. I think that's the best town of all."

Autry wore a sort of Hollywood version of a cowboy outfit all the time. It startled me when I saw him in his downtown office in tight-legged brown pants, brown fitted coat with trimmed pockets, flowing bow tie, big hat, high-heeled boots.

"What do you wear that rig all the time for?" I asked.

"Well," Autry said, "partly because I figure it's good business, and partly because I'm so used to it I'm uncomfortable in anything else. When I put on a pair of regular pants now, they're so big around the knees it feels like I was in a tent."

He didn't own a single pair of regular shoes. He hadn't worn anything but cowboy boots for years. He couldn't resist buying them and had a new pair made every time he saw some he liked. He owned a couple of dozen pairs. And since he had to have the best in cowboy outfits and change often, his wardrobe cost around three thousand dollars a year. But I'll bet he'd have been more comfortable in overalls.

Autry and his wife had been married six years, and had no children. She was from Missouri. Their closest friends were the chief of police of Burbank, Elmer Myers, and his wife. They spent Sunday afternoons together and played bridge after dinner. "I suppose we're together forty Sundays out of the year," Autry said. Jim Tully also was a good friend.

He liked Harry Carey the best of all the old Western stars. And the reason? "Because Harry Carey is the only one of the old-timers who ever came to me and said, 'Good luck to you, boy, I hope you make it.' The others resent a newcomer."

Autry played golf three or four times a week at the Lakeside Club, the only club to which he belonged. He was crazy about sports; he never missed a fight or a rassling match and was almost as keen about baseball. He had half a dozen saddles. The one he used in pictures was all covered with silver trimmings and was worth two thousand dollars. He had never been on one of those society "English" saddles. He was a good rough rider now, but they said he wasn't so hot when he first came to Hollywood.

On personal-appearance tours he drove from town to town in his Cadillac, followed by the other boys in the big truck and trailer with the horses. Kids went so nuts over the trailer that they nearly ruined it scratching their names on it. So now he charged it with electricity to give them a little shock. It wasn't enough to hurt them, but they weren't scratching names any more.

In some parts of the country Autry was so popular he had to eat in restaurant kitchens in order to get through a meal. Oddly enough, he got more fan mail from Pennsylvania than any other state. I looked through a stack of his mail, and found several from little towns on the Hawaiian island of Maui, where I had spent several days.

He didn't smoke—said he hadn't had a cigarette in his mouth in ten years, and one would make him sick. He turned down a radio offer from a big cigarette company, and said he'd had a lot of commendatory letters for doing so.

He had recently signed up for the use of his name as a trademark, and he loaded me down with samples. I left practically spilling over with Gene Autry thingumajigs. So as I sit writing about the No. 1 Western movie star, there is a cartridge belt around me, and a holster is on my hip. Every now and then I run to the bathroom and scrape off a few whiskers soaked with Gene Autry shaving cream. Occasionally I open the book and hum a Gene Autry song. I add up my expense account on a Gene Autry writing tablet. And after each paragraph I whip out my Gene Autry cap-gun and shoot my beloved right between the eyes.

Yakima Canutt had scars all over him, even on his face, but they weren't unbecoming. He was lucky to have any face whatsoever, because he was Hollywood's leading "danger man" for horse stunts—or anything else.

You might have thought he'd be ugly and rough-looking. But he was a fine-looking man who loved his home, and I never saw anyone around a studio better liked or more respected than Yak. He was forty-two, tall and fairly slim, and he had an easy western look about him. There probably wasn't a better rider in the movies than Yak Canutt. In his younger days he was one of the greatest rodeo cowboys that ever lived. He held the world's bronc-riding championship from 1917 to 1924, and was the all-around cowboy champion for five years. In 1923 he went into the movies and was starred in Western pictures, but when sound came in he lost out. His voice was too gentle and mellow.

That was when Yak turned to his riding ability and became a stunt man. He was making more money now than he ever did as a movie hero, and he appeared oftener on the screen—though usually anonymously as somebody's double. He free-lanced among all the studios, and had more work than he could do. He got as high as five hundred dollars for a single stunt, such as blowing up a speeding wagon full of dynamite.

He told me he was called to a studio one day and the director asked him how much he'd charge to fall off a horse. Yak said anywhere from five to a hundred dollars.

"What do you do for five dollars?" the director asked.

"I'll ride in at a walk, stop the horse, get off, and sit down," Yak said.

"And what for ten dollars?" asked the director.

"I'll ride in at a trot, get off without stopping, and sit down," Yak said.

"And for twenty-five?" the director asked.

"I'll come in pretty fast, jump off, and roll over."

"And for fifty?"

"I'll ride in at a gallop, do a good hard fall, and roll over several times."

"And for a hundred?"

"I'll do anything you can think up." The director compromised on the fifty-dollar fall.

Yak would wreck speeding autos, jump seventy-five feet from cliffs into water, do terrific fist fighting. But the basis of his work was horse stunts. He had probably fallen off horses at a dead run, been dragged by horses, ridden horses over cliffs, more than any other man alive. He said most of the Western stars rode well and could take pretty rough falls themselves, but they were so valuable the studios didn't gamble on their getting hurt.

Yak had been cut, bruised, and skinned hundreds of times, but seriously injured only twice. Once was when a torch he was carrying exploded. He was in a hospital three weeks. The other was when he was changing from a galloping horse to a "runaway" team hitched to a wagon. He fell between the horses; the wagon axle hit him on the back, broke his shoulder blade, and tore one

· 262 ·

shoulder to pieces. He was sent to the hospital again. He got pneumonia that time and almost died.

He said he had never fainted, but a couple of times the pain was so terrible that things went black and he would have fainted if they hadn't thrown water on him. He had never broken an arm or a leg.

I asked him if he could get insurance. He said yes, and without paying much extra. They investigated him thoroughly and figured he knew his stuff so well it wasn't very dangerous. He kept himself in excellent condition. He didn't drink except for an occasional highball. He rode a bicycle a lot to keep his legs in shape. He figured he'd begin to slow up in about five years, and then he'd probably get an executive position in the movies.

In the old rodeo days he earned as high as eighteen thousand dollars a year in prize money, but it got away from him. He said the most he ever "came in" with was six thousand dollars, and that was all gone by spring. But he'd been saving his money in the last few years. Just give him three more years, he said, and he'd be set for come what may. He had just finished a new Spanish stucco home on an acre of ground not far from Republic Studios. His little "estate" had a brick wall around it, and a badminton court, an outdoor grill, and a little orchard, and he was going to build a miniature speedway for his two babies to ride tricycles around. He drove a Dodge sedan, had deer heads and his old world-champion saddles in the den, loved California, got away once a year for a hunting trip to the Northwest, and had three pages written on his autobiography. Hell, he was better off than Gable.

I went to the Trocadero, one of the night clubs where the tourists went, thinking they might see a movie star.

Well, my visit turned out to be a sort of failure. In the first place, it cost so much I didn't sleep a wink for three nights worrying about it. And in the second place, every time I go to a night club I waste too much of the evening down in the men's department trying to find out from the whisk-broom boy how much he makes in tips. That's just what happened at the Trocadero, and since the boy wouldn't tell me I don't see how I can write much about it.

The Trocadero differs very little from any other night club I've been in. The tables are close together, the dance floor is small, the air is thick with smoke, and there's so much noise and chatter you might as well be eating in Childs.

At the Troc that night were Al Jolson and Ruby Keeler, Gracie Allen and George Burns, and Jack Benny and his wife Mary Livingston. The latter four sat together at a ringside table. I had already seen the Bennys in New York, so that made no difference. I never could quite locate Burns and Allen, so that didn't help. The only one that interested me was Ruby Keeler, and from where I was sitting I couldn't see her, and never did see her. Maxie Rosenbloom, the ex-prizefighter, who was becoming quite a rage in Hollywood, was the master of ceremonies. They say he is very funny, but I couldn't hear anything he said. There was a floor show, with dancing and singing and cartwheels. And after that the orchestra played and we all got out and milled around. And finally we paid off and went home.

This is a great life for people who like to do things like that. But unless a great change comes over me, I never expect to enter the doors of another night club.

Visitors with a little pull had become such a problem around the Hollywood studios that the movie moguls had decided to do something about it. Naturally everybody wanted to see how movies were made. And naturally nearly everybody knew somebody who knew somebody who could get him in. So many people knew so many people that it had got so there was hardly room for the actors on a set. So here's what they had in mind: They were thinking of setting up one sound stage just for visitors. All the studios would contribute to it. There would be a full movie-making crew at work all the time. Prop men would carry lumber around. Electricians would waste hours monkeying with the lights. Actors would emote and heave and weep. The director would yell, "Cut!" Thus the public could get the whole business in one eyeful, while the real working crews at the real studios could go about their business in peace and quiet.

There was just one thing wrong with this plan, and that was that it wouldn't work. It wasn't so much movie making that people wanted to see. It was the stars in the flesh, and there were only about fifty stars in Hollywood who would satisfy a star-seeker. So, unless they made each of these fifty stars work about six days a year on this phony set, there would still be just as much clamor to get into the real studios as there ever was. And as long as somebody knew somebody, they'd get in. There is one happy thought about this public movie making idea, though. My friend Cavanaugh, who had lived in Los Angeles for years and never been inside a studio, thought of it. Cavanaugh said, "Wouldn't it be funny if these people just going through the motions would turn out a better picture than the studios that are really trying hard?" Cavanaugh was always thinking up things like that.

I believe in the movies. One of my hates is the smart critic who hurls his words at Hollywood's disgraceful commercialism, its insane business extravagances, its illiterate executives, its failure to achieve any approach to real art, its refusal to broadcast a message. But then I'm not a typical movie fan. It seems impossible for me to see more than six or eight pictures a year, and I pick my pictures. The result is that I seldom see a bad movie. So I think the movies are wonderful.

As a matter of fact, instead of the usual "Why can't we make movies more like real life?" I think a more pertinent question is "Why can't real life be more like the movies?" A movie is a series of climaxes—little glimpses of high spots and low spots—and in the end there is the great climax, and the darkness, and no concern for the years of dying embers and the utter monotony ahead.

Why can't human beings too live only in climaxes, in great ecstasy or great despair, with all the long dull stretches left out? Who would mind being blinded in the war, if he could win the girl anyhow, and then have it understood that the rest of his life was to be an idyl and a blessing, with no dreary days or cruel, growing prongs of pity directed at him. And who would mind being the other fellow and losing the girl if in real life he could actually come to the end of the reel right there, and never have to brood about it, or hunger?

Of course, characters on the screen are made to suffer, but their suffering is dramatic and romantic, while ours here on the globe is the dull achy kind that embitters and wastes, with so little drama to ennoble it.

It isn't what the movies put in that makes them so wonderful —it's what they leave out. Wouldn't a movie be dull if it ran on for weeks and weeks, showing a man at his work? It's much nicer for the movies to show him working for just thirty seconds.

And in our little tragedies and despairs, and our big ones too, why couldn't we just go stare out a window and bow our heads and look grave and heartbroken for a few seconds, denoting a long period of grief and yearning, and not have to go through the actual months and years of it?

And our happiness too. Maybe you'd like to have happiness strung out, instead of just a flash and a kiss denoting bliss forever. But for me, I think not. Just a moment of happiness is all right, for then there is no dulling. Yes, just wake me up for the peaks and the valleys, and please have the anesthetist ready when we come to the plains, and the long days when nothing happens.

Death Valley

Chapter XIX ON A CALIFORNIA ROAD MAP YOU COULD SEE A place called Cave Springs. But when you got there you found it was not a town. It was not a village, not even a country post office. It was just a private home with two people in it. It was on the map because it was the only house in a stretch of a hundred forty miles. Mrs. Ira Sweetman and her cousin, Adrian Egbert, lived there. It was sixty miles to a store in one direction, eighty miles in the other. Either way, it was all desert. Sometimes you could hardly tell where the dirt road was.

"Do many travelers use this road?" I asked Mr. Egbert.

"Yes," he said. "There was a car past here just the other day."

Mrs. Sweetman and Mr. Egbert lived in this out-of-the-way place by choice. They didn't have to raise anything, or scratch for a living. They were simply retired. They were getting along in years—between sixty-five and seventy, I'd say—but they were lively and enthusiastic, and well-to-do in a modest way; they had every comfort and were on the desert because they liked it.

Their home was on the south rim of Death Valley, in a gap in the mountains thirty-six hundred feet high. From their door you looked down into the fabulous valley below sea level. At night you could see a campfire fifty-five miles away on the valley floor. On the north rim, a hundred thirty miles away, stood the isolated castle of Death Valley Scotty. The Sweetman-Egbert menage had none of the fame of Scotty's castle, and yet it was just as isolated, and just as unusual too, for while Scotty lived in an incongruously lavish palace, they lived mostly in caves! I know it is hard to think of desert cave dwellers as being sane, intelligent, educated people. But you wouldn't have known Mrs. Sweetman and Mr. Egbert from a couple of good Indiana neighbors.

We drew up at Cave Springs just at noon, after the sixty-mile pull from Barstow. I asked Mrs. Sweetman if she could furnish us a bite of lunch. "Why, yes," she said. "Come right on in. This is Mr. Egbert. I look a sight. Sit down and make yourselves at home." So they put on another can of chile con carne, and pretty soon we were all around the kitchen table, eating sausages and yams and chile and figs.

We stayed three hours, and they showed us all through their amazing place. They got out old letters and pictures, and we talk-talk-talked, and would have been there yet, I suppose, except that Mr. Egbert told Mrs. Sweetman she'd have to stop talking and make us go on, or we wouldn't get to Furnace Creek before dark.

Mrs. Sweetman first saw daylight in Richmond, Virginia. When she was ten she migrated with her parents to the Black Hills of South Dakota, where a good part of her life was spent. She loved the Black Hills, and she still owned stock in the famous Home-stake gold mine at Lead, South Dakota. She had been a widow for twenty or thirty years. She liked politics, and had been an active political leader in both South Dakota and Arizona. For several years she was postmistress at Daggett, California. Occasionally she went to Los Angeles to a banquet of the Black Hills Pioneer Society. "I never knew I was a pioneer till they started making over me a few years ago," she said.

She and her cousin had been at Cave Springs fourteen years. I asked Mr. Egbert: "How did you happen to pick this spot?"

"Well, sir," he said, "I rode through this gap in 1894, looking for a lost mine. There was hardly even a trail then. Many times after that I came up this way, and we always camped here because of the wonderful water in the springs. I liked this spot. Well, I had the flu in 1918, and I never really got over it. So in 1924 when the doctor told me I better go to the desert for good or I wouldn't live six months, I said, 'Doc, I know exactly where to go.' We bought ten acres here. We hauled lumber and everything for sixty miles in a Model T, and started building. We've been building ever since."

They lived in a three-room cottage and in half a dozen caves. There was nothing crazy about it. The caves were practical—and handmade; Mr. Egbert made them himself. He used to be a mining engineer, and he'd had construction experience. He had scouted mines from the Arctic Circle to Peru. He knew how to construct his little kingdom out of the rocky barrenness of Cave Springs.

Their house was perched on a small bluff alongside the trail. There was a good-sized living room with big windows taking in the sun. Behind this was one bedroom, which abutted a solid rock wall. And there was a kitchen, big like a farm kitchen. One of the caves led straigh᾽ back from the kitchen door. In it were long shelves stocked with canned goods, enough to live on for months. The next cave, where Mr. Egbert slept the year round, was a sort of apartment—two bedrooms in the back and a sitting room in front, all fully furnished. The temperature was never freezing in there in winter and seldom got above seventy in summer, even though outside it would go to a hundred fifteen. And it was never damp. A little shaft for ventilation led from the back bedrooms up to the surface. The walls and ceiling were jagged rock, whitewashed. "What do you think of this for when the Japs come to bomb us?" Mr. Egbert asked.

The next cave was a sort of workshop and office. And the next one contained the thing most important for life on the desert— water. It seeped through the rock and dripped into a tub. Mr. Egbert said it was the finest water in the world; he'd had it tested. Underfoot, covered with flooring, was a five-barrel tank, in case of emergency. There had never been an emergency.

The next cave was a garage where Mrs. Sweetman kept her new Dodge coupé. Mr. Egbert's old Model T sat out in the open. There were still other caves and semicaves, housing little chicken lots and various kinds of machinery. One of them was a little place for friends who might come to visit.

It had taken Mr. Egbert years to make the caves; he did it by drilling, and blasting with dynamite. The work kept idleness away during their first years at Cave Springs. But now they didn't need any more caves—and idleness was taking care of itself. Their days had no set schedule. There was an old alarm clock in the kitchen, but the alarm had never been set. They even lost track of the days. They would figure up this way: "You [Mrs. Sweetman] went to Barstow on Monday. We had steak Tuesday, fried rabbit Wednesday, and stewed rabbit yesterday. So today must be Friday."

Mrs. Sweetman drove sixty miles to Barstow about once a week for mail, a hundred fifty to San Bernardino twice a month for supplies, and occasionally on into Los Angeles. She always put her evening gown and slippers in the back of the car, in case she might be invited to a formal party. She was leaving in a few days on a three-month cruise to Central America.

Mr. Egbert hadn't been to town for three years. Just didn't want to go. And yet he was delighted when anybody dropped past. He was a great reader; he used a pair of glasses that cost sixty cents, and he subscribed to about ten magazines. He had a big radio, with storage batteries to run it. A little windmill generated power for the batteries. They burned oil in the cook-stove, for there wasn't enough wood within fifty miles to start a Boy Scout fire. Mr. Egbert smoked two Between the Acts cigars a day, drank beer, and let out a cussword now and then.

The only thing they raised was a few chickens. But that was hard, for bobcats kept breaking in. There were wild mountain sheep in the vicinity. "But," I said, "you're not allowed to shoot them; it's against the law." "Well, I won't let one come up and bite me," Mr. Egbert said. "Three or four have tried!"

He said they could live on about forty dollars a month. He must have meant just groceries, for that couldn't include the new car and gasoline and all the magazines. But anyway, they didn't have to worry. "We made our stake before we came up here," Mr. Egbert said.

I don't suppose one tourist in five thousand sees Death Valley from its south end—or, for that matter, ever gets into the south half of the valley at all. We didn't make the southern approach through choice or superior wisdom; the main paved highways were washed out, and it was a case of go in through the Cave Springs dirt road or not at all.

From Cave Springs you drop thirty-six hundred feet in a twisty, bumpy, fifteen-mile drive onto the floor of the valley. And every foot of the way down is a grandstand view of an appalling spectacle of desolation and silent, almost spectral beauty.

Death Valley is an immense slash in the earth. It is a hundred thirty miles long, and ranges from six to fourteen miles wide. It has a floor, and high sides. You can't see from one end to the other, because it is too far, and anyway it makes a turn. But there's no place in the valley where you can't look up and see the high, bare mountains hemming you in.

There is nothing consistent about the valley floor. I drove the whole hundred thirty miles, and there is hardly a five-mile stretch that is the same. Some places are sandy, some places very gravelly, with good-sized rocks. Some places are hard and black, like old lava, and others are actually swampy. Some are snow-white—salt beds. Most of the valley has a thin scattering of low shrubs— greasewood, bunch grass, small mesquite, and even some flowers —but occasionally there is no vegetation whatever. There is almost no cactus. The valley floor is seldom level; most of it rises and falls in long sweeps.

The famous "lowest point in the United States" is clear over to one side of the valley, only a few feet from the road, and you could go stand in it if you wanted to wade in a salt marsh. I just looked at the sign and let it go at that. It is two hundred eighty feet below sea level. If you built a twenty-story building there its spire would still be lower than a rowboat on San Francisco Bay.

Death Valley's terrific summer heat has been officially recorded as high as 134 in the shade—and there is none, except artificial shade. I would be afraid to drive into Death Valley in summer. Every summer, even in this modern day, somebody is lost—a prospector who should know better, or a tourist who leaves the road against advice, gets stuck in the sand, and it's goodbye. Even if you stay on the road—well, pulling up the gradual rise toward the north end, our radiator boiled, and this was at the end of winter.

And suppose you broke down? Changing a tire is dangerous. You can walk ten or fifteen miles in Death Valley in winter; but in summer, they say that often you can't see a hundred yards for the heat waves. Walking far is fatal; you and I would die in less than ten miles, even if we had plenty of water. Just lifting a jug is exertion. Many bodies have been found with water jugs beside them.

As far as I could learn, there is not a single, year-round private home in Death Valley. There are, however, two spots of lavish comfort for winter dwellers. One is the Stovepipe Wells Hotel, on the west side of the valley. The other is Furnace Creek, on the east side. At Furnace Creek there are a magnificent desert inn, a dude ranch, and the headquarters of Death Valley National Monument. Counting guests, employes, and government workers, you will find several hundred people around there in winter. But on May 1 the hotels close, and civilization in Death Valley locks its doors. Three or four people stay at Furnace Creek, and a lone watchman at Stovepipe Wells. The Indians of the southern end take to the mountains. If you wander across Death Valley in July and die, you'll die alone.

I cannot remember a time in my childhood when there was not a box of 20-Mule-Team Borax in our kitchen, but I never knew what borax was, where it came from, or what it was for outside of softening water. Now I have found out. It is a rather rare product with a hundred uses, and most of the world's supply is in the western American deserts.

There were some small borax workings in Nevada prior to 1880, but in that year a prospector named Aaron Winters discovered borax on the floor of Death Valley. He sold his claims for twenty thousand dollars. William T. Coleman bought them, and worked borax out of Death Valley until 1889. Then he was taken over by the Pacific Coast Borax Company, the biggest borax company in the world.

Borax, like gold, is mined in two ways—on the surface and in hard-rock shaft mines. The borax company built great mills right there in the valley, and did its own refining. But it had to get this borax to market, and it was a hundred sixty-five miles to a railroad. Out of this need came the twenty-mule-team borax wagons. They became a transportation service as daring and romantic in their way as the Pony Express or the Overland Stage.

The loads were hauled over the desert from Death Valley to Mojave, California, in immense wagons. A twenty-mule team always pulled two wagons, and a trailer with water and hay. The load was often as much as forty thousand pounds of borax, plus sixteen thousand pounds of wagons and water; twenty-eight tons —nearly a ton and a half per mule—up mountain grades and over parching sands. Each wagon carried a "swamper" and a driver who used a twenty-two-foot blacksnake whip, plus plenty of rocks and cusswords. The lead mules were a hundred twenty feet from the driver's seat. They say that a borax wagon driver had to be even more skillful, and tougher, than a stagecoach driver. The wagons made about sixteen miles a day—ten days for the trip to Mojave. There were ten stations, each supplied with water, for overnight stops. They didn't go in dead summer, but even so, the heat was so terrific that men's nerves went to pieces. They couldn't keep the same driver and swamper together for many trips.

Early in the century they started experimenting with tractors, and then in 1915 a railroad was built into the borax mill in Death Valley. So there hasn't been a twenty-mule borax team for many years, though they still use the trademark.

Two items in my borax lesson surprised me. One was that they hadn't mined a grain of borax in Death Valley for more than ten years now. And the other was that the concern that did most of the borax mining—the famous old twenty-mule-team concern— was a British company. In 1927 borax was discovered near Cramer, California, on the Mojave Desert. It was much purer than the Death Valley stuff, and it was practically on top of a main-line railroad. So they just shut down and moved to Cramer. There was enough borax around Cramer to last fifty years or more. When that ran out, the Death Valley borax would still be there.

And what do they use borax for, besides softening water? Well, in a general way, borax has the quality of taking out impurities. Borax is what makes glass so clear. Borax is what makes enamel so smooth. Borax is what welders sprinkle on two pieces of hot steel before putting them together. Borax is what the dentist stirs into his little cup of gold before filling your tooth. Borax is used to purify paint, and clean mechanics' hands. And the borax company is now working (with an eye in my direction) on a compound designed to purify men's souls.

The sign said "Road Closed." We sat and looked at it for a long time. Finally a truck came through, and we waved it down.

"Is it absolutely impossible to get through to Scotty's castle?" I asked the driver.

He said: "Well, two cars started through day before yesterday. They must have got through for we haven't heard from them. But they say the washouts are pretty bad."

I told the driver I couldn't bear the thought of being within twenty-five miles of Scotty's famous place and not getting up there.

"Well," the driver said, "if I was you I'd tackle it. Be careful not to straddle any big rocks. The road is good till you get within sixteen miles of there."

So we started. It was a gravel road, and though it lay on the open floor of the valley it had been terribly washed out by the recent floods that had come raging down out of the mountains. When we figured we were within sixteen miles I said: "Now let's time ourselves, so we'll know how long before dark we'll have to start back. It's just one o'clock now. No matter how bad it is, we can surely make sixteen miles in an hour and a half." Such is the sublime confidence of fools.

We were an hour going the first three miles. We were three hours going the next ten feet. After that, nothing mattered much anyhow. I built that road with my own hands for the next three miles. I heaved rocks, dug rocks, carried rocks. I filled up great chasms, and knocked off humps. I built grades, and causeways, and dikes, and roadbeds. With my bleeding fingers I dug out boulders big as houses and tossed them out of the way. Inch by inch we progressed. In a couple of dozen places the road was simply washed away and we faced a rock-strewn gulch. If I'd had any sense I would have turned back. But greenhorns driving in Death Valley don't have any sense. That's why so many of them are dead.

It was a stiff up pull all the way. The day was warm; the radiator and I boiled alternately. While it cooled, I built roads. By the time the car was cool, I'd be boiling over. Like all good desert travelers we had no shovel, no extra oil, and exactly one pint of water for the radiator and me. I drank the water and threw the bottle at the radiator.

Finally we accomplished the three miles. And then we came to something you could distinguish from the Grand Canyon only by the fact that it was in California instead of Arizona. This wasn't a washout—it was a cataclysm. My construction work here consumed nearly half an hour. Finally, hot and weary under Death Valley's March sun, I stood back and inspected my engineering accomplishments. "If I can just keep the car moving," I said, "I think we can make it across." The effort of making that remark took almost the last of my waning strength.

We made it one-third of the way across. At that point small rocks by the millions surged up around us and we were buried to the axles, as in a feather bed—made of rocks, I mean.

We unloaded every bit of our voluminous baggage. We dug with our hands and with wrench handles. We ruined our clothes. We spun the tires till they smoked. We got the motor so hot it would barely run. We jacked up the back end so the gear box would clear a rock, and that left no traction for the wheels. The thing was hopeless, and permanent. The sun dropped behind the Panamint Range. It looked like a night under the stars in Death Valley. It was twelve miles to Scotty's, all uphill, and it would take me at least four hours to walk it. Maybe longer. I wasn't sure I ought to start, without any drinking water. I sat down on a rock to think it over. And then suddenly two cars came out of nowhere and pulled up behind us at the brink of the washout. Some men got out, but I refused to speak to them, for I knew they were optical illusions and I have no truck with desert mirages.

Mirages or not, the men pushed and dug and threw rocks under the wheels, and pushed some more, and in a little while we were out. But the example was enough for them. They turned around and started back to Los Angeles, four hundred miles away.

And so finally, late in the afternoon, we reached our goal. Oily, dusty, sweaty, bleeding and weary, we pulled up in front of Death Valley Scotty's fabulous desert castle. A Filipino house-boy came out.

"Is Scotty around?" I asked.

The boy replied: "No. Scotty's in Los Angeles. He won't be back for a week."

Wasn't that just dandy! It was too late to go back over that same road. I wouldn't have tackled it after dark for any money. So I said to Walter, a cowboy who had charge while Scotty was away: "Can you put us up for the night? We would expect to pay, of course."

"Sure," said Walter, "we'll put you up for forty dollars apiece."

I didn't say anything. I guess Walter thought I was going to pass out on him, for he went on quickly: "We had to put the price up so high to keep people from staying. Last year so many people stayed that the hotels down in the valley got to raising hell."

"So you won't let us stay all night then?"

"For forty dollars apiece," said Walter. He was serious.

"I can't pay eighty dollars and wouldn't if I could. And I'm not going back over that road. Where can we stay?"

"Well, there's a dirt road into Nevada that isn't so bad. It's twenty-seven miles to pavement, and sixty miles to Beatty."

"Okay. At least now that we're here we can go through the castle, can't we?"

"It'll cost you a dollar-ten apiece."

"Okay. Let's go."

The public-at-large believed that Scotty was an eccentric desert rat who had some mysterious and unlimited source of money. Actually, people told me, Scotty wasn't eccentric at all. Most everybody in that sparsely settled desert knew him. They said he was a good fellow who'd got a good thing, and they didn't begrudge it. His money came from a man named Albert M. Johnson, who had been in the West years ago, in a bad way with tuberculosis. Scotty met him and invited him out to his desert shack, saying it would cure him. Well, Johnson went, stayed a few months, and was a new man. He returned to Chicago and became wealthy.

Although that story was known, it was usually accompanied by hazy concoctions about Johnson's fanatical gratitude to Scotty, how he had poured all this money into a castle for Scotty, and how Scotty had always refused to say where the money came from. But my impression is that Johnson built the castle for himself, and not for Scotty. The Johnsons weren't living in Chicago any more. They lived in Los Angeles, and they spent a great deal of time at the castle. They had their own regular rooms there and their wardrobes were stocked. Their private pictures were all over the place. The castle was largely designed by Mrs. Johnson, and furnished to her tastes. The ranch crest was J/S (for Johnson-Scott) in a circle, and it was on practically everything— dishes, tables, window hangings, and even on every fence post. I guessed that the castle belonged to Johnson, and that Scotty was a good friend and just lived there, and probably got plenty of spending money.

The building of the castle, started in 1926, was stopped after six years. The castle itself was finished, and all the fine outbuildings. But the great crooked swimming pool (the biggest one I've ever seen) lay unfinished, with bent reinforcement rods sticking wanly out of the rough concrete. Walter, the cowboy, said they quit building because they discovered some hitch about absolute title to the land. Now, he said, they'd sort of lost interest in doing anything more. But in a little Mojave Valley town, at a lunch counter one night, I heard an old desert rat say they stopped because Johnson lost forty-five million dollars in the depression.

Just a couple of years ago they had started letting sightseers in, and in the last year seven thousand people had gone through the castle. Walter said Scotty didn't like all the tourists coming —thought they were ruining the desert. Maybe they were. But the only thing that brought them to that part of the desert was a two-million-dollar castle, which itself was slightly alien to the desert.

The castle was just as elegant as I had always heard, and the surprising thing to me was that it was all in good taste. There was a warmness about it inside; it was a place you could live in. The building was not really immense. It had no great marble stairways or vast ballrooms. You wouldn't get lost in it. There was a sort of triple theme running through the house—Spanish-Italian for one; desert life for two; and just plain house for three. Oddly enough, they didn't clash.

There were lots of other buildings: a powerhouse, built like a county courthouse, with a big clockface in each of the steeple's four sides; and a long, fine-looking building which Walter said was the guest house. And there were stables, and a house for employes, and a garage and machine shop, and a big glass mechanism on the hillside where water was heated by the sun. There was a staff of six people—Walter, a guide, a bald-headed Chinese cook, the Filipino houseboy, and a couple of roustabouts.

While the castle's interior was luxurious, orderly, and spotless, the grounds had a run-down look. The site was not actually in Death Valley, but back up a wide canyon, about four miles from the valley proper. Why they picked that spot I have no idea. The earth had that black-streaked, washed-out appearance of West Virginia coal country, minus trees. There had been no attempt at landscaping, there was no grass, and the unfinished swimming pool gave the place a seedy look.

Walter took us around. He wasn't the regular guide, but he knew the spiel. And he wasn't a bad fellow at all. He got tickled at his own wisecracks. He had a sort of perpetual cat-ate-mouse smirk that indicated he thought the whole business—visitors, castle, and even himself—sillier than hell.

First, we had to put on flannel slippers over our shoes. Then we went into Scotty's bedroom—a corner room just off the living room. Walter showed us a little hole in the wall, with a slide over it. You could stick a shotgun in there and fire it, and the shot would ricochet at right angles and shoot past the window. "That's in case Scotty's wife ever comes around," Walter laughed. (She was living in Reno, and they'd had bitter divorce troubles.) On the walls were pictures of Scotty when he was with Buffalo Bill's show, and other pictures, including some of his son who was in the Navy.

We went upstairs into Mrs. Johnson's room. She had a built-in bed. Walter showed us how she could swing out an iron bar, pull down a panel on hinges from the wall, let it rest on the bar, and have her breakfast in bed. In the library Walter opened small double doors above the fireplace mantel, and there were tinted pictures of Scotty and Mr. Johnson, side by side. We went into the sun parlor—the solarium, as Walter called it. There was a sort of fountain there, with a background painted to represent the bottom of the ocean, and two big enameled bullfrogs. "They've been there ten years and haven't learned to swim yet," said Walter, practically splitting.

The dining room was really magnificent. The walls were stocked with more beautiful dishes than you ever saw outside of a store, every one with the J/S crest. We went into the big kitchen. "In that corner is a Spanish well," Walter said, "where we keep the garbage can and mops. It's genuine Spanish tile too." He smirked.

Finally we crossed the second-story catwalk, took a wink at three or four beautifully furnished "overnight rooms," as Walter called them (eighty dollars, ha!), and wound up in the big music room. This was the only place that looked like a museum. Some of the antique chairs had ribbons tied across so you couldn't sit down. On one side was a big fireplace, on the other side a dark little stage. In a corner was a pipe organ hidden by a screen. "You can play this either as a piano, as a pipe organ, or by mechanical rolls," Walter said. "Would you like to hear one?" We said yes, so he put on a roll, and the noise was so loud you could hardly talk. When that was finished he put on another roll. We listened that one through and then we asked if that was the end of the tour, and he said yes.

New Mexico
Revisited

Chapter
XX Ⅰ N NEW MEXICO Ⅰ PICKED UP A HITCHHIKER IN OVER-
alls, who turned out to be a professional milker of cows. Not a
farm hand, but a full-time milker in a dairy. I hadn't realized
there was such a profession in this world. And he wasn't a straight
milker, but a specialist: he stripped the cows after they'd been
milked by a machine. For this he got sixty dollars a month. As he
said, "It ain't much, but it's better than relief."

My hitchhiker said he could milk a single cow as fast as anybody in the world, but give him a whole string of cows and he
couldn't keep up. Why? Because not all cows milk alike. There
are three types of milking, all depending on the cow. In one type
you squeeze—that's where he shone. In another you just pull. In
the third you have to get way up high and press with your thumb
and forefinger. That was the hardest for him.

If you lay off a while and then start in milking again, your
arms get so sore it almost kills you. He said he had often walked
the floor all night with pain.

In New Mexico it is lawful to carry a six-shooter while traveling. But you must put it safely away within half an hour after
reaching your destination. Why half an hour? I have no idea,
unless it's to give you legal time to dispose of any citizens who
might be personally obnoxious to you.

It's useless to try to describe the Carlsbad Caverns. They aren't
just caves; they are another world. You feel like one of Walt

Disney's symphony children wandering in a dream world of unbelievable, impossible beauty.

The cavern entrance is out on the desert, twenty-eight miles from the town of Carlsbad, New Mexico. Around the entrance the government has built a group of distinctive stone buildings —Rangers' homes, a powerhouse, a curio store, a ticket office, and an elevator-shaft building eighty-seven stories high, three above-ground and eighty-four beneath. The shaft was put down in 1934, through seven hundred fifty feet of solid rock. But the government has discouraged use of the elevator, for you miss so much by not walking in.

There was just one trip a day through the caverns when I was there. You started at 10:30 A.M. and got out around three in the afternoon, during which time you walked about five miles. You saw less than one-third of the caverns, but they were the best part. Any more would have been an anticlimax.

The temperature of the caverns is fifty-six degrees, day and night, winter and summer. The natural ventilation is perfect; the air is fresh and cool, and there is no clammy feeling. A sweater under your coat is desirable, but don't burden yourself with a topcoat, as I did. You don't have to wear old clothes, for there's no place where you have to crawl. The trails are soft and easy to walk on and there are no ladders to climb. The entire route is electrically lighted, though you never see a direct light or a switch. Indirect beams are thrown onto the fantastic formations with an artistry that would make Hollywood jealous.

Rangers don't bore you to death with lectures every few feet. Our party stopped half a dozen times to rest, but I recall only three Ranger talks, all short and interesting. At the start, a Ranger explained in a few words the geologic cause of this underground Grand Canyon. If you wanted to know more, you could ask him or the other Rangers as you walked along the narrow trails, two by two. He said the Rangers already knew that the acoustics of the caverns were perfect, so we didn't need to whistle, scream, or laugh loud, seeking an echo, and we needn't make any jokes, either, because the Rangers knew them all. If any smart aleck had decided to be the life of the party, a Ranger would have taken him back up. They didn't give the pilgrimage a funereal aspect, but they did ask that it be dignified. And it was that. The crowd seemed to be awed and silenced by the mysterious wonders about them.

After an hour of walking you've seen some wonderful sights, but you still haven't reached what the Rangers consider the cave proper. When you hit it you come out from a narrow passage into a big room about a hundred fifty feet across, where millions of stalactites hang from the ceiling and stalagmites rear up from the floor. This is the Fairyland, the spot that only a fool would try to describe. From here on, it is beyond imagination—a world that surely can be nothing on or of this earth. Then an hour later you suddenly come out into a big room of civilization, seven hundred fifty feet beneath the surface. In the center is a little cafeteria settlement, and white tables and benches stretch as far as you can see. Your tray is already filled. You eat and rest and talk for forty-five minutes, and then step back into the dream world of half-light and shadowed fantasies. You have lost all feeling of reality. Your sense of appreciation aches, and your body feels a cool weariness.

The trail rounds a big rock, and ahead of you lies a white slope, roofed far overhead by solid rock. The light is dim, like the northern moonlight on snow. The dark world widens as you climb the slope. Finally you reach a height, and stop there with your fellow travelers to rest on the dusty white rocks.

When we were all seated, a large man in green uniform stepped forward and stood at the foot of an immense "candle-dripped" stone column. He was Colonel Thomas Boles, super-intendent of the caverns. All day he had kept in the background, one of the crowd. But now he took charge and asked for silence and complete attention. He got it, even from the children.

Colonel Boles told us how many were in our party—the number had been computed on the surface and phoned down—and what states and foreign countries were represented. Then he talked about the great stone column behind him. When the Pyramids of Egypt were being built it was already millions of years old. Drip, drip, drip—this great shaft has been built down here in total darkness at the rate of one cubic inch a century. Here it stands, tall as a house, big around as a room, hundreds of tons in weight—yet formed so slowly that since the time of the Pyramids it has grown not much more than the bulk of your folded fist. Sixty million years old, they say it is. I felt a great awe as I realized the ponderous patience of nature. They've named it the Rock of Ages.

"And now," Colonel Boles said, "we will see what it was like while all this was going on, in the past millions of years, before man came and made it visible. We will step back into time, and do honor to the Rock of Ages." He asked that cigarettes be doused, that no one talk or whisper. He waited until the crowd and the cavern were as silent as death. And then the lights went out.

You have never known darkness until you have sat in it eight hundred feet underground. You look around for a faint glow somewhere, a shadow, a movement. There is nothing. You are in a complete solid blackness. And the silence is as thick as the darkness.

And then softly, out of the darkness, came the notes of a song. Four Rangers, unnoticed, had dropped back down the trail, and somewhere off there they were singing "Rock of Ages." Suddenly there were dim reflections of light from the far end of the vast cave room, half a mile away. A few moments later, more light, nearer—another thousand-foot section had been switched on. And then at last, as the Rangers' voices sank almost to a whisper, the lights came on all around us.

They say government officials are stodgy, routined, unimaginative. Most of them are, I guess, but not those at the Carlsbad Caverns. A community sing would have made this spot ridiculous. A wrong word or a harsh note would have broken the spell. Overdramatization would have made it a Coney Island sideshow, but as it was that day, even the theater could not have been more dramatic.

When you get up, fall again into line, walk another short way through fairyland, and then rise swiftly through eighty-four stories of solid rock, out into the blinding sunshine, life suddenly is real again. It seems impossible that this gray, rolling plain of the earth's surface can conceal another world, so different and so near.

The Carlsbad Caverns were discovered in 1901 by Jim White, a cowboy who never even went through the third grade. He not only discovered them; he fully explored them, and tried to tell the world about their magnificence. But people are so smart, and know so much, that Jim White talked and argued and begged for more than twenty years before he could get another white man to go along and see for himself. In 1922 a party of thirteen Carlsbad businessmen finally consented to go down. When they came out, the world found out that Jim White wasn't a liar. The government took charge in 1923, and the cowboy's simple, unselfish dream began to be realized: others were able to see the wonderful things he had found. And by 1937 they were doing so at the rate of two hundred thousand a year. It isn't always that a discoverer gets credit in his lifetime, but every visitor to the caverns saw Jim White, who was now fifty-seven and still looked like a cowboy. He had a little stand down there where the tourists ate lunch. There he sold a booklet that told the fascinating story of his discovery, his explorations, and his long fight to make somebody believe him. He charged seventy-five cents a copy, and he dealt them out so fast that he resembled a chef in a Los Angeles hamburger stand.

Smoking is allowed in the caverns, as the natural ventilation is good. Two men with sacks come along behind the party (out of sight) cleaning up the trail. One of them, Louis Cocke, picked up seventeen hundred coupons of a certain cigarette in one year, and got a gold watch for them.

There is no life there except bats and crickets. The bats do not inhabit the part where visitors go. The crickets apparently have hopped out of people's lunch baskets, and are turning white from never being in the sun.

The oldest person ever to go through the cave was a man past a hundred. The youngest was a baby fifteen days old, carried by its parents on a pillow. Two men without legs had gone through. "If you're not sensitive about how you go, we can take you," Colonel Boles told them. They said they weren't. So how do you suppose they went? In wheelbarrows pushed by Rangers.

I asked Colonel Boles if people with claustrophobia ever tried to go through the caverns. Yes. But it got the best of them not far inside, and a Ranger conducted them back. About one in five thousand had to leave the cave for that reason.

One day Colonel Boles put a clicker in his pocket, to count the number of questions asked him. It was two hundred fifty-seven. Each Ranger probably averaged as many. The No. 1 question was "Where is the toilet?"

In their talks the Rangers made quite a point of asking people not to write their names on anything in the caverns. There wasn't a name on any of the rocks, and there was none in the men's washrooms. But in the women's, the Rangers said, there were ten thousand names. Figure that one out.

At Mesilla, New Mexico, George Griggs sat by the fireplace in his rocking chair and said, "Reach up to that third gun on the wire there."

"This one?" I asked. He nodded.

It was a small pistol with a short barrel that was split open on top, about an inch back from the nose.

"How did that happen?" I asked.

"Well, there was a Jew that kept trying to pick a fight with Billy the Kid in a saloon. Billy the Kid was tough, but he liked Jews and didn't want to hurt this fellow, so he just kept telling him to go away. But the Jew was in a bad mood, and he was bound to pick a fight. Finally the Kid gave him a shove and told him to get out of there. Then the Jew started to pull his gun.

"Well, Billy didn't want to hurt the fellow, so he pulled quick and fired right into the muzzle of his gun, in order to stop his bullet. That split there, that's where the Kid's bullet going in met the Jew's bullet coming out. It just split the barrel wide open." George Griggs got up and fumbled on the mantel. "Here are the bullets," he said. "See how they're all twisted up."

I looked a long time at the split barrel, and at the misshapen bullets, which were too big to go in either the split or the muzzle, and then at George Griggs. "Do you believe that?" I said.

He answered, "Well, I don't know much about guns. I'm not really very much interested in guns. I don't know whether to believe it or not. I guess it's true."

Mesilla was an old, old town with dusty streets and buildings of red-brown adobe. Flat. Colorless. The wind whirled the sand mercilessly, and you could hardly walk against it. Only the sand seemed alive. There was little other movement in old Mesilla.

George Griggs was born there. He had traveled far, but he had been back for a long time. He lived alone amidst his Billy the Kid collection and he fitted into it. He was tall and thin and stooped, and no longer young, and his pants were much too long. A scraggly beard covered his long, intellectual face, and he sported a huge bow tie. He spoke in a loud, confidential whisper. His Billy the Kid Museum was famous all over the Southwest. It wasn't like a museum at all; it was just a hodgepodge of stuff in an old adobe house, for which he charged tourists a quarter. In Las Cruces the businessmen told me: "Old George just barely makes beans out of his museum. Some days he doesn't even make beans." But he was independent and a little temperamental. If the wind was blowing, or he wasn't in the mood, he wouldn't go to the door when tourists knocked.

I was there two hours before I could get him to talk about Billy the Kid or show me any of his collection. The truth is that George Griggs didn't give a damn about Billy the Kid. He just had that stuff there for tourists; most of his collection was old pottery and blankets from Mexico. It disgusted him the way tourists got mixed up about him. Some thought he was a pal of Billy the Kid; some thought he was the man who killed Billy the Kid; and some, not so well up on their bad-man history, thought he was Billy the Kid himself.

As a matter of fact, Griggs saw Billy the Kid only once. Griggs was a little boy, and had been sent to the saloon for a bucket of beer. The saloon, incidentally, was in this very room where the Kid's guns now hung on baling wire. Little George Griggs went in the door and recognized one of the men in the saloon as the famous killer, and little George Griggs turned and ran as fast as he could go.

Lincoln, New Mexico, was the scene of more than one escapade in which Billy the Kid figured. He was captured and sentenced to hang, and a constant guard was kept over him on the second floor of the courthouse. About a week before he was to hang,

Billy, though shackled hand and foot, took a gun away from his guard, killed him, shot the other deputy from the courthouse window, and rode out of town, whistling. At this point the village of Lincoln died. It was still dead when I was there, sixty years later. And it was one of the grandest little spots I ever ran onto in that part of the world.

At twelve-thirty noon you found only Señor Miranda, the postmaster, stirring in Lincoln. It was siesta hour. And Señor Miranda wasn't really stirring—he was just sitting at his post-office window. But he came out from behind his mailboxes and stood on the porch.

No, said Señor Miranda, there wasn't any place in town to eat lunch. There had been a café, but it had closed. Well, how about the grocery store? Yes, that was it, the grocery store. So from Señor Romero, who was back from lunch now, we bought bologna, cheese, crackers. We walked up the gravel street to where it said "Bar." The door was locked, but from a nearby house a man came running. He was smiling and gracious, and he unlocked the door, invited us in, and fixed us chairs and a bench. With a pocket knife I carved the bologna and the cheese. We sat and ate, and Señor Roman Maes—proprietor and, as his sign said, "expert mixerologist"—stood and talked with us the whole lunch through.

Señor Maes owned the only bar in Lincoln. It was right across the road from the courthouse from which Billy the Kid escaped. Is your bar very old, Señor Maes? Oh, very old, as old as the town. Billy the Kid has stood there. And Sheriff Pat Garrett. All the bad men have stood there. Douglas Fairbanks was there once and bought the bar for one hundred fifty dollars. Of course he couldn't wrap it up and take it with him, so he left a twenty-five dollar deposit. He never came back after it. Señor Maes still had the twenty-five dollars, and the bar too. He wouldn't have taken several times one hundred fifty dollars for it now.

Lincoln was founded by Mexicans. Then the white man came and had his bloody day, but Lincoln eventually ebbed back into its gentle ways. Nearly all the people were Spanish American now; as in deep Mexico, they were friendly, quietly hospitable, and eager to tell you anything you wanted to know. You sensed that it was not decay but peace that had settled over the old village.

Maybe it was just the quiet, and the welcome heat of the sun. Or maybe it was thinking of the contrast with those days when a man, walking those same streets, never knew whether or not he would live to walk them tomorrow.

Lore of Billy the Kid was in every building—indeed, in nearly every mind. He was a hero around Lincoln. Francisco Maes owned the house where the Kid carved his name. The carving was on the outer door casing, and read simply "KID." It had been whitewashed over, but you could still see it.

There were many people in New Mexico who remembered the Kid, but only one was left around Lincoln. He was Francisco Gomez, eighty-four years old, short and bowlegged and spry as a cricket. He was sprinting down the road carrying a sack of beans when I saw him. We talked, through an interpreter, for quite a while. Señor Gomez remembered the Kid as a good guy.

The old ways in Lincoln were remarkably preserved. Most of the adobe houses were as old as the town itself. You saw women drawing water from old-fashioned box wells. There were hitching posts in front of the stores. Lincoln just dreamed nowadays, and it dreamed mostly about its hero, Billy the Kid. The place enchanted me. It is among the thousand and one spots where I shall retire when I retire.

Some tourists pronounce Taos to rhyme with "chaos." That burns the local people up. The correct pronunciation is Tah-ose, but the way it usually comes out it rhymes with "mouse."

Taos is a village way up in the mountains of northern New Mexico. It is seven thousand feet high, and in winter the temperature gets down to zero and they have big snows. There are high mountains right behind it, and long sweeping plains in front of it. Artists live there because of the landscape, the Indians, and the isolation.

Taos is small—probably not more than a thousand people, mostly Spanish Americans. I found it rather picturesque but not enchanting. There was a small central plaza, from which the village straggled out for a few blocks. Most of the houses were adobe, some of them falling down. The streets were hard clay when dry, and deep mud when wet. There were a few showplaces—

mansions built by rich people or artists—but not many. It was just as fashionable to live in an adobe shack. Until about 1935 the village had neither running water nor electric lights. Even when I was there the streets were not lighted, and you walked around at night with a flashlight. By nine o'clock the town was like a grave.

When you go to Taos, naturally you go to see the Taos Indian pueblo. It's only two miles out. There are two great adobe buildings, each five stories high, where about eight hundred Indians live. The buildings are immense at the bottom—at least a block long. Each story is set back, in irregular jogs, until the fifth story consists of only a few rooms, sort of like a penthouse. This is the type of native building that inspired the beautiful Santa Fe architecture.

As we drove up we saw blanketed Indians sitting on various roof levels. And out there in the desert, with bare hard dirt all around and dark faces peering from beneath soiled blankets, we felt that we must be in Arabia. We paid a quarter, and a guide came to show us through the pueblo. His black hair hung in pigtails behind each ear. His feet were in white deerskin moccasins. A bed sheet was draped around his shoulders and body. It was like setting out on a strange and romantic journey.

The guide said it was a nice day. We said yes, it was, and how old were the pueblos? The guide didn't know. Very old. The guide said he no speak much English.

We passed an anthill. The guide stopped and said, "What you call them in English?"

"Those are ants," we said.

"Ants," he said. "How you say it—ants? Never know what you call it in English."

We of the party looked at each other, and if our glances had been translated into a word, the word would have been "phooey."

At last the guide ushered us through a door into the pueblo— or, rather, into one room. On tables were homemade drums, crude pottery, moccasins, ears of colored corn.

"Maybe you want buy something?" said our guide, and went back outside. We realized we were merely in a curio shop. We smiled at the Indian boy in charge, and went out.

"Could we see inside the church?" one of the party asked.

"No have keys. Can't get in today," our guide said.

He walked some more, and we followed. Runny-nosed little girls called, "Gimme a nickel." Dirty little babies said, "Penny, penny."

"Where do you live?" one of our party asked the guide.

"I take you my house," he said eagerly. We saw only one room of his house. It too was a curio shop.

"Now I show you somebody else's house," said our guide. He took us through a door, and there we were in another curio shop.

And so we finished the one pueblo, and came to midway in our tour. We had seen five curio shops and not one other thing. We hadn't entered the pueblo proper; we hadn't seen a room where anybody actually lived; we hadn't got an honest answer to a single question.

We started then to do the other pueblo. I said to the guide, "What will we see in this pueblo?"

"Fine curio shops," he said. "I show them you."

"No, you won't," I said. And with that the entire party abandoned the guide, got in their cars, and drove away. He stood there looking after us, in his pigtails and bed sheet, cut to the quick. Or maybe not. Of course the joke was on us. We had paid to see something, and with a straight face we had been shown nothing.

"I guess it's all right," said my traveling partner at last. "They're just getting even for what the white man did to the Indians in the first place." And I guess that's right.

Some people out there get hepped, as they say, on Indian life and culture and philosophy. But I am more inclined to throw my eggs in the basket of an old-time stage driver in Taos. He had lived around there forty years, and knew the country like a book.

"Indians?" he said. "Hell, no, I don't know any more about an Indian than you do. And neither does any other white man. Talking to an Indian is just like writing a note and putting it in a prairie-dog hole. I don't pay any attention to them."

Eastbound

Chapter XXI WESTERN KANSAS, IN THE MIDDLE 1930'S, WAS THE saddest land I had ever seen. Coming in to Garden City from Colorado, you passed through both the sandstorm and the dust-storm region. Eastern Colorado is a mild form of desert, and hence rather sandy. When the wind blows there, you have a sand-storm. As you get into Kansas, the soil becomes richer and softer, and when it gets dry and powdery and the wind blows, you have a dust storm.

While we were still in Colorado we could see, far behind, old Pikes Peak lifting its snowy sides into the heavens. Far ahead to the east were faint, hazy clouds of sand, which meant we were running into a sandstorm. The yellow haze ahead grew heavier and darker, making the atmosphere a queer yellow—the way it is sometimes before a cyclone. To the right were rolling, fore-boding rain clouds, mixed with dust. And over to the left, over where the wind came from, were pillars of sand—giant yellow columns rising from the horizon miles away, like smoke from a burning town. It was frightening, and sickening.

The wind howled, roaring about forty miles an hour across the prairie from the north and drowning out our voices. It was hard to steer the car. As the sand steadily grew thicker around us, it darkened the atmosphere, and a little film settled on the inside rim of the windshield. On rises in the road, the sand-laden wind cut across the highway like a horizontal waterfall. Sand was not drifting, or floating, or hanging in the air—it was shooting south, in thick veins, like air full of thrown baseballs.

Cars we met had their lights on, and we wondered if it was really that bad ahead. It was. We went into the darkness as an airplane flies into fog. The air was black with sand; you could not see from one telephone pole to the next. There wasn't any sky. The tiny rocks smacked and pounded against the car windows. The wind was vicious, and the car was light on its wheels and inclined to weave. You couldn't hear the motor at all.

It didn't last long—no more than a mile or two—and then we popped out into rain. The air was washed clear; it was like coming out suddenly into fresh air on the windward side of a forest fire.

When we came into Kansas, it had been raining for twelve hours. The earth was wet, and we were thus spared the spectacle of a Kansas dust storm. But we saw what we could not have seen if the air had been filled with dust: the terrific desolation of western Kansas. You might honestly say there was nothing left of West Kansas. A few miles from the village of Lakin I stopped shoved open the door, and stood on the running board to look around. The land was as flat as a billiard table. The horizon was far, far away. Following the horizon around, as you sometimes gaze out from a ship at sea, I saw not a solitary thing but bare earth, and a few lonely, empty farmhouses. As far as the eye could see there was not a tree, or a blade of grass, or a fence, or a field; not a flower or a stalk of corn, or a dog or a cow, or a human being—nothing at all but gray raw earth and a few far houses and barns, sticking up like white cattle skeletons on the desert. There was nobody in the houses; the people had given up and gone. It was death, if I have ever seen death.

Because of the rain, the ground was now holding firm. But the day before it had given itself up to the wind, and the next day, after the bright sun, it would do so again. The air would gradually fill with the earthy powder, and people in its path would scarcely be able to breathe, and houses would be closed. And the soil would blow away from around the roots of things, and pile like snowdrifts against the barns, and fly on the wind southward toward Mexico, leaving nothing at all. As I drove along I thought of all the smart-aleck jokes about President Roosevelt's hundred-mile-wide belt of trees. I thought of the sneers about the "college professors" trying to improve the earth, and I wondered if any of the criticizers had ever seen a country that had died. A belt of trees, or a belt of soybeans, or a belt of billiard cues stuck in the ground—anything that might slow the march of the destroying wind across the face of our earth—seemed to me worth trying.

I spent an evening with a Garden City couple in their home—a beautiful, modern, suburban bungalow. They pulled up the Venetian blinds and showed me the windows. Every window in the house was sealed with surgeon's tape. The dust storms this year hadn't, they said, been so bad as the year before. The year before, they said, dust half an inch deep would collect on the window sills, even though the windows were sealed with tape. The year before, beautiful lawns were smothered by the settling dust. People even devised big vacuum affairs and went over their lawns, trying to draw out the dust from the grass roots.

I asked my Garden City friend to tell me all about the dust storms: what caused them, and what was being done about it, and so on. He said that western Kansas had always been grazing country, and that there had never been much heavy vegetation—just short grass. But during and just after World War I people found they could make more money in wheat than in cattle. They started farming, and money came easy. It was nothing for a man to buy a section of land and pay for it with just one wheat crop. People didn't put much back into the land, or till for the future.

Then came the drought. That year most of the farmers went broke. There had been a bumper crop, the market was flooded, and the price of wheat went down to nothing. With no money in hand, the farmers couldn't afford to let their land lie fallow—couldn't afford to have the doctor now, even though it would be cheaper in the long run. They continued to plow and plant. There was no rain. The wind blew. The raw ground dried, and started to blow.

My friend said dust storms are like a disease; they infect other land. The dust settles over an adjoining field and smothers out the vegetation. The blowing dust drills into it, gets a hold, bares a spot to the wind, and it's all over. Another field has been added to the desolation.

John Milburn Davis, of Hiawatha, Kansas, was eighty-three years old, had a long white beard and only one hand, and said he was the worst-hated man in Kansas. People hated him because he spent his money the way he pleased. What he pleased was to put up in the local graveyard a memorial to himself and his late wife. Estimates of its cost ran all the way from fifty thousand to a million dollars.

When I asked some people in Hiawatha about the memorial, they said, "Be sure and go see it. It's a monstrosity. There's nothing like it in the United States." So we drove out to Mt. Hope Cemetery, and there it was—eleven life-sized stone images sitting and standing around two marble-slabbed graves (one of which was still empty). Six of the statues were of Farmer Davis himself. Five were of Mrs. Davis, who died in 1930 just after their fiftieth wedding anniversary. They represented Mr. and Mrs. Davis at various stages of their fifty years together. All were sculptured from old photographs. They were not exactly grotesque, but they were daguerreotypish, and when you came up to them all sitting and standing around there, big as life and stiff as death, you got a spooky feeling. In one statue Mrs. Davis was an angel, with wings. There was also a big overstuffed sitting-room chair, carved in granite, with the words "The Vacant Chair" chiseled across the back of the seat.

We found Farmer Davis sitting on his front porch in town. He liked to talk about the memorial. He said he landed at Hiawatha in 1880, got married, and somehow he made a lot of money. (He was vague about this. "Always buy what somebody else wants," he said.) Mr. Davis didn't know what gave him the idea, but he decided to put up statues of himself and Mrs. Davis, facing each other across her grave. He wanted the best. He went to the local monument dealer, who advised having the work done in Italy. They sent old photographs and in due time the statues came back.

"I liked them so well," said Mr. Davis, "that I decided to have two more made. So I sent some different photographs. And when those statues came back I liked them so well I wanted some more. I started it in 1931, and it took three years. It's all through now."

In 1898 Mr. Davis was burning brush after trimming a hedge fence, and a flame licked up and burned his beard off. Consequently he was clean-shaven in one statue, bearded in the others.

Then in 1908 he was cutting hedge fence again, and accidentally cut his left hand off. So four of his six statues showed him with only one hand.

I asked him how much it all cost. He laughed and said that was one thing he didn't tell. Then I said, "Well, I guess it didn't cost a million dollars anyway." Mr. Davis squared around in his chair as though he was mad, and said loudly, "Have you got any real money that says it didn't?" I fished around in my pocket and could find only $3,800 and some Kansas tax tokens, so we let it stand at a million.

Mr. Davis said, "They hate me in Kansas because they wanted me to build a hospital and swimming pools and parks, and I wouldn't do it. It's my money and I spend it the way I please. There's one doctor that won't speak to me because I wouldn't build a hospital. Even the monument dealers hate the one that got my business."

Mr. Davis lived all alone in a big house and ate at restaurants. He was pretty vain about the memorial, and every Sunday when he felt like it he went to the graveyard and hung around. Lots of tourists would recognize him from his statues. Some complimented him and some abused him. One tourist came up with tears in his eyes and said, "You'll be blessed in heaven for this noble work." And a minute later another tourist came up and said, "You ought to be buried in a hole forty deep for this awful thing—and without even a headstone."

St. Joseph, Missouri, is the city where Jesse James was killed, where the Pony Express started, and where thousands of forty-niners equipped themselves for the awful journey to the California gold fields. Yet in the bookstores of St. Joseph you couldn't buy a book or a pamphlet on the fascinating tradition of the place. The Chamber of Commerce could give you the exact value of manufactured products in St. Joseph but it didn't know whether Jesse James was buried there or not.

However, I did meet one man with a Jesse James story. He was vice-president of a bank, he was eighty-three years old, and his name was Max Andriano. He left Germany when he was seventeen and went right to St. Joseph, where he had a cousin, and he said he fell in love with the place instantly. He had been a banker there now for more than sixty years.

In 1882 he was a messenger, daily carrying a big sack of money from one bank to another. We were sitting at his desk talking and he pointed out the window and said, "Right there on that corner, just across the street, is where it happened." He came out of the bank one afternoon with his sack of money. A tall stranger was loafing in the bank's doorway. The stranger said, "Young man, you're pretty young to be carrying so much money around alone. Don't you need some help? Better let me go with you." To which young Mr. Andriano replied, "I may be young, but I'm old enough to mind my own business, and that might be a good idea for you too."

The lounger laughed, and Mr. Andriano said he never saw such an evil leer on a man's face. Mr. Andriano went on alone, and delivered his money safely. That night Jesse James was killed. Mr. Andriano went down to the morgue the next morning to look at the corpse. It was the man who had spoken to him. "I wouldn't have talked back so smart if I'd known it was Jesse James," said Mr. Andriano. "I'd have given him a cigar."

In a hotel room at Springfield, Illinois, we found in the writing desk a telegram written out in pen and ink. It was dated the previous November and had the full names and addresses. It said:

WILL ARRIVE HOME TOMORROW, AND MEET YOU IN LOS ANGELES NEXT SATURDAY NOON OR LATER. CAN WE BE MARRIED AS SOON AS WE ARRIVE?

A woman's name was signed to it. I worried about the thing for a long time. I took down the man's address, and I suppose some day I'll have to write and ask him what he replied. If he told her "no," my only course as a gentleman seems to be pistols at dawn.

U.S. Highway 36, the transcontinental road known as the Lincoln Highway, might be called the road of great men's homes. Practically every fifty miles from Kansas to Ohio you pass through a town where some remarkable figure was born or spent his early days: Jesse James, St. Joe, Missouri; J. C. Penney, the chain-store man, Hamilton, Missouri; General John J. Pershing, LaClede, Missouri; Mark Twain, Hannibal, Missouri; Abraham Lincoln, Springfield, Illinois; and E. Trocadero Pyle, Dana, Indiana.

If any of the above gentlemen, or their heirs or assignees, object to being mentioned in the same breath with Mr. Pyle, let them go ahead and sue. All these great men were memorialized in some way or other by their home towns—all, that is, except the last one. At the crossroads where Highway 36 cuts past Dana, there might be a large marker saying:

> Three miles south is the house in which E. Pyle, Indiana's great skunk-trapper, jelly-eater, horse-hater and snake-afraider-of, was born. In his later years Mr. Pyle rose to a state of national mediocrity as a letter-writer, a stayer in hotels, a talker to obscure people, and a driver from town to town. The old house is in a good state of preservation, although the same cannot be said for Mr. Pyle. Historians say he has been falling to pieces for years.

Once when I stopped at home during my travels, my father and I were walking down the main street of Dana and we met Allison Goodwin, whom I had known since I was a baby. Mr. Goodwin didn't speak to me, and when my father sort of introduced us, Mr. Goodwin looked surprised and said, "Why, Billy, I never knew you had a boy."

So as soon as I get a little more money, say a couple of hundred thousand more, I'm going to do like that old farmer over in Kansas. I'll have six life-size statues of myself made, and instead of putting them in a graveyard I'll stand them like soldiers right across Highway 36 at Dana, so tourists will run into them and get wrecked. Then they'll know (or at least their heirs and assignees will know) whose home town Dana is.

My father was getting to be quite a man-about-the-country; in fact, you could almost class him as a gadabout. He rode clear to the Pacific Coast when my cousin brought my car out to Oregon. They came back on the train by way of the Canadian Rockies. Neither had been in a Pullman berth before, and their stories about not knowing what to do were good for several years of telling. My father called them "booths," and I guess they had quite a time undressing in such cramped quarters. Neither of them had pajamas—farmers just sleep in their shirts, you know. They saw other people in pajamas and bathrobes, and they didn't know what kind of faux pas they might be committing by sleeping in their shirts.

But my father was now prepared for travel anywhere. He had bought a pair of pajamas and a little brown zipper bag to carry them in. He had used them once already, for he was the Worthy Patron of the local Eastern Star lodge and had recently been a delegate to the annual convention in Indianapolis. He drove his car, full of women, the seventy-five miles to Indianapolis. He took his pajamas with him, had a nice hotel room for a dollar and a half, and sneaked off and saw two movies. One was *In Old Chicago;* he said it was a dandy, and showed the Chicago fire. My Aunt Mary said, "Why, Will, that must be an old picture. I saw that one in 1911." Although I hadn't seen *In Old Chicago*, I had a feeling it was not the same picture Aunt Mary was thinking about.

We were disappointed in my father and my cousin as tourists on their western trip. We persuaded them to come back by way of Canada so they could see Lake Louise, which I considered the most beautiful sight I had ever seen. I noticed that he never said much about it in his letters, so when we reached home next time I asked him about Lake Louise. Had they seen it? Yes, they even walked clear to the other end and back. And weren't they impressed by it, by that first breath-taking sight of the blue water and the great towering mountain and the white glacier at the far end? No, not especially. Well, what was the reason? No reason, just weren't impressed. The best thing they saw in the Canadian Rockies was when they got to Banff and went to a movie.

When I asked some friends what were the outstanding things about Cincinnati, they said, "Music, tories, and soap." So, since I didn't understand classical music, or tories either, that left nothing to write about but soap. Personally, I never touch the

· 298 ·

stuff. I hold that cleaning up is an affectation, practiced only by dudes to make the girls think they're hot stuff. And I've reached the point where even a clean face doesn't seem to impress the girls.

However, soapmaking is Cincinnati's leading industry, so I looked into it. There were several soap factories there, but my researches were carried on at the huge plants of Procter & Gamble, who were producing about forty per cent of all the soap made in America. The first thing I asked was, "What makes Ivory soap float?" I had to ask three people before I found one who knew. Ivory soap floats because it's whipped and beaten much longer than other soaps. It gets creamy, and full of tiny air cells. When it hardens, the air is sealed inside these cells, forming a sort of water-wing effect for the bar of soap. As far as I could learn, this extra whipping doesn't do the soap any good—or any harm either; it just makes it float.

I spent a couple of hours in the Procter & Gamble factory, but didn't see an awful lot. They were fairly cagey, and jittery about spies—like governments. It seemed there were lots of secret processes and machinery they didn't want other companies to find out about. I didn't blame them for being wary, for I was just the man to run and tattle to Colgate's. They also said part of the plant was dangerous for visitors to be in. And finally, I gathered, some of it didn't smell very nice. So we began our tour where the soap had finally reached the cooking stage.

There was a double-row battery of giant vats, made of battleship steel—a hundred of them, each three stories high. These vats were covered on top, but you could look down through a little window and see the boiling going on. And this soap cooking in there, which would eventually be a beautiful cake with a come-hither smell, looked exactly like the brown soap my mother used to make out of cracklins and lye in a black kettle over an outside fire.

I tried to find out how many cakes of soap Procter & Gamble made each year. They wouldn't tell. But I did find out how many whales they'd used until a few years before—twelve thousand a year! But the whale was becoming extinct, so coconut oil was now the main staple in soap. And Procter & Gamble were using about three-quarters of a billion coconuts every year. Think how many coconut trees that would be for the soft tropical winds to sigh through while you lay under them on a South Sea beach.

The making of soap is a process of chemical mixing. But what a chemist can do he can also undo. For example, a group of salesmen was entertained at a banquet in the Procter & Gamble factory. The meal was finished off with ice cream and cake. And after the last salesman had wiped his plate and licked his chops, the chemists announced that the cake had been made of Camay soap. They had just ground up some soap, disentangled all the elements that originally went into it, used the ones they needed for cooking, and made cake.

Of course I had to embarrass the soap people by asking them how about dead horses. "Do you still put dead horses in soap?" I said. The soap people were perfectly honest about it; they said they weren't sure because they didn't know the original source of their "animal fat," as it's called. They buy this from brokers who have thousands of sources all over the country—slaughterhouses, butchershops, disposal plants, and so on. The fat is rendered in the local communities, then shipped to Procter & Gamble in the form of tallow. It arrives just as white and pretty as a candle. "But," said the soap people in an orgy of frankness, "we wouldn't be a bit surprised if an occasional horse does stray into that tallow."

One more thing I learned about soap. You've heard the Saturday-night-bath gag all your life. Well, that joke is a bad understatement. Statistics show that the average American does not take even one bath a week. One in two weeks would come nearer to it.

Fourteen of the biggest soap companies got together and put on a terrific propaganda campaign designed to make people wash oftener. They spent two million dollars. And they might as well have poured that two million down the drain, or given part of it to me. Because, when it was all over and the checkup was made, they found they had not increased the national bath-taking average by even so much as the dabble of one toe in the bathtub. It was very discouraging. But even so, we are the best-washed nation in the world.

Almost every afternoon my Love had a number of her friends in for tea in my honor, there at Parkersburg, West Virginia. She introduced them around very carefully, so that I would get the names. Most of them were members of the Amiendern family, who were acrobats. There were also some friends named French-massy; I forget their profession, but I believe they were plasterers. They were all charming people. The only trouble was that, when I looked closely, they weren't there. But that was my fault, and I never mentioned it to my Love. I believe I can say honestly that my Love was not entirely unresponsive to my abject attentions. It was a little ritual of ours that she would not close her eyes in sleep until I had kissed her good night. When a man gets that far, he's doing all right. I had not yet asked her parents, point-blank, for her hand, but her father and I had discussed the thing casually. He seemed to have no special objections to me, outside of my face. He said just to let the thing float awhile. There was plenty of time, for my Love was only four years old. And her name was Claire.

Claire's parents, like all good parents, had a number of stories about their child. Unfortunately, most of them were slightly earthy, but I believe this one can be told. Claire's mother had to fly to St. Paul and was taking Claire with her. It was a drive of several hours to the nearest airline terminal. Claire's father took them in the car. They had not been long on the way when they stopped at a filling station. It was a disastrous move: Claire discovered filling-station rest rooms.

She was infatuated. From then on, not a filling station escaped her. Nature worked overtime on Claire, or so she made believe; in fact, a couple of times they had to stop and go out into wheat fields, impelled by Claire's wishful thinking on the subject. After eleven halts in thirty miles, things began to get on father's nerves. He stopped each time more reluctantly, and finally began to cuss. But Claire, all undaunted, continued her triumphant inspection march down the highway that was paved with rest rooms and father's dying hopes of getting to the plane on time.

Finally, with just a few minutes to go, nature called one last halt. And at this one father, amidst all his other troubles, slammed the car door on his elbow. Exasperated beyond endurance, he moaned, "Oh, God, I hope we make it."

Well, they did make it. It was Claire's first flight, but she loved it. (And to forestall a possible anticlimax, there are no more rest rooms in this story.) The plane was full of men. They were only a few minutes realizing that an angel was in their midst. Claire was a spectacularly beautiful child, and the men went completely silly. They were jouncing her on their knees; some even had her horsy-back in the aisle; gruff businessmen were saying "Quack, quack, that's how the duck goes." And Claire, the little devil, turned on the charm with her pale blue eyes and gave them the smile that makes you limp, and said perfect little childish things. She had that plane load of doting men right on the ropes.

They came finally to St. Paul. They banked and circled, the motors were throttled, and the plane settled silently toward the field. And then suddenly Claire, standing at the window, spoke. And she didn't speak as though she was praying. She spoke coldly and sophisticatedly, as Joan Crawford might speak in a movie. She said, "Oh, God, I hope we make it!"

Claire's mother said later that something electric and terrible went flashing around the plane cabin—something that hurt the souls of men who believe in little angels. And Claire looked at her mother without smiling or winking or anything. She just looked at her innocently, for which her mother could have slain her, because Claire wasn't any more frightened than the pilot was. She knew what she was doing, and she did it on purpose. Could you blame me for being in love with Claire?

Pittsburgh is undoubtedly the cockeyedest city in the United States. Physically, it is absolutely irrational. It is the only city in this country where I can't find my way around, the only one of which I can't get a mental bird's-eye picture. I've flown over it, driven all around it, and studied maps of it, and still I hardly know one end of Pittsburgh from the other. It's worse than ir- regular—it's chaotic. People who live there can't find their way around either. One friend of mine who was born and raised there said she could drive to almost any place in the city but probably couldn't go the shortest way. Another friend had lived there six years, and all he had ever figured out was how to get from his house to downtown. Every time he got off this path he was lost.

The reason for all this is the topography of Pittsburgh. It's hills, mountains, cliffs, valleys, and rivers. Streets never run more than a few blocks in a straight line. You may have a friend who lives half a mile away, but to get there you circle three miles around a mountain ridge, cross two bridges, go through a tunnel, follow a valley, skirt the edge of a cliff, and wind up at your friend's back door an hour late. Downtown, a freight train goes by a fourth-story office window. The main passenger line of another railroad runs smack through the center of a steel mill— right under its roof, even; there just wasn't any place else to put the railroad. Trolley cars run over the tops of houses one minute and through a tunnel the next.

There are more than two hundred bridges in Pittsburgh, for there are three big rivers right in the city. The Allegheny and the Monongahela twist around through town, and then come together within a stone's throw of the business district to form the Ohio. There are countless tunnels right in the city—tunnels for autos, for trolleys, for trains. The big Liberty Tubes through Mt. Washington are a mile long, and when traffic gets jammed the drivers start honking their horns and you think you're in a madhouse. And there are many inclined railways. I don't mean cable streetcars, such as San Francisco has. I mean the funny little things that run at forty-five degrees right up the side of a mountain, on tracks built onto steel trestlework.

And then the steps. Oh, Lord, the steps! I was told they actually had a Department of Steps in the city government. That isn't exactly true, though they do have an Inspector of Steps. But there are nearly thirteen miles of city-owned steps in Pittsburgh, going up mountainsides. The well-to-do people drive to work. The medium people go on streetcars and "inclines"— that's what they call those cable cars. And the poor people walk up the steps.

There's an old saying in Pittsburgh, dating back to the days when the steel mills paid off in gold—"No coal dust, no gold dust." Pittsburgh is a dirty city. It wasn't libeled a bit when it got that reputation. But Pittsburgh people, like people everywhere, love prosperity. And a dirty shirt collar there means prosperity. So people don't seem to mind.

While in Pittsburgh, I spent nearly the whole of one night in the steel mills. We walked for miles, we climbed our heads off, we got dirty, we got tired, we saw strange scenes that took on an exaggerated weirdness at three o'clock in the morning. In fact, we saw too much. The whole thing became eerie, and things merged into a sleepy-eyed dream.

But one outstandingly bright memory of the night was when the superintendent of the Jones & Laughlin plant said, "Now I'll show you something that no visitor to a steel mill ever sees." We got onto a huge freight elevator and went up and up and up. A door raised, and we stepped onto a wooden platform. Several men were up there, wearing pith helmets and thick gloves and doing nothing at the moment. They spoke to us. The superintendent handed me a pair of dark-blue glasses. "Now come over to the railing and look down," he said. I held on and peeked over; I was looking right down into the seething insides of a Bessemer furnace. "Now you know what hell is like," the superintendent said.

You would not dare look into that terrific fire without those glasses. They were so dark they made the eye-shattering glow look mildly purple, but you could see every detail. The molten metal didn't just boil. It leaped, viciously, against the sides of the furnace, like surf beating on a cliff. The temperature in there was around 2,900 degrees. Although we stood fifteen or twenty feet from the furnace mouth, the scorching heat was unbearable. My face felt blistered. The awfulness of the power in that golden maelstrom made me hold onto the railing as though I might fall, though there was no danger.

We went back down to the floor of the furnace room, and then up to another platform on the other side. Now we were below the seething mouths of the furnaces, but still we had to wear dark glasses to look up at them. These furnaces, I should explain, are three or four stories high, and built in the shape of an immense urn or vase—big at the bottom and curving to a smaller neck at the top. The only opening is at the top. They are set on huge cradles so that they can be tipped over and the molten metal can be poured out. We stood in a room of levers and valves, and a window opened onto the furnace room. "Here," said the superintendent, "pull on this lever, and then watch the furnace." I pulled, timidly, and in a second the whole urnlike furnace began to swing slowly over. I shoved the lever back to neutral, and was quick about it. "Go ahead," said the superintendent, "pull on it hard." I pulled again, and watched it move farther, but I didn't like it much. I could feel the pain of responsibility run up through my arm. If I had kept pulling that lever, and if nobody had knocked my hand away, I could have turned the whole vat over and dumped tons of molten metal all over the place, killing men, ruining machinery.

In my meanderings through three steel mills I was struck by how few men I saw working. Actually, there were thousands in each plant. You saw them coming to work, but where they went I didn't know. Maybe it was just that the plants were so big they got lost inside. Work in the steel mills goes on twenty-four hours a day, in three eight-hour shifts. But they aren't called shifts; they're "turns." Funny how different industries have different names for the same thing. On board ship your period of work is a "watch." In the oil fields it's a "tour," pronounced "tower." In telegraphy it's a "trick." In the mines a "shift."

Some terrible accidents happen in the steel mills. In one plant they opened the spout from the mixing furnace to pour tons of molten yellow metal into a vat on a little freight car. But the engineer got his signals mixed and didn't have his car under the spout at the right time. The metal came pouring out—2,900 degrees hot, bright and liquid—and it cut the locomotive squarely in two, just that quick. The engineer died instantly.

The Northeast

Chapter XXII — Put in Bay is in Ohio. But it isn't where the rest of Ohio is. It's on an island in Lake Erie. It was there that Commodore Oliver Hazard Perry defeated a British fleet in 1813, and it was from Put in Bay that he sent his message: "We have met the enemy, and they are ours."

But the most interesting thing about Put in Bay—to me, at least—was its little weekly newspaper. Among the personal items you'd run onto something like this: "The captain and mate of the yacht Sea Hag can usually be located sleeping on Roy Webster's woodpile." Or among the ads: "Bicycles for rent. Special rates to drunks." Some of the citizens of Put in Bay were afflicted with periodic bouts with demon wine, and would wind up soaking out in a mainland sanitarium. The local term for this affliction was "June-bug fever." So, in the columns of the *Gazette* you would read that "no cases of June-bug fever were reported to the Board of Health this week." Or that "So-and-so [actually giving his name] is eating ice-cream cones this week after a protracted case of June-bug fever." I envy anybody who can put out a paper so pregnant with freedom-of-the-press as the Put in Bay *Gazette*.

Since it is the ambition of most everybody to own an island somewhere, I asked a few questions about prices up in the Thousand Islands in the St. Lawrence River. There were plenty left for sale, and very cheap too. The boundary between Canada and the United States runs down the middle of the river, so about half the islands are Canadian, and half American. There wasn't any red tape about an American's owning a Canadian island. You didn't have to become a citizen; you merely paid county land taxes. Of course you could buy an American island, but that wouldn't be any fun. You could get a small island, big enough for a house and leg-stretching room, at anywhere from eighty-five up to five hundred dollars. And if you wanted to get into the big-island stuff, you could get one for a few thousand. I walked with the owner of Hay Island, who said he'd sell it for fifteen thousand dollars. Its area was several hundred acres, it had a number of houses on it, and you could raise hay, hogs, cattle, and chickens. The owner was tired of raising hay. But I too was tired of raising hay; I had got tired of it about twenty years before. That's the reason I write this stuff—so I won't have to raise hay. So why should I pay fifteen thousand for the privilege of raising hay in the St. Lawrence River? I'd rather live in Hawaii, anyway.

Captain Danny La Sha was the Fred Allen of the Thousand Islands. Captain La Sha (pronounced La Shay) ran tourists around the islands in his big speedboat. The trip would be worth the money if you never even left the dock.

Here's how Captain La Sha operated. He ran out into the river a little way, then throttled down his motor, turned around, and said, "See that lighthouse over there on that island? And see that rock shoal about a hundred yards away, with a pole on it? A lot of people ask what the cage on top of the pole is for. Well, up in this north country in November it gets to snowin' and blowin' and rainin' so bad the mariners can't see the lighthouse at night. So they bring a boy out from Gananoque and put him in that cage on top of that pole. And he sets there all night and holds up a lighted candle to guide the mariners. In the daytime he sells the *Ladies' Home Journal,* which tells all about light house-keeping."

That's the way it went all through the trip.

You pass some amazing places on that Thousand Islands boat trip. One island is so small that the house built on it covers the whole island. The boatman said it belonged to a Montreal man whose doctor had ordered him to take a long rest. He bought this small island so he wouldn't have any place to walk even if he wanted to.

Some of the small islands have little two-by-four shacks on them. Others, especially on the American side, have million-dollar castles. We passed one island with a beautiful house which was once the summer home of Caruso. We saw the summer home of Irving Berlin. And we passed the home of a Mr. Brachanbach of Pittsburgh, who was a fiend for boats. He had thirty motor-boats, a houseboat, a big cruiser, and even a fireboat which he sent out to all the fires on the islands.

There were two little islands, very close together, about the size of city lots. On one was a beautiful summer home, with lawn and boathouse and summer chairs; the other was a colorful little flower park. A footbridge of about forty feet connected them. Our boatman said this was the shortest international bridge in the world. He said the Canada-United States line ran right be-tween the little islands. Apparently the owner, a Mr. Cashmere of Philadelphia, believed it himself, for he had a British flag on one island and an American flag on the other. But later a fellow told me the whole thing was a myth, and got out a government chart to prove it. The line actually runs about six hundred feet south, which makes both islands Canadian.

On each side of the town of Williamsburg, Ontario, there was an unusual road sign which said, "VERY SLOW, PLEASE." You had to go very slow because the town was full of people walking jerkily and in pain, people with twisted bodies, people on crutches, people rolling down the middle of the road in wheel chairs. This was the town of Dr. M. W. Locke, the famous Canadian doctor who seemed to work miracles by twisting your feet.

For three-quarters of an hour I stood and watched the treat-ments of Dr. Locke. It was, in a way, one of the most fantastic rites I ever witnessed. In those forty-five minutes he treated about eighty-five people. Each one paid him a dollar. He did not speak to more than ten of them. Often a treatment was over in five seconds. With one exception, no person received more than thirty seconds of the doctor's time.

Dr. Locke treated patients in an outdoor pavilion next to his small white frame house on a cross street just off the highway.

By nine o'clock a couple of hundred patients were waiting around the pavilion. Many were in wheel chairs; many came on crutches; some could walk, limpingly, and others appeared outwardly to be perfectly all right. They brought folding chairs and camp stools, and sat around chatting as though at a picnic.

The pavilion was probably thirty feet square, and had a roof but no sides. From the outer edge, eleven chutes, formed by railings of ordinary inch-piping, led toward the center. At the inner end of each chute was an ordinary wooden chair for the patient. The eleven chutes did not quite complete a circle. There was a blank space left, big enough for three wheel chairs. Early patients had filled the first spaces. Fourteen patients in all, making a circle.

Suddenly the doctor appeared from the house. The sleeves of his blue shirt were rolled up. He walked to the center of the circle of patients, and sat down in his swivel chair. There were no preliminaries. Dr. Locke said nothing. He took the first extended foot on his knee. He did no exploratory feeling around. Quickly he placed his thumb on the inside, pressed, gave the foot a twist, then bent the toes down, and pushed hard. He reached for the other foot, and did the same. It was over.

He seemed to look a little to the left of the patient, or up in the air. Now and then he stopped long enough to take out his handkerchief and rub his eyes.

A couple of feet behind him, his son Parker worked. Parker took the patients' dollar bills and stuffed them into his dad's hip pockets. Once the doctor had to stop and empty them. He took out two enormous handfuls of dollar bills and pushed them into a side pocket.

Patients who were badly twisted got more than just the foot treatment. Occasionally Dr. Locke would take a hand, and bend and twist the fingers. Then Parker would take hold of the patient's shoulder and elbow, and Dr. Locke would apply pressure —trying to straighten a bent, rigid arm. Occasionally a patient would give a little cry of pain, but that came usually from those not in such bad shape. You never heard a sound from the wheel-chair patients, who suffered the most. That is what touched me most during those forty-five minutes—the casual stoicism of the people. What did a little more pain mean, after months and years of it, if there was a chance of cure?

Round and round the circle Dr. Locke swiveled in his chair— fourteen people at a turn, and five or six minutes around the circle. After each treatment the patient slipped on his shoes and left the circle, and another patient took his place. In those forty-five minutes I saw people of every class and description—cripples in old clothes and broken-down wheel chairs, women with so many diamond rings Dr. Locke could hardly get a grip on their hands. There seemed to be more women than men. There were a few old people, and a few children, but the majority were of middle age.

Dr. Locke told me that about a third of his work was charity, but of the eighty-five who received treatment while I watched there wasn't a single one who didn't pay. Handing over the dollar bill was about the only joke the patients could make out of the swift, grim business. One woman had her bill under her wrist-watch strap, and made Parker fish for it. A young fellow in a wheel chair had his wrapped tightly around his finger, and Parker, grabbing bills right and left, had to stop and unwind it slowly while the patient laughed.

While standing in a chute watching, I talked with a boy whose mother was next in line. She had had the flu, and it had left one leg stiff and without circulation. They had been in Williamsburg a week. The boy said his mother seemed improved. A few minutes later I stepped into a drugstore. Two women patients were passing the time of day. One of them said, "I've been here a week, and he hasn't helped me a bit."

Williamsburg had become a mecca after Rex Beach wrote about Dr. Locke's treatments in *Cosmopolitan* magazine, some six years before my visit. People had come by the scores of thousands. There had been Indian princes. There was a man there now from Jerusalem. Some went away improved, some did not. Some took only a couple of treatments; some stayed for months, and took two foot twistings a day. Dr. Locke said he told many after their first treatment that he couldn't do anything for them. The majority of the sufferers were arthritis victims, but they came with everything else, too—atrophied muscles, shoulders that had been out of joint for years, all kinds of muscular distortions. Some even came with syphilis.

I asked Dr. Locke to explain to me, in simple language, what he did. He said that most muscular ailments came from fallen arches, or flat feet. A fallen arch is a foot bone that has slipped out of place, thus creating pressure on certain nerves. It's usually caused by walking too soon after an illness, when supporting muscles are weak. What Dr. Locke did was work this bone back in place, relieving the pressure. I asked if this business of curing ailments by foot manipulation was a secret trick of his. "No secret to it," he said. "I just learned by doing. Anybody could do it. But somehow they can't seem to learn. Lots of them come up here and watch and then set up in business, but you never hear of them after about a month."

During the peak of the pilgrimages, there were as many as twenty-eight hundred patients at one time; Dr. Locke began work at four in the morning, and didn't finish till eleven at night. The town had prospered, along with Dr. Locke. But business was way off this summer; only five hundred patients were there now. Dr. Locke was just as well pleased, for he said he couldn't stand the grind any more.

They say all horse players die broke. But I'd be as safe from bankruptcy around the track at Saratoga, New York, as anywhere else. During a whole afternoon of watching the Sport of Kings, I never even figured out how to place a bet.

The only race-track word I know is "plater," and I have no idea what it means. Jockeys look silly to me, and I'm no horse lover. But it seemed like reportorial cowardice not to visit this glamorous track when we were so close, so we went. But we were out of tune with the spirit of Saratoga racing. The biggest mistake was in our clothes. I wore a blue business suit, with coat and trousers matching. To complete the rube effect, I even had on a necktie. That Girl had on the same gray tailored suit she had worn for two years. You'd think she could at least have put a bandanna around her head. Neither of us had binoculars, dark glasses, form sheets, or a worried look. I don't know why they even let us in.

Our first boner was trying to get into the clubhouse (where the Vanderbilts sit) on a mere grandstand ticket. After that rebuff, we were timid even about assailing the grandstand. When we finally got in, there wasn't any place to sit, so we stood in the aisle and got in everybody's way. Suddenly the crowd yelled, "They're off!" The only thing "off" I could see was an elderly woman standing in front of us, one arm high in the air, rigid as death except for her fingers, which went snap-snap-snap. It did thrill me to see such a plunger. You could tell by her grimness that her whole future was at stake. When the pay-off came, we saw she had a dollar on a horse to show.

When the crowd sat down, we decided to try to make a bet on the next race. We placed our faith in a man with a badge who was going around the grandstand, apparently taking bets. He stood near us and spoke as follows: "Seven is now fifteen and a half. Change the field to eleven. Lady, eight is now four, but I'll give you four and a half. What's nine now? Well, you can have nine at twenty and four. Six is still six and seven has gone to eighteen."

"Let's ask him about two plus two," I whispered, but just then the crowd yelled, "They're off!"

"We're not getting the hang of it," I said. "Let's try the betting ring downstairs." This place, under the grandstand, was about a block long, and jammed with thousands of men. Around the edge were about seventy open booths, like newsstands. In each one, men were grimly writing numbers on slates, others studiously figuring in ledgers.

We didn't see anybody pass any money. And everybody looked too busy for me to ask any questions. Anyway a cop came along and said, "No ladies allowed in here, cap." That made the Girl mad, so we got the hell out of there and went to look at the horses in the paddock.

The uniformed man at the gate said, "If you go in there you can't come back out." "Why not?" I said. "Because that's the field," he said. "What's the field?" I said. "That's where the cheap customers sit," he said. No man in my position dare be caught dead among the cheap customers, so we went away as fast as possible.

We found the paddock just behind the grandstand. We had passed it twice, and didn't know what it was. We were fooled because there weren't any horses in it. The horses were all out in the beautiful grounds behind the grandstand, walking around trees. There was a tree for every horse. That's the way they exer-cised them just before a race.

We picked out a horse, and looked wisely at it for some time. "What do you think of its hocks?" I said. Before the Girl could answer, they led the horse away for the next race.

By now we had missed four races, and this was the seventh and last. "Shall we go watch?" I said. We looked at each other, and simultaneously started for the car. When we got back to town I took off my shoes and lay down. By the time the thousands of elated losers were fighting their way out of the track, I was peace-fully napping.

That night a beautiful collie wandered into our restaurant. We petted him a minute, then he went to the next table, and the man and woman there gave him some meat. They told us the dog didn't have an owner, and that it slept in the park. That got us to talking back and forth, and these people asked if we had been to the races. We said yes, but couldn't make head or tail out of the betting. They said they couldn't either, at first.

After a while they moved over to our table. They didn't have anything to do after dinner, and we didn't either, so we decided to make an evening of it. They were swell people. We went from place to place, and talked and talked, till two o'clock in the morning. The man turned out to be, of all things, a bookmaker at the track.

He was sort of new at it. He had got into it by answering an ad in the paper; some guy wanted a partner with three thousand dollars. Our friend had three thousand and no job, so he became a bookmaker. He hadn't done very well so far; he was three thousand in the hole right now. The New York tracks ran only five months a year, and he couldn't operate in any other state. He had only about two months to recoup. If he did, they'd go to Florida for the winter. If he didn't—well, he knocked on wood, carried charms in his pockets, and rubbed Negro boys' heads. That's a race-track custom. While we were in a café, a little colored boy came in selling papers. The gamblers practically rubbed his head off.

Our bookie explained why everything seemed like chaos to us at the track. New York was the only state that had "open betting" on the races. All the others used pari-mutuel machines. In pari-mutuel betting you just go up to a window, say what horse you're betting on, hand over a minimum of two dollars, and they give you a ticket. You don't know how much you'll get back till the race is over. If you win, you go back to the window, present your ticket, and are paid off.

But in open betting nothing is centralized. There were more than a hundred bookies at the Saratoga track, each in business for himself. More than seventy operated at stands in "the ring," beneath the grandstand. Others just circulated through the stands, taking bets. Women had to bet with these, as they weren't allowed in the ring. Each bookie quoted his own odds. Your bet was a private deal between you and the bookmaker. Our bookie said all that gibberish we heard at the track and all the figures on the slates were merely the odds on each horse. He said it was simple as pie once you got the hang of it.

A bookmaker in the ring had to have at least six employes. And he had to lay the whole day's expenses on the line before the first race. It cost our bookmaker $197 a day before he ever took a bet. About three bookies at Saratoga went broke every day. But the bettors would be paid off just the same. The "office" paid off for the busted bookies. Frequently a flat bookie would promote money somewhere, pay up at the office for what it had dished out for him, and be back in business within three days.

You hear about race-track gamblers being free and easy, broke today and rich tomorrow, happy-go-lucky. Well, our bookie said he was that way before he started gambling, but race-tracking had just reversed him. When he made anything now, it went right into the bank. Off the track he carried only a dollar with him. His wife carried twenty-five dollars just for emergencies. For the first time in his life he knew the value of a dollar.

The state of New York owns the Saratoga Spa, which is fourteen hundred acres of flat land, about a mile from town on the Albany-Saratoga highway. Saratoga built up its name as a spa under private ownership, but in the manner of much private enterprise, the springs were drained almost to extinction. The state stepped in years ago to conserve the precious mineral waters, but it was not until the 1930s that it really went to bat to make something big of the Saratoga Spa. First, they capped most of the mineral springs, leaving twenty-four open for Spa use. Then millions were spent on the grounds and buildings. There were three huge bathhouses, a golf course, tennis courts, even horseshoe courts. There was a recreational center with a big swimming pool and a brick terrace with umbrella-shaded tables around the pool. There were a bottling plant, a large administration building, a drinking hall with marble pillars and Versailles chandeliers, and an orchestra from eight to nine in the morning to soothe the nerves of those who strolled and sipped the mineral waters. There were picnic grounds, forest groves, scores of acres of close-clipped lawns, and miles of walks. You saw little signs telling just what the grade of each path was. Sometimes it was only an inch in a hundred yards, but an inch is a lot to a bum heart.

When we walked around this elaborate outlay, there were very few people there. The Spa was certainly no Coney Island—no place for Us, the Masses, to have fun. It was a place for either the sorely afflicted or the fashionable rich. We saw practically nobody who looked as if anything was wrong with him. But we saw a lot of healthy, deeply tanned people in long black limousines, who looked as though they were at Saratoga because it was the thing for rich people to do. There was just one place to stay on the reservation—the Gideon-Putnam Hotel, and it was in the Rolls-Royce class. The common people had to stay in downtown Saratoga, a mile away.

The usual course of bath treatments lasts three weeks. Now, I could stand three weeks at the Spa, but three weeks in downtown Saratoga would give me the meemies, plus gastro-intestinal shrieks. One side of the street was Hollywood, the other was mammy plantation stuff out of the Civil War. Giant old hotels joined each other in a string that ran three blocks. You were charged double rates for a room with drooping wallpaper and exposed plumbing. The knotted-rope fire escape by the window was practically the city emblem. Saratoga had got it into its head over the years that it had only one month to make a living, and that was race month. The day after the track closed, everybody just gave up. And nobody was going to modernize a hotel that was open only one month a year. Yet thousands did come and take the baths, in spite of the inconveniences. Around a hundred fifty thousand baths a year were being given at the Spa.

So far as I could see, the only purpose of the Spa should have been to benefit sick people. It belonged to the state and should have been available to any citizen with an ache or a pain. The Spa officials themselves did not wish it to be snooty; they only wanted to keep it high-class. Yet prices were high. The recreation center was like an exclusive country club. There was no hospital. The medical director was not allowed to advise you or even suggest who was the best doctor in town. The walks and lawns and benches leaped at you with their emptiness. It seemed to me a shame.

The Indians discovered that the Saratoga waters were good for aches and pains, and white men have been using them since before the Civil War. The waters are full of minerals that taste like iron; they're the only naturally carbonated mineral waters east of the Rocky Mountains, and they are not sulphurous.

When I asked Cyrus Elmore, superintendent of the Spa, just exactly what the waters would cure, he said, "Well, they help so many things it really sounds like Dr. Johnson's Indian Snake Oil. We've had trouble convincing the medical world we aren't running a tent show here." People bathe in the water, drink it, inhale it, and pour it on themselves. Bathing in it is good for almost everything. Drinking it is good for your stomach. Inhaling it is fine for catarrh, hay fever, and sinus. Pouring it on you is good for skin diseases. People who can't afford the baths get water in tin cups from one of the free springs downtown and pour it on their arms and faces.

About a third of those who come for bath treatments have heart trouble. About a fourth have rheumatics of some kind or other—arthritis, neuritis, and so on. Then come stomach troubles, respiratory diseases, skin diseases, and on down to those who have merely worked too hard or "played" too hard, as the Spa people put it—meaning, I presume, those who come to soak out after a big drunk.

Some of the waters are highly cathartic, especially those from the Hathorne spring. There is an old Saratoga story about this. It seems there was a senator who visited Saratoga frequently. One morning he was stopped on his hotel steps by some ladies of his acquaintance who had just arrived. They raved to him about the wonderful Spa waters they'd been drinking.

"We stopped at one spring and had a couple of glasses of Hathorne water," they said. "Then we went to another and had a glass of Coesa. We also had a few drinks of Geysey water. Then we tasted two or three others we can't remember, and then had some more Hathorne."

Whereupon the senator tipped his hat, bowed, and said, "Ladies, do not let me detain you."

We were sitting in a hotel room at Albany one night when all of a sudden the whole town seemed filled with "Home on the Range" coming from nowhere. We looked under the beds and in the bathroom and out the window, and finally decided it was coming from the top of the City Hall tower. It was "Home on the Range" on bells.

Now, I've always hated music that comes from bells in tall spires. It is always a mournful hymn or something far too classical for my hotcha tastes. But when you hear bells playing "Home on the Range," that's different. I said to myself, "I'll have to find out about this guy." Next day I tracked down the heretic. His name was Floyd Walter. He was a big fellow with a short pompadour, and he was as affable as his music.

"What makes you play human on a carillon?" I asked. "Never heard of such a thing."

So he told me what he'd told a convention of carillon players, where they talked about nothing but Beethoven and hymns. "I don't know who is paying you fellows," he told them. "But I know who's paying me—it's the taxpayers. And if the taxpayers of Albany want 'Lazy Bones,' that's what they're going to have."

The Albany carillon was installed in 1928. It cost sixty thousand dollars and was bought entirely by public subscription. The city operated it.

There were forty-eight bells. The biggest weighed seven tons and was taller than me. The smallest was forty-five pounds, and wasn't much bigger than the old school hand bell. The carillonneur's room was right beneath the bells. You got there by going up a circular dungeonlike stone stairway until you were all out of breath. Carillon playing is hard work. On hot summer nights Walter stripped down to his underwear. Took off pants and all, and locked the door.

The keyboard was something like an old-fashioned organ, except that the keys weren't keys; they were wooden handles on the ends of levers, three or four inches apart. You pushed down about an inch to ring a bell. Down below were two long rows of foot pedals. These were duplicates of the hand keys, because in a fast piece two hands weren't enough. The carillonneur wore leather gloves with the outside of the little fingers heavily padded. In fast playing, he just pounded the sticks with the outside of his fist.

I wish you could have seen Floyd Walter playing. There he sat with a cigar stub gripped in his teeth, his face rigid, sweat rolling out, his hands fighting bees, his feet stomping out fire, his whole body jouncing as though in a fit, and the wooden sticks rattling so you could hardly hear the bells above. It was a funny contrast to the soft and soulful tones you heard half a mile away. Walter played two pieces, ran a few scales, then told me to give it a few bongs myself, just to see how it felt. People in the street probably thought the carillon had gone crazy.

Walter played on all holidays and Sundays. Whenever a prominent Albany citizen died, he played something sad and full of feeling. Then two evenings a week he gave a forty-five-minute concert of popular music. People sat in the parks and sang with the bells.

"Could you swing it?" I asked.

"Sure, I could swing it," he said. "But I don't. If I ever played swing music there isn't a carillonneur in the country who would ever speak to me again.

Lincoln, Maine, was just a little place, and its hotel wasn't even listed in the big AAA guide. The hotel was sort of old-fashioned, but it was clean as a pin and had an excellent dining room. When I mentioned casually to one of the clerks that I believed I'd write and ask the AAA to put it in the book, he said, oh, no, the owner didn't like publicity—just liked the old, old customers who had been coming there for years. I think that's wonderful. Also, it's Maine.

When I was a little boy in grade school we had to read and report on "The Great Stone Face," a story by Nathaniel Hawthorne. My hatred for this piece of fiction endures to this day. First, I hated it because I was compelled to read it. Second, the main character was called Ernest, a name of which I have never been overly fond. And last, I hated it because Ernest was just too nice a little boy for me to stomach.

As we studied our road maps one day I realized that Ernest's Great Stone Face was somewhere in the mountains of New England. It is also called "The Old Man of the Mountain." So we decided to seek it out. As we drew near to Franconia Notch in the lovely White Mountains of central New Hampshire, I wondered if we would be able to recognize the Stone Face once we were within sight of it. And then we came around a bend, and there painted on the highway in big yellow letters was "Old Man —Parking." Big yellow arrows led you off to parking areas, where there must have been five hundred cars parked. The area had been taken over by the state. Troopers were there to watch traffic; there were rest rooms, and a souvenir store, and a lunch counter, and benches and telescopes and bronze markers. The Great Stone Face was, I found, the No. 1 tourist attraction of the New England mountains.

You had to walk about a quarter of a mile from the parking place, and then you came out into a clearing and looked up, and there, high above, was Ernest's beloved Great Stone Face. It really is remarkable, no question about it—a sort of Abraham Lincoln face, old and solemn and full of character, jutting out from the very top of a granite cliff more than a thousand feet high. You see it from half a mile away, and it can be seen only in profile against the sky. If you were to walk or drive way around in front of it, you would see no face at all—just ledges of gray rock.

The face is formed of several granite strata which, over the years, have been pushed out into different positions by freezing and thawing. It was first looked upon by white men in 1805, and since then the face has changed its contour. The ledge that formed the forehead has been pushed farther out, giving the Old Man a heavy and intellectual brow instead of the receding dome he had a hundred years ago. In fact, the weathering action has been so rapid that had it not been for the enthusiasm of a New Hampshire preacher named Guy Roberts the face might already have been obliterated. The Reverend Mr. Roberts became interested early in the century in preserving the face, but it was not until 1915 that he got a granite engineer to climb the mountain with him. They found that the great forehead-stone was so nearly overbalanced that two men with crowbars could have shoved it off into the twelve-hundred-foot chasm below. So the state got interested, and paid for the work of saving the face. This was done by drilling holes into the slipping ledges, then tying them back to solid rock with heavy steel rods, tightened with turnbuckles. It was a tremendous task, as everything had to be packed by men up the high mountain, but it was accomplished in eight days.

So now the Great Stone Face is preserved for all future little Ernests who wish to become so noble in character. Despite my childhood hatred for the fictional Ernest, I found that I was genuinely touched by the power and solemnity of the stone face. If I weren't so old and solidly set in my habits (I like them, too, that's the hell of it) I might stand there myself and gaze until I became great and noble like that other Ernest, the little shrimp.

My first appearance in Boston occurred at a time when I was, to understate the case, in a financial predicament. I had a dollar and a half, and was supposed to be in Indiana the next day. A friend of mine had a similar amount and was in a similar position. We did not tarry to hear any symphonies or study the art exhibits. We simply started west. We left Boston on a Sunday afternoon. Our plan was to ride the subway to the end of the line and then start walking. The plan was all right, but our execution was bad. We failed to recognize the end of the line. When we finally got off, after riding an hour, we were right back where we started.

We made it the second time. We got as far as Worcester the first night, and stayed in a flophouse. The second night saw us deep in the comforts of a two-bit bed in Schenectady. The rest of the journey grows dimmer. We lived on coffee and doughnuts; we rode the blinds, we rode the running gears of logging trucks, we walked vast distances. And we rode for two days in a Model T Ford with a guy who bought our meals and put us up in hotels, yet absolutely refused to say a word to us. We got to Indiana on Friday evening. So all I remembered of Boston was that it was a long way from Indiana.

The second time I arrived in Boston, nearly twenty years later, I was prepared to dislike it. But I soon took a fancy to the place. Possibly it's because I was now full of culture. And for another thing, I got all around town without getting lost. Boston is famous for being the easiest city in America to get lost in; the streets are so twisty and cut up that you can make one turn, suddenly find the afternoon sun in the east, and swear that somebody must have pushed you. What's more, I encountered a couple of pleasant little incidents out of Boston life: one to uphold the cultural New England tradition, one to destroy it. I'm always happy when things reach an impasse like that.

The first came from a policeman. I pulled up to one at a corner to ask the way to Cambridge. (I wasn't lost—just slightly confused.) The policeman said I'd have to turn right. Since I was already halfway across the street, I asked if I could back up, then turn. The policeman was gruff, but no typical cop language came from his lips. What he said was exactly as follows, so help me: "Reverse promptly. I wish to use the street."

There weren't any words at all in the other incident. I simply saw a nice-looking couple about thirty years old come out of a cocktail lounge. The woman fell flat on her face twice within fifty feet. She fell down because she was (shhhhh!) d-r-u-n-k. Each

· 321 ·

time she fell, the man calmly picked up her purse and handker-chief, waited until she had sprawlingly staggered up under her own power, and then handed them to her. Do you suppose that somewhere, through those dim years between 1620 and 1938, the cold chivalry of New England could have crept silently around a corner and died?

Although I am an ignorant man, and could hardly be called even a bench warmer on the field of philosophic thought, still there has always been in me a deep veneration for those who have achieved high scholastic degrees. It has always been my thwarted ambition to be a philosopher—to become so wise that I might write like Emerson and think like Justice Holmes—hence I have always looked up to the Ph.D., the Doctor of Philosophy. There are all kinds of philosophers, including the corn-fed and those who hide in caves. But the Ph.D. is stamped with his intelligence, and wears it like an ermine wrap. The Ph.D. is a wise man, and he can haul out his sheepskin to prove it. He is one to whose feet the world may come for wisdom and a quiet discussion of the manifold secrets of existence.

And so, at Cambridge, Massachusetts, wearing a long-billed cap and a dirty shirt as badges of my own wretched ignorance, I slunk into the sacred halls of Harvard on a devout mission to find out what makes the philosophers so smart. Three hours of research took me through the entire list of theses upon which a thousand Harvard men in the past ten years had gained the all-knowing status of Ph.D. Just from the titles, I thought, might come some clue to a program of practical philosophy for myself. Here, if ever, was the source of a broad, placid design for living.

My first title read: *The Inheritance of Harelip and Fused in the House Mouse.* Audubon took his secret from the birds, and Thoreau achieved his philosophy from the growing things of nature. There are philosophers who have learned from the busy ant and the buzzing bee. But to sit at the feet of a harelipped house mouse (probably gnawing on cheese) is getting too damn philosophical for me. Even "and fused" is over my head.

So I had to seek further. Something simple, but well rounded.

This title caught my eye: *The Morphology and Syntax of the Periphrastic Passive in the German Works of Notker III*. When you know that, what else is there to know?

But I thumbed further along, seeking a treatise on life and death, a calm and usable understanding of it all. My answer was: *A Statistical Analysis of Fluctuations in the Price of Corn*. Howdy, Socrates, you old corn statistician, you.

The next title seemed to me to stack right up with any of Plato's writings. If I had a son I would want him to read and reread this volume, carry it with him, sleep with it, and apply it daily in his dealings with his fellow men. I refer to *Accented Vowels in the Northumbrian Dialect of Old English*.

And how would you like to read a little work entitled *Alpha, Beta Unsaturated Keto Sulfones*? I imagine Harvard would send it to you if you wrote them a nice letter. Personally, I always carry a copy in my toolbox.

I don't know whether you would call Darwin a philosopher or not, but he did work out a highly talked-about philosophy of existence called Evolution. The following philosophical work seems to fall right in Darwin's field: *An Investigation of Reconstitution Following Various Operations on the Tails of Frogs*. It is my understanding that this philosopher kept cutting off a frog's tail to see how far up he could go before the frog died. An old-fashioned conviction rendered this essay almost useless for me. I had gone through life believing that frogs had no tails. It was too late for me to change now.

I could go on for hours. In the reading rooms of Harvard I scratched down philosophical title after title: *The Life and Works of Thomas Sprat; The Variation with Pressure of the Phase Diagram of the Binary Mixture Na-K; Extensions of Partially Ordered Sets; The Limited Quadrennial Legislative Session of Alabama;* and on and on.

And late that afternoon you could have seen a weary philosopher named E. Tobias Pyle, late of Harvard, stumbling about Harvard Square. He held a flashlight above his head, and the startled homegoers of Cambridge heard him calling faintly, "Demosthenes, Demosthenes."

The plant of the American Optical Company, at Southbridge, Massachusetts, was the biggest one in the world, and they made so many million lenses a year that even the company officials wondered who bought them all.

I don't believe I was ever in a factory that went to as much trouble to get things just right. They had inspectors and light machines and strength machines and gadgets of various kinds behind every post. They had one whole building full of scientists —chemists, physicists, metallurgists, and worst of all, mathematicians.

There is an eye trouble known as aniseikonia, which means that if you're looking at a baseball, for instance, the ball will be one size in one eye and a different size in the other eye. This is not only absurd, but damned confusing. And it is very hard to fit glasses to eyes like that. You have to get mathematical angles, power units, refractory quotients, and so on. These are called "informations," and one man may have as many as eight informations in his eyes. Translating these informations into a lens of the proper corrective angle is a matter of higher mathematics— just how high you can imagine when you hear that it would take one mathematician a week to figure up how to grind one pair of such glasses. That's too wasteful, so they worked out a chart.

It took five years to make the chart. It was on a canvas about four feet wide and three thousand feet long, wrapped around two huge rollers. Two motors were needed to turn it. The whole three thousand feet of this chart were filled with weird lines and figures, from which the experts could work out mathematical combinations into infinity. You could knock out the answer to eight informations in no more time than it takes you to drop your glasses.

Seems as if it's almost impossible to bring up any subject without finding either Benjamin Franklin or the Chinese mixed up in it. Take gunpowder, electricity, printing presses, poetry—what have you got? You've got either Benjamin Franklin or the Chinese. And take eyeglasses. What have you got? Both of them. Eyeglasses were invented by the Chinese, and Benjamin Franklin invented bifocals.

Franklin had two pairs of glasses, one for reading, one for looking at scenery. If he was riding along the countryside reading a
book and suddenly wanted to see a cow in a pasture, he'd have
to change glasses. Often the cow would be gone before he could
get his other glasses on. That made him sore, so he had his glasses
cut in half and combined them in one pair of specs. That's all
bifocals are. They're still doing it that way today.

The desire to be somebody you aren't is almost a universal one.
There are only two people of my entire acquaintance, I believe,
who have become exactly what they wanted to become. It might
well be that the psychologists, if they were smart enough, could
find here the thing that keeps most of us from suicide. We con-
tinue to harbor, right up to the day of death from infirmities,
the belief that somehow we'll still get to be policemen, locomotive engineers, Indian hunters, or in some instances, millionaires.
As we passed a Connecticut farmhouse one day, there was a fellow
out in the front yard practicing with a lariat. It was an odd sight,
because Connecticut is far east, and anyhow we don't think of
Connecticut farmers as anything but suburban New Yorkers.
This fellow was pretty good. He was using what I would say was
a thirty-foot rope. As we passed, he went through a big windup,
swung his lasso with easy cowboy grace, and took a fencepost
right around the neck. This fellow will probably never get west
of Scranton, Pennsylvania, but the feeling that he may yet become a cowboy keeps him from hanging himself.

In my own case, I know quite well that some day I will win
the five-hundred-mile race at Indianapolis.

The hundred or so people who were in the Hofbrau at Mo-
hawk Lake, New Jersey, one Saturday about midnight would be
surprised to know the ending to this story.

On Saturday nights the Hofbrau was a very gay place. Everybody came—young and old, families and everything—and sat
around at tables and ate and talked. A little fellow in a white
suit played the piano and sang in an old-fashioned tenor, and
people were friendly and had a great time.

Things were going along like this one Saturday night when a

couple came in, bareheaded and in summer clothes. They sat on a bench, both on the same side of the table, and ordered something to eat. They talked and listened to the music but otherwise paid little attention to what was going on about them, or to the people who were making a generalized gabbing sound, or to the ones dancing in the aisles because there wasn't any real dance floor. Each seemed very much interested in what the other was saying, and since each one during his say had quite a long say and was animated about it, an impression got about the place.

The impression was probably born first in the piano player's mind, for he went over and asked what they would like him to play. They said play a couple of our old-timers—"Who" and "Lady, Be Good." So he started playing and singing, and they went over and stood behind him and listened, and helped him sing a little now and then when they could remember the words. The crowd thought it was great too and gave a big hand when it was over.

Then the piano player asked them if they weren't just married, and they said yes, just two days ago. The piano player must have spread the word, for three or four people went over and gave the girl a lot of earnest advice on how to live happily, how to handle a husband, what not to do, and so on.

Then the couple, left alone, got started talking again, and they must have been in a deep discussion about something, because they were facing each other now and were talking with their hands too, and being explosive about it, and another impression got about—that they were having a quarrel. Their first quarrel maybe.

But they were unaware that anyone was noticing, you see, so they were very much startled indeed when all of a sudden the piano playing stopped, and there was a great silence all over the place, and from somewhere out of the silence came a loud voice saying, "Aw, kiss and make up."

And that was followed by a louder and closer shout, sort of like an order, which said, "Go ahead and kiss her!"

The man and the girl looked around, and every person in the place was looking at them, waiting. So the man, being no doubt a gentleman, leaned over and kissed her—a great big one—and the wildest applause and shouting and handclapping you ever heard broke out all over the place. And then, one by one, everyone in the Hofbrau filed past and shook hands with them, and congratulated them on their marriage, and wished them long happiness and many good things. It wasn't any joke, either, for they were radiant about it, and serious too. The couple smiled and thanked them all. And as the last ones were filing by, the place was closing for the night, so the newlyweds left too, and got in their car with people still good-wishing them off into the night.

They drove away practically busting, because there was certainly a joke on somebody. Both of them had been married many years, and very happily too, but not to each other. So they drove on home and told their respective husband and wife about it, and everybody thought it was funny.

The man, for one—and probably the girl too—was quite happy about it, for all the people had been so genuine and enthusiastic. And then it was a little flattering too. Especially to the man.

I know this story is true, for I was there and saw it—I was the "bridegroom."

Siesta in Florida

Chapter XXIII YOU MAY NOT BELIEVE IT, BUT WITH THE EXCEPtion of one day we drove all the way from Maine to Miami in the rain. And we discovered that when it comes to just lighting out and driving all day long, days on end, we couldn't take it. Each evening we wound up very sore on our sitting portions, weary to the point of not wishing to eat dinner. We fell into bed. And in the mornings I had a feeling that the Grim Reaper at last had drawn nigh. It took me an hour to get out of bed.

In Miami it continued to pour rain. Back from dinner one evening, we parked the car behind our little hotel and made a dash for the back door. As we rushed in, we butted into the bell-boy and jack-of-all-trades. We had seen him around, carrying bags, painting floors, running errands. He was a nice-looking youth, and he had always smiled good-morning to us.

We made some usual remark about the rain. He didn't answer. That made us look closely at him, and we saw that he was crying. We stopped and asked him what was the matter. He just shook his head. I asked if he had been fired. He said no. We said, "Come on, now; tell us what's the matter." He kept saying, "Nothing. Nothing's the matter."

Have you ever seen a grown-up man standing by himself crying? I can't describe just what it does to you.

"You can tell me," I said to him. "Tell me what's the matter."

Finally he sobbed out brokenheartedly: "I'm just so lonesome."

We took him up to the room. He couldn't say anything for several minutes. He kept trying to get his tears stopped.

"Have you had bad news from home?" I asked him. "Is something wrong in your family?"

"I haven't any family," he said. "My parents died when I was four. I lived with an old man in north Alabama until I was fifteen. He was good to me, but I decided to make my own way. I've been on my own since I was fifteen."

"How old are you now?" I asked.

"Twenty-one."

In the last six years he had worked all over Florida—just little piddly jobs. When he left the old man he had gone through only the sixth grade, and his lack of education became a sort of phobia with him. He was an intelligent boy, and he realized acutely how doomed he was without an education. He could never be anything but a dishwasher, bellhop, gas pumper. And in Florida, where labor was surplus, you didn't hold even those jobs very long.

In those six years he had managed to get through the first year of high school, but he couldn't even go to school now. He worked from 6:00 A.M. to 6:00 P.M.—and after that he worked on till midnight to pay for his room. He barely had time to sleep, let alone go to school.

We talked with him for half an hour or so, and then he had to run—said he'd catch it for being off duty that long. We sat and discussed him for a long time, and felt like crying ourselves. What could we do? Giving him a few dollars wouldn't help. What he had to have was a key to another world, to an existence in which he could go to school, make friends, lift himself into a better job, and into a life where somebody might see enough of him to take an interest in him. We could be nice to him a few minutes a day, we could worry a little about him, but then we would say goodbye and go away and never see him again. We felt pretty useless.

That night Dick Merrill, the flier, came in on his regular Eastern Airlines run from New York. We had been friends for a decade, since long before he ever hit the headlines. He had breakfast with us next morning. Among all my acquaintances, I don't believe I knew a person who was better off than Dick Merrill. His life was packed with interest, and he made a good living by doing the thing he liked best in all the world to do—flying. He had friends by the thousand. He loved to hunt birds and shoot craps and play the ponies and know all the big names and eat at Lindy's and take long trips about the world. And he was constantly doing every one of those things that he loved to do. Even the monotony of flying airliners back and forth over the same route month after month was nectar to him. He said, that morning, "Ernie, every time I start my run, I'm starting on a joy ride. I love it. I've never got tired of flying."

We sat and talked, in the same hotel where a young man without any friends at all was down on his knees out in the hall, painting floors.

On our first day in Key West the following visitors either knocked at the door or else just walked right in: a woman looking for Shepherd Lane; two colonies of ants; a squadron of mosquitoes; several spiders; one scorpion; the iceman; and a little fat boy who said he was one of Jehovah's Witnesses. We used our new flit gun on the ants and mosquitoes and a house slipper on the spiders; the scorpion bit a friend of ours and we had to have the doctor; and we merely looked sternly at the little fat boy and he went away.

Maybe you would be interested in knowing about scorpions. In some countries, scorpions are harmless. In others, their bite is fatal. In Key West, they fall halfway between. Our friend was leaning over the icebox chipping some ice when the scorpion stung her on the foot. (A scorpion stings by sticking the sharp point on the end of its tail into you.) Well, we ran out and asked some people what to do. They said to rub the stung place with ammonia, which we did, and they said that in a few minutes the victim's tongue would get thick and lose its feeling. Sure enough, her tongue and lips and face got numb all over and full of little needles, the way your foot does when it goes to sleep. Her tongue didn't swell up—she could still talk. But she sort of had the jerks. Couldn't sit still. Knew she was doing it, but couldn't stop herself. And gradually the pain in her foot got worse.

We called a doctor, and he sent me to the drugstore for sleeping pills. But before I got back he had given the victim a hypodermic. He said she would fall asleep in half an hour, and be all right next day. But she didn't, and wasn't. She didn't go to sleep till nearly dawn, despite three sleeping tablets in addition to the hypo. By morning, the numbness had spread all over her. She spent all that day in bed, and the next night too. By the second morning after, she was fit as a fiddle. For one more day she was scorpion-shy (stepping gingerly and peering into corners) but soon she had practically forgotten about them.

I made some inquiries in Key West about scorpions, and gleaned the following information: that there were no scorpions in Key West; that Key West was full of scorpions; that our neighbor's gardener got stung three and four times a day, and just paid no attention; that the local treatment for a scorpion bite was an application of garlic and salt, mixed, and if you didn't have that, you used ordinary washing bluing. Some people even rubbed the bite with whisky, but this was generally acknowledged to be wasteful.

If I ever see another scorpion, I will pick him up in my bare hands, snap off his tail, and use him for fish bait. I'm no more afraid of a scorpion than I am of a rattlesnake.

For years I resisted writing a piece about That Girl who travels with me. Millions of people have written in, wanting to know who she is, where I got her, what she does with her time, and so on. One letter writer figured out she was a dog, and praised me to the skies because of my affection for animals. Another reader decided she was a parrot. Some think she is my mother, and some think she is my daughter. So at Key West I decided to straighten the whole mess out. But since she is modest to a fault, and is only reluctantly giving her consent to be written about, I must ask you to keep it all in confidence, and never tell a soul.

She is a Russian princess, who escaped in 1917 with a pack of wolves behind her. Her sleigh raced across the Chinese-Turkestan border just as the lead wolf got hold of the seat of her pants. But since the wolf was carrying a forged passport, he wasn't allowed to chase her after she crossed the border. She was one year old when this happened. Unless I am lying about it, that makes her twenty-two now. She speaks all known languages, and a few words of Spanish. She can commune with flowers and trees and telephone poles in their own tongue. The only thing she is afraid of is a bee. People invariably like her better than they do me, which naturally makes me sore. Many people think she is the brains of our outfit, but that isn't true. I am the brains of our outfit.

Her first name is Anastasia Petrovich. We met while I was working as a drugstore cowboy on a dude ranch in Wyoming. She was the millionaire's daughter. He disinherited her, but she has been a very good sport about washing her own stockings. She hates geese. She is six feet eight, and weighs forty-three pounds. She writes books under the nom de plume of Ernest Hemingway. She writes poetry under the name of Henry Wadsworth Longfellow. She writes music under the name of Cab Calloway. In mathematics, she is constitutionally unequipped to multiply two times two. She won't read anything that isn't printed in Greek. Sometimes she reads in the original Greek for weeks on end, without ever going to sleep. Other times she just sits and stares at spiders on the wall. I think she used to be a carpenter, but I'm not sure. She is not thoroughly dependable. Sometimes in San Francisco I'll look around toward her and discover she's in Denver. Other times, when I think she's in New York, I'll suddenly find she's right here in the room with me. She loves limburger cheese.

She writes practically all this stuff for me. That's what people like to think, and it is true. She runs them off on tissue paper, ties a red ribbon around them, and makes a pretense of giving them to me for Christmas. Although she is not an ordinary person by any means, I can think of only one real idiosyncrasy she has. That is her refusal to distinguish between left and right. Also, she cannot tell daylight from dark, but I consider that more a matter of personal taste. If she has any spare time, she spends it working double-crostics puzzles. She is the best double-crostics worker in America. She can swim and dive like a fish, too. She was in the artillery during the World War, and won the yacht-racing cup from Sir Thomas Lipton in 1904. I have never asked her whether she collects stamps. Her favorite baseball player is Eddie Rickenbacker.

During the terrible Japanese earthquake of 1923, she was in Stillwater, Minnesota. She has never seen a movie, killed a whale, or gone up in a balloon. She thinks telephones should be prohibited. Whenever she wants fire she strikes a match, instead of using her flint and steel. She says she'll never forget her experiences at Valley Forge. There are days when she thinks I am wonderful. There are other days when she has to hold an election to decide.

She has an odd way of walking, propelling herself by putting one foot ahead of the other. She does not knit, spin, weave, tat, or manufacture wallpaper. She could lasso a buffalo if she wanted to, but sees no sense in it. She is very conservative about such customs as serving toads in drinking water. She writes upside down.

I don't know whether this gives you a clear picture of her, but I've done the best I can.

On the Overseas Highway we stopped at a roadside combination of fish camp, lunch counter, and semirestaurant. It was run by a typical conch, who told us about the terrible crowds they'd been having lately, with all the tourists bound for Key West, or back.

"It's half past two now," he said, "and I've just now had time to eat my own lunch. Every table was full for three hours. They almost drove us crazy." There was a resigned resentment in his voice. "Seems like everybody gets hungry between eleven and two. I can't understand it." And then he added, as he sat on a stool and leaned philosophically against the counter, "I guess it's just a habit people have got into."

At St. Petersburg, Florida, we checked in at a hotel and I sent my suit out to be pressed. When it came back there wasn't any bill on it. "Compliments of Valentine Cleaners," the bellboy said. "No charge." You could have knocked me over with an ironing board. I don't know whether that sort of thing would have gone on indefinitely or not. Having only one suit of clothes, and not wanting to send it right back again, I didn't experiment further.

The St. Petersburg *Times,* which ran my column, got a call from a woman reader. She said she had read that I was flat broke, and she would gladly lend me a little money. She had misread the piece. I had written of somebody else's being flat broke. (As for me, I married money, and am so rich I can't sleep at night.) So we called back and explained to the woman, and thanked her.

That kind of good old Midwestern friendliness is the keynote of St. Petersburg, and the green sidewalk bench is its symbol. The green bench is to St. Petersburg what the lei is to Hawaii, the gondola to Venice, the rolling chair to Atlantic City, the sidewalk café to Paris. The green benches are where the winter residents sit in the sun and talk to each other and watch all the other visitors sitting and talking and sunning. When I was there the latest count showed 4,697 of these benches. About twelve hundred of them were owned by the city, and were in parks. The rest were owned by merchants.

The St. Petersburg sidewalks are very wide, and the benches are on the outer edge, at right angles to the street. One after another, like the rows in a theater, for block after block. By ten o'clock of a warm morning it's almost impossible to find a seat. And it is an unwritten law that you may sit down beside any stranger on a green bench and start talking to him. If he doesn't respond and talk pleasantly back, he is rude and we hope nobody ever speaks to him again as long as he lives.

It is a city law that all public benches must be green, and made of wood. And they must be repainted once a year. They're more than just something to sit on.

St. Petersburg has probably taken more drubbing from us writing fellers than any other city in Florida. That's because so many elderly people go there for the winters. St. Petersburg has been referred to as "The City of the Living Dead," and "The Old People's Home," and such things as that. This burns the civic leaders up. Of course, what they want to get over to the public is that you can whoop and holler in St. Petersburg as much as in other Florida cities. You can bet and go night-clubbing and fish and yacht and look at palm trees and parade in your sports roadster. But personally I'm at the point where I can yell "hotcha" about twice and then I want to go sit down somewhere. I think it's mighty nice to have a place like St. Petersburg where you don't need either a Blue Book status or eighty billion red corpuscles to have a good time.

A historical note: St. Petersburg's existence is due to two men —General John C. Williams, of Detroit, who chose this spot as a healthful place to retire to, and Petrovich Demenscheff, an exiled Russian who built the first railroad into the area in 1888. Each wanted to name the town. Williams was for Detroit, his home town, and Demenscheff held out for St. Petersburg, his home city in Russia. So they flipped a half dollar. Demenscheff won. General Williams died in 1892. And as for Demenscheff—it's a dirty trick to be telling this—he left for California in the 1890s, and never came back.

The Eady boys and I, we got along swell together. The only thing was, Bob said I ought to chew tobacco and get some hair on my chest. They were the town characters of St. Petersburg, and probably the finest natural divers in Florida. They'd dive for anything from a safety pin to a battleship. They weren't much on the English language, and despite all the water they got into, you could hardly call them scrubbed and shiny.

Oliver was thirty-nine and Bob twenty-seven. Oliver was a sort of exaggerated version of Harpo Marx. Bob looked like Robinson Crusoe; his red hair hadn't been cut for a year, nor his face shaved. His pants were halfway to his knees. He'd never had on shoes but once in his life. His coat was an old band leader's coat with black silk stripes down the back. He had no respect for anything, and called his older brother "Uncle Grandpa." He was loud and funny and yelled at everybody and cussed. Oliver was quiet and religious and kept his head down all the time. He was very short, and had a chest like a concrete mixer.

Tourists would gaze in awe at them. But these boys knew a great deal about a world that you and I couldn't venture into, and they were always happy. They owned a sinking rowboat and an appalling collection of gadgets, and a diving helmet they'd made out of an old kerosene can.

"How long can you stay under water with this helmet?" I asked Oliver.

"Aw, it ain't much good any more," he said. "You can't stay longer'n six hours with it."

The boys were born in St. Petersburg, and had been diving since they were children. Oliver was the better diver of the two. He could stay under water—and work—for three minutes, just holding his breath. Bob could stay about two and a half minutes. They did most of their diving without a helmet. They didn't wear rubber diving suits and they didn't strip down to trunks. They just jumped in with their clothes on, coats and all. "Helps you keep warm," Oliver said.

There were many stories about the Eady boys' diving. This was the best one: A Coast Guard cutter got a four-inch hawser tangled in her propeller. It was a diving job, and a tough one. They went over to Tampa and priced the professional divers. The price was thirty-five dollars an hour, and no guarantee on how long it would take. Then somebody suggested the Eady boys. They dived down to take a look. Then Oliver got an envelope and figured for a long time. Finally he said, "That's a mighty hard job. We can't do it for no less than four dollars." It took them two days. They cut the hawser loose with a butcher knife. The story is that the Coast Guard gave them a tip of a dollar seventy-five cents, but Bob said that if they did, he never saw his half of it. He said he didn't give a damn for money anyhow.

"I don't take anything from nobody," Bob said. "And then if one of them sharks down there bites me in two some day, ain't nobody gonna suffer from it." Oliver, somewhat less dramatic, said they've never been bothered by sharks at all. I asked Oliver what their biggest job was. He said it was raising a sunken ship. It took them fifteen days, and they got eighty-five dollars.

Their father had been a fish-bait man. He left them a little property, including the home place. The rest of the family was living there now, but the boys kept house in an old shed down on the dock.

"Oliver wouldn't sleep in that house for a hundred dollars a night," Bob said.

"Why?"

"Because the old man haunts him."

The boys loved "talking machines," as they called them. They had three down at the dock, and fifteen or twenty at home. They had hundreds of records.

"Let's go out home and see my mooseum of cooros," Bob said. "Things I've picked up off the bottom. All kinds of things. They're in a room out there. Wait till I get the key."

So we all drove out to the house. Bob couldn't get the "mooseum" door open more than a foot. The place was packed shoulder high with stuff, thousands of things, just thrown in on top of each other—anchors and sharks' backbones and broken talking-machine records and meat axes and things.

The best instance of the Eady genius came to light when we went to leave the room. I noticed Bob was locking up a little trap door in the panel of the wooden door. I asked what that was for. It seems they had lost the door key, so instead of getting a new key, they had sawed a hole in the door, put on hinges and made a little trap door, and bought a padlock for it. To get in, Bob would unlock the padlock, open the trap door, reach his arm through, and unlock the big door from the inside. When Bob explained it to me, I couldn't keep from laughing. Bob looked at me, and then at the door, and then he started laughing too. And then Oliver started giggling. And then their sister Florence, who kept saying "D-a-m-m-i-t-t, Oliver," joined in. And there we all stood, laughing our heads off, like a bunch of idiots.

There was a message at the hotel in St. Petersburg to call a Mr. Staats. Who could that be, I wondered. The only Staats I ever knew lived down the road from us in Indiana when I was a boy, and he must have been dead for years. But I called the number and gave my name, and the voice on the other end said right away, "Are you the boy who used to live at home?" Then I knew that Oll Staats wasn't dead. Who but somebody from Dana, Indiana, would say, without even identifying himself, "Are you the boy who used to live at home?" So I said I sure was, and I got in the car and went out to his address.

He was sitting in the yard under a tree, and he got up and walked out to meet me. We shook hands and he said, "Ernest, I'd a knowed you anywhere in the world."

I don't think I had seen him in twenty years. He lived a mile and a half east of us, and owned a big fruit farm. I used to pick strawberries down there for spending money. He always had "J. O. Staats" on his fruit boxes, but his name was Oliver and everybody called him Oll Staats. He was much older than my parents, but even so, as I remember it, he was considered rather a gay fellow. He was pretty well-to-do, and being a fruit farmer he didn't go around in overalls and gum boots like an ordinary farmer. He owned the first automobile in our part of the country, a one-cylinder Reo, and always wore a linen cap when he drove. Em Staats, his wife, died after I left home, and I guess that's how I got it mixed up and thought he had died too.

"Mr. Staats," I said, "you're sure looking mighty good. How old are you now?" He beamed under his sporty gray hat. "Next week I'll be ninety-three. They're going to give me a big birthday party out on a boat. There'll be about fifty people there. Doggonit, I wish you could stay over."

He had been coming to St. Petersburg for five winters now. He had a first-floor room, and walked ten blocks or so downtown almost every day. At ninety-three he saw and heard as well as I did. His speech was firm, and his mind didn't jump. He wasn't sick, and he had no aches. He enjoyed living.

"Seems like I know nearly everybody in town," he said. "Half of them I don't even know their names, but I talk to them all the time. And every time I see an Indiana car on the street I go up and talk to them. I go down to the park and listen to the band concerts. And I belong to the Three-Quarter-Century Club, and once in a while I give 'em a funny speech and they like it. I'm the only man in the club who can spell his name the same forwards or backwards. One day the chairman got up and waved a five-dollar bill and said he'd give it to anybody who could guess my age. And do you know what the highest guess was? It was eighty-five."

He asked if I remembered when I was in high school and making things in the manual-training shop. I said sure. Then he said that one day I rode down to the fruit farm on my horse and brought him two little bookshelves on brackets that screwed into the wall. "They're still in the house right there today," he said.

· 338 ·

I couldn't remember those shelves at all at first, but after I'd thought a while I sort of remembered them.

Oll Staats said, "Ernest, how are you doing in your work?" I told him I guessed I was doing all right. He said, "You know, I've been reading about your travels every day, but I never once looked at the name to see who it was. I never would have found it out if I hadn't seen your picture in the paper today. So I told 'em out here I knowed that boy when he was born. They said, aw, you've got him mixed up with somebody else. So I said, no, I haven't—I'm gonna call up the hotel and see. So I did."

Silver Springs is a small body of water in Central Florida, connecting with a river that wanders more than two hundred miles to the sea. In it there are salt-water fish which have swum the two hundred miles upstream and liked it so well they stayed. Surrounding the little lake are all kinds of curio stores, restaurants, concessions, and what not, but don't let them fool you. The main attraction is down under the water, where they've let nature alone.

You go out over the lake in glass-bottomed boats with seats along each side and a sort of manger in the middle. You lean on the manger rail and look straight down through the bottom of the boat. When you get in, the water is so shallow that the thick growth of underwater reeds is right up against the glass, but before you've gone fifty feet the floor of the lake suddenly drops off like a precipice, and you are staring into a hole more than fifty feet deep. The water is as clear as air. You see fish swimming around; you see an old dinosaur backbone; you see an old sunken boat of the Spaniards; you see a few empty whisky bottles. The formations are fantastic beyond description, with the exaggerated colored beauty of a Walt Disney epic. Down there you see mountains and glaciers and snowstorms in puppet fashion. And it's all natural—man hasn't monkeyed with it. You see dark-blue catfish so big you could hardly lift one. You see water reeds so violently colored that you say there just can't be such colors.

There was one old lady on our boat who had taken the ride every year for nineteen years. And there was a man who had been bringing his family there for four years, and waiting in the car while they made the boat trip. He had said, "Aw, nuts. It ain't worth while." But this time they wouldn't go without him, so he grudgingly went along. He was the most enthusiastic one in the bunch. "What I've been missing!" he said.

The ride takes an hour. A Seminole Indian runs the glass boat and explains what you're seeing. He stops over every beautiful cavern and lets you look. You probably aren't half a mile from the dock during the whole trip, and never more than a hundred yards from shore.

This year they had something new, called a photo-sub boat. Instead of looking down through glass, you descend into the deep bottom of this boat, sit down, and look out horizontally through underwater portholes. This ride amused us. People without heads would swim past. We could see their bodies under the water, but the surface of the water made a ceiling and we couldn't see up through it. The hull of a nearby boat was so weird we looked at it a long time before realizing what it was. We saw vast landscapes—one that you'd swear was a desert. We saw fish swimming by, and if the coloring of the reeds was wonderful from the glass-bottomed boat, from this boat it became unbelievable.

Silver Springs was privately owned. The owner and the two men who leased and operated the boats were making themselves a pocketful of money; but it was honest money if I ever saw any. I have yet to meet a person who wasn't overpleased at what he saw through the eyes of a fish at Silver Springs.

We drove up through north-central Florida toward Georgia. That part of Florida is no more like the winter-resort ads than an electric razor is like the Brooklyn Bridge. It is plain old deep South, except that it isn't so good-looking; it lacks the luxuriant vegetation, the greenness and freshness. It is a land of gray sandy soil, brown scrub pines, little farms, and many shacks. It is country that makes you melancholy.

The wind was blowing a steady, insistent gale. It was hot with an uncanny, foreboding heat. You had a feeling that this wind would slowly, relentlessly blow away north Florida. Queer clouds were in the sky. And then we began to run through dust storms.

From every open field the dust streamed across the road; from big fields it rose high into gray clouds. We had to keep running up the windows, and we were soon dusty all over and grit was in our teeth. Although we never had to turn on our lights, as we did in west Kansas, we said to ourselves, "This is an incipient dust bowl. It has every earmark of the desolated areas in Kansas and Oklahoma. The soil is light, and lifts more easily than the western loam. The timber is scrubby, and they're clearing too many fields. If the government doesn't start doing something, they'll be making moving pictures of the great Florida dust bowl in a few years."

We stopped in a town for lunch. I asked the woman at the counter if it blew like this every spring. She said, "Oh, no, this is the first wind we've had." I went up to two men on a street corner. They were farmers—typical overalled cracker farmers. I talked to them about the possibility of this section's blowing away.

"No, no," they said, "this don't amount to nothin'. Next month will be worse than this, but this country ain't blowin' away. We get lots of rain here, better than fifty inches a year. And there's lots of springs hereabouts. No, there's no danger of a dust bowl here."

This was corn, tobacco, and peanut country. I talked with the farmers a long time. I couldn't get the dust-bowl idea out of my head—for I had seen the real dust bowl, and they hadn't. I put one last question: "Have you ever had any bad droughts around here?"

"No, sir," one of them said, "we've never had a single one, except once. That was pretty bad. The water got up over the highway, and they had to rebuild the road. It drowned out all the crops around here. The water was even right up in the streets here in town."

That seemed to settle the question. I had intended asking if they ever had any floods, but after that I didn't see any sense in it.

In the Old South

Chapter **XXIV** **I** DROVE OVER TO POSSUM LANE NEAR POULAN, Georgia, and paid a call on Chase S. Osborn, who had once been governor of Michigan. In the winter he lived in a cabin there in south Georgia; in summer he repaired to a log cabin on an island in St. Mary's River in the Great Lakes country. It had been twenty-seven years since Chase Osborn was chief executive of Michigan, but he was still addressed as "Governor." He had officially, by the legislature, been made the No. 1 citizen of Michigan. It was the first time I'd ever heard of such a thing being done.

Osborn's career had been incredible, and his personality and mind at seventy-nine were incredible. He had made at least ten fortunes and given them away—and by a fortune I mean a million dollars or more. He had given away more than a hundred annuities to friends, relatives, and people who deserved something. These gifts ranged from three thousand up to a million dollars. Out of his last fortune he had bought an annuity for himself. Although he lived in log cabins, he had an income of around two thousand a month. That's pocket money in any society.

He had made as much as five million dollars in one year. For many, many years he made more than a million a year. He didn't give the money away because he was generous; he said it was plain vulgar to have more money than you needed. "And I can be vulgar enough without piling up a lot of money," he said. Osborn had given away both his Georgia and his Michigan landholdings, but retained the lifetime right to live on them. He had once owned more than a hundred choice islands in the Great Lakes, but had given them all away. And all this wasn't an old-age liquidating of his affairs—he'd been giving his fortunes away as fast as he made them, ever since the first one.

He had never bought a share of stock in his life and never sold one. Every one of his fortunes was made by discovery of "productive wealth," as he said—by finding veins of iron ore and stands of timber, and selling them. He was prominent in many fields, but it was as "Iron Hunter" that he was chiefly known. He had prospected, dug, and sniffed for iron over the entire world, and had found great deposits in South Africa and Canada and Tibet. He was a naturalist, explorer, big-game hunter, author, statesman, engineer, and philosopher. He was a Major Hoople, except that it was all true. I believe he had more knowledge in his head than any other man I've met.

It is entirely possible that had he been politically ambitious he could have been president. He served as governor of Michigan from 1910 to 1912, but that was just an interlude, and then he went iron hunting again. Two years later he was renominated for the governorship. He didn't know about it, as he was in Persia. He almost got elected anyhow.

Governor Osborn had traveled more than any other man I'd ever met. He mildly boasted that he had been everywhere, and I believe he had. He had been in every country on the globe. He had written a two-volume work on the Andes countries. He had been to Tibet three times. He had been within ten degrees of the North Pole. When I told him I'd been up the Paraná River in South America, he said, "Isn't that Iguassu Falls some sight?" He had been in buildings where one whole end of his room was torn away by earthquakes and he, sitting at the other end, was unharmed. He had been on the lonely Pacific atoll near which Amelia Earhart was lost. He believed he had shot every animal known to big-game sportsmen. He was said to be the only man who ever killed an African lion with an ordinary shotgun.

At seventy-nine he had practically all the faculties of youth except good eyesight; he was totally blind in one eye, and the other was more than half gone. He could read only headlines, yet he rarely missed a shot. Every afternoon he tramped through the Georgia woods with his dogs and shotguns for two hours. Just two days before I met him he had killed three quail with three shots.

At his hidden-away camp, which he called Possum Poke, there were a main house and several cabins. The main house was just an old-fashioned cracker farmhouse. He had lots of people around him: his daughter Stellanova, who served as secretary and collaborator on his writings; two assistant secretaries; seven servants; and usually half a dozen relatives or guests stuck around in lofts or cabins—a household averaging about fifteen people.

He had eccentricities by the bucketful, yet he was not one of those balmy characters. There was a basic reason for everything he did. For example, he always shaved in the dark, standing on one leg, to maintain the equilibrium of youth. And by jiminy, he had maintained it.

Governor Osborn was a big man, well set up. He carried himself well, and his actions were quick. He rassled big firelogs around easily. His daily routine was inviolate. He was up every morning at three o'clock. He didn't use an alarm clock, but he never missed 3:00 A.M. by more than one minute. First he built the fire in his own room, then in the cook's, then in his daughter's. He hired men to build fires, but did it himself. Meanwhile, his water had been heating, so then he would shave, standing on one leg, as I've told you. He'd have used an electric razor, but there was no place to plug it in. There wasn't even a phone in the camp. After he'd shaved, he bathed. As soon as he was dressed, he straightened up his room and washed out his towels. He had a housekeeper and a laundress on the pay roll, but he did these things himself.

"There are two things I really pride myself on," he said. "That is, that I'm a good janitor and a good woodsman. I believe I'm probably the best natural woodsman in the world. I don't believe there's any place you could turn me loose where I couldn't live off the woods." In all his explorations and prospecting in the jungles and wild mountain country he had never taken a local guide.

He called his daughter at five o'clock. They ate at six. After breakfast he spent an hour cleaning his false teeth. He called them "dunkeys," because he said they made you look like a donkey when you grinned. False teeth were one of his hobbies; he had given away forty sets to the crackers around Possum Poke. If he'd had his way he would have pulled everybody's teeth at twenty-one.

At seven o'clock he went over to his "office cabin" and went to work. The cabin was just plain lumber, sort of like a rustic lodge. There was a big fireplace, and there were lots of pictures on the raw pine walls, many shelves of books, an army cot, and several desks piled with stuff—not the dusty stacks of an old man, but the neat desk of a busy executive. His correspondence was terrific. Mail came in by the sackful. The morning was spent in dictating, lending money, settling people's troubles, receiving old friends, and getting some work done on his latest book. The book, incidentally, was concerned with an idea of his that some day Canada and the United States would merge and become the last stamping ground of English-speaking people. I wouldn't be surprised if he was right.

Anybody from Henry Ford to a Negro boy wanting to borrow two-bits might drop in. He would give each of them some of his time, but not an unlimited amount. He kept to his routine. While I was there a Negro came in and stammeringly asked to borrow five bucks. Governor Osborn said, "Ray, what do you want it for? What've you done now? Yes, you can have it. When will you pay it back?" He put all these loans down and made them pay, for their own good.

After lunch he rested a while, then did a couple of hours' more work. Then, rain or shine, he went rambling through the woods for two hours by himself. He was a naturalist at heart, and a self-educated one. He knew every tree and weed and bush. Among the scores of weird things he had done was to trace the source of a firefly's light. It took him twelve years, and he wrote a book on it.

He was deeply religious—not the pious kind, but an absolute believer. He felt that the answer to everything—all truth—was to be found in the Bible. He was also very dry. "You're not a fanatic on it, are you?" I asked. "Yes, I'm a fanatic on it."

I noticed that every time one of his secretaries came in or went out, he half rose in his chair. "I always do that," he said. "It's another one of the things I do to preserve the equanimity of youth." I'll bet he got up two hundred times a day. Personally, I think women are fine; but if you have to keep bobbing up and down like a cork all your life, I don't know.

In the summertime, when the governor lived on his island in the Great Lakes, he slept on a cot of balsam boughs out under a tent, and often cooked his own meals out of doors. He verged on being a faddist, but wasn't quite. His dress was not eccentric. He wore an ordinary business suit, with blue shirt and gray tie. His shoes were the thick-leathered cheap shoes of the cracker farmer. His talk rambled, but he was always saying something definite. And when I said something, he paid attention. He asked me all kinds of questions about myself.

There was nothing mystic or psychic about him, yet he pulled one that had me on the floor all through our conversation. When I went in he said: "Oh, a farm boy from Indiana, eh?"

I said, "How did you know that?"

He said, "Oh, I can tell. Thought transference, maybe."

I certainly hadn't been thinking about being a farm boy as I walked up to the door. I knew that he had never heard of me in his life. I asked him about it two or three times during our talk, but I never found out how he could tell. It haunted me.

But I got even with him. In fact, I think I made quite a hit with him. When the word "farther" happened to be used in the conversation, he looked at me sternly and said, "Do you know the difference between 'further' and 'farther'?"

"Sure," I said.

"What is it?" It was like a cop's saying, "Did you kill this man?"

So I tightened up my courage and spoke: "Farther is used in speaking of actual distance; further means delving on into something—in research, for instance."

"You're right," he said. I almost fainted from surprise. In a crisis I generally get things backward. "But I've got a better definition of 'further,' " he said. "It's an 'extension of continuity.' " And so it is. I hope.

The governor made some remark about my nose. I said yes, that my mother had always kidded me about my nose, saying it was exactly like hers. He said: "Don't you worry about your nose.

It's a good nose." I guess it's all right at that. I can get air through it.

When we sat down to talk, he wrote down my full name on a piece of paper. Then, throughout the conversation, he would alternately call me Pyle, Ernest, or Ernie. He said, "Ernie, has anybody ever said you resembled Frank Murphy?" I said yes, several people had. He said, "You look so much alike I can hardly believe it." (Note to Mr. Murphy: Never mind our looks; we've got hearts of gold, haven't we?)

Chase Osborn was a native of Indiana himself. He was fond of Indiana, though he said he ought to hate it for the dire poverty he knew as a child. He went to Purdue University when it was in a barn, and quit two years before graduation. Twoscore years later, I believe it was, he studied and got his degree. He had been offered honorary degrees by the dozen, but wouldn't take them until he could earn one.

He was a Republican, but he liked President Roosevelt personally. He had known all the presidents since Taft. He had made as high as nine hundred speeches a year. He said he had written a thousand books; that was an exaggeration, unless you counted all the pamphlets and speech reprints. Most of his books had been privately published for friends, and never put on sale.

He invited us to come and stay in one of his cabins. "But you can only stay a month," he said. "I'd probably be tired of talking to you by then."

I didn't see how it was possible for one man in a lifetime to do all that Governor Osborn had done—to travel so far; find all that ore; be such a public figure; make all that money; accumulate all that knowledge; and above all, achieve a sort of serene inner self that suited him and did the world good also. One of these days he would die, and it would be over. If the world could only be arranged so that for every Chase Osborn who died two would be created, then there might be some basis for a belief in ultimate perfection.

Warm Springs is seventy-five miles south of Atlanta and not far from the Alabama line. It is in heavily wooded pine country, very rolling, and about as beautiful as you will find in the South.

This is the only sanitarium in America that accepts nothing but poliomyelitis cases—"polio" for short. Even the patients refer to each other as "polios." The place seemed to me more like a college than an institution. In fact, the officials called the grounds "the campus." You saw patients around everywhere—in wheel chairs, on crutches, even on wheeled stretchers. From their faces, you would never have known they were invalids; the tragedy of polio seemed never to show in the face. Only the withered limbs and the braces on legs told the story. Yet, although polios are in pitiful shape, there is nothing pitiful at all about the atmosphere at Warm Springs—and I believe that is as important as all the scientific treatment. Back home a stricken individual gets to brooding, drops out of the stream of life, and is often the victim of melancholia, thinking of himself as a hopeless cripple. But at Warm Springs that feeling is almost invariably wiped out. Patients see others of their kind all around, having a good time. "Polio" ceases to be a hushed word, spoken with self-pity. They make up songs about themselves, such as "From the tops of our heads to the tips of our toes—we're paralyzed." Back home they were invalids. At Warm Springs they are human beings.

President Roosevelt came to Warm Springs two or three times a year. Everybody there loved him, and his visits were always high spots. His little settlement of private cottages was about a mile from the hospital grounds, back in the woods. Neat signs pointed to the "Little White House." His own cottage was a spreading six-room house with two baths, on the slope of a hill, nearly hidden by pine trees. There were also a guest house and a house for servants. When the President was not there, the houses were closed tight, and Georgia National Guardsmen stood watch in a little sentinel house out front.

When he was there he went every day about noon to swim in the polio pool, but not until the other patients were about to leave. And as one polio said, the secret-service men, by hanging around ahead of time and looking grim, made you feel so unwanted that you just didn't stay to see the President swim.

The President's own car—a Ford V-8 convertible sedan—was at Warm Springs all the time. The Georgia license tag had on it simply "F.D.R." instead of numbers. When he was away, he turned it over to Fred Botts, the registrar, who was himself a polio. Botts was a tall, sensitive-faced man, sincere and jovial, and I could see why the President liked him. It was Botts who so impressed me with the change that Warm Springs brings to the mental attitude of paralysis victims. He said that for the first nine years of his own helplessness he just lay around and pitied himself, and gradually went down and down into a complete funk. He got interested in Warm Springs from seeing pictures of Mr. Roosevelt and Annette Kellerman swimming there. He was one of the first to arrive—in 1925, while Warm Springs was just a resort for wealthy Georgians. Around 1926, when Mr. Roosevelt began to visualize what might be done there, he bought the whole resort. Then when the foundation was formed, the land was turned over to it.

Botts could walk on crutches with difficulty. He got around mostly by wheel chair. Like the President, his paralysis was in his legs only. To see him sitting down, you'd never have known he was crippled. Warm Springs hadn't cured him, but from a hopeless, sour cynic, he had become once more a regular guy.

The President drove quite a bit around Warm Springs. Several of the other polios had cars too, and drove around by themselves. Their cars were fixed up so they could be driven with hands only. The clutch and brake were operated by one lever, within easy reach on the left-hand side. If you pressed down so far, that released the clutch. If you pressed still farther, that put on the brake. You used a hand throttle under the steering wheel, as in the old Model T Fords. That's all there was to it. The gear shift was the normal one.

Frequently the President stopped his car out in front of Georgia Hall, the main building, and chatted with anyone who came up. He didn't often go into the hall. But he was always there at Thanksgiving—ate with the polios, laughed his head off at the amateur show they put on, then gave a little talk, and finally shook hands with everyone.

The newspapermen who came with the President rented two cottages half a block from the main building. They mixed with the polios, and everybody had a great time. When the newspapermen were there, officials practically had to go around with a whip to get the patients to their rooms by ten o'clock. Everybody wanted to stay up and not miss any fun.

One of the guardsmen told me that about five thousand cars a month came by to take a look at the Little White House. He said they didn't have any trouble with people tearing off things for souvenirs. But down at the hospital they hadn't had such an easy time. They used to let tourists go through the grounds and talk with the patients, but you know how some tourists are. Some emotional old lady would go up to a polio and burst out: "Oh, you poor pitiful thing! What a terrible shape you are in! Oh, isn't it awful! Oh me, oh my!" And then she'd start bawling. All of which, you can see, would be very fine for the patient. And some tourists had even had the effrontery to walk right into the infirmary, lift the sheets, and stare at the casted legs of recently operated-on patients. That was too much. Tourists were still allowed to look around, but the intimate impudence of well-meaning fools had been stopped.

Among the patients I saw at Warm Springs there were cases in all stages. Some were bedridden, couldn't move a muscle, had to be fed; these were a minority. Others were learning to walk again. And some were in the condition of President Roosevelt, but there were few of these, because when they got that well they were sent home. There was an occasional one with acute melancholia, but ninety-nine out of a hundred were mentally perfectly natural. You could see sharecroppers' young sons playing Chinese checkers; you could see a girl wheel her chair past and push another girl's head just for fun; you could see what was apparently a New York theatrical producer devouring *Variety*. There had never been a suicide at Warm Springs.

All except the bedridden patients ate in the big dining room, mostly at tables for four, men and women together. The food was swell, and it was like eating in a big hotel. Everybody put on his best clothes for dinner. The patients were encouraged, if at all possible, to leave their wheel chairs at the door and walk to their tables on crutches, no matter how awkwardly.

There was a movie three times a week. The front two-thirds of the theater was merely blank floor. Colored girls wheeled the patients in and then sat in folding chairs down front. Behind them was a row of bedridden patients on wheeled stretchers. Some of these were propped up with pillows, and looked straight ahead at the screen. Others, who had to lie flat, watched the movie through hand mirrors. Behind the stretchers were two or three rows of wheel chairs, and at the back, rows of comfortable raised seats for able-bodied people.

There was a little chapel on the grounds, just recently finished. At the back were benches, but the whole front was blank floor for the stretchers and wheel chairs. There was a nine-hole golf course on the grounds, which was a godsend for the able-bodied employes way out there in the woods with nothing to do in their off time. There was one polio who played golf, but only one. A number rode horseback.

A man polio and a woman polio were not allowed to go driving together unless there was an able-bodied person in the car. The excuse was that they might get a flat tire and be in a pickle. But the real reason, damn the officials' hides, was May, sap in the trees, springtime. Boy Meets Girl. Love Comes to Andy Hardy. There had to be a chaperon along. Even so, chaperons and steel braces couldn't keep the love bird from flitting. There had been cases where polios met, fell in love, and were married, right there. There were some beautiful girls at Warm Springs, even one lovely debutante. And one girl had been a player with Warner Brothers in Hollywood; she was bedfast, unable even to feed herself.

When a newcomer arrived, the others always gave him a big heigh-ho in the dining room the first evening, and the same when a patient was leaving. In the fall, all who were able were taken in buses up to Atlanta or over to Columbus to see the football games. And whenever Fort Oglethorpe put on a big horse show or something, the Army sent a couple of dozen cars and took the polios over to see the show.

Time didn't hang heavy on the patients' hands. In the morning they were taken by bus down to the pool, where they swam or were given muscle treatments by attendants or nurses. There was an electric crane that lifted a stretcher from its running gear, swung it around, and let the patient down flat into the water.

Attendants rolled him off and floated him over to an underwater table, where they exercised his arms and legs. The temperature of the water was always ninety degrees. It is not true that the Warm Springs water has intense curative powers. The water is, in fact, a very minor but very pleasant item in the treatment.

I spent some time at the outdoor platform where people were learning to walk again. There was one alleyway with bars on each side, to which they could hold. There was another alleyway where people were trying to walk with crutches. An attendant stood directly in front and another just behind, to catch them if they fell. There was another place for those who were getting along pretty well. They walked down a black line painted on the floor. At the end of the line was a full-length mirror. They watched themselves as they walked, and saw their own mistakes. I saw one boy in a Boy Scout uniform walking down this line normally, though slowly. He did not use crutches or have on braces. He had arrived on a stretcher just a year before.

It is possible that Warm Springs may have become overrated in the minds of the public—overrated not as to its efficiency and good work, but as to its capacity for real benefit to the afflicted. The average person, I believe, has a hazy idea that if you have polio all you have to do is to go to Warm Springs and get fixed up. That is completely wrong. First, you don't fix up the majority of polio cases. You can bring them back to a useful place in society, but only infrequently to complete normality. And in the second place, it would take a hospital twice as big as the city of Atlanta to handle all the polio cases in America.

There has been some criticism of Warm Springs from people who couldn't get their afflicted ones in. The selection of new patients from the stacks of applications is a terrific headache, and I suppose nobody could do a perfect job on it. The foundation tries to take, first of all, recently stricken people; there is so much greater chance of help if treatment starts early. And it tries to select adults whose rehabilitation would directly affect large families. The criticisms have made the officials touchy about publicity—especially, I gather, the foundation officials in New York, who have the responsibility of money-getting. There is a little story that helps explain it. The magazine *Life* had a spread of pictures on Warm Springs, taken by Margaret Bourke-White. I thought it was a fine set of photos, but official Warm Springs didn't care much for it. One picture showed a pre-Thanksgiving party in the home of a well-to-do polio who owned his own home at Warm Springs, and paid his own way. Everybody was sitting around smiling and gay, just like a party in New York. "Well, what's the matter with that picture?" I asked. And here is what was the matter: many people who donate money to such places as Warm Springs don't want the recipients of their charity to seem happy. "So that's what we're giving our money for, eh? People laughing and having a good time. All right, we won't give any more money, then, if they're not going to have long faces."

I was shocked by this revelation. Why, happiness is the best cure for almost any ailment. I think it's a hell of a commentary on the so-called charitable spirit of you, and you, and of me.

They call Birmingham the "Magic City," because it grew so fast. In less than seventy years it climbed from nothing to almost a quarter of a million. Unlike most southern cities, Birmingham has no Civil War history. It didn't exist then.

It is the Pittsburgh of the South. All the ingredients are right there—iron ore, coal, and whatever is that other thing it takes to make steel. Why, there's one mountain right alongside, covered by the city's finest residential section, that they say is practically all iron ore. Some far day, I suppose, it will all be chewed up by the machines. Beauty versus the Beast.

Birmingham is, I believe, the most beautiful industrial city in America. The downtown part is neat and modern, and the residential sections are superb. There are hills and mountains all around, and up on the hillsides, on winding streets and back among trees are the homes—homes ranging from the ones you and I might buy on the installment plan, on up to the castles of the millionaires. I talked with many people whose business had brought them temporarily to Birmingham, and who had stayed and bought homes, expecting to remain forever. The only thing I didn't like about Birmingham was that when you blew your nose in the morning you wondered if you hadn't been cleaning chimneys in your sleep.

When we had been in Birmingham three years earlier I'd written something about George Ward, twice mayor of the city and still one of its first citizens. Mr. Ward had one eccentricity that set him off from all other Birmingham citizens. That eccentricity was Roman history. With Roman history he was like a kid with a new Christmas train—or at least he used to be. I guess he had read and reread every word of Roman history ever printed. Then he built himself a round Roman temple, which he called Vestavia (after the goddess of the hearth), and in which he lived alone on a mountaintop, surrounded by a 360-degree view and an acre of roses. For years now he had spent his days in the offices of downtown Birmingham, and his nights in the Rome of his own creation. He strolled each evening in his Roman grounds. He gave his Negro servants Roman names, and his dogs too. And at night he sat alone and read his Roman history.

Hearing we were in town again, Mr. Ward sent a Roman runner to invite us up to lunch at his mountaintop temple. There were just the three of us—and the two Roman servants. We had lunch in front of the huge fireplace, and Mr. Ward had even typed out a Roman menu for us. The main course was Pavo Potpourri re Caesar, or, in other words, peacock hash. It was wonderful. Lucullus and Cicero stood at our backs, attentive to every call. Each wore a long linen toga—which looked mighty like a garage foreman's coat to me—and a bright tin helmet with curlicues and Roman festoons. You could tell that the colored boys loved it. Mr. Ward loved it. And we loved it. Rome is very nice—in Birmingham.

I was interested in seeing what three years had done to Mr. Ward, because he was getting along. For one thing, he'd had a slight stroke, but recovered from it. He looked and acted younger than three years before. He was in a brokerage partnership, and drove his own car downtown over the winding mountain roads every day. I think he had grown a little weary of Roman history. I asked if he still read it and he said, "No, it's all I can do to keep up with the newspapers now." The same two Negro boys, whose real names were Robert and Jerry, were still with him. They were enthusiastic actors in the Roman drama but they, like Mr. Ward, played at it only occasionally nowadays. I got that when

Mr. Ward suddenly wanted something, looked up at Robert and said, "Say, what's your name?" Robert answered with a big proud grin, "My name's Lucullus."

Mr. Ward, like a real monarch, was cut off from the world, at least at nighttime. It was a long drive to his mountaintop, and the wind had an unmerciful moan up there in the dark. He was lonesome. But I didn't feel sorry for him, as I had the last time, for though the thrilling enthusiasm of first love was gone, he had now settled down to complacency in the arms of his hobby. It was nice to get early into his canopied bed, and smoke his pipe until he grew sleepy, and to know that Cicero was down below, to protect him, and that if you couldn't remember Cicero, you could just yell "Jerry," and an Alabama boy in overalls would come, and do just as well.

There was a town in Alabama that had two names. The whole town was split up and mad over it. And since I am just a frail youth and do not like to get into fights, I'll call the place by both names—Crumly's Chapel and Westwood. When I first heard the story it sounded awfully funny, but when I got there and nosed around I saw there wasn't anything funny about it. This was a village of about a thousand people, some ten miles from Birmingham. It was made up mostly of schoolteachers, middle-salaried commuters, and a few farmers. It had a store and a church and a school and a graveyard. The community was as old as Birmingham.

It had always been called Crumly's Chapel. That was because the first man through there was named Crumly, and the first church was Crumly's Chapel. There wasn't any town then, but when a town grew up it continued to be called Crumly's Chapel. Lately, though, some of the more modern elements had decided it would be nice to call the village Westwood. They said the town never had a name in the first place, and if you told people you lived in Crumly's Chapel they thought you lived in a church.

The majority of the town was for Westwood. A small but persistent minority was for Crumly's Chapel. So the fight started. "Westwood" road signs put up by the highway department were tarred and feathered. A "Crumly Chapel School" sign was smeared with tar; the sign was taken down next day, so the town school now had no name at all. The Parent-Teacher Association was split on the thing. Neighbors wouldn't speak to each other. Families were divided, even mother against son. Some residents were in the phone book under Westwood, others under Crumly's Chapel. A deacon, after passing the plate at church one Sunday morning, found a threatening note among the nickels and dimes. Two relatives, out fox hunting, got into an argument over the name, and it wound up with one getting his teeth knocked out and the other getting stabbed. Four scurrilous letters were received by people on the Westwood side. One was to the postman; he turned it over to the United States postal inspectors—and when those boys move in, you better watch out.

I started out to talk to both sides, so I could be fair. For the Westwood side. I was directed to Mrs. Graydon Newman, whose husband taught school and practiced law on the side. Mrs. Newman herself was a relief teacher. The Newmans were what the Crumly's Chapel faction called "squatters," or newcomers. They'd been there only sixteen years, and hardly knew their way down to the crossroads. You never saw anybody nicer than Mrs. Newman. While the baby kept crawling around and untying my shoelaces, she told me their side of the story. She could see the funny side of it, and even said that some of the old families on the other side were the most accommodating people in the world till this thing came up.

I went to the other side—the side of the "old settlers." And then I saw that this was as grim as a Kentucky feud; there was raging hatred in it and outsiders weren't welcome. "You'll have to go farther than this to get any talk," one man said. He was very suspicious and tried to find out who sent me to him. I had been sent by somebody who had nothing to do with the feud, but since he wasn't talkin' I wasn't either, so I never told him. We parted with stiff courtesy, and not much of that. I tried another of the Crumly's Chapel side. The man and I talked on the front porch, and a woman came out. I spoke, but she didn't. She sat listening and giving me the old fish eye. "I won't allow you to print anything about this business," the man said. When I told him he was getting a little out of his field, he said, "Well, you won't get any talk from us." You couldn't call them downright discourteous—they didn't order me off the premises. But they made it pretty plain that the sooner I got, the better it'd be.

Small-town hatreds like that, verging on civil war, have happened everywhere in this country: over a man's shooting a neighbor's dog; over one kid's slapping another; over a dead relative's will; over which farmer was first in line at the grain elevator; over hiring a new preacher. It's small and disgusting, but it's America. And I reckon we might as well get used to the idea that people are going to be mean and ornery at certain times of the moon. Where this one would end, nobody knew. There was tension in the air. If the residents had only listened to me, I could have settled the whole thing. Why not compromise, combine the two names, and call the place Crumwood?

Never have I met a man who towered above Dr. George W. Carver in nobility or intelligent greatness. He was one of the greatest men in the South; he was a scientist; he was a Negro.

He was getting old and had been sick when I went to see him. He was sitting behind a desk, hunched over almost in a half moon. He shook hands weakly and apologized for not getting up—said the doctors made him rest every little while. He said he could talk only a few minutes, and his voice was tiny, sharp, and high. I had the feeling that my story was lost—that my interview would be short and futile. Now, I don't know whether this was a little trick of Dr. Carver's or not, but when we got to talking, the first thing I knew he was sitting up and his voice was strong. Within five minutes we were out in the laboratory, and he was showing me things and walking around rapidly like an enthusiastic young athlete.

Dr. Carver was born in Missouri, probably during the Civil War. Night raiders stole his parents and sold them at auction; he never saw them again. But Amos Carver, the white plantation owner, was good to the little boy. He gave him his own name, as was customary in those days. The Negro boy became George Washington Carver. When he grew up, he went to school in Iowa, where he specialized in science and rapidly got his degrees. Then he turned southward to his own people. He went to

Tuskegee Institute, the South's famous Negro school in Alabama, and had been there ever since—a lifetime.

Dr. Carver was a dark prophet, in the dark. He had worked like an inspired man for forty-two years to help the South—not only the Negroes, but the whole South, black and white. His work was of the soil and of the things that grow from it. For forty years he had been preaching the dangers of erosion. He tried to tell the poor farmers how to improve their land, though only a few would heed. And all through the years he was also working in his chemical laboratory. It seemed impossible that he could have done so much, even in forty-two years. He had found dozens of uses for almost every plant that grows in the South. His discoveries of practical commodities that could be made from sweet potatoes and peanuts ran into the hundreds.

The South has been labeled by the government as the nation's No. 1 economic problem. The South as a whole resents that. The rich people, who don't do much about it, resent it; the poor people, who are both unable and loath to do anything about it, resent it even more. The South is fundamentally rural. Except for a steel city like Birmingham, and a few textile towns, the whole heart and soul of the deep South spring from its soil. And the soil and its tillers have sunk to a point that is not pretty.

And I believe that the clue to southern reconstruction lay right there in the laboratory of this humble Negro scientist. Some far-seeing administration could take Dr. Carver's discoveries as a basis of planning, and rebuild a new and varied and prosperous South. It would take money and intelligence. The money might come from the federal government, as money has a way of doing; the intelligence could come from the Southerners, if they would form themselves into a sweeping movement to do better by themselves. If farmers would rebuild their soil and open their minds to something besides cotton, if industry would set up factories to manufacture the things that Dr. Carver knew could be made from the varied plants of the South, if it could be done in an organized and forceful way, then it seems to me that within twenty, forty, fifty years the old, old South could again become the nation's garden spot, and no longer either Tobacco Road or that No. 1 Problem.

I had read that Dr. Carver was seventy-eight. I asked him if that was right. He said, with sadness and futility in his voice, "I don't know. I was born into slavery. I was a chattel, the same as the cows and pigs. We were all chattels. They didn't keep records of us. I don't know how old I am."

Dr. Carver had lived a lifetime on the underside of racial prejudice and taken it with silent grace. He had been ignored by intelligent white men and run out of town by ignorant ones, but he would not discuss these things. His colored assistant said Dr. Carver would not speak of them even to him: he passed them over.

He had no relatives. He had no money. He had turned down scores of offers—even one from Thomas A. Edison to work with him. All his discoveries had been given free to the world.

Dr. Carver never married. For forty-two years he had lived in an apartment in one of the dormitories on the campus of Tuskegee Institute. He got up at four every morning, and for two hours worked at his books and calculations in his room. He ate breakfast at six, then went to the laboratory. He was in bed by nine-thirty. Like many scientists, he was careless about eating. Often he'd forget to eat at all, and if they didn't watch him, he'd revert to slave diet of fat meat, meal, and molasses. He had anemia now, and looked older than seventy-eight. He was very tall, and his clothes hung loosely on what had been a large frame.

He was extremely religious. He did not smoke, swear, or drink. On the other hand, he didn't bring pious phrases into his conversation. And he saw no quarrel between science and religion. Fun had been poked at him because he said his plants talked to him. I don't think that was funny. They were living things; they were human to him.

Dr. Carver's genius seemed unlimited. Right now most of his time was going into experiments in the use of peanut oil on infantile paralysis cases. And once more he had run into prejudice—not only Negro prejudice, but a stern "hands off" from the medical world. He was not a physician, therefore he must not presume to try. He had massaged paralyzed muscles with some forty different oils and had found peanut oil the best. He thought he had had some success in enlivening atrophied muscles.

During most of Dr. Carver's lifetime at Tuskegee he had never allowed himself an assistant—never felt he could trust anyone to share his work. Then, about four years before I saw him, along came a fine-looking young colored man from West Virginia, just out of Cornell. His name was Austin W. Curtis, Jr. For four years now this young man had been Dr. Carver's assistant, and he was proud of the honor. His position was somewhat like that of a young lawyer who had become the private secretary of a Justice Holmes.

One summer Curtis made an auto trip through Missouri, where Dr. Carver was born. Dr. Carver himself had never been back since he came to Tuskegee. "Did you find any of the white Carvers still living?" I asked Curtis. Yes, he did—three. They were all farmers, all very old, and they were out plowing. They stopped their teams and leaned on the fence to talk to Curtis. The youngest was seventy-two and the oldest eighty-four. Curtis said they all seemed proud to remember Dr. Carver.

After talking with Dr. Carver, I sat for a long time with Curtis. When finally I went to say goodbye, Dr. Carver was hard at work in his laboratory, but he wiped his hands on his white apron and came out. He hoped so much that I would come back and see his new museum when it was finished. He said he was no good on names, but he'd know my face even if it was five years later.

I am not especially emotional, unless I sit down by myself and get to thinking. But when I said goodbye to Dr. Carver I could hardly speak for the lump in my throat. When I came back, he might be gone.

I had always wanted to see Tuskegee Institute. It was founded by Booker T. Washington in 1881, and with private endowment it had become a model in Negro education.

It looked like any Midwestern state university. It covered a lot of rolling ground; the campus was beautiful; there must have been three dozen handsome brick buildings scattered around; streets and sidewalks wound about; there were dormitories and a stadium and a gymnasium. Outwardly it wasn't different from a college for whites. The few differences were under the surface.

Many white visitors—businessmen, students, writers—came to

visit Tuskegee; consequently, the institute had facilities for putting them up. We stayed in Dorothy Hall, in a room that would shame many hotels. Our wing was presided over by Mrs. Sarah Martin, a retired teacher of Tuskegee, who had been there thirty-three years. We ate in a little dining room of our own and were served by a tall and gracious-mannered colored girl who was working her way through school.

There was not a white person in this whole school, even on the faculty. There were 1,150 students—680 boys and 470 girls—and a large faculty of about 250. Most of the students were from the South, but others came from all over America and from nine foreign countries. The students dressed like college students anywhere. Discipline was more strict than in the ordinary college. There was no smoking on the campus. Boys could smoke in their rooms; girls couldn't smoke at all. I saw an ash tray on the desk of only one faculty man. Drunkenness and rowdyism didn't go. Only a few special students were allowed to live off campus. All the others were in the fourteen big dormitories, two in a room, under pretty close supervision. No student was allowed to have a car. Attendance at church, twice on Sunday and once on Wednesday evening, was compulsory. So was military drill. The boys had to keep their own quarters clean. Everything at Tuskegee was as neat and clean as a pin. You didn't see a speck of dirt anywhere; you never saw slovenliness or freakishness in dress. But despite the strictness, there was plenty of student social life.

When Booker T. Washington founded the school, no Negro who yearned for knowledge was turned away; the most ignorant, raggedy barefoot boy could walk in and start learning. But things had to change. Nowadays the student had to have a certain amount of money for clothes, and had to have a high-school education. As one official said, "The bulk are from our middle-class families, if you can say we have a middle class." The tuition was seventy-five dollars a year and every student had to work out at least half of it. Board and room cost only twenty dollars a month, and could be worked out. Practically all the institute's daily labor was done by students.

I had thought that Tuskegee was a school of higher learning— a Harvard of the Negro race. I couldn't have been more wrong.

Booker T. Washington started it as a trade school, and a trade school it remained. It taught Negroes to work. Courses in forty-one separate trades were offered. In two years you could get a certificate of fitness in a trade, or you could go on another two years and receive a Bachelor of Science degree. By 1938 forty thousand students had enrolled and six thousand had gone clear through.

Booker T. Washington's spirit was still around there, and in just a couple of days you "got it." He never thought the Negro race should consider itself equal in all things with the white race. He said, "It is important and right that all privileges of the law be ours, but it is vastly important that we be prepared for the exercise of these privileges." That's where Tuskegee still stood. It wanted only to prepare students to work, diligently and honestly, and develop their characters, generation after generation, until they would be capable of becoming a real and natural part of the civilization into which they had been thrown so suddenly, unwilling and bewildered.

Almost any student was sure of a job at the end of two years in Tuskegee. Of the previous year's graduating class, every single one had been placed and was working by September 1. In many departments the school had many more requests for employes than it could fill. Teachers, chefs, nurses, dietitians—all these could snap up jobs.

Tuskegee had had three presidents. Booker T. Washington, the founder, presided until his death in 1915. Both he and Mrs. Washington were buried on the campus. Dr. Robert R. Moton had served for twenty years, and retired. Dr. Frederick D. Patterson had been president since 1935. He was a young man, big like a football player. His wood-paneled office was large, and there were deep red-leather chairs for visitors. Ten years before, President Patterson had been a veterinary teacher in a small college in Virginia. Then he got an offer to join the faculty at Tuskegee. "That was the height of my dreams," he said, "to have my own veterinary department at a school like Tuskegee. I came in a hurry."

"I guess you never pictured in your wildest moments that you'd be president of Tuskegee some day, did you?" I asked him.

"I certainly didn't," he said. "Such a possibility never entered my head."

On our first evening I took a walk around the campus before supper. To my astonishment every student I met, boy or girl, spoke to me. Later I asked if the students were instructed to do this. They said no, it was just an old Tuskegee custom. Friendliness and courtesy, the students were taught, would help them in life after they left school. For two days I hotfooted it around from 7:00 A.M. till late at night. I visited departments by the score. I talked with instructors and students and deans till I was out of breath. We went to the gymnasium to see the basketball games. Although the gymnasium was packed, we were the only white people there. Throughout the game I talked—when it was possible to be heard—with the colored girl who sat next to me. And the thing that impressed me most was that in not one instance did anybody make me aware that he or she was black and I was white.

As most of us know Negroes in our daily lives, they are either in lowly jobs and "keep their place," as we say, or else they are "educated" Negroes, sometimes with an I'm-as-good-as-you-are chip on their shoulder. Those two attitudes don't exist at Tuskegee. Both faculty and students treat you exactly as one gentleman treats another. If all the Negroes in America could come to Tuskegee, and if all the white people could go to a similar school that taught the dignity of association that Tuskegee teaches, how much greater harmony there could be between our two races.

The town of Enterprise, Alabama, is the place that put up a monument to the boll weevil—the insect that destroys cotton. That's like putting up a monument to a hurricane, you'd think. The story was that when the weevil wiped out the only crop those parts had ever known, the townspeople woke up and turned to other things, and were better off than they had been with cotton.

But the monument was really a kind of accident. In 1919, when new street lights were installed at Enterprise and things were torn up, the town built a circular pool and fountain in the middle of the main street, with a statue of a woman something like

· 363 ·

"Liberty" in the center. So many passers-by stopped and asked the workmen what they were doing that finally one of them, just wisecracking, said, "We're putting up a monument to a boll weevil." A traveling salesman overheard it. He went on to Montgomery, called a newspaper office, and told them Enterprise was putting up a statue to the boll weevil. The paper came out with a big story the next day. Then the town had to live up to the story. It put a bronze plaque on the statue base which read: "In Profound Appreciation of the Boll Weevil and What It Has Done as the Herald of Prosperity, This Monument Is Erected by the Citizens of Enterprise—December 11, 1919."

There wasn't a boll weevil at all on the monument; but so many people had come to look, and had gone away disappointed, that they were thinking of putting up a real boll weevil statue.

But the story I came to Enterprise for—of how the citizens turned to varied farming and got rich—would make a good entry for the Liars Club contest; it wasn't true. After cotton, the farmers did turn to peanuts. And, true, Coffee County's annual peanut crops soon became worth five million dollars, in contrast to cotton's one million dollars. But that didn't keep up. Peanut prices went down; the depression came; farm tenancy, one of the banes of the South, kept increasing. Things were getting worse all the time. But I found another story, about what the government discovered there in 1935 and what it was trying to do about it.

When the government took a hand in 1935, six out of ten school children in the county had hookworm. Every other baby died at birth; one mother in ten died in childbirth. The average mentality was third-grade; one out of ten adults couldn't read or write. Three-fourths of the farmers were tenant farmers, and most of them had never been out of debt in their lives. They averaged only one mule to three families. And this was in Coffee County, which stood third among the counties of Alabama in the value of its agricultural products. Those figures were not the scandalous revelations of some brain truster from the North; they were from a survey made by Southerners. Sure, you'll find wealth and grace and beautiful homes in the South—homes as pretty and people as fine as anywhere in the world. But you drive the back

· 364 ·

roads, and you won't see one farm home in a hundred that would equal the ordinary Midwestern farmhouse.

Coffee County became a sort of experimental station in Alabama—not by design, especially, but because government people and the local agencies got enthusiastic, and it just grew up under them. Federal, state, and county agencies all had a hand.

I had heard of hookworm, but I'd never known exactly what it was. Since it was the worst scourge of Coffee County, and probably of most of the deep South, I investigated a little. It is a tiny worm, just visible to the naked eye, which moves through the bodies of human beings, wasting them away. Children get it from going barefoot around backyards where hookworms are in the ground. They get in the skin between the toes; an infection starts, gradually spreads through the system, and winds up in the intestines. Here the worm multiplies by the hundreds, feeding, sapping your blood. It could eventually kill, but it seldom gets the chance; it so weakens your system that something else—pneumonia, whooping cough, diphtheria—carries you off.

You can tell a hookworm victim by his paleness. Even I could tell. The lobes of the ears get pale, then your whole face becomes a ghastly corpselike white. You become listless, lifeless, ambitionless, just sick all over, till you finally do nothing but sit on the old porch in a daze and let life roll by.

Hookworm is curable, and quickly. You eat a light supper and no breakfast, then take some capsules the doctor gives you. This medicine dislodges all the hookworms. You follow that in about three hours with a strong laxative. But if you walk barefoot, you're soon infected again—that is, unless there is a sanitary toilet, so the hookworms can't spread. The farmers call hookworm infection the "ground itch." They have all kinds of home remedies for it, but all too few will do anything modern about it.

Pellagra, which is another major scourge in the South, is caused by improper diet—not enough vegetables. It produces sores and bloating, and is a horrible disease. There would be no pellagra, especially among farmers, if they had the ambition to provide themselves with vegetables. The average tenant farmer in Coffee County had no garden, though vegetables grow wonderfully in the South. But the people were becoming increasingly garden-conscious, and there was a movement on to get women to can vegetables.

I stopped by one of the Farm Security Administration homes, which was an old house remodeled into a comfortable bungalow. Half a mile down the dirt road you could see the old shack where the family used to live. The woman took me out to the shed where she kept her canned stuff. There in the meat-and-meal South it was like an oasis—in neat rows, shelf after shelf. The previous year she had canned three hundred fifty quarts of vegetables, fruits, and meat—twenty-nine different kinds of things. They'd been eating real meals all winter. I asked her if she had ever canned anything before this program started. She said no, she never had. I asked why. She said, well, just wasn't interested, she guessed. My mother had canned things like this as far back as I could remember, and I'm sure my people had been doing it for generations before. But down in Alabama, where the growing season is long and things flourish, half the people had starved themselves sick because they weren't interested. Half the rural South was sick—physically sick. And what can you expect of sick people? If you felt continually lousy, would you care whether you were honest or not, whether you got out of debt, whether you had what people call "character"? I'll bet you wouldn't.

W. L. McArthur, who was county head of the Farm Security Administration, had no highfalutin theories about the rehabilitation of the South. His theories were simple. He said that absolutely the first thing to do was to get the people well again, get the disease out of them, get them to eating right. The other stuff could come later. They had made wonderful progress in just three years. The nurses were responsible for lowering infant mortality from 55 to 19 per cent in a single year, and deaths of mothers at childbirth had fallen from 10.4 per cent to 6.6. But it would take generations to educate the poor people to want to be well. They'd been used to feeling rotten too long to change overnight.

One of the government men said the FSA couldn't, of course, tolerate a farmer who was a perpetual drunk. But he said that down in his heart he couldn't blame the guys for taking a few snorts. "My God!" he said. "The only time in their lives they ever feel halfway human is when they get a coupla shots of bad liquor in them."

They have a way in Alabama of using the word "sorry" which I've not heard in other parts of the country. A listless, no-good, poor-paying fellow is known as sorry. You can be poor without being sorry; you're sorry when you just ain't got no character.

Of Coffee County's forty-two hundred farmers, six hundred were under the Farm Security Administration when I was there. The FSA set them up in new or remodeled little houses on decent land, gave them a small loan for getting started, and then supervised them. They didn't hand out much on a silver platter. For instance, they didn't put bathrooms in the houses. That would be mighty nice, but as McArthur said, "Lots of them won't even use privies now. What would they do with a bathroom? Wait till they get healthy and out of debt and grow up to a bathroom. Then they can put one in themselves."

He was also strict about their debts. The government was getting back most of the money it lent them. Those who were just plain sorry and wouldn't try to make a crop were kicked out. As McArthur said, "When you put a premium on sorryness, you might as well quit."

They told me that southern farmers could get really well off in only three ways: by inheriting a lot of land; by being scrooges and denying their families everything worth living for; or by skinning somebody out of it. Just one of those three.

Probably half the land in Coffee County was washed away, not fit for raising anything. They felt that reforesting and terracing could bring much of this back. "But it's not submarginal land that puts us in our sorry shape," one man told me; "it's submarginal people." And when you got right down to it, you couldn't say that conditions were caused wholly by cruel landlords, by sharpster supply merchants, by erosion. You couldn't blame any individual, least of all the poor people themselves. As McArthur said, all landlords weren't bad. In fact, many southern farmers were better off under a capable and interested landlord than they would have been on their own land. And he said you couldn't blame the "supply merchant" who carried the people on credit, either. There were some bad ones who skinned people and kept them always in debt and reaped high profits. But there were some mighty good ones too; they carried people who didn't pay them for years—people who otherwise would have starved. And they took an awful chance. Many and many a supply merchant had gone broke in Coffee County. What was wrong was a combination of the landlord and the supply merchant and poor land and low prices and sickness and ignorance—in other words, it was the whole system.

It would take a long time—maybe ten generations—to purge America of the disease of "sorryness." Maybe I get too worked up about things like this. Sometimes I think maybe a fellow should just shut his eyes and drive fast. One night, there in Alabama, I went to see a movie called *St. Louis Blues*. Dorothy Lamour was in it (how beautiful she is in clothes!) and the setting was on the Mississippi, and it was all very romantic and full of the lovely old things of the South. I came away in the dumps, thinking that I was all wrong, and that Hollywood was right. I should have written about Coffee County as romantic, and full of guitars, and happy, happy Negroes, and sweeping bows to the ladies. Maybe I should—I don't know. But Hollywood has never seen all the pale dead people walking slowly around the red clay countryside.

I heard of one big landlord who had more than a hundred families sharecropping for him. They were treated so badly that a third of them moved away every year. This landlord sold fertilizer to his tenants. Under the rental agreement, they were to pay half and he was to pay half. The price he put on it was thirty dollars a ton. That sounds fair enough—except that he had bought the fertilizer for fifteen dollars a ton. At four tons per family, it was a nice profit of six thousand dollars a year. But, in fairness, the local people told me that less than half the landlords were like that.

When the government tried to talk one backward Alabama tenant into moving to a decent place, he said no, he wouldn't move because his grandfather had once owned all that land. In two generations the family had gone down the scale from comparative wealth to grinding poverty. His ragged children sitting on the porch had sores all over their legs. The government man suggested taking the little girl down to the doctor and getting her fixed up. The man said, "Naw," as soon as he could get four dollars he'd take her back over the hill to a doctor who had fixed her up before—a Negro witch doctor who used potions of manure, and weird incantations.

It was part of the new program to get all rural families to equip their places with sanitary toilets. That was the only way hook-worm could be stamped out. The approved toilet consisted of a pit in the ground, sealed on top with concrete, and a "riser" lid on it. The riser cost four dollars and a half, and the farmer could build the rest himself. The response was fairly good. But one day a county official went out on an inspection tour of these modern Chic Sales. He went into one, lifted the lid—and the whole pit was full of hay. It had never been used as a toilet. The whole family, women included, preferred to go out behind the barn.

You general farmers around Indianapolis who may read this, you beet farmers in Colorado, you citrus farmers in California, I don't believe you can possibly conceive of what life is like for half the farmers in the South. A young man and woman marry. They are of sixth-grade intelligence, and sunk in the hopeless-ness and listlessness of one-mule, sharecropping, debt-owing farming. Their parents can't help them, so they go to a supply merchant for "furnishing" and start life in debt. Thereafter, the girl gets pregnant as soon and as frequently as possible. They live on fat meat and corn meal, three meals a day. She has never heard of a women's club. The house is filthy and stays that way. She car-ries her little baby down to the fence row, lays him down, and works in the field. She knows only a few neighbors. Maybe twice a year she goes to town. She doesn't read anything and they have no radio. They use coal-oil lamps and the floors are bare. Likely as not, they don't even have a privy. The children are half naked and covered with sores. Soon she is old, and her sickly brood goes out to repeat the process. She chews snuff, spits at the fireplace, hits the wall, and there it stays for posterity—her mark in life. These people are not Negroes; they are whites.

Remember that bellhop in Miami who was so lonesome? Well, people all over the country wrote in, offering him everything from money to a complete turning over of his affairs to God. We gave his name to those whose letters seemed to indicate they could really do something for him. It wasn't charity he needed, for he had a job and small spending money. His great need and wish was to learn his way into a better job through schooling.

He wrote to us twice. He had changed jobs shortly after we left Miami and was now head busboy in a big restaurant. He had left the hotel where we knew him. But when the letters started coming in, the owner had him return and gave him his room for just a few chores. But out of all the letters he had had from people with good hearts, only one was concrete and offered him the kind of help he felt he needed. That was from Los Angeles, from someone who offered to give him lodging and help him through school. He had corresponded with this person, and things looked hopeful. As things stood now, he intended to go.

Most of those who wrote in were poor people. Which goes to show—or something. Many of those who wrote could offer nothing but sympathy. But toward those, just as much as the others, the boy felt, and I felt, the greatest gratitude.

This is a legend about islands and buzzards that I picked up at Biloxi, Mississippi. All along the Gulf Coast near Biloxi, a mile or so from shore, are long narrow islands, almost like beads on a string. They are all about the same length and width, all exactly alike. One of them is called Ship Island. Back in the early days it was inhabited by Spaniards, but smallpox or something swept through, and most of the people died. They were buried in the shallow sand there on the island. Years passed. Then came a great storm. The wind blew and the waves washed the island, disintering the dead. Buzzards did the rest.

So enraged were the remaining residents by this viciousness of storm and fowl that they all packed up to leave. But the old padre had a solution. He said he would consecrate the island against buzzards, and so he did. And to this day, they told me in Biloxi, there was not a buzzard on Ship Island. Captain Bill Reed, who told me about it, said that for years he'd had a standing offer of twenty-five dollars to anyone who could show him a buzzard on Ship Island. They infest all the other islands; they swarm over them by the hundreds and swoop down to take anything that dies. Yet a cow can die on Ship Island and lie there forever without attracting a buzzard. They said a buzzard would not even fly over Ship Island.

This is a story of the last battle of the Civil War. It was fought in Mobile Bay, in 1905, some forty years after you thought the war was over. It was told me by a friend, and he said the story was true.

Steven Quayle, we shall call him, was a Mississippian of gentle birth and scholarly parts. He went north in search of adventure and fortune. He worked in many northern cities, and being frequently appalled at the climate and the bleakness of manners, he longed at times for gentler scenes. At length he adopted a definite routine. He would work diligently for six months, and then for the next half year, with his savings, he would travel on the magic carpet of strong liquor. He would move physically too, and always, of course, southward. It was during one of these periods that he found himself in Mobile. That particular night he had slept in a park. At dawn he wandered to the waterfront. He was penniless, and lank for lack of food. He sat down on a bench to watch the spectacle of sunrise over Mobile Bay.

Presently a small rowboat came across the waters. It tied up, and the oarsman came ashore. He gave good morning to Steven and sat down to talk. Now, Steven had a courtesy of manner that would make the courtiers of the old French courts look like stumblebums. Poor or rich, drunk or sober, he was of the school of chivalry. The newcomer, it developed, was of the same school; his polished manners also knew no bounds. Gracious conversation began. They told their confidences. It rapidly developed that Steven was the son of a Confederate general. And by an odd coincidence the man from the rowboat was too. Companionship grew.

Steven told how he had fled north to wrest his fortune from the damyankees. The other man had been even more thorough. He had spurned the very continent where such things as Appomattox could happen. He had pre-empted an island off the mouth of Mobile Bay and lived there alone. He was an Unreconstructed Rebel, and had built himself a hermitage. One day a month he rowed ashore for supplies, liquid and staple. This happened to be the day.

Eventually the saloon and ship chandlery, before which they were sitting, opened. Our man invited Steve to join him in a little something. Steve explained his position, and our man became his enthusiastic host from then on. They filled themselves and also the demijohn the oarsman had brought along. Eventually they loaded it into the boat and left for the island—for by now Steve had been invited to spend a month, and had accepted. They alternately rowed and paused to sample the demijohn. Above the rowing and the sampling was the hum of erudite conversation, confined largely to the War Between the States and its intolerable ending.

In the midst of this, Steve espied a smudge of smoke on the horizon. They sat and watched. Soon the vessel was nearly abreast. Then the two friends recognized her as a battleship, flying the hated flag of the United States of America.

Now, it seems that that man from the island always placed a fowling piece in his boat when he set out on a trip. Steve, eyes agleam, seized the rifle and dropped a load across the bows of the battleship, calling upon her, in a loud voice, to heave to. The gun's pop attracted no attention whatever. Steve reloaded and fired at the foredeck, and again, at the bridge. He drew attention that time.

The battleship hove to in a hurry, a gig was swung down, and a rough bos'n's mate placed the men in the rowboat under arrest and took them to the battleship. Steve demanded that they be brought before the captain. This was done. The Confederates demanded immediate surrender of the battleship.

Now this, I understand, is all in the records of the Navy Department in Washington. I am sorry I have not had access to those records, so that I might give you the name of a captain in the United States Navy who possessed not only rich manners and a quick command of a situation, but also a sense of humor. The captain invited the Confederates to be seated. He politely offered them cigars. With courtliness he begged for a discussion of terms before he should turn over his sword. If I remember the story correctly, three bottle of champagne were ordered up and served. The conversation was heavy with elegance, and gradually became lightened by a certain bonhomie that grows between respected adversaries. It ended there in the captain's cabin with the drawing of a formal truce between the Confederacy and the United States.

This treaty of peace was signed and sealed in duplicate. Under the terms, the battleship was allowed to proceed to Mobile, but not to sail near their island, and the captain was permitted to retain his sword. The captain escorted the Confederates on deck. They were piped over the side with all the dignity that naval formality can bestow, and assisted into their rowboat, which they found almost dangerously loaded with cases of champagne and other ardent beverages. A launch was waiting to tow them back to their island, and at a signal it shoved off. Steve stood in the forepeak of the dory, seized the old fowling piece, which had been restored to him, and fired a salute. The battleship fired a salute in return.

Thus, in 1905, ended the last battle of the War Between the States.

Texas

Chapter XXV AN OILMAN WILL NEVER TELL YOU HOW MUCH he's worth; he's probably afraid he'll be broke by the time he gets back to the office. But he'll tell you how poor he used to be. Five years before I met him, Glenn McCarthy was down to three dollars. And now at thirty-one, his friends told me, he was probably worthy twenty million. It made me ashamed. I was past thirty-five, and I don't suppose I was worth a cent over ten million.

McCarthy was tall, broad-shouldered, slender—a perfect physical specimen. He dressed handsomely, talked quietly, and chewed gum. He had a $200,000 home in Houston and a summer place on Galveston Bay. He had lots of autos, and a riding stable, and five children. He wore a diamond ring and a diamond tiepin the size of your thumbnail.

He was born in the famous Spindletop oil field near Beaumont. His father was an oil-field worker, and the boy was brought up in the game. He didn't hanker for oil; he wanted to go to Annapolis. But his family didn't have the influence to get him in. So he thought he could get there via the enlisted man's route. He joined the Navy and served two years. On a sunny deck off Havana one afternoon, his captain told him he didn't belong in the Navy, and that an enlisted man's chances for Annapolis were slight indeed. McCarthy had found that out for himself, and was ready to leave.

So he went to school in Texas, married as soon as he came out, and got a job as a distributor for a big oil company. He worked day and night, and in no time ran his salary from $12.50 a week up to $250. He saved some money too, but he was ruining his health. So he picked up a few leases he'd had his eye on, quit his job, and took a whirl at the big time.

"But it takes around $125,000 to drill one of these ten-thou-sand-footers down here," I said to him. "How does a little fellow ever get that kind of money?"

No little fellow, of course, ever has $125,000 handed to him on a platter. But by trading some leases for cash, selling part interest in whatever oil he might find for more cash, getting some credit from the supply companies, and borrowing here and there, McCarthy got together enough to drill a well. That was when he was twenty-five—and he drilled a dry hole. It broke him, and then some. The story of his financial maneuvering—trading, finagling, twisting, and turning for the next year and a half—is something that only an oilman could understand. At one time he was $48,000 in debt. He produced some good wells, but it took everything he made to pay off. He kept drilling away with rattletrap machinery. On one well he was so broke that his father and brother worked as drillers while he fired the boilers; and then he'd take his own turn as driller at night.

But finally he hit it, and he hit it big. After only a year and a half of trying, he jumped into the millionaire class. He had had one setback since then, but he pulled out of it. He had drilled about two hundred twenty-five wells in those last six years and discovered five new fields. He sold one of them for seven million dollars. His father and brother were still working for him, in charge of production on his various fields.

McCarthy didn't have to wear overalls any more, or fight a drill all night. But the terrific responsibility that was on him, with millions tied up in drilling rigs, keeping his eye out for new fields, watching his debts like a condemned man (for they'll get you in the oil business)—all that kept his nose to the grindstone. He didn't even dare leave for a vacation trip. For all his mansions and autos and big diamonds, he actually had no more time for small things or pleasure in them than before. The biggest dif-ference was that, whereas he used to work so hard in the field he'd be ready to drop at night, now he had to go in for tennis and riding to keep himself in good physical shape.

You have to know these oilmen to realize it isn't just the money they're after. Maybe it is at first; but once they've got it, then it's "the fever." They want to be BIG; they want to be smarter than the others, make bigger finds, drill deeper wells, see what's under that ground, outgamble the other fellow. It's the same thing as Monte Carlo or Wall Street.

McCarthy said it was his ambition to drill the deepest oil well in the world. And he'd probably do it too—or go broke trying. If ever that twenty million slipped out on him some night, he could go right back and put his own big shoulder to the drill for a fresh start. With five children and the oil fever, what else could a man do?

In Houston I met a man who had served in Alcatraz. I won't give his name because I don't want to do him any harm, but I assure you he is not fictitious. He came to my hotel room at my invitation early one morning, and we talked till after noon.

This man, a Texan, was sent up for transporting narcotics. He said he was carrying it all right, and he knew what he was carrying. But he said the fifteen-day circumstances that led up to it were a frame. He served twenty-two months of a two-year sentence, the last seven months in Alcatraz. He went to Houston when he got out, and he had been there for two years. He had had nothing but picayunish jobs—ticket-taking, dance-hall bouncing. "But that's no work for me to be in," he said. "You have to throw drunks out every night. And if somebody fights back and you defend yourself, a man like me is on the spot."

There were a dozen things this former convict could do. He was an experienced oil-field worker, he knew steam boilers, he had done office work, he had done selling. He made a good appearance, and there had never been any thievery in his record. But people just wouldn't have a man from Alcatraz working for them. Many people, I suppose, were afraid to have him around. Others were afraid of public opinion.

Naturally he was known to the Houston police. Some of the cops had been good to him; others had gone out of their way to tattle when he had a job, and cause him to lose it. But there had been one Good Samaritan in this gloomy picture—a substantial Houston businessman who had been like a godfather. He had seen to it that the man had a hotel room to stay in and, I imagine, had handed out a little money when the going got too tough.

This man out of Alcatraz was tall, slim, and impeccably dressed. His hair was black and he had a little mustache. He was in his early thirties, I would say, and physically powerful. He did not hesitate to look you in the eye. There was something arresting in his face which told you that if you were his friend he'd fight the whole world for you; and if you were his enemy nothing would stop him from crushing you. He was intelligent, his manners were perfect, his speech was correct and quiet. His mouth was firm, and he almost never smiled.

I remarked on that. "Did you used to laugh a lot?" I asked. He smiled then. "Yes," he said, "I used to laugh all the time. If I'm going out among people now, people often ask me why I never smile. It burns me up to be asked that." He also said he used to dance a lot—but not any more. Just didn't feel like getting out and cutting up. I commented, too, on the neatness of his appearance. "I've made a point of it," he said. "I figured if I ever let myself get run down at the heels I wouldn't have a chance."

He was one of a big family, but none of them was able to help him. I asked, "What is your mother's feeling toward you after this business?" He grinned again, with real pleasure. "Well," he said, "I guess she's like a lot of mothers. I'm the black sheep, and yet I guess she likes me almost best of all." She was in Texas, and about twice a year he went to see her. He said they joked and scuffled around. You could tell he was crazy about her.

I don't believe the time in the penitentiaries, as such, had affected this man's spirit. He was not cowed. But these two years as a free man had done something to him. They had stopped his smiles; they made him suspicious; and he didn't dare think about himself too much. He stayed in his room as little as possible, to keep from brooding and getting too blue. He just used the place to change clothes and sleep a little. He said he wasn't much of a reader.

What would eventually happen to this man with the brand of Alcatraz on him? Well, I didn't know, and neither did he. He had three irons in the fire for good jobs, but they might go the same way as the others. In the end he might be driven back to

Alcatraz, for want of a better deal. But by staying two years in the same city, showing his hand and showing it clean, surely he had pulled his end of the load.

There was a street in Fort Worth with the simple name "Boulevard." When Vernon Castle, the great dancer and war hero, was killed in a plane crash at Fort Worth in 1918, a movement was started to call the street, then nameless, "Vernon Castle Boulevard." But no. Castle was a dancer; dancing was evil. Some residents of the street filed objections, and the proposal was voted down. The street was still just "Boulevard." But I hoped they would bring it up again. Bluenosing had lost considerable favor since then.

At a coffee shop in Fort Worth they used checks of stiff cardboard. And we noticed that the waitress always turned up one corner of the check when she put it on the table. We puzzled over this. I thought it was some kind of code signal to the cashier. That Girl thought it had something to do with the bookkeeping. The longer we pondered the deeper we got. At last, thoroughly baffled, I said to the cashier, "What do they turn up the edge of the check like this for?"

And she answered, "So you can pick it up easier."

A guy like me sure goes around making life difficult for himself.

I don't know that Mrs. Roosevelt and I had anything especially in common, except that we both wrote columns and saw a lot of country. But I'd been in her camp for a long time; I considered her a mighty fine woman. And I thought it would be nice if our wandering reportorial paths should cross some time. I hoped it might be out in the country somewhere, where she wouldn't be so busy, and we could sit down and chat—just one old columnist to another.

Well, our paths crossed. In San Antonio, Texas. We two Washingtonians, meeting so far away from home.

I'd had it all planned how I'd send a note to her secretary and ask if I might come up privately and say hello. They say she's awfully nice about such things. And after all, our two columns had run side by side for years in many newspapers. But do you know what I did? I lost my nerve. I fought with it a long time, and finally lost. I just couldn't send a note. So I got blue and lay down on the bed and said to myself, "Well, some other time, maybe."

But I had a friend on a San Antonio newspaper, and he said, "Why, you damn fool, you mean two travelers like you and Mrs. Roosevelt have never met? Why, this is news. Go on up and see her. If you're afraid to send a note, you can at least go to her press conference with our local reporters."

So, under his goading, I went. There were four local reporters, four photographers, and four high-school journalism students. And me—the thirteenth. She stood at the door, smiling, and shook hands with each of us as we introduced ourselves. I guess I really went because I hoped vaguely that Mrs. Roosevelt might recognize the almost unforgettable mug that ran in the column alongside hers. Or that she might catch the name as we introduced ourselves. But she didn't. She smiled upon me as upon all the others. I blushed, and sat in the corner with the two high-school boys. Mrs. Roosevelt looked at me frequently. I'm sure she must have thought, "How admirable it is for a bald-headed man to keep on trying to get through high school."

While the other reporters took notes, I just sat and watched how Mrs. Roosevelt handled things. Her graciousness had been mentioned many times, and I could see it had not been exaggerated. There wasn't a question she declined to answer, and she did practically no hedging; I've never seen anyone treat strange reporters with more intellectual honesty. And she was kind, even about the dumbest questions. During the embarrassing silences when we country reporters couldn't think of anything to say, she would fill in by elaborating on the last answer. She had a beautiful enunciation. She also split an infinitive now and then, which further warmed me toward her.

During her lecture tours Mrs. Roosevelt would be on the go from about six in the morning till late at night. Every minute was full; everybody tried to see her. She had almost no privacy.

Thinking of my own seemingly full days, I said to her, "Don't you get terribly worn out on these tours?"

She said, "Oh, no. They're much less strenuous than when I'm in Washington and have to keep up with the social routine." She looked right at me when she spoke, and I thought to myself, she knows I'm from Washington. She's trying to place me.

Then one of the reporters asked what her program was for the day. She said she was to go out riding with some friends shortly, and after that she had to get back because "I've got a daily column to write, you know." She laughed when she said that, one of those "between us newspaperfolks" laughs. She started her smile at one end of the group, and bestowed it clear around the circle to me on the other end. It seemed a sort of knowing smile when it settled on me. Ah, she's got it, I thought. Now she knows who I am. She'll say something later.

We talked with her for about half an hour. One very intelligent and pretty girl reporter did most of the questioning. The high-school boys were so scared they never once opened their mouths. One high-school girl asked for an autograph, and got it.

"Is there anything else?" asked Mrs. Roosevelt. There wasn't. So we all stood up, and once again filed past, to smile and shake hands and say goodbye. I was the last in line. I guess maybe I hung back on purpose so I could be last—I don't know. I still had one faint hope that she really knew. I thought she might lean over and whisper, "Stay behind a minute, Ernie. Let's talk about our columns." But it was not to be. In that brief second of her smile and handshake I couldn't have been any more anonymous if I'd been a fish in the sea. And so—onward, and out the door.

That's how I met Mrs. Roosevelt.

They called him Ad, which was short for Adolph. They called her Plinky, because when she was learning to shoot she'd keep saying, "Throw up another one and I'll plink it." Ad and Plinky Topperwein of San Antonio were one of the greatest shooting teams in the world. A gun-toter in the old Southwest wouldn't have stood a show if he'd had to draw against Ad Topperwein. Yet Topperwein had never been called upon to defend his life with a gun. The nearest approach was many years ago when an escaped lunatic tried to get in the house. And on him Ad used a club!

Ad, the son of a gunsmith of German descent, was born a few miles north of San Antonio. He started shooting when he was six. He would be seventy on his next birthday, and apparently he was shooting as well as ever. He and Plinky had a farm outside of town where they went to shoot whenever they could. Their son Lawrence was telling me about his father's pulling off a series of difficult shots out there. And about Plinky's saying, "Isn't he wonderful? I don't see how the old fool does it." Which I suspect was slightly rhetorical because, if there was anything Plinky Topperwein loved more than shooting, it was her husband. She almost got tears in her eyes when she talked about him. They'd been married nearly forty years and earning their living together all that time by fancy shooting, and she still adored him.

Topperwein was also an artist. His first paying job was as a chalk etcher on one of the San Antonio newspapers. Even now drawing was his hobby and an outlet for some of his nervous energy. He always carried crayons in the breast pocket of his coat, and he sketched on trains and in restaurants whenever he felt like it. His drawings could be found on windows, walls, doors, and mirrors all over the Southwest; the owners were proud of them. His favorite subjects were Indian and cowboy heads and comic-strip characters. Lawrence was even better at it than his father. He too had worked for years as a newspaper artist. But now he was a reporter, and he loved the newspaper business. Incidentally, he couldn't hit the Municipal Auditorium at twenty paces.

When he was young, Ad Topperwein traveled with a circus doing trick shooting. The Winchester Arms Company heard of his prowess and hired him to go about the country giving sharp-shooting exhibitions. That had been thirty-nine years ago and he was still at it, for the same company.

On one of his early visits to the Winchester plant in New Haven, Connecticut, he met a girl and married her. Things were pretty tough for her at first. She either had to stay home or else go on those exhibition trips and just twiddle her thumbs. She didn't like it. So she made Ad teach her to shoot. It wasn't long before she was as good a shot as her husband. And then Winchester hired her too. For twenty-nine years the world's greatest shooting couple traveled the North American continent together. But always, the home they came back to betweentimes was San Antonio.

Six years ago the Winchester people, probably for economy, had dropped Mrs. Topperwein. It almost broke her heart. Left at home, Plinky turned to other things for recreation, for she was a large woman with tremendous energy. She started bowling, and joined four bowling clubs. She was so interested that for a year she hardly shot at all.

Then one day her husband, somewhat critically, said he felt she'd been bowling too much and had forgotten how to shoot. You have to know how intense was their pride in shooting to realize what a sting that remark carried for Plinky. To them, their guns were human, and their marksmanship was an emotional thing. To neglect it was like neglecting your family. So they drove out to the farm. Plinky was not only hurt but scared stiff too. Maybe I *have* forgotten how to shoot, she thought. Maybe I *have* been bowling too much. If Ad was right, she was as disgraced in his eyes, and in her own too, as if she had struck their child. They got out there, and Ad started tossing targets into the air. One by one, Plinky picked them off. Her old confidence came back, and she called for more and more difficult shots. Before they were through, she had gone through their entire old routine without missing a shot. There was never a happier woman.

Friends told me you could start an argument anywhere in San Antonio by saying that Ad was a better shot than Plinky, or vice versa. But the Topperweins said there wasn't any argument; Plinky was better at some kinds of shooting, Ad was better at others.

I spent a fascinating evening with the Topperweins. It was just luck that I caught Ad at home, for he was on the road most of the time. If he liked you, he'd talk guns all night. And Plinky was emotional—loved everything almost to heartbreak. We sat for hours in their den, which was a remarkable, helter-skelter, gun-infested room. There were guns everywhere—in cabinets, hung on the walls, standing in corners. And from under the couch Ad would pull suitcase after suitcase, each one full of six-shooters; there must have been scores of them. He took special ones out and fondled them, always looking to see if they were loaded. He said he had found cartridges many times in guns that he absolutely knew were not loaded.

And that brings up what was, to me, the most amazing thing about this couple's long career as professional crack shots. In forty years of almost daily shooting, they had never had any kind of accident. Never a split barrel, never a stray shot hitting anybody, never any kind of accident at all.

I asked about the wild west custom of "fanning" a gun, and Ad showed me how fast he could do it. Fanning means knocking the hammer back with the back of your hand, instead of pulling the trigger. He admitted you could fire faster that way, but he said there wasn't any advantage in it; when you hit the hammer it threw the gun out of line. "You might fire three times while the other fellow was firing once," he said. "But your shots would be wild, and the other fellow would kill you with one good shot."

One day Plinky started out the front door, and there was a rattler coiled on the porch with its head up. It may have escaped from the reptile museum a block away. Anyway, its head went off with one blast from her six-gun. Next day she heard her neighbor screaming. She grabbed a rifle and ran over. The rattler's mate also went to heaven via the Plinky route.

Ad and Plinky held some remarkable records. In 1907 Ad shot steadily eight hours a day, for ten days in a row. He was firing a .22 rifle at 2½-inch wooden blocks tossed into the air. He shot at 72,500 blocks, and missed only nine. Out of the first 50,000 he missed four. He had a number of runs of more than 10,000 without a miss, and one run of 14,540. But the strain of it, day after day, almost drove him insane. His muscles and nerves were in painful knots. At night he had horrible dreams: the blocks would be a mile away; the bullets wouldn't come out of the end of the gun. As for Plinky, her trapshooting record of 1,952 hits out of 2,000 targets was a world's record for anyone, man or woman. She shot for five hours straight, using a pump gun. It raised such a blister that a few days later the skin came off the whole palm of her hand.

Neither of the Topperweins drank, but Ad smoked cigars and Plinky smoked cigarettes. She wondered why some of the cigarette companies didn't ask her for a testimonial, since smoking hadn't hurt her nerves. "Now, you don't want any stuff like that," Ad said.

When I started to go, they refused to let me call a taxi, and drove me downtown. They said the next time we were in San Antonio we had to come out for dinner or get shot. All right, I'd come. But not because I was scared. I figured they've never shot at anything as thin as I am, standing edgewise.

Stopover
at Dana

Chapter
XXVI I HADN'T BEEN HOME FOR A YEAR WHEN I WENT BACK
to Dana in 1939. It had been three years then since my mother's
first stroke and two years since her second. After a full life of
farm work, life in a bed and a chair were hard for her, but she
was swell about it, as she had been about everything else in her
life. She had taken it with her chin out. Certainly she didn't like
inaction, but she accepted it, and that was that.

I was immensely pleased to see that my mother's face had filled
out again, and had color in it, and was almost the same as it
had been before her first shock. But she was semiparalyzed, and
could get around only with help. She didn't attempt to move
unless my father was there to lift her and steady her. When I was
home she liked the novelty of my helping her.

She was up around six-thirty every morning, had her breakfast, and sat and listened to the radio for a couple of hours. If
she stayed up too long she got a headache, so she would lie down
on the davenport a little while in the morning, and again after
lunch. In the late afternoon her chair was moved out onto the
concrete cistern top east of the house, and she sat there with her
back to the road. "I'd lots rather watch the cows and chickens
than the people passing on the road," she said. The folks in our
neighborhood were still kind and thoughtful. Hardly ever did
one of the clubs or lodges meet but that they sent her a box of
gifts.

There was a time after each stroke when my mother couldn't
speak, but she could talk now, very slowly, until she got tired.
Then her words played tricks on her. That was her greatest dis-

appointment and frustration when I was at home. When I was leaving she would cry and say, "I didn't get to talk to you."

She was able to ride in the car, but didn't go every day, because it was too hard to get her into the seat. She enjoyed riding around, though she got frightened easily. Once when we were out driving and I decided to turn around, I backed into a neighbor's driveway; there was a rise, and the back end of the car tilted up. My mother grabbed the door handle and started to whimper. "Why, what's the matter?" I asked. "We're all right. You were never afraid of anything." "I know," she said, "but I'm not well like I used to be. I get scared so easy. Storms nearly drive me crazy. I just can't help it."

My mother sat and watched the little world of her neighborhood. Her interest was not in gossip, and never had been; it was in the actions and thoughts of growing young people, and the welfare of old neighbors. She had always had an innate sense of fairness and justice, and it seemed to me that she saw through and into the true worth of people more acutely than ever before. She had no deep interest in that bigger world that constituted the news of the day. Although she wouldn't miss hearing Lowell Thomas each evening, still I believe Hitler and Japan meant no more to her than the noise of a passing truck. When I was home, she never asked me about any of the places we had been. I asked if she would like me to send her a big map so they could keep track of us. She said, "No." And she said, "Whenever you're going to fly, don't let us know about it till after you've got there."

Occasionally my mother would get a rash of the giggles, usually when they came to the most difficult point of lifting her into the car. And then it would get so funny that my father and Aunt Mary would get to laughing too, and they would just have to cease operations and hold her up till the giggling was over. I suppose those giggles were caused by her acute sense of the ridiculous—a woman like her having to be helped around was just too ironic.

At last my mother got a little dog. For a long time she had wanted one. She loved dogs anyhow, and now that she had nothing to do but sit all day a dog would be company. But the family verdict still seemed to be "No"—I never could find out why. It was none of my put-in, so I didn't go around looking for a dog, but one night fate took a hand. The folks heard a man out in the yard, whipping a dog. It was dark and they couldn't see, but then they heard the man go away, and the whipped dog came to the house.

My father said the dog couldn't stay. My mother said she wanted it to stay. When I got there she told me she wanted a collar and chain for it, so when I went to town I got them. I really didn't mean to take any hand in it, but I guess that collar and chain had some bearing; my father didn't say anything more about sending the dog away. Finally I saw him petting it, and teaching it to stand on its hind legs to ask for candy.

The dog was part collie and part just dog. She was about six months old, brownish black, and as friendly as a politician. She still thought she was going to be whipped, but I figured that business would soon be gone from her memory.

My mother called the dog "Snooky." My Aunt Mary called her "Betty." It didn't seem to make any difference; the dog answered to either name—when she felt like it. Along toward evening she would get so happy and full of vinegar you'd have thought she was going to bust. She would run wildly in circles out in the yard, with her head out and her belly close to the ground. Then she'd wind up with a straightaway dash for the porch, give a headlong leap into my mother's lap, and almost eat her up. That was a problem. The puppy's teeth were like needle points, and she liked to chew on people's hands, as all friendly dogs do. She tried to be tender, and not to hurt, but my mother didn't have quick use of her hands, and two or three times a day she got bitten. You should have seen her hands and wrists; they were so badly torn that I wanted to send for the doctor. But she pooh-poohed the notion. She swore it didn't hurt.

Although the dog was smart, she didn't really know anything yet. She hadn't become attuned to the whims and feelings of her human friends. She barked at the wrong time, played at the wrong time, didn't lie still at the right times. She gnawed playfully at my mother's feet. And when we raised my mother from her chair, or set her down, the dog was always wholeheartedly in the way.

My mother decided she could start training the dog by using a little switch. So we cut a switch from a tree. But my mother just sat and held it, and let the dog chew her. She said she couldn't switch Snooky, even lightly, when the dog meant so well.

I wonder what makes dogs afraid of some things and brave about others. Betty (or Snooky) was deathly afraid of little boys. I had a two-year-old cousin who came to our house sometimes, and Betty-Snooky was petrified at the sight of him. At night the folks shut the dog up in the smokehouse and, like a child, she hated that. But when the little boy came, she ran whining to the smokehouse door and, when we opened it, went in like a shot. We left the door open, but she stayed there all day, quiet as a mouse. The minute the little boy left for home she was out in the yard again, running and jumping as though she was the bravest dog that ever lived.

While I was there, no formal verdict was handed down as to whether or not the dog was to stay on at our house, but I'd have suggested putting two dollars on the proposition that the William C. Pyle household had a dog permanently in its midst.

Nature was pulsing that spring, and there was a thriving of life in the country around our house. The grass and the trees had never seemed so beautiful to me, so fresh and green. The spiraea bushes were out in a wild white, and if you hadn't been hot with spring warmth, you'd have sworn the bushes were covered with snow.

In all my early years I never saw a fox around there, but they said the country was thick with them now. They would go right up to the edge of Dana, and set the dogs wild. Wild rabbits were sitting all around the old gravel pit up by the barn. Never had quail been so abundant. And as I walked through the country it seemed to me the grass and the bushes were alive with birds —birds I'd never seen before, birds I didn't know the names of, new birds in our country. There were more rats. And more cats too. Enemies flourished side by side. Trees and bushes bloomed, and bugs and things by the thousands buzzed and flew around.

At night I couldn't read in bed for the hard-shelled bugs roaring at the screen, trying to reach the light. Nature was rampant again in our farmed and paved and tractored country. I don't know what it was. The farmers didn't know what it was.

The groundhogs were thick; all the neighbors were bothered with them. At our house there were three big dens of them on the hillside beyond the barn. Outside their dens they had piled up mounds of fresh sand from their burrowings. My mother said, "Ernest, why don't you go borrow Jack Bales's gun and see if you can't kill some of those groundhogs while you're home?" So I drove over to the Bales's house. Nobody was there, but I went in anyway, as neighbors out there do, and got Jack's little .22 rifle, just a single-shot gun. I took it home and loaded it and walked up toward the barn. Groundhogs are nasty things, and I don't like them.

I went sneaking around behind the barn on tiptoe, like an Indian. I peeked around the corner of the barn—and there it was, sitting out in the middle of the barn lot, right out in the open. I was between the groundhog and its hole.

I took two steps out from the barn, and the groundhog saw me. It stood motionless for one second, puzzled, as though it could not conceive of being cut off from its den. Then it ran swiftly, at right angles, toward the barn. I fired across the fence. It was a good forty yards, and I had no idea of making a hit. But as the gun cracked the groundhog rolled. It gave me a thrill, I can't help admitting. The groundhog rolled once, and landed on its feet again, running. This time it ran straight toward me —instinct, I suppose. Instinct and hurt and a numbing fright drove it toward its den, man in the way or no man.

I had an extra cartridge in my hand, and it took me only a second to reload. I had the sight dead on it when it was within ten feet of me, and was pressing on the trigger. And then the groundhog staggered. I never fired the second shot. The ground-hog fell once to the right. It pulled itself up and fell once to the left. It kicked twice. It wasn't a yard from my feet when it twitched out its last breath. I stood there looking, fascinated and horrified, as it died.

My father came, and said, "Well, that's good. You'll have to bury it now." So I got the spade and dug a deep hole in the bottom of the old gravel pit, and tied a string around the groundhog's leg, and dragged it into the hole, and covered it up. The groundhog was chubby, and there would soon have been young ones. I tramped the earth down hard over the filled hole.

That night just before bedtime I went outdoors. Our country is very quiet and very dark in the nighttime. I had a feeling of something up toward the barn. It sounds foolish. But there was a life less, and I had taken it. Sure, a groundhog is no good, and ought to be killed. But there was a home in the hillside without a tenant. Maybe a groundhog enjoys living, too. I could sense a presence in the darkness . . . a spirit kicking pitifully at my feet . . . eyes looking up, and slowly glazing . . .

I stood there in the dark for a long time thinking about it, out there under the maple trees, and I just felt like hell.

Dana is a pretty town. Nearly every street is a cool, dark tunnel, formed by the great arching maple trees from either side. People who have been around say Dana is a medium-good town. I really don't know whether it is or not. I never felt completely at ease in Dana. I suppose it was an inferiority hangover from childhood; I was a farm boy, and town kids can make you feel awfully backward when you're young and a farm boy. I never got over it. I should have, of course, because all that was long ago, and the people I saw on the streets were people I'd known all my life, and many of them were our farm friends who had moved to town in their declining years. But just the same I felt self-conscious whenever I walked down the street in Dana, imagining the town boys were making fun of me.

Four Corners
and Thereabouts

Chapter **I** HAD BEEN HOLDING MY BREATH FOR YEARS FOR
XXVII fear Mrs. Roosevelt would beat me to Four Corners, but, as far
as I know, I made it first. This is the only place in America where
four states come together.

Way off in the mountainous desert, the corners of Colorado,
Utah, Arizona, and New Mexico all touch each other. There's
nothing there except a concrete post, and two swallows that
keep flying around, and nobody but a screwball would have
thought of going there to write about it. We drove thirty miles
west from Shiprock, New Mexico, on a dirt road, and then went
uphill for eight miles on a track that was full of rocks and drifted
sand. It took three-quarters of an hour to go the last eight miles.
Our destination was a little plateau, a block or so square. From
there the land falls away, or rises, into vast, rolling, desolate,
windy country. The sight is majestic in all directions. The concrete post, about two feet high, was put up by the government.
On top of it is a bronze plate, and stamped on the plate are two
lines, about an inch long, crossing in the middle. Those are the
boundary lines of the four states.

We got kind of silly there. First thing, I had to sit on top of
the post, which made my rather scant bottom repose in four states
simultaneously. I don't care how big your bottom is, you can't
do better than that. After that, I leaned over the monument, and
had my picture taken with one foot in Utah and one in Colorado,
one hand in New Mexico and one in Arizona. Didn't even feel
ridiculous while I did it, either. Then we got out our sandwiches,
and I sat on the post eating in one-twelfth of America all at once.

When we finished I threw a handful of banana peels and pieces of bread up in the air, and they desecrated four states. The dirtiest tourist in the land can't outdesecrate me.

Very few people go to Four Corners; at Shiprock they said that one car a week would be stretching it. For one thing, most people never heard of it. For another, those last eight miles are just an old Navajo wagon trail that isn't even on the road maps.

Not a hundred yards from the marker post are the crude stone walls of a crumbled building—a trading post that went broke.

This is an account of fifteen minutes at Teec Nos Pas, Arizona. Teec Nos Pas is an Indian trading post. There are scores of them scattered about the big Navajo reservation, mostly quite isolated. You drive, and you look, and you say, "Lord, what wastes! This is utter emptiness. How does anybody make a living?"

Our road had become a mere trail. We jounced over thousands of acres of flat solid rock, like fields of concrete. The end of nowhere. We came around a rough little hill, and there in the valley was Teec Nos Pas—just a store and a few outbuildings, that's all. Loafing Indians, wearing red bands around their heads, lay on the porch, lounged against stone walls. Indian ponies, saddled and blanketed, were tied here and there. We stopped and walked towards the store. One of the two white men lounging on the porch got up and went in ahead of us. All the loafing Indian eyes drilled us coldly. In the West there is usually a friendly greeting between strangers, but not at Teec Nos Pas. The unfriendly stare, the sinister eye, is the greeting at Teec Nos Pas.

The store was old and dirty inside. Lying on the floor, flat on his back, was an old Indian. Just lying there, doing nothing, looking at nothing. We wanted to buy something, to break the ice. "I'll have a Coca-Cola," said my friend. "No cold drinks here," said the white trader. My friend bought a sack of Bull Durham.

"Can you tell me anything about that old building up at Four Corners?" I asked.

The trader leaned one elbow against the high candy case. He

pulled at his cigarette, held his head back, blew high. And then he said, with finality, "Don't know anything about it."

I waited a while and then said, "Never even heard of it, huh?"

The trader waited a while and then said, again closing the subject, "Yes, I've heard of it."

Then I waited a while and said, "You been out here long?" And after a while the trader said, "Yes, quite a while." And then he said, "I thought you were tourists. I hoped you were tourists and gonna look at a rug."

We kind of laughed to ease the tension, and I said, "Well, how can you tell we're not tourists? Do we look too poor to buy a rug?"

The trader said no, that wasn't it.

One by one the porch-sitting Indians were drifting in and standing around, with no expression of any kind on their faces. They stood and stared, like so many animal eyes around a campfire. There was no conversation except between the trader and me, and it was toilsome and unwelcome conversation to us both. I tried again.

"I hear somebody tried to start a hotel. That old building up there."

The trader said, "No, it wasn't a hotel. It was a trading post."

"I'd heard it was a hotel," I said.

"That's the Indian agent out there on the porch. He can tell you what you want to know."

After a bit the agent drifted in. He did not speak. He sat on the high counter across the store, and studied the old army shoes my friend wore. Waiting us out. Our move.

"How long has it been since you sold a rug to a tourist?" I asked the trader.

He blew a disdainful answer of smoke through his nose. "God, I don't know. Tourists never come here. Nobody ever comes here."

The Indian agent continued his study. The Indians watched to see if my friend could actually roll a cigarette. He could. Their expression did not change. The old Indian on the floor never moved. The heat was oppressive, and the needles in the air grew sharper. My friend and I sensed each other's wishes without looking.

"Well, I reckon we better shove along," I said.

"I reckon we better," my friend replied.

Stares propelled us out the door. The rocky road away from Teec Nos Pas seemed like a ribbon of velvet.

We felt as though we were in a new country when we got to Monticello, Utah. It was just a little place, seven thousand feet high, on the slope up to Blue Mountain. People are nice there, in that great, warming way of people who are somewhat isolated, but not isolated into sourness.

One of the first settlers around Monticello was a Mormon named Parley Butt. He was one of the first into the town of Bluff, to the south, and into Dove Creek, across the Colorado line to the east. He was a character if I ever saw one. He was in the Mormon scouting party that first penetrated southern Utah, a member of the fated group that made Mormon history by their experiences at "The Hole in the Rock." They spent a whole year crossing the Colorado River, and many of them died. Parley Butt was in Bluff in '78. He owned the first store in Dove Creek, but he was renting it out now. "I don't rent it out," he said. "My wife rents it out. She's bigger than I am."

Parley Butt was a lovable rascal. He must have been close to eighty now, and ugly as a mud fence, with huge queer gold teeth in his lower jaw. He doddled around Dove Creek with a fly swatter in his hand and an ornery grin on his face. I'd have liked to know him better. He had been rich in his day. Was a great Mormon cattleman, and owned thousands and thousands of acres of land. Probably the first citizen of southeastern Utah. He had lost a great deal of that, but he was doing all right. He was having a good time.

He ran for the Utah legislature once, and got elected by one vote. He said if that was the best they could do, nuts to 'em. He refused to go to Salt Lake City. He served three terms as sheriff of San Juan County. I was told how he tracked three desperadoes into the desert, found them all asleep, took their guns, and then just sat quietly till they woke up, and laughed at them.

Utah and Colorado would miss Parley Butt when he was gone. He had a sense of ironic humor that you seldom see in this day and age—you find it mostly in Alaska, among the old boys. When the Albuquerque friend who was traveling with me started to leave, Parley Butt said to him, "So long, kiddo." And when I said goodbye, he said, "Well, give my regards to all the good-looking people in the world."

Out in the desert, where vast space puts a frame around every little thing, you find that actions, too, are somehow magnified. Incidents that are small elsewhere become big incidents out there. They come back to you again and again, and you laugh to yourself if they're funny or sit and think about them if they're not. There is time and room not to have things killed in the rush.

In the very old village of Bluff, Utah, we sat on the concrete doorstep of the one-room store. A couple of local men were slowly telling us about things.

"Is this town all Mormon?" I asked.

"Yes, all Mormon," said one of the men, as he squatted and drew a line in the sand with a rock. "That is, they're all Mormons but me. I've been here so damn long I don't know whether I'm Mormon, gentile, or Jew."

Maybe that wouldn't be funny in New York, but it was funny in Bluff.

Once Bluff was alive. There were cattle there, and people were rich. But that was long ago. Bluff was dead now, and well it knew it. The immense square stone houses, reminiscent of past wealth, stood like ghosts, only one or two to a block. Sand was deep in the streets. People moved slowly, for there was no competition. Nobody new ever came to Bluff.

When we started that long trip into the desert country, we prepared ourselves as though we were going from the Cape to Cairo. We replaced two tires with new ones. We brought a shovel. We carried a five-gallon can of water for the radiator and a gallon thermos jug for ourselves. We bought a tire pump, a can of patches, an extra fan belt, and two quarts of oil. We took a first-aid kit, and a snakebite kit. We had a funnel and a tin cup. We had a small board on which to place the jack in sand. We had old gunny sacks to put under the wheels if we got stuck. We had two cans of sardines and a box of crackers, just in case. We had a .22 rifle and a German Luger revolver. These were just for fun, and not because we thought we'd need them. We wore overalls and heavy shoes.

Of all this paraphernalia, we had no need for anything except the two cans of water, the funnel, and the tin cup. We never saw a snake. We never saw anything to shoot at except some prairie dogs. We didn't eat our sardines, and the fan belt didn't break. Yet if I was making the trip again, I wouldn't eliminate a thing. For it is possible to need all those things in the desert, and when you need them, you need them bad.

The first day out we drove too long with the top down. Result— bad sunburn. I can take it when my arms catch fire and even when the itching sets in. I can take it when my nose turns red, and the freckles come out, and even when the water blisters start and my forehead gets scurvy-like from the ragged peeling. But when a man, three days after a sunburn, can reach up and peel big patches of skin right square off the top of his head, then the time has at last come to admit he's plumb baldheaded, and I find it exceedingly hard on my Romeo complex.

Blanding, twenty-seven miles north of Bluff, is the jumping-off place into the vast unwashed desert land of the Navajo country. When you leave Blanding, coming south, you've left the last group of buildings that can call itself a town and keep its face straight.

Blanding is a farm community. It is Mormon, staid and conservative. There was a CCC camp there at the time, filled with boys from New York and New Jersey. The boys found Blanding a bitter pill. Beer was not sold there. And the boys said there was even a highway sign, on the edge of town, warning visitors that smoking wasn't allowed. We didn't see any such sign, so I asked the proprietor of a store in Blanding about it. He stopped unpacking a box of merchandise and stood up.

"I know just who told you that," he said. "It was a filling station in Monticello. They've got it in for us. Of course there isn't any such sign. People smoke here. I sell cigarettes. We're no better and no worse than other people. We just try to make a living and live decently and have a good time. Just like anybody else."

Small towns are like small people. They enjoy running each other down.

In each of the little settlements of the Navajo country there is usually one white family that stands out. One such family was the Nevills, of Mexican Hat, Utah. It was Norman Nevills who kept the newspapers in hot water for more than a month in the summer of 1938, with his expedition down the treacherous Colorado River. The party was forty-two days making the six hundred sixty miles from Green River, Utah, to Boulder Dam; for weeks they were supposedly "lost." But they came through, and if you've ever shot a rapids with Norman Nevills you'll understand why.

There were two families of Nevills at Mexican Hat—Norman and his wife and little girl in one house, and his parents in another. The elder Nevills was a California oil engineer. He had arrived in this majestically bare part of Utah in 1920, and had been there ever since. He was in poor health; he said that even to say a few words exhausted him.

Norman and his mother ran the Indian trading post, and a tasteful little lodge where they put up occasional wayfarers. But to Norman, those things were sidelines. The river was his main life. He was a college graduate from California, and had studied engineering. They'd had a lot of money at one time, but shot it all in oil, and didn't get it back. Norman was glad, now, for otherwise he might never have stayed at Mexican Hat so long, and today he loved it there above any other place in the world.

He was, I would say, not much over thirty. He spoke some Navajo, and dickered impatiently with the Indians who brought in rugs to trade for supplies. His mother said he offered the Indians too little. He said she offered them too much. But the Indians must have liked it, for they were always hanging around.

Norman had been playing with the rapids of the San Juan River for years. But it was the expedition of 1938 that was likely to provide him a livelihood for many years. It publicized him as a river guide, and it was from the river, mainly, that he made his living. His schedule was full for the summer, and far into the fall.

What he did was take summer parties on an eight-day boat ride from Mexican Hat, on the San Juan, clear down to Lee's Ferry, on the Colorado. He charged sixty-two dollars and a half a person for the eight-day trip, and that included grub, a cook, sleeping bags, a long taste of the simple outdoor life, much scenery, and many thrills. On the ninth day he pulled his boats from the water, loaded them on trailers, and in one hard day's driving over rough Navajo roads was back again at Mexican Hat. And on the tenth day he would be headed downriver again with a new party. "See the desert by water" was his slogan.

Norman told some whoppers about the force of the rapids, and I believed them all. For instance, he used to wear a stocking cap on the river to keep his hair from flying. But once, in particularly bad rapids, the water came over the whole boat with such terrific force that it pulled the stocking cap right down over his face, clear to his neck, and he couldn't see a thing.

He said he had never overturned a boat. In all these years the river had never nicked him, but he had an intensely respectful fear of it.

The greatest aviators I know are those who are always a little afraid; they're the ones I like to fly with. And so it was with Nevills, and the river he loved and feared. We were a little skittish about riding with Nevills. "I wonder if this guy can really row a boat?" my traveling friend asked, the night before. Before another twenty-four hours we knew damn well he could row a boat—and how!

We were up early. Nevills was up ahead of us, overalled and dirty, smearing black tar on the boat bottom with his hands. "I don't think it will leak much," he said. It was a fifteen-foot plywood rowboat, very thin. We lifted it onto a trailer, and drove twenty miles north, to where the road crossed Comb Wash. Then we headed the car right down the dry stream bed, dodging rocks, until at last we bumped up to the shore of the San Juan River. We put the boat in the water, and we two passengers put on life jackets. By river, it was nineteen and a half miles back to Mexican Hat. Nevills said we would make it in five to six hours.

There are many odd things about boating on a river full of

rapids. The very first is that you float down backwards—in other words, stern-to. This is so the oarsman can sit facing forward and see where he's going. Also, the boat takes it better.

Nevills took off his shirt before we started. He was a smallish man, but his muscles were powerful and steely, from much rowing. The first thing I knew, we were floating sideways. And, although the waves were a couple of feet high, we seemed to rock across them like a blob of oil. "In small waves, we always go sideways," Nevills said. "That way we don't smack the waves, and don't get so much water aboard. But when they get bigger, we have to switch around stern-to, or the boat would swamp."

For the first couple of hours the rapids we went through were small. To be sure, they looked bad enough to a novice. But we handled them so simply that my friend and I were disappointed.

It was beautiful to watch Nevills handle the boat—just fishing around, easing the boat through the big waves like an eel. Often we would go into a rapids stern-to, switch sideways in the middle, and come out into smooth water bow-to. Water oozed in through the seams of the boat, and soon we were wet. Every fifteen minutes or so one of us would bail with a tin can. "This boat can't leak," Nevills said, "but it's sure doing a good job of going through the motions, isn't it?" On dry land, that would have been a swell joke.

The hours went on. Nevills told us river tales. And always, as he gracefully oared that little boat through the rushing waves and around hidden rocks, he would sing or whistle. I think he must have made up his songs as he went along, for I'd never heard any of them before.

The riverbank rose gradually, and before long we were riding along between canyon walls a quarter of a mile high—frightening, forbidding cliffs of solid rock that would have been impossible to climb. Eating lunch on a rock ledge in those narrows, we were a little apprehensive, and kept our eyes on the boat. It was tied to a small jutting rock of the canyon wall. If it had broken loose, we sure would have been in a pickle. The ledge was cut off by canyon wall behind, and deep, rushing river in front.

It was just a little after noon when Nevills rowed over to a sandy beach, jumped out, and tied it up. "This is Eight-Foot Rapids around the bend," he said. "Hear it? It's bad. We'll walk down and see how it looks today." The personality of rapids changes from day to day, it seems.

It developed that Nevills didn't expect to take us through this rapids with him; we'd have to walk around, and he'd pick us up farther along. We walked down. The rapids didn't look bad to me. Nevills studied them, and finally said, "I guess maybe I could take one of you." I wanted the experience, and since I was the smaller of the two passengers, it was agreed that I could go. We left my friend alongside the rapids, and Nevills and I walked back to the boat. He really did a build-up on Eight-Foot Rapids. He said lots of boats had been lost there. He put on his own life jacket, for the first time. He told me just how to sit.

We got all ready to go. And then I learned something else— that it's a custom and a tradition among rivermen, just before shooting a big rapids, to—how shall I put it?—to go to the gentlemen's room. We honored the tradition.

I was excited and eager as our little boat eased off from shore and the swift current caught it. We were around the bend in a few seconds. Going through was just like having an automobile accident. It was a blur—over so quickly I never caught any details at all. I only know that even right in the middle of it, I was let down, for it wasn't bad at all.

Our friend walked on down to us, and we started on. I'm afraid we disappointed Nevills, for two or three times he said, "I'm telling you, twenty-five per cent of the people who make this trip are scared speechless." And later he said, "You two are the only newspapermen who have ever shot rapids on either the San Juan or the Colorado. The rest are scared." Maybe I'm making this sound as if we were too brave. Just wait.

The afternoon was tame. The sun grew hotter, and the rapids down below were milder. For long stretches we floated on smooth water. We all got sleepy. Finally we came to the bluff above which sits Mexican Hat. Nevills started calling, hoping his family would hear and send the car and trailer down for us to the landing, another mile downstream. He yelled a weird, half-musical "Moo-hoo!" over and over again. And then he sang little nautical chanteys, made up as he went along. "Three men in a boat, yo ho, sailors three. Ahoy, we're home. Come and get us."

"We're almost there," he said to us. "Just one more little rapids, if you want to call it a rapids. Gyp Creek. Doesn't amount to anything."

We were bored with small rapids by now. We hardly paid any attention. We hurt from five hours of sitting on a board seat. It had been a swell day, but we were ready to quit.

And suddenly we saw what we were in for. Nevills saw it at the same time, but it was too late. Gyp Creek rapids, usually placid, had turned into a maelstrom. We were caught, and going like the wind. The roar ahead of us was terrifying. The sand-laden waves reared up ahead of us like a painting of a furious sea. Nevills was magnificent. He didn't sing this time—he was working too fast. He turned us, switched us, played the boat through those waves as though he was fingering piano keys. But we hit a hole. It was a terrific smack, like dropping down a roller-coaster and then ramming a blank wall. The water came over our heads in a great swoop. Boy, it was cold! It knocked off the dashboard in front of us, which was fastened on with long screws. It threw us off balance, but we held on.

The boat came up a third full of water, and logy. We grabbed the cans and started bailing. Nevills jerked off his sun helmet and bailed with it, a gallon at a time. We were soaked to our ears. But we were joyous, elated. We felt as though someone had handed us a million dollars. What a dramatic surprise! And what an end to a perfect day!

Within two minutes we were at the little landing. The water squished deliciously in our shoes as we stepped onto the safe white sand.

Wonder if that guy can really row a boat? we had thought the night before. Haw, haw, haw! Could he row a boat? By the Horny-handed Oarsman on the River known as Styx, that guy could row a boat!

Harry Goulding was a good old cowboy who had everything whipped right down and tied in a hard knot. He had simply retired on the desert, there in Monument Valley along the Utah-

Arizona line, without waiting to make his fortune first. He was so far away from anything else that his home was on the road map. Yet he had running water and electric lights. And I don't suppose there was anybody in America who ate better.

How did it all happen? Well: "Me and another old boy come ridin' through here with a pack outfit in 1920. And when I saw this valley I said to myself, if they's ever a chance to throw my hat on one of these rocks, I'm gonna do it." The chance came in 1924. The valley was opened to homesteading, and Harry threw his hat on a square mile. He was the only one, I guess, who bothered to file a claim. His hat had been on that rock now for fifteen years. It had grown into an oasis that you probably couldn't have bought for thirty thousand dollars. Goulding made his living from his trading post and his few guest cabins, by taking visitors through Monument Valley in a car with big air wheels that would go anywhere, and by taking pack parties deep into almost unexplored country.

He looked kind of ageless, but probably was around forty. His wife was called "Mike," and she was nice. Their home was a real home.

Goulding was a cowboy type if I ever saw one. Tall and skinny as a rail. When he squatted to talk, with his back against a wall, he folded up so perfectly he looked like a letter "N" squeezed tight. Talked slow and easy and very low. Rolled cigarettes out of corn papers, and held them long after they went out. Wore a big hat and overalls, and a black kerchief around his neck, held with a silver Indian clasp. He spoke Navajo, and could wait just as long to speak as an Indian could. I doubt that he had had much formal education, but he used surprisingly apt words, colorful and meaningful.

He was full of wonderful little philosophies. He talked cowboy talk that would have warmed the heart of a dude. I suspect he preened it a little on purpose, but it sure sounded good. For example, after calling him "Mr. Goulding" a while, I asked him his first name. "Harry," he said, "and I handle better that way, too. That Mr. Goulding kind of throws me."

Goulding was a sort of rail-fence Chamber of Commerce for Monument Valley. He had been trying for fifteen years to let the world know about this spot, and he was making headway. He was responsible for having the movie *Stagecoach* filmed in Monument Valley, some of it right there on the flats in front of his house. When he heard they were going to make a film of that type, he drove to Hollywood, and stayed there three days. Didn't get kicked around much, either. He sold them on Monument Valley.

The little group of buildings that formed the Goulding home was like a few grains of sand lying in the corner of a room. On two sides of the house, a solid rock wall, sleek and bare and brown, rose straight up for eight hundred feet. It was an immense butte— one of those gigantic ghosts left standing after the millions of centuries had eroded the valley out from around it. Goulding built his home in a nook of this butte, high on a slope of crumbling rock and soil. From his front porch you could see sixty-five miles straight ahead. And if you turned a little to the left, you could see mountains a hundred twenty-five miles away. But even that didn't satisfy Harry Goulding. He wanted to build a house right on top of the butte where you could see at least a hundred miles from every window. Up there you would be isolated to extinction— especially if you wandered off the rim of the butte some night in your sleep. But the Goulding home, as was, satisfied me. It had a fireplace set with petrified-wood inlays, and beautiful desert paintings by artists who had been out there. And books and desert doodads, and everywhere the gentle, softening Navajo rugs. I counted nineteen in one room.

Next day Harry took us down through Monument Valley, and on into the Valley of Tsay-Bege. He took us in his car with the big air wheels—the car he could drive right over the tops of sand dunes without getting stuck. Monument Valley is a vast depression, some sixty by thirty miles, and it is all Navajo Indian reservation. It is called Monument Valley because in it stand hundreds of monumental stone formations. Name almost anything you want, and you'll find its likeness there. You can see a great medieval castle, or the United States Treasury, or a mule lying on its back with its feet up, or the profile of Joseph Smith the Mormon, or a figure of the Pioneer Woman, or a totem pole, or a pair of mittens. Distances and shapes are deceptive amidst all that space. You can hardly credit the statement that the castle stands fourteen hundred feet high above the surrounding flats, and that on its level top you could build a whole city. Most extraordinary of all, to me, was the Totem Pole—a solid shaft of rock, sticking straight up out of the desert for more than seven hundred feet. It stands there all alone, fantastic, impossible. To me, it is one of the Seven Wonders of America, and offhand I can't think what the other six are.

There are scores of great natural bridges. There are vast caves, where the Navajo shepherds herd their flocks for refuge. There are weird sand spouts rising into the air. There are crude ruins of Indian homes a thousand years old. There are sounds, and unearthly presences. Harry Goulding could stand and shout a cowboy whoop, and it would come back many-voiced, from all sides, again and again, like a surrounding enemy. You would come around the rocky pinnacle of a butte, and there under the cliff would be a wood-and-mud hut, and darting through the door a dark-skinned woman in vividly colored dress, and all around would be sheep and goats grazing and bleating—almost as close to ten centuries ago as the dark shepherds of the Persian deserts. The sight of a camel would have surprised you less than the fact that you didn't see one.

You see and know only a few of these things if you drive just the main north-and-south road across the valley. And yet you must not venture off this road in your own car; they might be days finding you. The only way to go is with Harry Goulding. Even if it was possible to drive in and out by yourself, still the only way to go is with Harry Goulding, for he is almost a spiritual sexton of Monument Valley, and he transfers his love for it to you.

Harry stopped the car in a peaceful little valley-within-a-valley. We walked a hundred yards, and stopped before a pile of brush. "This man was a friend of mine," Harry said. "He was a leader among the Indians. See what they sent with him." There were the bones of a horse. "They knocked the horse in the head," he said, "so its spirit could escape and go with the old man." And there was a coffeepot, with a hole in the bottom. "They knocked the coffeepot in the head," Goulding said. "And the saddle too. Everything was knocked in the head, so its spirit could go with the old man." The things were lying all around there in the sand among the sage bushes. This wasn't a museum, or a storybook, or a legend. This was genuine, right there at our feet, genuine as life and death.

"I don't know of anything better than being buried out here," said Harry Goulding. "I wouldn't mind if they'd put me right alongside the old man. I got a few nice things to take along. We could join up when we got up there. We'd have a horse and saddle and coffeepot, and we'd knock my car in the head and take it along."

The Navajos, the biggest tribe of Indians in America, are a pastoral people, constantly moving with their sheep and cattle and horses. They do little farming; they have no towns, or even permanent homes. Wherever they go they build new houses, or *hogans,* which are round, one-room huts made of logs and brush and chinked with mud. The Navajos still stick to the beliefs and customs of old. When a Navajo dies in his house, it is never used again. The family smashes in the back of the house, and there it stands, sacred and taboo, till it falls down. Sometimes white men tear down the ruins and use the logs for firewood. The Indians don't object, but they won't go into a house heated by that wood. You can build yourself a campfire with some logs from a deserted hogan and boil some coffee. The Indians will sit at a distance and watch you, and there will be no hard feelings. But they won't think of getting close enough to absorb any of the heat from that fire, and they won't drink a cup of the coffee boiled over it.

The Navajos, who numbered about fifty thousand in 1939 and were increasing, occupy a reservation that is roughly a hundred miles square. Most of it is in Arizona, but it extends into Utah and New Mexico. It is a sparse, dry land, and you ask as you travel through it, "How in the world does anybody make a living here?" Yet life can be abundant on what appears to the untrained eye an utter waste. The Navajos run large flocks of sheep, and we were constantly startled by the fatness of the sheep and the butter-ball condition of the horses. But still the Navajos are poor. They don't even have enough to eat, we were told, and they are susceptible to tuberculosis because of undernourishment.

They need a more extensive market for the things they have to sell. Navajo ponies, for instance, are the prettiest little pieces of horseflesh you ever saw—good-natured, wiry, and tough as steel. The Navajos are overrun with horses; in fact, people told me that a Navajo measures his wealth by the number of horses he has, even though he doesn't have use for more than a couple. Consequently the ranges are full of Navajo ponies, eating their heads off and doing nobody the slightest good. The government had started a horse-reduction program, to free the sparse ranges for the Navajos' sheep, but the Indians didn't like it. Just before the program started, a horse buyer came through a certain section, offering ten and twelve dollars a head. He didn't get many because the Indians wouldn't sell. But in a few weeks they had to sell those same horses for two dollars a head, to be made into fertilizer and dog food.

The rest of America doesn't know anything about Navajo horses. A good high-powered press agent could have this country buying thousands of Navajo ponies every year—if the Indians would condescend to sell—and he could run the price up to a fancy fifty dollars a head, instead of two dollars for dog food.

That isn't all a press agent could do. He could sell America on Navajo rugs. The Southwest is fully conscious of their beauty, and you seldom go into a white home there without finding it filled with Navajo rugs. But aside from this, and a few tourists, Navajo rugs have no real market. As one trader said, anybody in the United States who can afford a nice home could well do with an Indian room in it; not because he's Indian-crazy, but simply because a room of Navajo rugs and Indian trinkets is a pleasant room, a room of softness and grace.

All Navajo rugs are made by the women, from the wool of the sheep the Navajos raise, and they could make a lot more of them than they do. The designs all mean something in Indian tradition. And it's absolutely against the gods for a woman ever to make two rugs alike. The most prominent of the Navajo symbols is the swastika. They tell a story of a new clerk in an Indian trading post who sent back in high dudgeon a bunch of blankets that had swastikas on them. Either he was fired or he should have been. The swastika was a Navajo emblem centuries before Hitler thought of it.

When a rug is finished, the Indian man gets on his horse, rides to a trading post, bargains with the trader, arrives at a price, and takes that much out in supplies. The tourists never buy rugs direct from the Indians. All the rugs in the fancy shops in Albuquerque and Gallup and Flagstaff have first come through the hands of traders. And, like oranges in California, you find the poorest selection of rugs right out where they're made. The best ones are shipped off for sale in the cities.

It takes a lot of time to trade with an Indian. He'll sit and think all day. He'll ride in for thirty miles to trade off a three-dollar rug. He'll hang around two or three days and nights while the dickering goes on. He'll ride another fifty miles to get an extra dime.

It'll be a long time before the desert is spoiled, in the sense of becoming a mecca for tourists. It is Indian reservation, and the government has no notion of putting in hard roads for sightseers. And ninety-nine tourists out of a hundred, when they see "dirt road" on the map, go elsewhere.

But desert accommodations are superb. You'll have coal-oil lamps and a bowl and pitcher in many places, but the beds are fine and everything is clean. You'll eat right at the table with the folks you spend the night with, and you'll discover human beings again, more than likely. You'll find yourself sleeping like a log and eating like a horse.

It's perfectly safe for anybody to go through that country, if he is prepared; it's not unusual for women to drive through alone. If you want to, you can drive straight through the area in two days, but if you do, you might as well stay home. The only way to feel the country is to pause in it; sit on a rock and don't worry about getting up; lie around as long as there's anybody to talk to. After a few days you'll find it's possible not even to wonder in the evening what happened in the outside world that day. I'm not one of those isolationist fanatics who think everything can be solved by seeing, hearing, and knowing nothing. But in the desert it's likely to occur to you that our daily lives in the cities are full of seeing, hearing, and worrying over a great many things that are of no damn consequence whatever.

The friend who made the trip with me was E. H. Shaffer, editor of the Albuquerque *Tribune*. Although Albuquerque itself is in the heart of dry country, he had never seen anything like the desert before; he fell in love with it. For the first time in twenty years he wasn't worrying about the next edition, or what the world was coming to. In fact, it was sort of startling to see how much this country and its spirit affected us both. We felt that somehow we belonged out there, and that nowhere else could be so satisfying. And when we came back into so-called civilization, we were so mad we could have bitten all the tourists in two. Pavement never felt so unwelcome, even after nearly a thousand miles of rough, dusty road. A few miles from Tuba City, Arizona, we could see black smoke coming out of a big chimney. My friend pointed and said, "Ugh! White man smoke. Me no like. Ugh!" And when we drew up at the nice lodge and coffee shop in Cameron, Arizona (and Cameron, itself, is just a crossroads), and saw all the cars with various state licenses, and all the smooth-road tourists in their fancy clothes, we were so smug and contemptuous that we could have been shot for our thoughts.

Some National Parks

Chapter **M**ESA VERDE PARK, IN SOUTHWESTERN COLORADO,
XXVIII is one of America's national parks in which my interest had always been at a white-hot standstill. But, like a lot of other smart
alecks, I didn't know what I was missing. You don't have to be a
steeplejack to enjoy Mesa Verde Park, but it helps. This region
is cut up with canyons about half a mile wide and a thousand
feet deep. On each side the wall is straight up and down for a few
hundred feet. Then it slants off, making a V bottom to the canyon.

When the Indians lived there in caves a thousand years ago,
the hardest cave to get to was the best one to live in, because of
prowling enemies. So the caves were usually from fifty to two
hundred feet below the rim of a canyon. Two trails led from each
cave—one to the flat and fertile mesa above, where they did their
farming, and the other down into the canyon bottom, where they
had to go for water. You could still see many of these old trails.
Most of them were steep and treacherous—just tiny footholds in
the rocky cliffsides. Many new trails had been built by the park
people, but in places they were primitive enough to make you
wish you were either an Indian or else home in bed. You had to
climb ladders set against perpendicular walls, toe-hold across
slanting cliff faces holding onto a chain, crawl through tunnels,
look back down at hundreds of feet of space below you. This was
all perfectly safe if you had a good heart and didn't get dizzy—in
other words, if you didn't fall off. There had been a number of
broken arms and legs in small falls at Mesa Verde, though no one
had yet been killed in a fall. We modern tourists needn't be
ashamed if we have a touch of cliffside jaundice now and then, for

the Indians themselves often came a cropper. The Rangers said they had found dozens of battered skeletons at the bottoms of those old trails, indicating that Indians had fallen and been killed.

Thanks to a scientist named Dr. A. E. Douglass at the Steward Observatory in Tucson, Arizona, the Rangers of Mesa Verde can tell you the very year an Indian dwelling was built, even if it was a thousand years ago. Dr. Douglass' forte was not archaeology, but weather. In the 1920s he worked out a sort of history of weather, based on the rings in the cross sections of trees. In wet years trees grow fast, and so the rings are thick; in dry years they are narrow. In the rings of just one old tree he could find a yearly weather record for two hundred years back. Well, he got to using logs in old houses, in order to push his weather records further back into the past. He made charts showing what kind of weather this region had as far back as the year 1000. And then one day it dawned upon him that he had the key to something the archaeologists had been seeking for years. As simply as falling off a log, he could go up and date those Mesa Verde ruins. And he did.

There is no guesswork about it. The science of tree-ring dating is as exact as the science of fingerprinting. The Rangers explain it to visitors, but they say they just can't make the public understand. So I guess I'll take a whack at it. Say we go out and cut down a big tree. We study the rings on the stump. The outside ring (anybody knows this) grew only last year, so we count the rings inward. Let's say, to make it easy, there are exactly two hundred. That means the tree sprouted and began growing two hundred years ago. By the time the rings are photographed and the pictures are enlarged, you can see as much difference between the rings of two seasons as between two thumbprints. Furthermore, any tree of the same type and from the same area will show the very same weather differences. The ring grown in 1848 will be the same on all trees of that species.

All right, we've got rings for two hundred years back. Now let's go into an old mission and saw off the end of a ceiling beam. We study these rings. And now let's say, to make it easy again, that we find the thirty outer rings of this beam show up exactly the same as the thirty inner rings on the tree we have just cut down ourselves. That would mean that the tree in the old mission was cut down just thirty years after the tree in our yard started growing. If the tree in our yard began growing in 1738, and if these two trees overlapped by thirty years, then the log in our old mission house was cut in 1768. So we count its rings toward the inside, and find that it was three hundred years old when it was cut. That means it started growing in 1468. Right in those two trees we have a weather record and a year record for four hundred seventy years.

Dr. Douglass, by sawing off beam ends in old houses and missions and Indian ruins all over the Southwest, had carried his tree-ring datings back to the year A.D. 11. A log was found in Mesa Verde Park that had started growing when Christ was eleven years old. They were still looking for old logs, and they expected Dr. Douglass to plunge into B.C. almost any time.

The new mummy and I arrived at Mesa Verde the same day. Fortunately I had a White House press card in my pocket, so the scientists had little trouble distinguishing between us.

It was, they said, the finest mummy ever found in America. It had been discovered by Carnegie scientists in a cave over near Durango, some forty miles east of Mesa Verde. The Carnegie people studied it all winter, and then gave it to Mesa Verde Museum. It arrived by express, in a big wooden box marked "This Side Up." Ranger Don Watson, the park's naturalist, invited me to the uncrating.

Don pried off the top board and then started taking out wadded-up newspapers by the score. About halfway down we came to the mummy. "Well, there's Susie," Watson said. He lifted her out and put her on the carpenter's workbench. Then we spent half an hour just standing around and peering at her. She was as dry and hard as petrified wood, in such a perfect state of preservation, after hundreds of years, that she practically turned your stomach.

The mummies found in America are not like those of Egypt. The Egyptians prepared the bodies and then wrapped them round and round with cloth. All our Indians did was just drag the dear departed to the back of the cave and leave her there amidst the trash. The thin, dry air did the rest. The body simply dried up.

Susie's legs were drawn up against her stomach, for that was the burial custom at the time. Her toes and fingers looked as natural as though she had died just a little while ago. Her hair was brownish-black, cut in a sort of boyish bob. She was about twenty when she died, and she was a buxom lass, with an enormous chest. It's a good thing the Indians didn't have clocks in those days, for Susie's face would have stopped them all. I believe she would have stopped a sundial. Apparently she had died a horrible death, for her tongue was curled up over her upper teeth, as though she was biting it in pain, and her expression was one of agony. But there were no marks to indicate violence.

We put Susie on a set of kitchen scales. She now weighed sixteen pounds. In her heyday she had probably tipped the beam at a hundred forty. Don carried her up to his office and put her on top of his desk, and stood and looked at her. "Here I've been waiting for this moment for months," he said. "And now that we've got her she's so hideous I hate to put her on exhibition."

Next morning I peeked in the museum window and Susie was still lying there on the desk, as nonchalant as a paperweight. She hadn't got any better looking during the night.

Most people think the Grand Canyon is in Colorado. Used to think so myself. Don't know where we get that idea—I suppose because the canyon is made by the Colorado River. But it is wholly in Arizona.

The Grand Canyon really is a whopper. When you stand at the big lodge on the North Rim, you are only fourteen miles from the hotel on the South Rim. Yet if you want to drive over there, you have to drive two hundred fifteen miles around the east end of the canyon, or six hundred eighteen miles around the west end, over Boulder Dam. And if you send a letter from one rim to the other, it takes four days to get there. But you can cross the canyon in two days by muleback. It cost thirty dollars when I was there, and for that you got a mule, a guide, your meals, and overnight lodging at Phantom Ranch in the bottom of the canyon. I had thought of taking this trip myself, but two things stopped me—the thirty dollars and fright.

"Is the trail scary?" I asked the man at the lodge desk.

"No, it isn't scary," he said. "Of course, there are stretches where you look straight down for a thousand feet. But the trail is eight feet wide, and you couldn't push a mule off with a locomotive."

My great worry was not over the mule's staying on the trail, but about my staying on the mule. I decided to wait till I got braver.

The North Rim of the canyon is a different world from the South Rim. It is a thousand feet higher—about eighty-five hundred feet above sea level. It's chilly all summer long. There are no nights when you don't sleep under blankets and shiver in the evening.

I liked the North Rim better, though. It wasn't so crowded. The great central lodge run by the Union Pacific was magnificent, but you didn't have that Coney Island feeling you got on the South Rim. True, the view of the canyon from the North Rim is not so good as from the South. But to me the North Rim was a place where you wouldn't mind spending a vacation, while on the South Rim my impulse was to look and move on.

Most people don't know it, but there is a tribe of Indians living right in the bottom of Grand Canyon—the Havasupais. There are about two hundred of them, I was told. As I understood it, they were chased down there by bad Indians back in the 1880s and had never come out. A white Indian agent stayed down there with them. I asked an old cowboy about them—whether they were smart or not. He was the kind of man who would never say anything bad about anybody. He said, "Well, I'd say they're about average. Yes, just about average." Meaning, I judge, that there weren't any Einsteins down there.

There is something very ironic about Zion National Park, in Utah. The government spent a million dollars to build a road so people could get in to see the park, and the road turned out to be more wonderful than the park. It's the truth. That road is so marvelous that the park is an anticlimax. It took them, if I remember, three years to build it. It goes through a tunnel more than a mile long, which slopes all the way and has curves in it. Every once in a while they've blasted out a big cave in the side of the tunnel, leading to outdoors, where you can pull over your car and look out. The road cuts off scores of miles of driving, and it enables you to see Bryce Canyon and Zion Park and Grand Canyon all in a day, instead of hanging around a while and appreciating them as you should.

Zion Park relieved me of a queer obsession. You know, there are some scientists who spend all their time worrying about the world's running out of oil, and others fret about the eventual exhaustion of all our coal. Still others spend a lifetime stewing over the day when our forests will all be gone. Well, I'm like that, only I have a field all to myself. I have always worried about running out of rock. I've caught myself sitting straight up in bed at night, screaming, "My God, we're out of rock!" But now my worries are over. In one day we saw enough rock to keep all the armies and contractors and little boys of the whole world in rock till the end of time. There are whole mountains of solid rock. And I don't mean big, rough-looking rock covered with trees and gullies and dirt, like the Canadian Rockies; I mean just bare, slick, clean, hard rock—as far as you could see, nothing at all but rock. The slopes and the valleys and even the creek beds are solid rock. You could drive for miles and not see two bucketfuls of dirt.

Bryce Canyon, in Utah, is a sort of Carlsbad Cavern outdoors. You stand on the rim of a precipice and look down into a valley covered with a forest of tall and erratically carved stone spires, rising as high as five hundred feet. They look like gigantic stone tree trunks without limbs, or like a solar pipe organ, or ten thousand pink flagpoles. Or they look like what you see if somebody hits you on the head with a mallet. All these poles have weird knots and projections and toppieces. It is probably the best spot in the world for sitting and picking out images, better than seeing faces in clouds or in fireplaces. You can find a camel, or William Jennings Bryan.

The finest time for looking is just before sundown. Then the dark shadows of those thousands of spires reach across each other, and they make a scene of such chaotic fantasy that you just have to stand there and look till the light is gone.

The bus from Sun Chalet in Glacier Park, Montana, to the top of Logan Pass was full of Easterners making one of those circle tours before reboarding their train to go on to the coast. The man sitting next to me asked where I was going, and I told him with great casualness that I was just starting out to walk to Canada. He seemed impressed. He must have told the other passengers after I got off, for ten minutes later, when I was well on the trail and hundreds of feet above the highway, the bus came along below me and every passenger in that open-topped bus stood up and waved and waved at the little figure way up there on the trail—the brave little figure on his way to Canada.

It was a warm morning, pleasant for walking. About an hour later I met a man in green slacks and a woman with a handkerchief around her head, walking very rapidly. We exchanged curt hellos in passing. Those were the only human beings I saw all day. But the mountains were full of woodchucks and gophers and, as I climbed higher, of marmots. The squeak and whistle of the gophers and the marmots was almost constant.

Glacier is my favorite of all the national parks. With the exception of Carlsbad Caverns, I wouldn't trade one square mile of Glacier for all the other parks put together. The vast valleys that you look down into, and the unbelievably great peaks and ridges rising above you, and the hidden passes, and the surprising banks of snow, and the incongruous meadows on the high flats, and the tumbling white streams, and the flowers and the silent little lakes around a bend—all have an isolation and a calm majesty that to me make Glacier Park more than just a place.

The spots where you spend the nights are almost the best parts of a walking trip through Glacier Park. Granite Park Chalet, where I spent my first night, was a log house with rooms upstairs and three or four units of cabin-rooms in rows out back. You could get there only by walking or on horseback. And that night the entire guest clientele consisted of myself.

Miss Patricia Whitwell said yes, indeed, I could have a hot

bath. In a few minutes I saw her hurrying up the outside stairs carrying an old-fashioned tin washtub. Then she made trip after trip with porcelain jars, and she carried up a teakettle of boiling water for the finishing touch. It was the first time in more than twenty years I had bathed in a washtub. And I'll bet that Mahatma Gandhi and I are the only two men in the world who can sit right square down in the bottom of a tin washtub, feet and all.

After dinner Miss Irene Eldred, the manager of the chalet, said to me, "We've been reading out loud every evening to entertain ourselves. Would you like to join us?" I said sure. We all gathered closely around the stove. The wind howled louder and louder, the doors rattled, and we had to poke in firewood frequently. They were reading *Prologue to Glory*, out of one of Burns Mantle's collections of best plays. Miss Eldred asked if I wouldn't do the reading, but I told her I had never been to school. So Edison Spriggs, the woodchopper and all-around boy, did it. He read well, without self-consciousness. He put laughs and tears and great feeling into his reading, and when Ann Rutledge died and Abe Lincoln was suffering, we suffered too.

We stopped a few times during the evening's reading. Once when Edison upset the gasoline lamp and scared us all stiff. A couple of times to listen in on the party line and hear how the new forest fire was getting along. Once when Mrs. Eisenman went out and got great dishes of ice cream that she and Patty Whitwell, the waitress and all-around girl, had made by stirring it with a spoon in a bucket set in the last unmelted block of snow back of the chalet. And once when the mousetrap went off in the kitchen.

Next morning the wind was blowing so ferociously and it was so cold that Irene Eldred wanted me to stay over. That tin stove full of roaring wood was an awful temptress, but then I thought, After all, am I mouse or man? It was with great reluctance that I discarded the pleasant mouse theory. But two little sweaters might as well have been mere handkerchiefs wrapped around me. So Miss Eldred lent me her leather jacket, and said to leave it at Fifty Mountain Tent Camp—they'd send it back by the first pack train. I was glad I had it, for the trail hung along a steep mountainside raked by the wind that came roaring out of the vast valley below. The backs of my hands turned blue.

When you walk through the Rockies it is not often you can see your trail very far ahead. You approach each bend with the excitement of an explorer, never knowing what vast scene will be revealed. It was around one of those bends that I came upon Ahern Pass and Ahern Snowbank. One minute I was walking along level, on an easy trail across a gentle slope, and the next I was looking down hundreds of feet over sheer cliff. There was really no danger. The trail was six or eight feet wide. You'd have had to have St. Vitus's dance to jitter yourself over the side. Yet one cowboy I know, who has ridden every foot of Glacier Park, told me Ahern Ledge scared him worse than any other place in the park. The first time he crossed it, he was riding a horse that was blind in one eye. It happened to be the outside eye, and the cowboy said that horse tried to see how close to the edge it could walk.

So far as I knew, there had never been an accident at Ahern Pass. But there had been one recently at Swift Current Pass, east of there. At one place, they told me, the trail wound crookedly along the ledge, and it was straight up and straight down for hundreds of feet. A long string of horses was being deadheaded up into the park, roped together according to park regulations. Well, the last horse in the string reared or something, lost its footing, and plunged over the side. One by one, it dragged the other horses over after it. The cowboy saved himself and the top-horse only by quickly cutting the rope. Five horses went over. They dropped hundreds of feet before they struck. It was heartbreaking to hear their cries as they went down. When they finally hit, they were, mercifully, killed instantly.

Just beyond Ahern Ledge was the snowbank. It was about a block wide, and it stood on end at better than a 45-degree angle. The trail builders had hacked and dug a path across it. Right in the middle of the crossing I thought, "Cutting this path has weakened the whole bank. My weight will break it loose, and the whole thing will go sliding and roaring down the valley, with me in it." Later some cowboys said, no, it was packed and frozen as hard as concrete. It would be there all summer. But I was glad to put my feet on solid earth again on the other side.

In the northern end of Glacier Park it is just like being in Alaska: the weather is chilly even in August, you are isolated, people are few, and everybody knows everybody else. The occasional traveler is the only line of communication between camps. At one camp you discuss the people at other camps and the people on the trail ahead of you. You know that Willie Bennett lost the bacon from his supply train and you know who found it; you'll recognize the Franger party from San Francisco when you meet them; you know the dudes have had to help chop wood at one camp; you know Indian Joe is coming up the trail today, leading a horse. And, as in Alaska, it gives a tenderfoot tremendous satisfaction to walk into a strange and faraway camp and put his feet up by the stove, and know exactly who is meant when a name is spoken, and even himself add a little spot of gossip.

Fifty Mountain Tent Camp was the most isolated of all the Glacier Park camps. As at Granite, I was the lone guest at Fifty Mountain. Just me and Willie Bennett, the supply-train cowboy, and the staff of three women and a young man. After supper we lit the gasoline lamp, and kept throwing wood in the tin stove in the main tent, and sat there joshing and talking. Viola Marti, the cook—who normally was a school executive in Minneapolis—knew how to tell fortunes with coffee grounds. So we had a fortunetelling evening. She got pretty personal with Willie and me, too. She told me that I didn't take long hikes because I enjoyed the physical sensation of walking, but because I liked to be out alone. And that was true. She said that as I walked I did a great deal of daydreaming. That was right too, I guess, for when I walk alone I am quite a hero. Oh, I win auto races, and have movie actresses after me, and come back from the wars very sad-looking and with one arm shot off, and my column runs in seven hundred papers, and even the savages in darkest Africa know who I am. And out there on Ahern Pass there hadn't been a soul to tell me I was a damn liar.

And she said that, mainly, walking gave me a great sense of power. And I guess maybe it does, though perhaps a better word would be superiority. I love to be able to do things my friends

· 418 ·

can't do, and not many of my friends could walk a dozen miles a day over those rocky trails for two, three, and four days.

Those who are thrilled by wild animal life would love those tent camps. Each one sets out a salt cake, and at sundown there'll be half a dozen deer just outside the tent door, licking at the salt. That night at Fifty, all night long, a dozen deer were leaping and playing around within a few feet of my tent. Their hoofs made sharp thuds on the hard ground. And you could hear the coyotes yipping and howling on distant ridges. And down at the corral, a porcupine was gnawing on one of Willie Bennett's saddles, thrown across the corral fence, though, of course, you couldn't hear that. And the bear—oh, yes, the bear. They had quite a bear at Fifty Mountain Camp. Every night he would come around and help himself to something. One night he ate all the butter.

The Colossal Pyle Walking Expedition from the United States to the Dominion of Canada arrived in the little village of Waterton Lakes, Alberta, at 2:27 P.M. Not a soul even looked up. The expedition had covered some fifty miles in four days and nights. While actually on the trails it had averaged the sizzling speed of two miles an hour. The expedition arrived without a single blister on its heels, and with one Hershey bar left over. The expedition's homemade knapsack—homemade by That Girl —not only worked perfectly but was the object of much admiring comment all along the way.

Expedition Leader Pyle was in high spirits over the completion of the hazardous journey. "Hurrah!" he said. His face was gaunt, and there wasn't much hair on top of his head. Just before disbanding the expedition (which consisted of changing its socks), Leader Pyle declared everything a complete success. With true exploratory spirit, he declined to take any credit for himself. "Our brilliant crossing of the Rockies into this charming land," he told a bootblack in Waterton Lakes, "was due solely to the fine spirit of co-operation and sacrifice on the part of my two legs. Without those legs, we would never have got here."

I walked into a rustic little hotel at Waterton Lakes with my pack on my back. The lady at the desk was very British. I knew she would be impressed when she found how far I had walked. She would be proud to have me aboard, sir, I knew. So I registered smugly, and didn't say a word, just letting my dusty overalls and my tanned and weary countenance spray their full import upon her. She looked at the register card.

"Oh," she said eagerly, "did you walk from Washington, D.C.?"

Up in Glacier there's a mountain called Triple Divide Peak. From its snows, three different rivulets start trickling down its sides. Farther down they become leaping mountain streams, white and silvery and roaring. And of those three streams, one eventually flows into the Gulf of Mexico, one into Hudson Bay, and one into the Pacific Ocean!

Some of you may wonder why, in all this park visiting that summer, we didn't go to Yellowstone. The answer is—we did. We got in there at six o'clock in the evening, everything went wrong, we got sore as boils, and left at eight o'clock next morning. Yellowstone was too popular for us.

Down the
West Coast

Chapter
XXIX THE ROGUE RIVER IS MANY THINGS. IT IS A TREACH-
erous and bounding mountain stream which runs through one
of our few remaining frontiers; it is a fisherman's paradise; and
it is the path of one of the oddest mail routes in America, from
Gold Beach on the Oregon coast up to Agness, thirty-two miles
inland. For years Indians carried the mail up the river. They had
to pole their boats through the slower riffles and drag them
around the bigger rapids. First it took as long as three days;
finally they got it cut down to one long day. Then about 1930
the government called for bids on round-trip daily service. The
Indians' equipment wasn't fast enough, so the contract fell to a
man named Roy Carter.

Carter built special boats that were rugged and fast and could
do twenty-eight miles an hour. They were really homemade
speedboats—open-topped, wide-bellied, flat-bottomed, with big
Buick engines in their open holds. He rigged up a rear-end apparatus by which the propeller could be raised in shallow rapids.
The boats could carry sixteen people, or, with the seats removed,
a caterpillar tractor.

The line had seven boats in 1939, and there had been times
when all seven made the round trip every day for weeks on end.
They hauled in all the heavy steelwork for a big suspension
bridge near Agness. They hauled up a complete CCC camp. It
was the most isolated camp in America, but it worked itself out
by building a road over the mountains for thirty-seven miles
to the north. Now you could get from Gold Beach to Agness
either in two hours by boat or by driving all day over rough

· 421 ·

roads for one hundred fifty miles. Most people took the boat.

The boats ran all winter, rain or shine, making about twenty mail stops on the way up. They just slid along the bank, threw out a sack for somebody in the woods, and roared on without really stopping. At one place there was a dog that met the boat every day and carried the mail sack in its mouth back to its master. Tom Fry, a Rogue Indian, was the pilot on the boat that took me to Agness. Passengers sat behind a windshield on board seats in the bow, with freight and mail piled behind them. And in the stern stood Tom, one hand on his rudder-wheel, one on the throttle. He was always peering ahead. The boat plowed through riffles of green water that leaped and lashed themselves into whiteness, and ground slowly over rocks that crunched against the bottom. The water was so shallow that you could reach down and grab a stone from the bottom. We roared through torrents that in some places were rushing downstream at fifteen miles an hour. We saw lovely summer cabins, and gardens fenced off to keep out the deer. We saw goats sunning on the rocks, and at the right time you'd probably see bear. Ducks and graceful cranes were common. High-booted fishermen might be standing in midriver as we swung round a bend, but they would be out of our way, for they could hear the roar of our motor ten minutes before we got there.

Just after we passed through one shallow rapids, our boat vibrated and rattled all over, and Tom Fry throttled down the engine. We all looked back. Tom was unconcerned. He said, "I hit my wheel. It don't go so good now." That was an understatement. It not only didn't go so good—it didn't go at all. Tom meant that the propeller had hit a rock and was bent. We drifted over to the bank, and he poled the boat in. He jumped out into water above his knees without taking off his shoes or rolling up his pants. He felt around in the water, found a big rock and, holding it against the propeller, pounded on the blade with a hammer. We were soon on our way again.

At another narrow rapids, the leaping waves threw us over into sidewater so shallow that the boat grounded. We looked back again, full of concern. Tom gave a couple of grunts and said,

"Didn't make it that time, did we?" We drifted back fifty yards, took another shot, and made it.

A confirmed fisherman is one of the world's weirdest animals. He is usually a businessman who sits in an office fifty weeks of the year. He has a secretary and a family and a nice home; he is comfortable and demands comfort. And then he goes up to Agness—or to any one of a thousand such places—to fish for a week or two. He drags himself out of a cold bed before daylight and dresses by coal-oil light. He shivers into old damp clothes, and over them he pulls a cumbersome pair of "waders," or high-waisted rubber pants. He walks sleepily for a mile or two, goes a mile or two in a boat, then steps out into the ice-cold water and stands there in it. From daylight till noon he walks around on the rocks, waist-deep in water. He bruises his tender feet on the stones; his soft muscles grow weary and constrict with pain; he casts out and reels in, casts out and reels in, like a robot. And when he stops at noon he has had only one little bite, and that one got away. He repeats the performance in the afternoon. By the time he gets in at dark, it is dankly cold. He eats supper and listens to the radio a few minutes, then goes to bed to try to get warm.

The only comfortable thing about his whole experience at a fishing camp is the marvelous food they serve. All the rest is chill, wet, weariness, monotony, and disappointment. Yet such is the philosophy of the fisherman that he wouldn't trade it for a palace and two yachts. I consider a fisherman a screwball, and a fisherman considers me an ignorant fool.

The fishing guides at Agness told horrible stories about people getting fishhooks embedded in their flesh. One fellow got a hook deep in his upper lip. The guide held his face and yanked it out with a pair of pliers. "Some meat came with it," the guide said. "The fellow winced."

Another man told how he got a hook through the end of his finger, under the nail. Up there you're far from a doctor, and he had to get out the hook all alone. "I took my old barlow knife, and just sawed down through about half an inch of flesh," he said. "I didn't think I could do it at first, but I did. It was uncomfortable."

Another fellow got a fishhook through his eyelid. It was too delicate a job for the guides to monkey with, so they put him on a boat and rushed him to Gold Beach. The doctor filed off the barb and pulled the rest out backward.

Larry Lucas, who ran the fishing camp at Agness, had got a hook right between the shoulder blades. He said it felt like a bullet. When three people insisted on fishing from the same boat, he charged them two dollars and a half extra. "And I tell them the two-fifty is just for dodging that third hook, and nothing else," he said.

One of the guides told how his two city fishermen got their lines tangled one day. The guide took the lines and started untangling them, while the fishermen held to their poles. All of a sudden one of the fishermen gave his rod a hard jerk and yanked the hook right into the guide's hand. "It was just like he had suddenly hooked a fish," the guide said. "In fact, the fellow told me later that he was daydreaming, and actually thought he had a strike. He was sorry about it."

Mr. Stuart X was the only great man the human race had ever produced. He said so himself and he wasn't lying. Mr. Stuart X, for the benefit of those who must have a man fully identified, was Henry Clifford Stuart. He changed his name years ago because he knew of at least ninety-nine other H. C. Stuarts, and didn't want to be confused with them. Once he got a check for seven hundred dollars cashed in Pocatello, Idaho, where he wasn't known at all, simply because they figured a forger wouldn't think up such an odd name.

A dozen years ago, Stuart X had decided he wanted a hideaway in the woods. He hunted the United States over from coast to coast, looking for his ideal spot. He was just about to give up and go to Canada when a drunk told him about the Rogue River country. At that time, the only way to get upstream was by a forty-mile boat trip up a narrow river full of rapids, and that suited him fine. But now the CCC had built their road in from the north. They almost built it right through his front yard, but he finally got it diverted a quarter of a mile away. He had spent seventy-five thousand dollars on this hideaway where he passed his summers. It was large and comfortable and midwestern in architecture, and the color was yellow. He had another home in Berkeley, California.

He was an immense man, tall and thick, seventy-five years old. He wasn't fat—just powerful. His head and face were large, and he had a woodsy gray beard, pointed. Around the house he wore riding pants with colored socks to his knees. Outdoors, in cap and tweed suit, he looked like a vacationing scientist. His first wife had died, and his second was a lovely woman.

He considered nearly everybody a fool, and most of his actions were the result of somebody's saying he mustn't or couldn't do something. In spite of his irascibility, he was hospitable and friendly, and he had a marvelous satirical sense of humor. He liked to talk, and swore hugely.

Stuart X had had great experiences. His personal memory went back fifty thousand years before Christ. He had been in the Garden of Eden and had met Adam and Eve. He said, "You may think I'm an egotist, but I'm not. I really am the greatest man that ever lived. Because I know everything."

He was born in Brooklyn. Much of his life had been spent in Central and South America; Spanish was practically a mother tongue. For years he managed railroad and steamship lines. He said he had never cared for money, but he'd always had an easy ability to make a great deal of it. He claimed that the government took most of it, but I noticed that he still lived extremely well. He had done countless odd things. He had lived in foreign capitals, and belonged to the best clubs. Once he'd had great gold-mine holdings in Nevada. His raising of five hundred thousand dollars for that venture was the greatest financial achievement in history, he said. Another time he ran a chicken ranch and lost ten thousand dollars. Once he went to Denver with hardly a cent and within a year was giving monthly dinners for every prominent person in town at ten dollars a plate. That came from real estate. He lived in a huge house on Scott Circle in Washington for ten years, including the World War period. He didn't know how he kept out of jail, because he badgered the government to death about the way it was running that war.

He kept a can of snuff in his pocket, and paused about every two minutes to stuff some up his nose. He wasn't drinking or smoking when I met him, though he hadn't actually stopped. He got started drinking in Central America, when he had to take long rough trips into the interior and always seemed to be sleeping with natives' feet in his face. One time in Costa Rica, he'd visit the officers aboard the American and British warships every afternoon at cocktail time and do away with about two quarts of free whisky. At the same time he was also consuming some fifty cigars per diem. Then he quit drinking, and didn't start again till prohibition. That so disgusted him he took to the bottle again. He considered quitting when repeal came, but thought better of it.

As a young man Stuart X went to law school for a month. Suddenly it dawned on him that his teachers were assigning him twelve cases a day, whereas, he said, the Supreme Court took twelve years for one case. He knew he was smarter than the Supreme Court, but not that much smarter, so he figured law was a fake and quit it.

Even then his vast wisdom hadn't reached its full flowering. It came upon him like a bomb shortly thereafter. He was in bed in a San Francisco rooming house. Suddenly he was awakened by a terrific light in the room, like "globular lighting," which apparently is colossal. Stuart X was scared and thought his time had come, but it hadn't. Do you know what that light was? It was merely a second lobe in Stuart X's brain bursting forth, making room for his wisdom. "All my strength went to my head," he told me. His brain had to expand. It had never happened to anyone else in history. And he was only twenty-two then.

Stuart X was always a reader. He had immense libraries in his homes, though he didn't find one book in a thousand that had an idea in it. On desks and chairs in his study were rows of colored pencils. He underlined everything he read, the color of the underlining denoting the degree of wisdom (rare) or nonsense (common). He was a great man for words. He had worked out what might almost be termed a new language; it was English, but full of dashes and double-meanings, not to mention a thick sprinkling of puns. He said he was the only man in the world who was qualified, through his knowledge of the true meaning of words, to write a competent book review. He was a prodigious letter writer. For decades he had been writing letters on important subjects to friends, acquaintances, and practically everybody else. He had kept carbons, and he said these letters formed the only real literature ever produced.

I read over some of his 1914 war letters, and they really were spookily accurate in their predictions of what would happen to the world after the war. Six months before we entered that war, he volunteered his services as commander in chief of the United States Armies, because nobody else was capable of doing it. A man named Pershing got the job. Three times Stuart X offered his services to J. P. Morgan the elder, twice as a philosopher and once as a fool. He never heard from Mr. Morgan. He corresponded with George Bernard Shaw till one of his statements so stumped the famous playwright that he couldn't think of an answer, and quit writing. In reading over some of these letters I came upon this typical Stuartism: "Shaw, you weary me."

The Secret Service got after him for the letters he wrote to Woodrow Wilson. More recently he had sent a flock of letters to Washington, written in his new language. The Dies committee thought he was a Red, and sent for him. He didn't go.

Stuart X had a marvelous facility with English, and could get the best of any and all opponents through sheer bulk and lyricism of words, irrelevantly put together. The only thing he ever did in his life that he was ashamed of was when he was a guest of Sitting Bull: the great Indian chief served him dog soup and Stuart X couldn't eat it. He had hated himself ever since for that weakness.

A few years ago he'd had to have all his teeth pulled, and he had a set of four-hundred-dollar false teeth, but he never wore them. "When I get them in my mouth," he said, "I can't get anything else in." He kept them in a bureau drawer, wrapped in cloth, to remind him what a damn fool he was.

Mr. Stuart X told me all these things himself. If they cause some of you to raise your eyebrows, let me warn you that you'd better be careful. Stuart X was, to begin with, one of the most vastly informed men I ever met. And, in the second place, either he was actually the one and only great man the human race has ever produced, or else he had the biggest tongue in the biggest cheek in the land. I don't know which he was, but I do know that Stuart X had a mischievous glint in his eye.

There are people who travel clear across the United States and spend the winter in the town of Newport, Oregon, just to go out on the beach every day and hunt for rocks. They are agate fiends. An agate, as you know, is a pretty rock; it is extremely hard, and when you cut through it or polish it you're likely to find any picture from Whistler's "Mother" to "The Battle of Waterloo," all drawn out for you by nature. An agate in the raw looks just like any other rock. That's where the fascination of agate collecting comes in; you don't know what magnificence you have uncovered till you stagger home and polish your rocks on a grinder.

Agates are by no means rare. They're found on seacoasts, in mountains, on the desert. But that little Oregon town of Newport comes about as near to being the agate capital of America as any place you could name. For seventy-five miles up and down the beach are found the greatest variety anywhere. The agate hunters fall into two groups—the professional and the amateur. The professional goes at it coldly, but the amateur—ah, there you have a man with butterflies in his heart!

Newport's greatest amateur, probably, was a gentle ex-newspaper printer named Will Grigsby. He and Mrs. Grigsby had come to Newport in recent years. For eighteen years he had been a printer on the Kansas City *Star*. "I'm poor and half sick," he said, "and I don't know what will happen." But he kept on hunting agates, good weather or bad, when he felt so rotten he could hardly move. He had hundreds and hundreds of beautiful agates on shelves in his house; he had a shedful of whirring wheels for grinding and polishing; in the yard lay a ton or two of waste and discarded rock; he traded rock collections with people all over the country.

Will Grigsby never sold an agate to a tourist. He sold only on mail orders, and that came to just a few hundred dollars a year.

He did it only to get a little money to support his hobby. The most he ever got for an agate was three dollars.

Another agate collector was James F. Baird, the mayor of Newport, but his fever heat had worn off. There was a time when he had every agate wrapped in a separate cloth, and got them out every night and studied them. Now they were just dumped in pasteboard boxes, and he saw them only when some interested stranger came along.

Probably the most fascinating and the best liked by tourists is the moss agate. It has a weird little design of mossy tendrils—sometimes hundreds of them—around which transparent rock has formed. It is the moss agate that produces the fantastic pictures. A rather rare specimen is the water agate. It has a water-filled cavity in the center, and in the water is an air bubble. When you hold the rock in front of a light bulb, you see the bubble move back and forth. Will Grigsby said the average among hunters was about one water agate out of a thousand rocks picked up, but he seemed to have a knack. He had found more than two hundred of them. They really weren't of much value, and would dry up inside if you weren't careful. Will Grigsby kept his in a bowl of water.

An agate is the seventh hardest known stone. It has to be cut with powerful circular saws running in diamond dust. Earl Ruddiman, who ran one of the agate shops in Newport, used a hundred fifty dollars' worth of diamonds a year. He bought raw diamonds and hammered them into dust himself. He had been an agate man for nineteen years, and his father had been one before him. He didn't think much of the agate business, though, and I was inclined to agree with him.

Nobody has seen all of America until he has driven through the redwood forests of northern California. You get an eerie feeling there where it's so dark, with those great trunks rising around you so thick and so straight. They don't seem like trees at all, but more like spirits or werewolves—something half human and half ghost. Everybody I've ever talked to about it has felt that way. You wouldn't be surprised to see an immense, gnarled wooden hand reach out and snatch you away into nowhere.

In 1939 the oldest grapevine in California was 169 years old. The state had half a million acres in grapes, and five hundred wineries. In October you could drive through Napa and Sonoma counties and actually smell wine in the air. It smelled pretty good, too.

Out there they had a Wine Institute which put out handsome cookbooks, watched legislation, and got publicity in the magazines. It was the Institute's mission to make Americans drink more wine. They wanted each person to drink three and a half gallons a year. At that time we were drinking only half a gallon each, which must mean that you drank a gallon, since I don't like wine. It isn't that I have any moral objection to wine drinking; it's merely that my taste runs more to opium and wood alcohol. I had a friend in Los Angeles who drank up his whole year's quota in two nights, but the Wine Institute said that wasn't the way to do it. My friend said so too, the next morning.

California winemakers met two big stumbling blocks in their campaign to make America wine-conscious. One was the usual belief that wine isn't much good unless it comes from Europe; the other was the average person's idea that you have to follow a set of uppity rules about serving and drinking wine, and that if you don't observe them you're a greenhorn. As for the first, the California vintners had been regularly taking their wines to the European expositions and coming away with the highest prizes. They said that we made just as fine wine as the Europeans, and that when it came to lousy wine Europe made more than we did. As for the etiquette of serving wine—the "proper" and "improper" ways—the Wine Institute said that was all bosh. The proper wine to drink with any given course is whatever wine you happen to like best. And the proper glass to serve it in is any glass that doesn't leak.

We had dinner in Jack London's house at Glen Ellen, California, where he spent his last eight years. It had been twenty-three years since his death, but you had a feeling that he was just out walking in the moonlight and would be back in a minute.

The place is in a valley—they call it the Valley of the Moon, and somehow the moon there does seem to give out a peculiarly vivid light. The home that Jack dreamed about, and spent money on faster than he made it, was never finished; it burned just as the last touches were being put on. He had planned to start rebuilding the next spring, but he died before spring came. Its great stone walls still stood high and silent and made an eerie shape among the trees in the moonlight.

The house in which Jack lived while he was waiting for his dream home was an old winery converted into comfortable living quarters. There he wrote and entertained and loved and fumed his heart out. Now it was the "Jack London Guest Ranch." It was still in the family's hands, and was run by Irving Shepard, the son of Eliza London Shepard, Jack's beloved sister. She was still living there in the ranch house, but was not well. Life there was family-style: guests ate at a big table with Shepard and his family. There was no museum effect about anything. Much of Jack's stuff was right out where you could see it and touch it—just part of the ordinary furniture. The Shepards kept horses, for Jack loved them, and there were miles and miles of riding paths. There was even a private lake in which guests could fish. It was at the end of a winding dirt road through the hills, and you had a feeling of peaceful isolation. You didn't see cars passing, or tourists nosing around. The ranch covered about twelve hundred acres in soothingly beautiful country fifty miles north of San Francisco. Jack chose the geographical spot for peace, though he never found it in his own heart.

The Shepards were easy people, and they enjoyed talking about Jack London. They resented, as did all the family, the intimations that he committed suicide. Irving Shepard, who was around forty when I was there, was away at school the day Jack died, but he knew all the details and remembered his uncle very well. He had read most of London's books, but not every one. He liked especially to get out old letters in Jack's handwriting and show them to friends.

The ranch house was far from pretentious. It was just a rambling one-story building in two units, with a yard and a driveway between. In the dining room were fine chests that Jack had brought from Korea, and Russian samovars. The floors were thick with Navajo rugs. Jack didn't collect them; his sister Eliza did.

In the dining room there was a glass-doored bookcase containing a first edition of all the fifty books that Jack London wrote—all, that is, except one. Once a large party came there from an organization of women writers, and they looked and admired. After they left, one of the first editions was gone.

I could hardly bear to leave the wing where Jack worked and slept and finally died. His workroom had windows on three sides. His desk, where he sat for three hours every morning and wrote in longhand, was set out from the wall. Everything in the room was about as he left it, including a phonograph with a morning-glory horn. Up a little flight of wide stairs was his library. All his books had been taken over to Mrs. London's home, but there were no empty spots on the shelves. They were filled with pictures, old letters, mementos from friends, Polynesian knick-knacks. On one group of shelves were scores of pasteboard boxes containing Jack's notes for his writings. He always wrote from notes; in fact, he made so many notes I don't see how he ever got time to write books. We dug into half a dozen boxes and found outlines, chapter headings, skeleton plots, choice phrases—for books written and unwritten.

Just off the library was an enclosed porch, where Jack slept, and where he died.

Charmian London, Jack's widow, shared with him the greater part of his adult life. From what I have read their marriage was not a notably happy one, yet on her side there was a consistent and compassionate understanding. After Jack's death she built a house of her own on the ranch, about half a mile away, and she lived there alone. It was a minor castle made of stone and enclosed by trees. She was in the East then, and we did not get to see her. They said she was a charming woman, and that she had a rippling command of the English language that was like nothing you'd ever heard before. She herself wrote a two-volume biography of Jack London.

Hers proved to be less a home than a private Jack London museum. The rooms were immense, and they were packed with stuff from the South Seas—gifts sent back to Jack by the hospitable Polynesians after his cruise in the *Snark*. Charmian was on that trip with him. Great wooden sculptures, some almost life-size, stood around the walls; the curtains were of Hawaiian tapa cloth; every room was a Polynesian exhibit room. And in the basement were stored tons of South Sea stuff—the overflow from upstairs.

Jack's personal library consisted of nearly fifteen thousand volumes, covering every subject under the sun. You could easily pick out the books he took with him on the *Snark*, for they were splotched and faded from salt spray. The library had copies of his books in scores of languages, some of which we couldn't even make out. There were secret closets, opened by removing a few books from a shelf, where Charmian kept Jack's scrapbooks and some of his rarer volumes.

Mrs. London had gone to Europe early that summer, because German publishers owed her a great deal of money on royalties from Jack's books, and the only way she could get it was to go over there and spend it. They gave her all she needed to travel about Germany, or even to nearby countries and back to Germany, but they wouldn't pay her way from one outside country to another. And they never would give her an accounting of the royalties. Jack's books were among those Hitler burned—Jack was a socialist—but they were still selling there.

When we went back to the ranch house half a mile away, we learned further that it had been open to guests for five years. There were accommodations for twenty-two guests in private rooms and in cabins out under the trees. Although Jack London was one of America's most notable drinkers, liquor was not served at the ranch. The ranch had no objection to drinking, though, and guests could go right into the kitchen and get glasses and ice for their own highballs any time they wished.

Most guests came there the first time because it was Jack London's place. But there was one man that summer who was different. He was from the East, and he came up for dinner with some San Francisco friends. He got to talking with Irving Shepard, and said to him, "Say, who was this Jack London, anyway? I hear everybody talking about him."

"Don't you really know?" said London's nephew.

"No," said the man, "I never heard of him."

"Why," said London's nephew, "he was the greatest brick-layer in California."

"Is that right?" said the man. "Well, I'll be darned!"

You ought to be around San Francisco when they have a heat wave. The local people are a riot. You see, it practically never gets hot in San Francisco, winter or summer. The wind from the ocean keeps it cool and the fog keeps it dark, and when a nice warm day wanders in by accident San Franciscans think the city is catching fire.

We encountered a heat wave there that lasted a week. It got all the way up to ninety-seven degrees. The city practically stopped turning; schools closed; people told me they saw cops without their coats for the first time in their lives. During that week I never heard a single conversation upon any subject but the heat. People actually died from it, and those who lived apparently would have welcomed death.

While walking along the street in San Francisco we noticed a dignified-looking, middle-aged man sitting in a restaurant at a table next to the window. A woman and her little girl passed on the sidewalk. The little girl lagged behind, stopped at the window, and peered at the man eating his lunch, whereupon he stopped, flattened his nose against the pane and looked cross-eyed. The little girl giggled and went on. The man continued his lunch, looking pleased with himself.

We met a young woman on the street. She was walking along unconcernedly, rather slowly, paying no particular attention to anybody. There wasn't anything unusual about her—except that she had nothing on but a chemise. Everybody stopped and stared, too surprised to laugh or say anything. The girl paid no attention. She didn't seem drunk or doped. Possibly she just liked to walk around in a chemise.

The St. Francis Hotel every night washed all the silver money it had taken in that day—did it in a whirling machine with washing powder and BB shot. The money came out looking as if it had just been minted. They said the idea originated at the Davenport Hotel in Spokane.

As I myself am a rather persistent traveler, I decided to go around to the San Francisco branch of Travelers Aid to see if I could get some aid. Since I wasn't out of money, didn't need a job, hadn't run away from home, could speak English, and wasn't about to become an unwed father, there wasn't much they could do for me. But I hung around long enough to ask them what they did. There were sixteen people on the staff; they spoke half a dozen languages, and met every overland train and bus. Runaway children constituted a large proportion of their clients. The age of the runaways would almost span a century: there were children hardly big enough for kindergarten, and the oldest runaway was a man of 102, from Illinois. He got tired of staying around home, so he ran away. When he showed up in San Francisco he said he had a pal who came out to the gold rush in '49, and he hadn't heard of him since and thought he'd look him up. Did the Travelers Aid happen to know his pal? No, they didn't. They sent the old gentleman back home.

One day two little children got off a bus. They were so tiny they didn't even know their own names. Travelers Aid had nothing at all to work on. The newspapers co-operatively ran the children's pictures. Next day their mother called up from Bakersfield, three hundred miles away. She said she and her husband had put the kids on the bus, hoping to hitchhike through to San Francisco before the kids got there, and meet them at the bus station. But on the way up they got a harvesting job in one of the vegetable fields, so they just stopped and went to work. That's one way to raise a family.

The director of Travelers Aid in San Francisco was Miss Emilie Taylour, a youngish woman from Buffalo who had sung in grand opera. After twelve years in the helping-hand business, she was still a sucker for a good story. She had got so she didn't believe anybody, but she knew you could be in pretty bad trouble even if you lied about the reason for it. She wound up by taking the biggest liars under her wing and shelling out some help for them from her own pocketbook.

She was telling me about an 87-year-old man from Texas, who showed up in San Francisco with no coat or vest, walking with two canes. He told them he had been in Hawaii when he was a boy, and always remembered the beautiful brown hula girls on Waikiki Beach; he wanted to see them again before he died.

Miss Taylour, supposing he was broke, asked, "Have you got money to get to Hawaii on?"

"Of course I've got money," the old man said. "I just sold some lots in Texas."

"Well, can we see the money?" asked Miss Taylour.

"No, you can't see it, because I've got it sewed up inside my pants and I'm not gonna take my pants off in front of all you women."

So they got him a pair of scissors and left the room, and he cut six hundred dollars in cash out of his pants.

Well, Travelers Aid was stumped. They didn't think he ought to make the trip to Hawaii, and yet it wasn't any of their business. They got in touch with a brother back home, and he said he had tried to dissuade him too, but without success. So Travelers Aid monkeyed around over it for several days. They kept stalling him off, and saying they couldn't get steamship reservations. And finally, somehow, they got him started back to Texas.

Unwed mothers came to Travelers Aid like bees to a hive. There was one every three weeks. Travelers Aid did the best it could—calmed them down, made a "plan" for them, either sent them back home or got them into a hospital in San Francisco, provided layettes, and kept an eye out afterward. Most of the mothers turned out all right. In fact, it was so damned successful that one wayward girl had been back five wayward times.

When my Aunt Mary decided to make a trip to the San Francisco Exposition, Travelers Aid wrote me and said they'd be pleased to help her in any way they could. I wrote back and thanked them, and said Aunt Mary wouldn't need any help, but in case Travelers Aid got lost or something, Aunt Mary would be glad to help *them*.

Beniamini Bufano had designed a giant statue of St. Francis of Assisi which might some day stand atop the highest of San Francisco's hills and look down upon the city.

I spent an afternoon with Bufano. If everything he said was true—and I suppose he intended me to believe it—then his life had indeed been fantastic. He was born in Italy, apparently around 1900. The whole family came to America when he was two years old. He was one of fifteen children, and all of them, and his parents too, were still living. He was brought up in New York City.

He ran away from home when he was eleven, but ran back again. He studied the violin and became a considerable musician, and he studied art. Then during World War I he did something weird: he cut off the index finger of his right hand and sent it to President Wilson as a protest against our entering the war.

"Why did you do that?" I asked him.

Well, he said he was very artistic at the time. It seemed to him that war was destroying all the beauty and sensitiveness in the world, and he must cry out against it. Also, he was then an intense Bible student. He remembered a passage that read: "If your right hand offend you, cut it off." His own right hand hadn't offended him, but the actions of mankind had, so he decided to cut it off anyhow—or at least part of it. He got his mother's meat ax from the kitchen, sterilized it and put peroxide on it, and whacked off his finger. Then he walked three miles to a doctor he knew. When he walked into the doctor's office and showed him the finger, the doctor fainted. As soon as the doctor came to, Bufano fainted. After the fainting was all done, the doctor trimmed the stump of finger and made a neat job of it.

Bufano never did get an acknowledgment of his finger from President Wilson, or even from a third assistant secretary.

Well, with that behind him, he started out to see the world. He lived on the Gold Coast of West Africa with the savages, doing sketches and portraits to pay for his meals. He lived several months with Gandhi in India. He disguised himself as a Brahman and spent a week inside a holy temple. All the time he was in India he never slept in a bed. In Hong Kong he was a beggar on the streets for three months, sleeping on the sidewalk. He joined the Chinese revolution in 1920, fought with the Chinese, and later was taken in by Sun Yat-sen and lived with him for months. Once he was shot in the wrist by one of Sun Yat-sen's sentries who didn't recognize him. In Italy he was in jail for weeks, accused of anti-Fascism. In Paris he lived for three months on nothing but cabbage. He had been in Rio, and had spent days inside the Hopi kivas in Arizona. He knew all the artists in Santa Fe, spoke three languages, belonged to the San Francisco Press Club, and gave you the impression that he wouldn't be cutting off any more fingers.

When we got to San Simeon, we thought Mr. Hearst might be out in the middle of the road to flag us down with an old shirt or something, but I guess he forgot. We saw his famous castle from the road anyway. It sits back up in the hills, probably five or six miles from the highway, but even at that distance it looks mighty big. Down in the tiny seacoast village of San Simeon, there are two big telescopes on pedestals outside the grocery. A sign says: "See the Castle—Ten Cents." You put a dime in the slot and stand there in the sun with one eye squinted, and become a ten-cent Peeping Tom upon the fabulous Hearst in his castle five miles away. The telescopes, incidentally, are lousy. I don't see why Mr. Hearst doesn't buy the grocery a couple of new ones, the better for us tourists to see him with.

Sunset Cox never was like the usual run of men. For fifty years he lived his own free life, doing as he pleased, not working too hard, keeping mildly adventurous, delving with an immense interest into everything in sight. And now at sixty-seven he had tuberculosis and was lying in the Veterans' Hospital at San Francisco, California, and he thought it was the most wonderful experience of his life. I don't mean he was a Pollyanna. Far from it. He simply had such a gnawing curiosity that no matter what happened to him, he enjoyed experiencing it. Everything was wonderful to him. It always had been.

Sunset went out to the Philippines in 1898 as a sergeant in the regular Army. When the soldiers came back, he stayed on. For forty years he lived in China and the Philippines as a sort of adventuring newspaperman—sometimes working straight jobs, sometimes running his own little sheets, sometimes straying into the mysterious world of Oriental "advisership." In all those forty years he came back to the States only once. In 1929 he was back for a few months and spent some time in Washington; it was there we became friends.

Sunset was about my size—of medium height and very thin. He was old enough to be my father, but I never thought of the difference in our ages. He was straight and walked with a little swagger. His graying hair was parted in the middle, and he had every hair he'd ever had.

He had written us as soon as he got back from China and landed in the hospital, so we stopped by to see him. We arrived during nonvisiting hours, but he had everything fixed. He had a way you couldn't say no to. If he had been in the operating room, I'll bet he'd have got us in.

When we entered the room, he jumped out of bed, jumped here and jumped there, ran out in the hall and dragged in chairs, all the time rattling off his amazing delight at merely being in this wonderful place.

"Oh-h-h-h," he said, "you don't know. This is the most wonderful place. Am I lucky to be here! This is one of the Veterans' Administration showplaces. There's a nurse for every two patients. We get the best of everything. The doctors are fine. And just look at those mountains out my window. Aren't they beautiful?"

To our surprise, he wasn't the least bit homesick for China. Hadn't had time to think about it, I guess—too many interesting things around, and new things. He had heard his first baseball game by radio, and his first football game. He listened to the war broadcasts, cut out all the maps, even made maps of his own.

"And say," said Sunset, "they've got food here that I had forgotten existed. Things like fried cornmeal mush. And what a kick it is to eat green vegetables without having to wonder if they came from an inspected garden!"

The thing he couldn't get used to was seeing white people doing all the work. "White men out there mowing the lawn," he said. "And big strapping white fellows sweeping and straightening up the room. It doesn't seem right."

Some men lying in bed at sixty-seven would gaze out the window with melancholy and see nothing but gray, but not Sunset. He thought the mountains were so wonderful he had pictures taken from his window and sent them to friends. He had bought a book on fir trees, so he could study every tree on the hillside. He had another book on California missions. And he had ordered one on birds, so he could identify all the birds he saw out the window. When he first came he loved the hummingbirds so much he'd throw his breakfast orange juice through the screen, and they'd come and suck on it. That was fine till the juice attracted several million ants, and hospital workers had to climb up and spray the screen.

Sunset's room looked like a hobbyist's den. All over it were magazines and papers and books and letters. There were scissors and pots of glue. He cut out clippings by the score. He read my column in the Los Angeles *Daily News* every day. Not only that— he made everybody else read it. And when he had saved up six, he sent them to his sisters in New York.

He carried on a terrific correspondence and read mystery books and California history. And on his second day in the hospital he wanted to tour the whole place, so he could write a story for the *China Press* about it. The doctor suggested he wait a few months. A couple of weeks before I saw him they had operated on him, and Sunset was sore as a boil because they covered up his eyes. He wanted to watch his own operation and write a story about it.

Sunset Cox was no sickroom despondent. If you were in his room an hour, he wouldn't be still during three seconds of it. He was zestful, incorrigible, and probably immortal. If death ever did come to him, he would hate it only because he couldn't stay on to tell people what it was like.

There was a rugged individualist at Carmel, California. I never did see the man, but I can swear that he was.

One morning I went into a little coffee shop there, and gave the waitress my breakfast order—orange juice, one egg medium-boiled, crisp bacon, dry toast, and coffee. The girl looked at the menu and said: "That would be No. 3, but No. 3 is a poached egg. You can't substitute."

So I said, gaily but politely, "Well, I don't care whether it's No. 3 or No. 27. I'm not trying to substitute. I'm just ordering what I want."

And the girl said, "But the cook won't boil one egg. He'll poach one, but not boil one."

So I said, "Well, a man can get one boiled egg if he's willing to pay for it, can't he? How much is the breakfast I ordered if you make it à la carte?"

So the girl, looking extremely doubtful, disappeared into the kitchen to find out. In a little while she came out. She looked a little scar d, and said, "The cook won't boil one egg under any circumstances, for any price!"

And so I left, my vexation completely overshadowed by my admiration for such a man.

Leslie Crowe was probably the best wood carver in the United States Navy, and where did it get him? It lost him a five-dollar bet to his wife, that's all. The way it happened was that Mrs. Crowe wrote me a letter, telling me that every single thing in their home was made of wood carved by her husband, and inviting me to come and see it when we visited San Diego. Then Leslie Crowe had to sail away on his destroyer. Before he left he said to his wife, "I'll bet you five dollars he never comes."

So when I walked up the front steps of the Crowes' little house, it cost the sailorman five bucks.

I believe the only things in the house that Crowe hadn't made out of wood were the refrigerator and the gas stove. He made the bed and all the chairs. And they were not just carpentry—they were pieces of distinction. All the knives and forks had handles carved by Crowe. They ate off wooden plates, they drank from wooden cups. The walls were decorated like a sportsmen's club. There was a fine moose head, and over the door an old-time blunderbuss; Crowe carved them both. Also the flintlock pistols. Massive Chinese chests stood against every wall—made by old Chinaman Crowe. And the bedroom was thick with candlesticks and altars and crosses, for Mrs. Crowe was Catholic. She burned candles for her husband when he was at sea. And one night when she read about our having to make a forced landing in the Andes, she got out of bed and lighted candles for That Girl and me.

Looking back, I cannot remember a tenth of all the wooden things in the Crowe home. There were easily two hundred separate pieces of cabinetwork or sculpture, from a great mahogany bedstead to intricate little Japanese dancers carved onto chair backs. As we were going along, looking at wooden hangings, we came to the fullface of a dog in bas-relief. Its white lower teeth jutted up in doggish ferocity. "He didn't think you'd come," Mrs. Crowe said, "but just in case you might come, just before he left, he made that for you. That is yours." She took it down from the wall and handed it to me.

Crowe was a farm boy from Minnesota. He had been in the Navy twelve years, and was a machinist's mate. His work had nothing at all to do with wood. Even in his boyhood farm days he had done nothing with wood. This business had just drifted in on him, like a perfume or a pleasant morning, some five years before I dropped in. He had never had a lesson of any kind. All by himself, he had progressed from rickety little manual-training tables to sculptures of graceful figures.

Of course sailors don't make much money, so the Crowes didn't live very high. Every spare cent went for wood and tools for Crowe and food for Mrs. Crowe's two little trained dogs. She was cooking up eleven pounds of stuff for them while we were there.

The Crowes didn't have a telephone or an auto. They never took any tourist trips. They seldom went to the movies. Neither one drank. Mrs. Crowe rolled her own cigarettes out of Bull Durham—one of the half dozen women I'd seen who could do it. She even had a quilt made of Bull Durham sacks.

She remembered that piece about my getting a one-armed fellow in Idaho to teach me to roll cigarettes with one hand. "Was that really true?" she said. "Madam," I said with dignity, "everything I write is true."

"Yes, of course," she said. "But can you roll one now?"

"I cannot roll one now," I said, "because I am out of practice."

"Well," she said, "just show me how a one-handed roller starts out."

So, not wishing to be impolite, I got out my papers and tobacco and began showing her how you start, and I kept on showing her, and the first thing I knew right there in front of my own eyes I had as nice a one-handed cigarette as you ever saw.

It was pleasant to be in the Crowe home. When Sailorman

Crowe was off on a cruise, Mrs. Crowe just relaxed. Didn't clean up the house for days. Boy, it was comfortable. She would light a cigarette and throw the match on the floor. Just to make her feel at home, I did too.

There was a club in San Diego known as the Bottom-Scratchers Club. The only way you could get into it was to bring up three abalones from the bottom of the ocean in thirty feet of water, and then bring in a live shark by the tail with your bare hands. I am willing to be quoted as standing rockbound and steadfast on a platform of to hell with being a Bottom-Scratcher. Only five men had been able to meet the club requirements. One of the five had had to retire because of busted eardrums; another was practically emeritus, because he turned blue in cold water.

The club's president had the title of Chief Walrus. The club was only about five years old, and the first incumbent was still Chief Walrus. His name was Glenn Orr. He was a friendly well-built man of thirty-one who ran a crane for the city of San Diego whenever the city wanted something built, which was all the time. He worked six days a week. On Sundays, summer and winter, regardless of wind, snow, sleet, or mail carriers, he was out in the water diving and crawling around the bottom of the ocean. His feet were cut up from walking on the bottom, his shoulders were scratched and scarred from scraping against barnacles on underwater ledges. And in the small of his back there was a big scar where a sea lion had bitten him; he was down on the bottom prying loose abalones when the sea lion came plunging down from above. He never even saw it coming. He had to go to the hospital for that one.

This bottom-scratching was done purely for sport. They didn't use diving helmets or anything; they just went down and held their breath. Not one of them but had been caught by some circumstance, and held his breath almost to the dying point, and come to the top roaring sick at his stomach. Each man always carried a long sharp knife when he dived to the bottom. Sometimes it was strapped around a wrist, sometimes stuck in a sheath inside his trunks. Once a sea lion bit Glenn Orr's underwater flashlight right out of his hand. He got to the top and wouldn't go back after the flashlight unless somebody went with him, and I don t blame him. Twice he got his knife caught in an underwater rock crevice. That wouldn't have been so bad, except that the knife was tied around his wrist, trapping him there. On each occasion he gave a big yank and broke the cord—a feat he probably couldn't accomplish if he was doing it just for fun.

The Bottom-Scratchers could hold their breath underwater for three minutes. Glenn's chest had expanded four inches since he had been diving. Furthermore, he had taken on considerable weight. The cold water did it; he said nature was providing him with blubber against the cold, just as it does a walrus.

The Bottom-Scratchers did their diving just off the breakwater at La Jolla, a half hour's drive north of San Diego, where the water usually seemed to be clearer. Mainly they were after abalones. An abalone is a thing in a shell, sort of like a clam, only the shell is about as big as a plate. It has suction cups around its rim, and it glues itself to the rocks on the bottom. A man could no more pry one loose with his hands than he could fly, but if you slip a knife underneath, it comes off easily.

Glenn Orr had been swimming so long it was second nature to him. He was the first swimmer I'd met who didn't make fun of me because I couldn't swim. He said some people just naturally couldn't swim, the same as some people couldn't swallow swords.

He was not the least bit afraid of sharks; they were just a nuisance. They would dart around you and get in the way when you were trying to pry abalones loose. He wouldn't say that a shark would not attack a man, but he had never been attacked. Killing a shark was nothing at all in his life. He couldn't even estimate how many he had killed—sometimes three and four in one Sunday, and other mild things like octopuses and sting rays.

About those sharks they had to bring up by the tail for their initiation: these were little sharks, only three feet long. Little and harmless, you know, like small rattlesnakes.

We have been many times to California. You could not count on the fingers of both hands the number of our trips out there. But always we have avoided coming right out and admitting that we liked California. We would say yes, it might be all right if you could get back east once a year. Or we would make fun of their sunshine claims, for we had seen California in flood. Or we would join the intellectuals and hoot at all the Iowa farmers in Los Angeles. But maybe as we grow older we grow more honest with ourselves, or maybe we just reach a stage where we aren't ashamed of agreeing with the majority. Whatever it is, I am at last ready and willing to admit that I think California is wonderful.

Sure, it has spots I don't like. You couldn't hire me to live in agricultural Bakersfield, nor in far-north Eureka, nor in the sham of Hollywood. But you don't have to live in those places. There are hundreds of miles of startling seacoast, aching to be lived upon. There are thousands of magnificent little valleys, placidly waiting for man to come and despoil them with his enjoyment. There are deserts where those with a feeling for sand and wind could find peace. And there are mountains for the virile, and forests for the woodsy people, and fog for those who hate the sun. Yes, in full honesty, we admit that California does have everything. And we were sad at leaving because, in the way of all things, no man knows but that this backward glance over the shoulder may be his last glance forever.

Hoosiers

Chapter
XXX **D**AVID ROSS, WHO HAD BEEN REFERRED TO AS "Indiana's No. 1 Citizen," was sixty-nine, and had never married. He was an inventor, an engineer, a chemist, a manufacturer, a farmer, an educator, and president of the board of trustees of Purdue University. He was all wool, without embroidery. He had Jack Garner eyebrows, except that they were steely instead of white. He pursed his lips, folded his hands across his stomach, and paused long and frequently in the middle of a sentence, and you wondered if he'd forgotten what he was saying. But he hadn't.

Ross graduated from Purdue in 1893, and he had been paying back his alma mater ever since. He had an almost religious sense of obligation to the world for what it had done for him. He had given the university a lot of his time, and more than a million dollars. Among his gifts to Purdue were its airport and, with George Ade, the Ross-Ade Stadium. Purdue was his life—the only family he had, and Purdue students made him a father confessor.

When he went to Purdue it was for an engineering course, but shortly after graduation he almost died of typhoid, and the doctors told him he'd have to stay in the open. So he went back to the farm, and never left it for thirteen years. Out there on the farm, he thought up his first invention, a steering gear for autos. When he was thirty-five, he ventured into the industrial world. He built his first factory in 1906, and now in 1940 it was still going. Many of our 1940 passenger cars were steered with Ross gears, and more than half the trucks on America's highways.

Later he built another gear factory, and one for making a processed shale composition that looks like stone. He had scores of patents. But once he had invented and perfected a thing, he was through with it—never wanted to monkey with it again. He had retired from his factories long ago, and stepped back in only when they needed pulling out of a hole. He had never worked for anybody a day in his life. Always his own boss. And he had never kept on doing a job himself a minute after he had trained someone else to do it. He said he had never had any desire for money, and yet almost everything he touched made money.

He owned about a thousand acres of farm land, and had three families running it. He didn't call them tenants, but partners. Two of them had been with him nearly thirty years. Ross himself was living on one of his farms, eleven miles out of Lafayette. It had been farmed continuously by the Ross family since 1820, and he said it was in better shape now than the day it produced its first crop.

Ross drove to his office in Lafayette every morning, carried on the business of Purdue University, received callers and students, made decisions about his factories. At noon he drove back to the farm and stayed there. If you visited him in the afternoon you'd find him wearing only "three pieces of clothing," as he put it— two shoes and a pair of shorts. He liked to get his hoe and monkey around out in the sun.

One day in 1933 Ross's tenant farmers, Ona Myers and Harry Bartlett, said to him, "Our bins are all full. Our haymows are stacked to the roof. Our outside cribs won't hold another bushel of anything. What shall we do?"

Ross looked at them a long time, from under his bushy eyebrows, and then in his short, bluff sentences he said, "Indiana has one of the best state park systems in the country. There's a World's Fair in Chicago. You've got relatives in Dakota. You've got enough money. Take a year off. Quit farming for a year. Put everything down to clover, and then go see this country."

The farmers were aghast. "What will the neighbors say?" they asked.

"I don't give a damn what the neighbors say," said Ross.

And so the two farmers packed up their families and went away to see America. Next spring they were back. The granaries were still full. "You've still got money, haven't you?" said Ross. Yes, they had. "Take another year off, then." So they did. That year came the western drought. Hay was at a premium. They sold every ounce of all three cuttings at twenty-five dollars a ton, and made more money than they ever had before.

One day they came into the office and said, "Things are bad out in the Dust Bowl. Cattle poor and dying. Feed scarce out there. We've got plenty of feed. We could pick up some of these weak cattle pretty cheap in Nebraska."

"What the hell you stoppin' here for?" said Ross. "Get on your way."

So they went to Nebraska, brought back the cheap and half-starved cattle, fed them out, and sold them. Made more money than ever—made enough in those two "vacation" years to buy a farm apiece. So Ross started looking around for new "partners." The two farmers heard about it and came storming into his office. "Well, you've bought farms of your own, haven't you?" said Ross. "I'll have to have new tenants, won't I?" No, he wouldn't. "Those farms are for us to retire to in our old age," they said. "Until then, we're staying with you." And they were still with him in 1940, prosperous and happy.

George Ade was a wonderful man. He was one of that famous quartet that made Indiana great in letters. The others were James Whitcomb Riley, Booth Tarkington, and Meredith Nicholson. Riley died before I got around his way. Once I drove for half an hour around Tarkington's home at Kennebunkport, Maine, and never got up nerve enough to go in. I spent an evening with Meredith Nicholson in the American legation in Nicaragua, when he was United States minister. And now I wanted to meet George Ade.

Ade was seventy-four, and he had not been well for several years. I didn't know whether he would see anybody or not. So a friend at Purdue called his farm near Brook, fifty miles away, and left a message. In a little while Ade called back. Sure he would see me, and I'd have to stay for lunch.

I found him sitting on a long couch in the cool living room of the comfortable home he had built thirty-five years before. He had on gray trousers and shirt, summer shoes, neat tie, no coat; he was spick and span as a bandbox, tall and slender and graceful as a youth. It took a minute for him to place me, and then he realized it was my columns he read every day in the Miami *Herald* in the wintertime. I was tremendously flattered. He called them my "letters."

"And so you're from Indiana?" he said. "From down around Dana? Yes, I know Dana. You find Hoosiers no matter where you go, don't you?"

He liked to revert to the old days and tell stories of Riley and Tarkington. He was full of yarns about Riley, and as he told them he would laugh and laugh. He said Riley was without question the most amazing and interesting personality he ever knew. He had framed letters from him in his study, and the drawers were full of them.

Ade's kind are the salt of the earth—sharp, witty, gently caustic, quick on the understanding, and blessed with an ordinariness that helps to make them great men. Ade had a humility that I loved. Not a studied humility, but just a plain Hoosier appraisal of himself. It showed when he was telling how Indiana University gave him an honorary Doctor of Laws degree in 1926. "They gave them to Tarkington and Nicholson and me," he said, "and that was pretty fast company for me to be moving in!" And he meant it. He beamed over that degree like a little boy.

He had received three degrees—his original one from Purdue, from which he graduated in 1887; a Doctor of Humane Letters from Purdue; and his I.U. doctorate. He had all three diplomas on his study wall. "But I can tell you one degree that will never come my way," he said, "and that's Doctor of Divinity. No, sir, I'll never get that." Then he told about the cyclone of the year before. He had missed it by going over to Rensselaer to a movie that afternoon, but it swung across his farms, touching nothing on either side, and smashed down four different sets of his buildings and most of his beautiful shade trees. "People around here said it was a visitation of divine wrath for the way I've always lived," he said, and he laughed. "That's all right as far as I'm concerned, but why did it pick on those tenants of mine? They live all right." And he went on: "That divine-wrath business was blown up, you know, when the San Francisco fire left a block-square warehouse full of whisky standing right in the middle of a whole section of the city that was absolutely burned down."

Ade told things like that with chuckles and a born storyteller's zest. And if divine wrath were really holding sway, I doubt that it would pick on George Ade at all. He had done too much for his fellow man.

He had always been generous, and in his younger days had been famed in Indiana as a host. He had an unusual capacity for enjoyment, and he could make other people enjoy themselves. Nearly thirty years earlier he had started a golf course on his farm. He gradually enlarged it, and finally gave it to the community. It was called the Hazelden Country Club. Ade himself hadn't played golf for several years, although he was once of championship caliber. He seldom walked out of the house nowadays, though indoors he seemed agile and not at all in poor health. He spent nearly all his time reading and playing solitaire. He had occasional callers, though not too many, and he still loved picnics— had a picnic ground and swimming pool and dance hall right on his lawn.

Ade had contributed to Purdue nearly all his life, probably close to a hundred thousand dollars, Purdue officials told me. He had helped build the Sigma Chi fraternity house, and, of course, the Ross-Ade Stadium. He and Dave Ross were old and fast friends. The stadium was Ross's idea, and he badgered Ade into coming in with him on it. Then it came time for a name. "Purdue Bowl wouldn't do," Ade said, "because it wasn't a bowl. So I thought why not get my name on it? Hell, I wanted my name on it. I was shameless about it. Why, a hundred years from now nobody will remember me for any books or plays or fables I wrote, but they're gonna remember me for that stadium. Yessir, I wanted my name on there." He didn't seem to realize how much he had contributed to the gaiety of the world with his pencil. (Yes, pencil, for he never learned to use the typewriter.)

Ade was born at Kentland, a few miles from Brook. After leaving school he worked on newspapers in Lafayette, and then for two years with a patent medicine company. "We guaranteed absolute cure of the tobacco habit," Ade said, "provided the patient faithfully followed the directions on the bottle. The very first direction was, 'Give up the use of all forms of tobacco immediately'!"

It was from newspaperwork in Chicago that he sprang into the literary limelight around 1900. He said he never did have much ambition, that somebody else pushed him into every good thing that ever happened to him. By 1905 he was rich. He bought the farm at Brook and built his house that year. He had lived there in the summers ever since. He spent his winters in a rented house at Miami Beach.

He always used to go to Florida by auto, but the trip now exhausted him so that he went by train. "The trouble is I want to see every damn thing," he said, "and I sit there for four days jerking my head from one side of the road to the other like somebody watching a tennis game, and when I get there I'm dizzy." He had his first auto back in the days when they guided the things with a handle bar instead of a steering wheel. But he hadn't driven a car himself since 1910.

He never married. His household consisted of Katie Krue, who was combination housekeeper and nurse, and a cook, a gardener, and a chauffeur. The house, which was large and rambling, looked like a gabled country clubhouse of a generation ago. In a corner of the first floor was his study, where thirty years ago he had written some of America's most popular books and plays. There he wrote *The College Widow* in three weeks. The study was lined with old photographs, medals, and letters from people like Riley. On one side was a large safe which contained most of his manuscripts. The house was full of little statues and images and trinkets that he had brought back from his travels. He had been around the world two or three times.

He had achieved real fame and fortune, yet at the height of his career he had come back there a few miles from his birthplace, and built a home to spend the rest of his life in. He was the compleat Hoosier.

About twenty miles east of Indianapolis there is a town with four names, and it will answer to any of them. It is registered in the county courthouse as "Carrollton," the name on the highway sign. It is on the road maps as "Finly," the name recognized by the Post Office Department. On the railroad depot you see neither of these, but instead, "Reedsville." And to the inhabitants thereabouts it is known as "Tailholt." This is the town that James Whitcomb Riley immortalized in his poem "The Little Town of Tailholt." Personally, I shall always refer to it as "Joe."

Being a stodgy fellow who seldom does anything spirited, I admire people who do things on the spur of the moment. I knew a girl in Indianapolis who worked at a rather dull job, and it nearly got the best of her. One night, in a frenzy of despair at the monotony of her life, she gathered up all the money she could find, took a taxi to the airport, got on a TWA airliner and flew clear to St. Louis, and then turned around and flew right back again. It was the first time she had ever been on an airplane. She concluded her epic voyage through the starry skies at two o'clock in the morning—cleansed, refreshed, and able to face the world once more. Everybody who heard about it thought she was nuts. I thought she had discovered the secret of sanity.

Cannon Ball Baker was an Indianapolis institution. In that automotive city he had been making a living for thirty-five years by setting automotive records, and at fifty he was still doing it. He held more auto records than any five other men combined. The Baker home was full of silver cups and medals and testimonials. He had driven forty thousand miles on the Indianapolis Speedway in test work, though he drove in the big race only twice. He had driven five thousand miles just up and down Pikes Peak. He had crossed the continent a hundred eighteen times, and had driven hundreds of miles in the western sandy deserts on railroad tracks, before there were any roads. He had ridden across the Isthmus of Panama before the Canal was finished, following railroad tracks and foot trails. He had ridden a motorcycle the entire length of Cuba, around the island of Oahu, all over Australia, and across Tasmania.

There was a time when speed records were being set right and left, but like the hoop skirt and the hair on my head, those things were gone for ever now. Autos had become so perfect that all of them could go too fast. So Cannon Ball Baker's records nowadays were of a different stripe. They were records of mileage per gallon. He had proof that he had motored at the rate of 55.8 miles to the gallon of gasoline—that was with the wind. But when he drove right back again against the wind and averaged up the two, he came up with 39.2 miles to the gallon. He did it with a manifold-and-carburetor development of his own. He'd been working on it for years. He said it was perfect now, and he expected it to make him a million dollars. He had it installed in his own Graham sedan, and he said that car would go farther and faster on one gallon of gas than any other car in the world.

And he had another thing, a perfection of the old rotary-valve engine, which he had worked out in a one-cylinder motorcycle. With that motorcycle he had got 154 miles on a gallon of gas. Furthermore, the thing was so smooth that he could ride uphill and down at five miles an hour without a buck or a tremble. This thing would make him another million. That makes two.

Cannon Ball Baker was a hearty fellow. He had a big hooked nose, and loved to talk and laugh and show you around. I went out to the house to see him (used a pint and five-eighths of gas getting there) and spent the afternoon with him and Mrs. Baker. His real name was Erwin George Baker. He started motorcycle racing in 1906, then began setting transcontinental records on his motorcycle. As his records grew, he acquired such names as Demon, Warhorse, Daredevil, and The Fox. But it was when he rode into New York in 1914, at the end of a new transcontinental, that he got the name Cannon Ball; a reporter on the *Tribune,* George Sherman, gave it to him. He was in the Indianapolis phone book as Cannon Ball Baker, but Mrs. Baker called him Erwin, and friends called him Bake.

As late as 1934, he was racing across the continent on the public highways at speeds as high as a hundred miles an hour. But not any more. His top limit now was the same as mine—fifty miles an hour. He liked to set records at that speed. Once he shook hands with the engineer of the *Lark* just as it was leaving Los Angeles, and then beat the train into San Francisco by forty minutes, though he never drove over fifty miles an hour. He said it wasn't so much the speed as the gawking around that got you into trouble. You had to sit there one-minded and staring, as though you were shooting a gun—which you really are, only you're riding on the bullet. He said one of the first requisites of safe driving was to get your stomach right up against the wheel, so you'd have a good purchase on it, and then keep your eyes peeled.

It was fun to listen to Bake. He frequently said "motored" where you and I would say "drove." His grammar, incidentally, would take the booby prize in any university, but I found out long ago that grammar and achievement don't necessarily go together. He was a tremendous eater. He weighed 225 pounds, and he thought that if God had one special piece of work it was a big thick steak. He was the steak-eatingest man I ever heard of. Sometimes ate four a day. And, boy, I mean big ones—the kind that would ordinarily do a whole family. On these devastating coast-to-coast runs, where he drove on and on with no sleep or rest, he existed solely on steaks, hash-brown potatoes, and black coffee. On one fast trip he wired ahead to a restaurant friend in Santa Fe, New Mexico, to have the biggest steak in town ready for him. It was ready, and a yard long. Baker downed her with relish, and then his restaurant friend told him it was horse meat. Baker hadn't known the difference.

On his first transcontinental trip by auto, in 1914, he had only four miles of paved road in the whole distance. And that same four miles was still in existence today, he said, on U.S. 40 between Marshall and Waverly, Illinois.

On the whole, I am ill at ease in the company of artists, for so much of the time I don't know what they are talking about. And yet I invariably like the places they have made into colonies. And so it was with Brown County, Indiana. I fell head over heels for the place, and the people, and the hills, and the whole general air of peacefulness. Good Lord, I even liked the artists there!

All northern and central Indiana is as flat as a board. Neat farms checker it, and the roads are straight as a ruler. Big barns and regular fences and waving fields of grain splash across the endless landscape. But some thirty miles south of Indianapolis the land begins to undulate, the hills are covered thick with forest, the roads wind, and the fields become patches on slopes. It is hill country because this is where the great glacier stopped and melted away and left its giant rubble piled.

Into this hill country of Indiana more than a hundred years

ago came people from Virginia and Tennessee and Kentucky, pushing on into their new frontiers, though never out of the hills, for they were hill people. For a long time they lived their own lives in the woods and the tobacco patches and the little settlements, asking nothing of any man, and eventually they came to be known to the rest of Indiana as "quaint." That is what first attracted the artists to Brown County early in this century— the log cabins, the lounging squirrel hunters, the leaning sheds, the flowers and the autumn leaves and the brooks and hillsides. That, too, is what eventually attracted the sightseers. Brown County in the fall of 1940 was overrun with tourists and sight-seers, and a few outsiders who genuinely appreciated not only the wildly colored hills of autumn but also the spirit of the people themselves.

Brown County was not the same as it was when the artists discovered it. The artists no longer considered it picturesque. They said it was "spoiled." They would have gone away, except that they said it was better than anywhere else. Fine roads and hotels had impinged upon the hills and villages. The patch farmer who lived up the holler was nearly pushed off the sidewalk by the gawkers from the city. There was little privacy left. And yet the deep fine attributes of the people endured. The native of Brown County was innately courteous. He would do anything for you, and not think of pay. His honesty was almost old-fashioned. Few people in Brown County locked their houses, and when they did they hung the key on a nail outside the door. They worked in a way that would paralyze an assembly line, yet their work got done, and friends told me there was something fundamental in the Brown County air that compelled an honest day's work for an honest day's pay. The typical Brown County man played a guitar, and sang in harmony, and loved to square-dance, and didn't get lost in the woods, and raised a little tobacco, and went to church, and drank whisky, and was a dead shot with a squirrel gun. Some-times he was prosperous and sometimes he didn't amount to a damn—but it didn't matter whether he lived twenty miles up the crick in a clapboard cabin or worked in the garage downtown and wore a derby hat, still his code of gaiety and of honesty and his innate sense of dignity remained the same.

The log cabin is the mark of Brown County. I don't mean the log cabin of the western mountains, built of round logs with the bark still on. I mean the old-fashioned hewn log, roughly adzed into rectangular shape, and left unpainted and graying with age. The kind Abe Lincoln was born in. Such log cabins, modernized, have become a fad in Brown County. When people from the city build summer homes there, they are almost always log cabins. But don't let the term "cabin" fool you. I stayed in a little six-room-two-bath-and-basement log cabin, and there was a new one in Nashville that was said to have cost thirty-five thousand dollars. But it was still a cabin, and you'd better not call it a house.

A genuine cabin can't be built out of new logs. No, it must have antiquity. So you scout around the country and spot an old log house, or maybe a barn. This is called a "set of logs." Then you dicker with the owner, and buy it. You number the end of each log, take the whole place apart, haul it to wherever you want to build, and put it together again, with whatever improvements you want. Sets of logs are getting scarcer and scarcer. Walter Snodgrass said he had driven thousands of miles over the back hilly roads of southern Indiana, and even into Kentucky, looking for sets. He believed he knew every available log within two days' drive.

From the first, I knew I had no chance to become a great man, because I wasn't born in a log cabin. But I certainly know of nothing now to prevent me from dying in a log cabin—provided the people of Brown County would let such an ornery fellow die in their midst. So I guess I'll start looking around for a set of logs and a good undertaker.

Nashville, the county seat of Brown County, is only an hour from Indianapolis, and the road from the city is always heavily traveled. In the fall, when the leaves turn red and golden and yellow, Brown County seems to become a shrine for all the Midwest, and the local people have to stay home, for it is impossible for them to get anywhere. On autumn weekends, cars stand motionless in traffic jams for miles. On just one Sunday eighteen thousand people passed through the gates of Brown County State Park. But they were all gone by eight in the evening, because they were afraid of the hills and of the darkness, and they wanted to flee before the night engulfed them. It made us old Brown Countyites snicker, but we were glad they'd gone, anyway.

Outsiders have never been too popular in Brown County. Too many of them stand on the street and laugh at the courthouse, which is certainly nothing to laugh at at all. They ask whether people can read and write. They are amazed to find there is a school in Nashville. They stand looking in a store window, and laugh and laugh, and the people inside don't like it. They make fun of the girls, and rudeness is on their tongues. The Nashville people tolerate a great deal in silence, but once in a while the younger ones break over into an old, old custom known as "egging"—which means just what you think it does. It doesn't happen often, and when it does it is more than deserved.

Nashville, the only settlement in the county that could properly be called a town, had a population of around four hundred in 1940. The only railroad in Brown County went through Helmsburg, eight miles away, but there were broad black roads out of Nashville in all directions. The town had no movie, but it had an old, old hotel that had been modernized, a tavern and a restaurant, an old log jail that was now a museum piece, a grocery and a hardware store and drugstore, shops for the craft buyers, and an art gallery. Nashville had no water system, and when a fire got started it was liable to be dangerous.

The courthouse lawn was always dotted with men sitting and talking, or lying in the grass asleep in the shade. Under one tree was a bench known as the Liar's Bench. Some years ago Frank Hohenberger, the photographer, took a picture from behind of six men sitting on this bench talking. The picture became famous, and was sold in every state in the Union. The bench I saw was not the same one, but people still sat on it all day long.

Nashville still abided by the old custom of taking up a public collection for people in distress. Flowers for the dead were the main reasons for collections, but if anybody burned out, or was caught by some calamity and needed help, the people helped him. It had gradually fallen to Mabel Calvin to be the town collector. She was in the hardware store with her father, and when somebody died the townspeople automatically started dropping in at the store next morning, leaving anything from a quarter on up. She estimated that in six years she had collected for a hundred funerals.

You didn't see artists trailing around Nashville in arty clothes. They didn't have a favorite bar where they congregated to discuss their genius in mystic tongues. They simply worked hard and lived like normal people, and hoped to Heaven somebody would buy their stuff. And practically all of them were self-supporting through their art—which speaks for itself. In many summers there were at least sixty artists painting in Brown County. They had rented a huge store building on Nashville's main street and remodeled it into an art gallery, which was open from late spring until early fall. The exhibitions were changed twice a year. In addition, each artist had a home studio, where visitors were welcome. Adolph R. Schulz became the dean of the Brown County art colony upon the death of the famous Theodore C. Steele. Schulz came from Wisconsin in 1907, and he left Wisconsin because, with the growth of dairying, the cows "ate up all the scenery." He was a tall man, slender, striking in appearance, youthful-looking despite his years, animated in his conversation, and frank in his expression.

Close to Schulz in tenure was Will Vawter, of all the artists probably the most loved by the townspeople. He was a big man, heavy, with a large head made even larger by an immense thatch of white hair. He and Schulz both looked like artists, and yet Will Vawter also looked just like somebody's nice grandpa. Vawter illustrated one edition of Riley's poems. He had a nice sense of sarcastic humor about himself. Somehow we got to talking about smoking. He didn't smoke, but he chewed gum avidly and constantly, even when he was at a funeral looking at the corpse. He used to smoke cigars. He said he never could smoke halfway; he had to smoke perpetually or not at all, and it used to interfere with his art. He would load up his car of a morning with all of an artist's necessary junk, drive out in the country and find himself a likely spot to paint, then unload everything and set it up. "It was like setting up a circus," he said. "I'd get out my easel and fix it just right. And then the canvas. And then get my paints and brushes all out and ready. And then my stool. And finally set up a big umbrella over the whole thing, practically like a tent. Then I'd sit down to paint, and reach in my shirt pocket for a cigar. And of course I'd have left them at home. And do you know, I couldn't paint a stroke. So I'd jump in the car and rush back to town, taking corners too fast, killing chickens on the way, and being a general public menace. I'd lose an hour getting back to get those cigars so I could paint. So I just quit, and took up chewing gum."

Will Vawter talked about art the way I like to hear people talk. He said you go out and paint something the way you see it; somebody comes along to look at it, and if that scene happens to strike some memory, or cherished little scene, or a spot of appreciative beauty in whoever is looking at it, then he likes the picture, and if he's able he buys it. That's all there is to art. Nothing mysterious about it. When a man can talk like that, and still have no sense of time or direction whatever, and doesn't recognize his own house half the time when he sees it, then I say he has combined the functions of artistic detachment and common horse sense to a degree that nearly reaches perfection.

There are some fascinating village names in Brown County, such as Gnaw Bone, Bear Wallow, Stone Head, and Pikes Peak. There are various legends about how each one got its name, but I like the Pikes Peak one best. It seems that back in the middle of the last century a fellow from Brown County got the western fever. He sold his patch of ground and all his furniture, stocked up his wagon with several months' supplies, and started west. On the side of his wagon he painted: "Pikes Peak or Bust." Well, roads weren't so good in those days. It took him a week to get to the Ohio River. By that time he was so homesick he couldn't go on, so he turned around and came back. There he was home again, with no house, no land—nothing but a wagon full of supplies. So he set up a tent for a home, and started peddling his supplies to the people around. It got so people would say, if you needed something, "Why don't you go down and get it from that Pikes Peak feller?" And that's how the place got its name. And the funny thing is, it's down in a valley, and there isn't a respectable hill within half a mile.

I was caught shorthanded and without a sign of a present when I arrived home and discovered that it was my mother's birthday. So I improvised one. My mother's right side was useless, and her right hand was becoming more and more drawn. The hand was permanently closed, and since her fingers lay constantly against the palm of her hand, the skin there had become acutely tender and sensitive. She always gripped a handkerchief in that hand to take up the perspiration, but the handkerchief held the heat and the trouble continued. So I said to myself, why couldn't she grip a piece of wood instead of a handkerchief? It would hold her fingers off the palm of her hand, and allow the skin to toughen again.

I found a little stick and sat down beside her on the front porch and started whittling with my pocketknife. After a while she asked me what I was doing. I said I was making a stick for her to hold in her hand. The way she laughed, you'd have thought I was a half-wit. After a while, more in self-defense than anything else, I said, "I'm making it for your birthday." That was the wrong thing to say. If simply making a plain old stick was the subject for riotous laughter, then making a stick for a birthday present was thoroughly sidesplitting. I began to think so myself, but I kept on whittling.

Finally the stick was smoothed off and shaped to her hand. She let me slip it underneath her fingers. After an hour or so, she said it was too thick, and hurt her fingers. So I whittled some more, and that seemed to work. She gripped it all the rest of the afternoon.

Next morning when I came out to breakfast, there was the stick in her hand, still with her. She hadn't let go of it all night, even in her sleep.

"When are you going to leave?" my mother asked.

"I've got to leave right after breakfast," I told her. "I'm way behind in my work."

And she said, "Aw, you're always in such a rush."

"Yes, but I've got to go," I told her.

And she said, "Do you know what?"

And I said, "No, what?"

And then she laughed a while before she could speak, and finally she stopped and reached out for my hand, and said, seriously, "Some of these days you're going to die. And when you do the world will get along just fine without you. Do you know that?"

And I said, sort of on the defensive, "Yes, I know it plenty. But as long as I'm in the world I've got to keep rushing around and trying, haven't I? A fellow's got to. You always did yourself. You wouldn't want me to just stop and go on relief, would you?"

And then she said, no, she wouldn't want me to go on relief. And that's all we ever said about it.

Vagabondage

Chapter **T**RAVEL, THEY SAY, IS EDUCATIONAL. AND SO WE
XXXI have found it in our first five years of constant wandering. Why,
if I had been sitting at a desk instead of busting around, I never
would have learned that Pocahontas was buried in England, or
that most laundries insist on putting starch in white pants, and
I'm sure I never would have got it into my head where Patagonia
is. Neither would I have known where the Red River is, but I
now know of so many Red Rivers that I don't know which one
the song was written about. And if I had been behind a desk, I
never would have ridden with a long-unseen cousin dragging
redwood logs down out of the California mountains with a caterpillar. There is one thing, however, that travel has not taught me:
what makes the noise come out of a radio.

We have traveled by practically all forms of locomotion, including piggyback. We have been at least three times into every
state in the Union. We have been to every country in the Western
Hemisphere, except two. We have been in every city in America
of more than a hundred thousand population, except one. I
won't tell you what it is. We have stayed in more than eight hundred hotels, have crossed the continent exactly twenty times,
flown on sixty-six airplanes, ridden on twenty-nine boats, walked
two hundred miles, and put out approximately twenty-five hundred dollars in tips. We have worn out two cars, five sets of tires,
three typewriters, and pretty soon I'm going to have to have a
new pair of shoes.

We have not spent a Christmas in a home in four years. I spent
one Fourth of July in hip boots, sheepskin coat, mittens, and
stocking cap. And we've celebrated New Year's three times in
shirt sleeves. Travel is so confusing. And speaking of confusion,

my most confused moment was at the airport in Mexico City. The ladies' and men's retiring rooms there were labeled "Señoras" and "Señores." That's an awful lot alike, so I walked smack into the ladies' room. No harm was done, however, and I walked right out again. Then I took my bearings, consulted my Spanish dictionary, lit a cigarette for nonchalance, and this time walked confidently and correctly into the men's department. And I'll be damned if there weren't two old ladies in there! Americans too.

People often ask me how we have stood all this travel. Well, there is almost no way for a constant traveler to fill his fountain pen, but the life has some compensations. You don't have to make your own beds. You don't have to buy coal. You can make new friends and go before they find out how dull you are. You don't have to get up at four in the morning and milk the cows.

The reason we've done all this traveling is to make a living by writing a piece a day for the Scripps-Howard newspapers and some others. In five years those columns have stretched out to the horrifying equivalent of twenty full-length books. The mere thought of it makes me sick at my stomach. In sending the columns to Washington from odd spots all the way from Nome to Asunción, I haven't lost one. Once I went for five months without seeing my own column in print. Two men I interviewed have died before the columns about them were published. We have no figures on the number who have died of shock after seeing themselves in print.

Where this wandering business will get us or where it will end, I have no idea. Five years ago my boss in Washington got tired of my pestering him about the travel idea, so he said, "Oh, all right, go on and get out. Try it a little while as an experiment. We'll see how it turns out." From that day on he never mentioned it again.

When we started I weighed 108 pounds, had two bad colds a year, felt very tired of an evening, and was scared to death at meeting strange people. But now, after five years and 165,000 miles of travel, I weigh 108 pounds, have two bad colds a year, feel tired of an evening, and am afraid of people. Travel is indeed broadening.

The longest I ever went without sleep was forty-four hours,

riding a truck from Albuquerque to Los Angeles. The earliest I ever got out of bed to get a column was at 1:00 A.M., when I went out with the Italian crab-fishing fleet from Fisherman's Wharf in San Francisco. Twice in strange towns we were roused from our sleep by nearby fires. Each time I got up and dressed and ran to the fire. One was in Yuma, Arizona, the other in Pembina, North Dakota.

The dirtiest I've ever been was on a horse-packing trip in the Cascade Mountains of Washington State. It was so cold I didn't wash my face for four days. The mosquitoes were bad, and I rubbed on a heavy coating of mosquito paste about every hour. The rising dust from the trail settled into the mosquito paste and gradually turned it into mud. At the end of four days you couldn't tell me from a mud pie on horseback.

The weirdest dishes we've eaten were guinea pig in Peru and that iguana in Guatemala.

The deepest I've ever been in the ground was twenty-eight hundred feet, but I've forgotten whether it was at Cripple Creek, Colorado, or Butte, Montana. The highest was in a plane flying across the Andes—sixteen thousand feet. The longest we've ever been on one boat was three weeks. The longest we stopped in those five years was a month in Hollywood. Occasionally we would intend to stay three or four days in a place, but got the heebies for no reason at all and moved on the next morning.

The farthest we've driven in one day is 570 miles—from a ranch in the center of Arizona clear into Los Angeles. I'll never do that again. A friend of mine claims to have driven from Los Angeles to Washington, D.C., in three days and eight hours. I think he should have his driver's license taken away.

A fellow gets awfully sleepy driving, especially right after lunch on a hot day. Several times I have had to stop and walk up and down the road to wake up. Once we stopped on the desert for me to take a little nap. I have never heard such intense quiet. That Girl who rides with me was reading a newspaper. This sounds incredible, but the slight rustling of her paper made so much noise in the desert stillness that I couldn't go to sleep, sleepy as I was. I never said anything to her about it.

When I first started on this roving assignment, I would clip along at seventy miles an hour. I remember once, on a long straight road in Arizona, the speedometer got up to eighty. When I saw it, it scared me almost to death. Even though I have always driven cautiously, I finally figured that seventy miles an hour was too much for day-in-and-day-out traveling. Even if you're careful, the law of averages will catch up with you. So I have gradually slowed down to fifty-five and lower. Usually, on a straight, the speedometer stands at forty-eight. After all, why should I hurry? I ain't goin' no place especially, as they say. And I've got all day to get there.

The steepest hill we've ever driven was at the far end of the Gaspé Peninsula in Quebec. It was like driving up over the roof of a barn. The most frightening road we were ever on was a mountain trail just west of Lowman, Idaho, right after a cloudburst. It was one car wide, and hung over an abyss. The outside was caving off in little washouts, the inside was banked up with small landslides. It makes me weak to think about it.

The car got stuck only once. That was in Death Valley, and if it had been summer I'm sure we would have died.

We have had a few narrow escapes. There were two or three times when, if we had been driving like the other fellow, we wouldn't be here to tell about it. And he wouldn't either. It is amazing the number of positively dangerous drivers you see on the road. The weavers, the speeders in heavy traffic, the passers on hills. The passers make me madder than anything else, and yet I have never seen an accident caused by them. We have seen a lot of accidents, though. One snowy and sleety afternoon in North Carolina, the day before Christmas, we counted thirty cars piled into the ditch within a hundred miles. One car skidded, hit a bank and rolled over twice, just after we had met it. I saw it all through my mirror. I was the first one back there, to pull out the corpses. But they weren't corpses—just two badly scared women, without a scratch. In New Mexico we came across a car hanging by two wheels over the edge of a cliff. The driver, a traveling salesman, had simply gone to sleep. He admitted it. We were afraid to try to pull the car back up, for it looked as though if you blew on it, it would fall over the cliff. So we got a towline onto each end, and while one car pulled sidewise toward the road, another pulled him forward and out.

Twice we ran out of gas. Both times, as far as I could figure, thieves had siphoned it out the night before, for I should have had enough for another hundred miles. Once was in New Mexico, and talk about luck! The car went dead right in front of a ranch house, and there wasn't another house for seventeen miles in either direction. The rancher gave me gas from his gasoline engine. The other time was on a dirt road in Minnesota, after midnight. It wasn't thirty seconds till a car came along, took me to the nearest town for gas, brought me back, and the fellow even took the can and said he'd return it the next morning.

The hardest thing for us to keep in the car was a flashlight. Garage mechanics wouldn't think of stealing a topcoat, but flashlights seem to be free game. We lost a dozen. Outside of flashlights, we had only two thefts in five years. One was in Portland, Oregon, and it was my own fault, for I forgot to lock the car door. They cleaned us out. The other theft was a tire, right off the wheel. They put an old one back on, so I didn't notice it for maybe a long time. We were in Franconia Notch, New Hampshire, when I happened to see it. And the old one they put on lasted as long as the new ones they didn't steal.

In five years of cashing traveler's checks all over the country, I've had trouble only once, and that was in a town where I was known. Make your own deductions.

The store clerks in New Orleans, in that last crowded, destroying week before Christmas, are sweeter and kinder than it is possible for human beings to be. When the Negro hotel maids in towns around Lake Okeechobee in Florida knock at your door and you say "Yes?" they always say, "It ain't nobody but me." The Ben Milam Hotel in Houston sends a bowl of fruit up to each new guest. The Alcazar in Miami brings up a huge glass of orange juice. The Franciscan in Albuquerque gives free breakfasts to guests.

The most prized possession I picked up in those travels was a godchild. Met her pappy and mammy on a stern-wheeler going down the Yukon River. When she was born and they wrote me I was a godfather, I was embarrassed, for I didn't know what a godfather was supposed to do. Still don't know. Just beam, I reckon. Her name is Vondre Bush, she lives in San Francisco, and every day she is getting handsomer and handsomer, like her godfather.

I think the happiest I have ever inadvertently made anybody was when my column about William Andrew Jackson, an old ex-slave of Knoxville, resulted in his being invited to Washington, where President Roosevelt gave him a cane and the keys to the city.

The best compliment I ever got was from the old firebrand sculptor, Gutzon Borglum, in Rapid City, South Dakota. I stopped him in the hotel lobby, and asked if I could come out next day and see his faces on the mountain and have a chat with him. With characteristic brusqueness he said, "Come ahead, I'll talk to you all day if you act intelligent!" We were there all day.

I suppose the following assertions will draw forth screams of righteous wrath, but I say every man is entitled to his opinions. The prettiest girls are in Salt Lake City. The best-dressed women, outside the coastal cities, are in Memphis. The friendliest public servants are bus drivers. The nicest rain is in Seattle. The American town with the most spectacular setting is Ouray, Colorado, completely cupped by terrifically towering mountains. The most beautiful single scene on this continent is Lake Louise, in Canada. There is no really perfect year-round climate in America. Of all the places we've been in, we'd rather revisit Hawaii. In the States, we are partial to New Mexico. The happiest people in America are not those who are wondrous wise, but those who are a little crazy.

I am probably the only solvent person in America (and I don't mean too solvent) who literally has no home, no place to hang his hat, no base to go back to and start away from. We have worked up a whole new continent-wide list of intimate friends, and we consequently keep up a personal correspondence with about three hundred people.

But it is still in Washington that most of our friends are to be found. And our visits to Washington are so infrequent and so brief that we always leave with a feeling of frustration. We realize that, although we have talked to lots of friends, individually we have talked to nobody. It isn't our fault, nor our friends' fault. We are prodigal sons, home for a brief moment, and if we are to see our friends we have to see them all at once. There is no time to sit down with one alone and say, "All right, now let's talk about old times." We are afraid that our friends will gradually come to think we aren't worth bothering with— we are too hectic and discomposed; we do not conduct ourselves placidly, because of haste and many little duties; we are not ourselves. Always, after we leave Washington, we visualize the day when this disappointment in us will have wearied all our old friends, and we see ourselves eventually returning to Washington with nobody at all to speak to us.

The question most frequently asked of us is "Aren't you getting awfully sick of traveling by now?" The answer is an honest no, though it isn't impossible that some of these days we might come to hate the impermanency of travel. I've tried to figure out myself why we haven't tired of it. And my conclusion is that our travel is a means of escape. We don't have to stay and face anything out. If we don't like a place, we can move on. If something happens that isn't pleasant, we can leave and settle it later by letter, or just let it go forever. Stability cloaks you with a thousand little personal responsibilities, and we have been able to flee from them.

But just as important with us, I suspect, is the fact that we can't stay long even in the places we love. There is no opportunity for lingering disillusionment. I remember that once, years ago, we loved Arizona so much that when we crossed the Colorado River for the last time we could hardly talk for the lumps in our throats. We left Hawaii with broken hearts. We can hardly speak of the people of Sun Valley, Idaho, without bubbling over. We hardly dare go to Albuquerque, we hate so to leave. And we still love all those places because we always had to leave before the sweet taste could turn to vinegar. And also before they could find out about us, and kick us out.

Index of Persons
and Places